A WYATT
BOOK for

W

— ST. —
MARTIN'S
PRESS

A Wyatt Book *for*
St Martin's
Press

HoNKY TONK LOGIC

TOM HOLLIS

Book design by Gretchen Achilles

Hollis, Tom.
    Honky tonk logic: a novel / by Tom Hollis. —1st ed.
        p.   cm.
    "A Wyatt book for St. Martin's Press."
    ISBN 0–312–13981–0
    I. Title.
PS3558.03548H66   1996
813'.54—dc20   95–38854

First edition: March 1996

10   9   8   7   6   5   4   3   2   1

HONKY TONK LOGIC

prologue

I have never seen a night like this, so full of shooting stars. In fact, I have never seen more than one shooting star at a time, but tonight the sky is going haywire like a cartoon or video game or something. Zip, there goes one; zap, there goes another. I just went outside and stood there for a good ten minutes drinking it all in. Other people in this motel were slouched in their doorways doing the same thing. Traveling salesmen were squinting upward and dealing with the sight the best way they knew how—spitting and shaking their heads and making these "Woo-ee" noises that would bring hogs a-running where I'm from. Tourists were slapping their hands against their sunburned faces and calling to one another like old friends. They were saying things such as "Have you ever seen the like?" the way strangers do when the Virgin Mary pops up on a refrigerator or a taco or the last place you would expect to see her. One boozy old gal has been out by the pool all night, sprawled in an aluminum chair and shaking her fist at the skies. I can see her through the blinds now in her baseball

1

cap made of Budweiser cans. I can hear her hollering, "Shine on, but I ain't making any wishes." She's looking around now to see if there's anybody she can share a laugh with. Everybody else ignores her, but I waggle my fingers at her and give her a grin. Rave on, honey, I know just where you're coming from.

The other funny thing is the sheer number of regular old stars up there, the kind that just stay in the same spot and twinkle. It might make sense if this was Alaska or someplace where they take the northern lights for granted, but, Lord, this is the Oklahoma Panhandle. I wonder what it means. I bet it means something. This kind of stuff usually does. Who knows?

In other words, it's not a night for sleeping, although this room is as quiet as the Egyptian pyramids. Of course, you could play a hockey game on this shag carpeting and not hear a damn thing. And I'm sure this ceiling, the kind that looks like rhinestones and cottage cheese, must do its part in swallowing up motel racket. They sure didn't put it up there in the name of beauty and high-class living.

So on this night, quiet and warm and star-spangled as it is, I have decided to do something that's been simmering on the back burner of my mind ever since a woman at a truck stop in Washington State gave me the idea. She and her husband, grimy, travel-weary people, were selling their belongings out of the back of a station wagon with Arizona license plates one snowy night.

She peered into my face and said, "You know, I think I've seen you somewhere before."

I pulled the hood of my jacket up over my head and muttered something about how lots of women look like me. She probably figured she had seen me on *America's Most Wanted* or something, but I didn't care. I was just too damn cold and too damn pooped to go into a long-winded explanation of why so many of America's television viewers find my face sort of familiar. We chitchatted while I poked through her books and pot holders and hamburger candles and I warmed up to the sturdy young gal whose hands were as red and chapped as mine. She was trying to raise money to get to Vancouver, where her husband had a job lined up. I rattled on (bragged, to tell the truth) about the hazards of driving an eighteen-wheeler in sleet and snow, since I was on my way to Spokane with a load of refrigerators and this was my first time out driving a truck that big. After I bent her ear a few minutes, she said, "Here! Here's what you need," and shoved this big old GE tape recorder toward me. It was the old-timey kind, the size of a picnic basket, and I told her I couldn't use the thing.

"Sure you can," she said. "You can tell your life story into it."

Well, she made me an offer I couldn't refuse—ten bucks for the bunged-up recorder plus half a dozen tapes, and I've been lugging it around ever since, thinking, hmm, well, I do have a story to tell.

Before I flipped this machine on, I bowed my head and prayed that the Lord would see fit to get this story out where it could help people realize that they do have the power to change their lives if they are willing to commit themselves and not be afraid to take a chance. And I'm not talking about just the young folks all full of dreams. I'm talking about anybody that feels like they're all used up.

Then after I said amen, I bowed my head again and said, "Lord, I wouldn't mind making me a little money on this deal, either."

And if all goes right, my girlfriend, Dot Struthers, and I ought to come out at least a little bit ahead on this self-publishing idea that she has whomped up. I would never do it on my own, but Dot has a nose for business, plus she can type, and if she says we can write a book and publish it ourselves and make a little money, well, I don't argue. She is going to make us some little wire racks out of old coat hangers and my job will be to see that every truck stop in the United States of America has one of these racks sitting on the counter, stuffed full of copies of *Honky Tonk Logic,* the story of one woman's life, namely mine. I'm not ashamed to say that I'm telling my story for money. After all I have been through, I feel like it's the least I deserve. Furthermore, if, in the process, I have to give up my privacy, then so be it. If I become the toast of *Entertainment Tonight* or live to see some ex–Charlie's Angel portray me in a miniseries, then just spell my name right. That's Raylene Stout from Lake Gladys, Louisiana.

3

Oh, Lake Gladys. Excuse me while I heave a big all-purpose sigh. On a road map, Lake Gladys looks bigger than it is, probably because there's plenty of blank space between Lake Charles and New Iberia to write the name of the town without scrunching it all up. However, small as it is, a population barely into four figures, Lake Gladys is the big apple to the people that live up and down our stretch of the long, long Bayou LeJeune or along the banks of the Pawhusky River that passes by on its way to the Mississippi, or by the lake itself, which is just a little muddy puddle of a thing, but they had to name the town something. Lake Gladys does have one claim to fame: if you watch TV or read the papers or have been anywhere except under a rock for the last ten years, you may recognize the name of Lake Gladys as the hometown of that noted saver of souls and America's favorite defrocked televangelist, Dr. Leroy Lazarus. He has always liked to call attention to the fact that he is just a good ole boy from a small town in the bayou country, not the least bit susceptible to whoring and highway robbery, praise the Lord. I'll have more to say later about the good doctor, whose ten-dollar Ph.D. was conferred upon him via the U.S. mails from a university in Florida that advertises in the back of a magazine called *Bikes 'n' Babes*.

People are friendly and sociable in Lake Gladys, and at night the lemony smell of magnolia blossoms can break your heart provided you're far enough away from the shrimp factory, where, after a heavy rain, the waters of the bayou lap right up over the piers. I won't talk about the mosquitoes and the less said about the water moccasins the better. But it was home. It's where I grew up as the only child of one of the singing Keating twins of southwest Louisiana fame (like true celebrities, they never went by their married names) and the only granddaughter of the parish judge, who was a legend in his own time, not only for the length of time he spent in office but for his fiddle shaped like the state of Louisiana that he carried with him everywhere like Matt Dillon carried a six-shooter. He could whip that thing out in an emergency and play a two-step that would put a smile on the face of a tax collector. And he always wore a suit, too, Bible black, even going fishing. People like their judges to look dignified, he always told me. My granddad was named James Raymond Keating, though I never heard anybody call him anything but "the judge." He had been married to my grandmother, a beautiful Cajun girl named Viola, less than a year when he decided to run for parish judge and, to everyone's surprise, he won a landslide victory. A lot of people in town said that the quiet and mysterious "Miss Viola," as everyone called her even back then, had worked some Cajun mumbo jumbo on the outcome of this election. They talked about the hundreds of banana-scented candles that she burned day and night in the windows of the little house during the campaign. There was also talk that people passing by late at night could hear Miss Viola chanting some kind of Latin-sounding something or other over and over. Other people said the candles were nothing more than mosquito repellents and that the chanting was just some crazy Cajun kind of music. Who knows? I do know that a lot of bayou people respected my grandmother as a *traiteur,* or a treater, because she was left-handed and able to cure warts, and I know that she had her own ways of doing things.

Before the judge's first term of office was completed way back in the mists of time, Miss Viola gave birth to her twin girls, Eilene and Earlene. Their names were suggested by the judge's friend and adviser, an up-and-coming young lawyer with a fine mind for politics named Huey Long. It was a good idea because, thereafter, the Misses Eilene and Earlene Fournier, the rich old maid sisters who owned half the parish, not only sent valuable birthday presents to the little twins each year, but supported the judge in every campaign.

I just want to mention in passing another item about the early life of the judge and Miss Viola. (Don't you hate these biographies where, before they get to the grit of the story, they go on and on about which way the wind was blowing when the ancestors came over on the *Mayflower?*) I don't want to make a big thing of this, because my story, as you will see, has enough credibility problems as it is, but a lot of people in Lake Gladys claimed Miss Viola's little poodle, Poupée, had been able to talk. However, you know how people like to stretch a story. The truth, according to Miss Viola, was that old Poupee could indeed communicate by saying "Uh-huh" for yes and "Uh-uh" for no with the appropriate head shakes. The other thing he could do and often did, for his own amusement and with no coaxing, was walk around the house and yard upright on his hind legs for hours at a time. So Poupée was kind of a special dog and my grandmother had been very devoted to him. When I was growing up, Miss Viola always wore a ring that the judge had given her when Poupée died of old age. The ring was set with little emeralds and diamonds in the shape of a little poodle.

The judge swung a lot of weight in Lake Gladys over the years, and when his buddy Huey became governor and dropped by for overnight visits during reelection time, people thought he was a big shot sure enough. However, as important a man as her husband was, Miss Viola was the ruler of the house, and even Huey Long wasn't allowed to smoke cigars in the front parlor. My grandfather consulted his wife about everything from his wardrobe to her opinion on the poll tax laws, and she had the final say on most subjects.

The twins were inseparable and did everything side by side, including falling in love, when they came of age. In a town where most weddings included a lot of crepe paper, the judge went all out to marry off his daughters in fine fashion. He rented out the Hotel Lake Gladys's banquet room, where the crystal chandelier was said to be a duplicate of one in the governor's mansion in Baton Rouge. For entertainment he hired the Sonnier Brothers, who held forth with old-time Cajun music till well past midnight. At one point in the evening, the twins stepped up to the bandstand and sang along with Antoine Sonnier on "La Jolie Blonde" in such perfect harmony that even the dignified Miss Viola was seen to wipe away a tear. When a decent interval had passed after the big wedding, Eilene had a son and named him James Aubrey Clayton to honor both her daddy and her husband, Uncle Aubrey, who sipped Dr Pepper mixed with Dr. Tichenor's Antiseptic all day long and who probably never received (or deserved) another honor in his lifetime. James Aubrey was always known as Jamie, a kind of a cute name that I wouldn't have minded having bestowed upon me since it works well for either sex (and this would turn out to be convenient in the years to come, but not another word about that, because that would be getting ahead of my story). So it fell to me, when Earlene gave birth mere hours later—and nobody will ever know how the twins accomplished this, but their ways were always baffling—to enter the world as Raylene Viola Arceneaux and to do battle forever after as a Raylene in a world full of Pams and Debbies. This was when all you Kimberlys and Tiffanys out there were just twinkles in your daddies' eyes.

By the time I was born, the judge was smoking dollar cigars and driving a brand-new Mercury every year, which I guess we all could if we got into politics and stayed there fifty years the way he did. After the twins married, they moved into little white clapboard houses—matching, of course—on either side of the house they grew up in, known forever after as "the big house." Miss Viola still devoted her time to sewing matching outfits for them and inventing new hairdos for them. Later, she took it upon herself to oversee the activities of Jamie and me. She ran a tight ship and made sure we brushed our teeth and took our naps and didn't track up the kitchen floor. She spent hours with us, playing Scrabble, telling stories about the old days, teaching us to read. She taught us about the bad luck an upside-down loaf of bread can bring and how to court good luck by eating seven kinds of greens on the Wednesday before Good Friday. She told us how to get rid of unwanted visitors: wait till they leave, then stand a broom upside down behind the door, slap a dishrag over it, and plunge a fork through the dishrag. They won't come back. It works. I've tried it many times. Miss Viola seemed to know everything worth knowing. Lord knows, if the mothering duties had been left up to the twins, Jamie and I would have grown up like wild-eyed banshees. Jamie and I were as close as pages in a book when we were real little and we even looked alike, everybody said, much to the delight of our mothers, who dressed us in matching outfits till we were big enough to put a stop to that nonsense. After we were dressed, however, the twins practiced their music and did their hair behind closed doors. Did they worry about their kids? Not much. The twins were staunch members of the "shit happens" school of child raising, and it was Miss Viola who took up the slack. And, for me, Jamie. On rainy days I couldn't have done without him. It was Jamie who found the Morse code in the *Compton's Encyclopedia* and tapped out messages to me over the telephone with a spoon. It was me who kept saying "Slow down," as I looked up each letter in my own encyclopedia (the salesman from Compton's had given the twins a two-for-one-and-a-half deal). Jamie was the one who discovered the notch in his backyard oak tree, the perfect hiding place for secret messages. We had a lot of those. It was Jamie's idea, when we were barely in school, that if we dug a hole in his backyard and just kept on digging we'd eventually get to China. So dig we did for one whole Saturday, till Uncle Aubrey came running out and pitched a fit that the neighbors talk about to this day.

Jamie's mother and mine were identical to the point that you wanted to slap them. They dressed alike, walked alike, talked alike, told the same lies, and went everywhere together till the day they died together. If Mother went on a celery-and-water diet, as she often did, so did Aunt Eilene, because the twins were obsessive about how they looked. If Aunt Eilene went to bed in the middle of the afternoon with a sick headache, I always knew I could go home and find Mother upstairs flat on her back with a wet washrag over her face. The twins enjoyed poor health, as my grandmother said time after time, and Jamie and I learned how to tiptoe as soon as we could walk. Their lives seemed very separate from mine and Jamie's, with their movie magazines and *Evening in Paris* and open-toed shoes, but we were grateful for every glimpse they gave us into their secret world. They had a collection of a hundred silk or semisilk scarves from every place they had ever been and Jamie and I spent hours unfolding and admiring these treasures. The inscriptions—like Hot Springs, Vacation Paradise, or St. Louis, Gateway to the West—seemed as exotic and remote as those perfumed creatures we had for mothers.

Every couple of years around election time, the twins would rally from their headaches and sniffles, because this was when they were most appreciated. The twins, or "the songbirds of South Louisiana," as the judge proudly introduced them, sang and played the piano at every stumping in Burton Parish and you can bet they produced a respectable number of votes for my granddaddy over the years. My grandmother often said the twins could have been much bigger in show business if only they had not been such high-strung girls. But high-strung or no, they sure could harmonize. Just turn 'em loose on any of the old backwater Cajun songs. And play the piano? Honey! They would sit side by side on a piano bench, Eilene playing the right-hand part, Earlene the left, and the arms not in use clasped around each other's waists. They'd start out on something slow like "Mockingbird Hill" and wind up with their fingers flying in a blur up and down the keyboard to some fast and sassy Cajun two-step normally played on fiddles and accordions. It was something to see. And they got more applause than any of the candidates for the parish offices, you can bet. The country people that gravitated to the political speaking events generally just milled around chewing toothpicks and tobacco and shooting knowing looks at one another in response to the candidates' promises. They weren't "in touch with their feelings," as they say on the talk shows these days, but, when the twins got through with them, you never saw such a commotion—whistling, cheering, clapping, and carrying on. And nobody clapped harder than little Raylene, but sometimes I would have to stop and actually hold my hand over my heart to keep it from jumping out of my chest with pride while the twins bounced around blowing kisses at the frenzied crowd. Attention was what the twins lived for, it was why they spent all the time and money keeping their hair blond and curly and perfectly duplicated down to the dinkiest little spit curl. I can still see their flushed little faces, curtsying and grinning as they stood, barely five feet tall, beside the towering judge at the end of their act on a flatbed truck that served as a stage.

Jamie and I inherited our mothers' size, or lack of it. As we entered high school, our reputations were already well established: Jamie was the class cutup, always running here and there with his friends, chasing after fun and mischief, stealing watermelons out of moonlit patches, sneaking off for joyrides in the judge's Mercury. And the movies, always the movies, he never got enough of the movies. I wasn't exactly a wallflower myself. People called me "sassy" and "cute" and I blossomed as the head majorette for the high school band, the Marching Muskrats. Jamie worked on the school newspaper and read a lot of books, though he acted like he didn't have a brain in his head—always joking and two-stepping at the weekly fais-dodo. Once, in the tenth grade, we went to a costume party as each other, me as him, him as me—his bright idea. It was fun till a certain Shirley Jack Crabtree sidled up to Jamie and pointed out that he was a cuter Raylene than Raylene. You'll be hearing more about Shirley Jack later. Way too much to suit me.

As teenagers, Jamie and I were still close, but we spent less time together just because there were not enough hours in the day for me to practice with the band and do all the other extracurricular activities I was involved in—football games and pep rallies and popularity contests. Sometimes the kids in our class would use words like "weird" or "strange" when Jamie's name came up, but to me, when he took more of an interest in decorating for the prom or the latest gossip from Hollywood than in the record of the mighty Muskrats, well, hell, that was just Jamie. Sometimes, at age sixteen, he would take a Greyhound bus to New Orleans and spend the weekend all by himself. And that was just Jamie, too.

Two events, one when we were nearly seventeen and another less than a year later, sort of put the lid on my childhood and Jamie's. The first was the night the twins committed suicide. It happened in the fall after a summer when nothing went right. First they auditioned for a weekly spot on the *Louisiana Hayride,* a radio show out of Shreveport. They were crushed when they lost out to another sister act, the Pomada Sisters, who not only sang like angels on any Kitty Wells song you could name, but accompanied themselves on talking guitars as well. Then Uncle Aubrey lost his job at the paper mill, went on a drinking binge, and ran his pickup slam into the Daughters of the Confederacy statue on the courthouse lawn, totaling both the truck and the statue. And then no sooner did Uncle Aubrey sober up than my own dad confessed to my mother that he was in love with Tammy Crack, a pretty young grocery checker at Piggly Wiggly. It didn't surprise anybody that this series of disasters plunged the twins into a deep depression. Lord knows, they had taken to their beds many a time before over much less serious matters. This time, they wouldn't eat, sleep, talk, nothing. For days, they sat in my mother's bedroom, their eyes like vacant store windows, as they thumbed through old sheet music and cried. What pushed them over the edge was a grapefruit-and-pine-tar-based hair dye of champagne blond sold to them by a smooth-talking salesman who appeared at our front door one day. The twins dyed each other's hair one Saturday morning and an hour later their hair began to come out in handfuls. By sundown they were completely bald, and, as you can imagine, completely hysterical. As shook up as I was by the situation, there was nothing to be done, and I went on out to the movies with Nick Tarkington, my high school honey. Later, as we sat holding hands at the Cameo and watching a James Bond movie, a flashlight suddenly went on at the end of the aisle. I heard somebody say my name in a hoarse whisper and it was Mr. Averett who owned the theater. When I saw Miss Viola standing, stunned and weary, on the sidewalk outside the theater, she didn't need to say much.

"Raylene," she said, "Raylene, I have something to tell you. Something has happened. Your mother and your Aunt Eilene . . ."

Somehow I knew.

"They're dead?" I asked.

Miss Viola stared into my eyes and nodded. She looked different, sort of haggard, and that's how she looked the rest of her life. The twins had been found in the garage of our house. They sat peacefully holding hands on the backseat of my dad's Studebaker, a garden hose rigged up from the exhaust pipe to a window. Their heads were swaddled in matching scarves, souvenirs from a town in the Ozarks so hilly that you enter the church through the steeple. They wore their new red sling-back pumps from Sears. Their nails, just as red as their shoes, were perfect.

For months I would wake up in the middle of the night thinking that it was all a bad dream. Miss Viola worried about me. During the day, I could feel her watching me. Her eyes would brim over with her feelings, but words didn't come easy to my grandmother, especially the kind of words I needed at the time. One night, she came to me on her back porch where I was sitting all alone, feeling sad and watching the lightning bugs flit around the honeysuckle.

She said, "What are you doing out here, Raylene?"

"Just thinking," I said.

She said, "You think too much, honey."

She seemed to be waiting for me to reply, but I didn't. Suddenly, she sat down beside me on the porch swing and said, "Raylene, I want you to have something."

She slipped a ring off her finger and laid it in my hand. It was the ring the judge had given her after the death of her dog. She knew I loved that ring and I knew how she treasured it. It was her only real jewelry besides her wedding ring.

I said, "Oh, I can't take that."

"Yes, you can," she said, and slipped it on my finger. "I want you to have it. As a gift from your grandmother."

I didn't argue. Nobody argued with Miss Viola. I held out my hand and looked at the little dog made of emeralds and Miss Viola disappeared into the house without another word before I had a chance to thank her.

As for Jamie, he went into his room and hardly came out for weeks. Aunt Eilene had always acted as sort of a buffer or maybe a referee between Jamie and his dad, who could be pretty forceful in a disagreement, especially when he was drunk. Many times, Jamie retreated with his bruises to the big house. He began to spend more and more time alone. I can remember standing outside his room with my ear pressed to the door.

"Jamie?"

"I'm reading."

"Oh."

I worried about Jamie. However, I did have something else going on in my life that was pretty distracting: I was in love. For the first time. With Nick. And we all know about these first loves, don't we?

There's nothing like 'em. Oh, the tortures and the raptures of high school romance. The mountains made out of molehills. The hours spent on the phone. The revolutions made around his block by me and Dot Struthers in her daddy's pickup. I could never get over how bland and blank Nick's little white frame house looked, how similar it was to the ones on either side of it. This was the house so privileged as to contain my sleeping, bathing, laughing dreamboat? The house where he thought the tenderest kinds of thoughts about me and relayed them by telephone? Where he spun his PP&M records (as he always called Peter, Paul, and Mary. Oh, he was so cool.). And this was where he splashed on his West Indian Lime cologne? This house with the concrete steps and plain old rectangular windows? It seemed to me like the windows ought to turn up at the corners in a big proud smile. And how come the sidewalk didn't sport a bright red carpet to celebrate his comings and goings? Nick was dark-haired and soft-spoken. He had just moved to Lake Gladys from Tallahassee, Florida, the year before and, oh, he was so polite and so slick-looking and so different from the other guys. He sat next to Jamie in the trumpet section of the school band and the two of them became fast friends, much to my delight. Whenever Nick came over to Jamie's to study or shoot hoops in the backyard, there I'd be. "Oh, hello, Nick, what a surprise!" After weeks of hint dropping and eyelash batting on my part, Nick asked me to the shrimp festival dance. We went out together off and on throughout our senior year and he always made me feel like somebody special—never any of this backseat grappling or talking dirty. By graduation time I had just about made my mind up about Nick Tarkington.

"He's the one," I told Jamie one night as we sat playing Monopoly in his room.

"You're too young," he said.

"I couldn't do any better," I said. "I'm gonna marry him."

"Has he asked you?"

"Well, no, but . . ."

The next night—well, it was my idea—Nick and I exchanged rings, which is what all the kids did to show they were going steady.

He gave me his class ring, but when I handed him mine, he said he wanted to wear the other one, Miss Viola's ring.

I said, "I can't. My grandmother would kill me," but he convinced me to let him wear it just for a little while and went home with the ring on his little finger.

As I said, there were two events that final year of high school that Jamie and I would never forget. The second one, Nick's drowning, happened only a few nights after he and I exchanged rings. It was the night of our high school graduation party at Dot Struthers's dad's camp house out on the river. Nick and I had split up on the phone a couple of nights before because he had broken a date with me for the second time in a row. Miss Raylene Arceneaux did not cotton to such behavior. Always his excuse was the same: his mother, a divorcée, was creating big drunken scenes over this and that and he didn't want to leave her alone. He said he was afraid she might hurt herself or wreck the car or something.

"It's true," Jamie told me. "His mom's nuts. You ought to be more understanding, Raylene." But I didn't listen because Jamie always took Nick's side in any of our little lovers' spats, and besides, Bo Portier, fullback for the Mighty Muskrats, was giving me a big rush and I knew Nick was jealous, which suited me just fine. Oh, yes, I was a teenage Jezebel.

I arrived at the party with Bo and looked around for Nick. He wasn't there. When he showed up a few minutes later with the widely grinning Shirley Jack in tow, the party was ruined for me. Shirley Jack had been chasing him for months and this was her night of triumph. The festivities were centered around the big screened porch of the house that sat up on the bank of the river, but there were hot and cold running kids all over—drinking beer and making out in cars, hanging from trees, floating down the river in canoes, though swimming was out. Heavy rains had swelled the river till it overflowed its banks and the current was going full tilt. A couple of guys got into a fist-fight over God knows what and all the kids gathered in the yard to watch and hoot and holler. I watched Miss Shirley Jack right there on the sidelines yelling her fool head off, while Nick stood talking with Jamie and some other guys under a tree. I was bored with the whole scene and real unhappy when I left Bo's side and wandered into the house. I was kneeling on the darkened screen porch, petting Dot's old hound, when I heard somebody behind me.

"Raylene?" It was Nick.

"What?"

"Are you still mad?"

"Yes," I said, with my back to him.

He said, "I wish I could explain everything to you," and he said it in such a tone of voice, exhausted and sort of hopeless, that I gave the dog one final pat and turned, ready to make amends or at least to get my ring back.

Then the screen door squeaked open and slammed and I heard an all too familiar voice say, "Nick! I've been looking all over for you! Oh, hi, Raylene."

"Hi, Shirley Jack." And I made myself scarce.

I was just coming up for air from a hot clinch with Bo Portier in the front seat of his Pontiac when I saw three people walking toward us through a thicket of pines. I looked closer. In the dim light I recognized tubby Karen Hebert and treetop tall Johnny Capp, but who was that dead weight they were supporting between them? Shirley Jack. And the three of them were wailing like Judgment Day was here and they were not among the chosen.

Well, their voices began drifting over to us and what Shirley Jack was saying was, "He's dead, he's dead." And what her friends were saying was, "Don't cry, don't cry."

Nick had jumped from the bridge. When I found out what had happened, I became hysterical. Just beside myself. I bolted from Bo's car and ran through the crowd looking for Jamie, but there was so much confusion, I couldn't find him. The next day, Nick's body washed ashore a few miles downriver. Weeks later, feeling miserable,

I got up the courage to ask his mother about the ring. She looked at me a long time before she sighed and said, "I don't know anything about a ring."

The night of the drowning, Bo took me home to the big house, where I was living with my grandparents since my dad and Tammy Crack had married and lit out for Lake Charles to start a new life. I went straight to the phone to call Jamie. He answered the phone sounding all distressed.

I was sobbing myself. I said, "Jamie, I need to talk to you."

I could hear Uncle Aubrey yelling in the background, but couldn't make out what he was saying. Jamie said he couldn't talk right then, he would call me later. I sat by the phone and waited but Jamie never called.

I cried myself to sleep. Just before daylight it began to rain and I got up to close the window of my bedroom, which still felt like Miss Viola's sewing room to me. If I had got up one minute later, I would not have seen him, but there was Jamie, loping across his backyard like a burglar under the oak tree that was big as a church. He wore jeans and a T-shirt and carried a little suitcase. I watched him steal across the lawn toward the point where our backyards drop off into a ravine. I thought he turned for a moment and looked toward my window, but I might have been wrong about that. If he did see me he didn't let on. He just headed down into the ravine. I remember standing there a long time with my hands pressed against the window. Seemed like I was hypnotized by the ribbon of darkness where he had waded through the Johnson grass. And the cold glass against my fingertips was sending a message up my skinny teenage arms. I remember thinking Jamie was gone for good. And I was right.

One

The big Wal-Mart out on the New Iberia highway forced my hardware store out of business. I wasn't all that sorry. My feet were calluses up to the ankles from twenty years of standing on a concrete floor, shucking and jiving with the customers all day long. When it got so bad that selling a three-speed fan was a cause for me and my cashier, Myrtis Broussard, to share a bourbon and Coke in the backroom, I decided the time had come to close the doors on Raylene's Hardware and Tool Rental. I was tired, anyway. I was about shucked out.

"What are you gonna do now, Raylene?" people asked.

"I'm gonna watch some TV, go bowling, drink some beer, run around on my husband," I would say with a ha-ha-ha.

But I began to notice that people didn't ha-ha-ha back at me. What they were giving me was more like a sympathetic smile and a quick change of subject. Hmm. Well, well, well. It didn't take me long to figure this little mystery out. It was pretty obvious that jokes about my marriage did not exactly strike my friends as humorous. It was pretty obvious that someone had been leaking confidential information, someone privy to the loose bundle of heartaches and frustrations that I called my life. So, one night I marched right down Singletary Street to the house where my lifelong best friend and confidante Dot Struthers, has lived her entire life. After I made sure her mother and daddy were safely tucked away (Dot waited on them hand and foot and worked full-time and still managed to be the state bowling champion, female division), I said, "Dot, you and me need to have a talk."

Well, she was busy trying on a new dress, squinting into the mirror, snapping her gum. She looked at me out of the corner of her eyes and said, "Pertaining to what?"

"Pertaining to my husband and that big mouth of yours."

I guess I had better point out right here that I talk to Dot any damn way I please and vice versa, which is one of the most important advantages of having a lifelong best friend. Well, she swore and be damned that she was not guilty, Your Honor, in the case of the tattling tongue. And of course, she carried on so, a-cussin' and a-wailin' and calling me every name in the book, that I was sorry I came. In fact I ended up apologizing to her. That's me. That's how I am. Plus Dot is not somebody you want to mess with. If you're ever in the vicinity of the Tick-Tock Tavern out on Highway 49, check out the eight-by-ten glossy of her hanging on the wall: six times in a row she's won their annual ladies' arm wrestling championship and she's still going strong.

I said, "I'm sorry, Dot. It's just that you're the one that pouts if I don't share every detail of my life with you. And let's face it, honey, you do have a mouth like the Grand Canyon." I was just trying to get a rise out of her. She looked so put out with me.

She waved me away and went back to looking in the mirror, pursing her lips, squaring her shoulders, loosening up a little bit. Dot had too much sense to hold a grudge, especially when she knew I was really upset, or had my tail over the dashboard, as she would put it. She tried to change the subject.

"Let's face it," she said, "I do look like a million bucks in blue."

But I wouldn't let her distract me. "So who spilt the beans?" I said.

Well, that set her off again. She wheeled around and said, "Raylene, let's talk about big mouths here. I told you not to tell Sue all that stuff. . . ."

I said, "Dot, Sue Fontenot moved to Abbeville six months ago, as if you didn't know."

"Raylene, were you under the impression that there's a statute of limitations on gossip?" Dot was in charge of issuing driver's licenses down at the courthouse and she liked to throw all these legal terms around.

I said, "All right. The word is out. My husband is catnip to the ladies."

"Your husband," she said, "would screw anything from a stovepipe to a horse collar," and she commenced to spring a brand-new story on me. Whispering so as not to disturb her folks, she told me she had seen Buck and Marie LeBlanc in his car out at the A&W one night the week before, drinking root beers in a very lovey-dovey fashion (whatever that means; I pictured them doing the one mug–two straws thing like Judy Garland and Mickey Rooney). This Marie wasn't exactly a nun. Everybody in town had lost track of her divorces, not to mention the color of her hair, which changed about once a week. Plus they say she spent every dime she made on her collection of lacy black underwear that showed more than it hid, and there was plenty to show, as this was a woman so fat she'd roll off your lap. Not that that ever seemed to present a problem with the captivating Marie. As they say, "More to love," and that's enough about the attractions of hefty women right now, though it's a subject I will touch on again a little later in my story.

"What were you doing," I said, "saving that story for a rainy day?" After all, she and I were on the phone practically every night, breaking down the latest Lake Gladys gossip and rendering our verdicts.

"Raylene," she said, "I didn't want to hurt you."

By the time I got up to leave, I was beyond hurt. All I felt was a heavy, gray fog between my ears that was beginning to take shape as a headache. I didn't need trouble from Buck. I had my hands full with unloading the hardware store and trying to cope with my sixteen-year-old daughter, who was giving me more trouble than I could say grace over. Staying out till all hours with a fast crowd and drinking and probably taking all kinds of dope. And her clothes! I don't know how it is in the rest of the country, but in Lake Gladys, I believe the teenage girls hold a contest every morning to see who can go off to school looking like the biggest slut.

Seemed like I was always "at" her, like I had been such a prim and proper little thing when I was her age, which I definitely wasn't.

"Leslie, you go wash that face! I don't know how you can see out of those eyes with that much Maybelline on 'em!"

Or, "Les, are you sure that skirt's short enough? I can't quite see your behind."

That very morning we had had a face-off about the state of her room.

"Well, I can't help it, Mother. I'm always on the run."

"Well, fine, young lady. You can run right over there and pick up those dirty socks and then you can run right over here and take care of this wet towel and then you can run right out to the washing machine . . ."

Of course I had to stand right behind her the whole time. And, Lord, she set up such a howling and a carrying on, you would have thought I had a gun to her back, marching her down to the river to pound her clothes against the rocks.

Oh, it was always something, and if I had known she would run off and marry Bobby Bridges and move to Chicago in less than a year's time, I guess—no, I *know*—I would have nagged less and I would have managed to spend more of what they call "quality time" with my daughter, but you never realize these things till it's too late and I don't want to think about it right now.

According to Dot, Buck's little affairettes had numbered about double the ones I knew about, and once she got up a head of steam, she ticked them off on her fingers—Patsy Birdsill, Odile Boudreaux, and even the tacky Poison Ivy Lefever, who had been three times widowed at age thirty, and legend has it that at least two of those husbands died of heart attacks while having sex with Ivy. (I say let the buyer beware on that one.) But, oh, I'm not going to name all of Buck's women. There was a bunch. Take my word for it.

Well, like I said, my tail was a-dragging in the mud when I left Dot's, but if you think I slumped into the house that night, laid my keys on the table with a hopeless sigh, and ran a hot bath to drown my sorrow, you've got another think coming. I had had just about enough. Oh, yes. If you think I didn't upend the kitchen table and break half the dishes and snatch all the pictures off the wall and send 'em crashing to the floor, then you don't have a clue as to how upset I was and how tired I was of turning the other cheek in regard to Buck's general sloppiness in every area of his life. And this was before the man even got home! When he did pull up in the driveway well after midnight, he tiptoed through the door. He knew something was up. You bet. Well, maybe it was the venetian blinds I had yanked off the living room window after they had pissed me off somehow and, of course, every light in the house was on. I have to smile now at the picture of me waiting for him, holding a rolling pin behind my back like in a Maggie and Jiggs cartoon, but, boy, smiling was the last thing on my mind at the time. What I had in mind was something along the lines of: Wham! "That's for Marie LeBlanc!" Wham! "That's for Patsy Birdsill!" Et cetera, et cetera, et cetera. What came to pass was a couple of wild swings on my part and some fancy dodging and fast talking on Buck's part. So he survived. We even made up. Oh, yes, we made up. Why? I've often wondered. Calling Dr. Joyce Brothers! Well, I guess it was because my husband and daughter were the only family I had left. My dad didn't last more than three years after he moved off to Lake Charles. Heart attack. I guess he couldn't keep up with Tammy. I assumed Jamie was still breathing out there in the world somewhere. Over the years, he had sent me postcards from New York and Madrid and Amsterdam and Hong Kong and places I had only dreamed of visiting, but after Miss Viola died ten years before, we had gradually lost contact and I wasn't even sure what country he was living in.

So, since Leslie only dropped by to change clothes, it was usually just me and Buck in our little house on Singletary Street, a block down from the house I was raised in. After a couple of decades and the little cracks and creases this man had put into my heart, I was still with him, though sometimes I would have to shake my head and moan and wonder why.

But there we were. Mr. and Mrs. Buck Turner. Only one kid, much to Maw Turner's often-expressed concern, as if she didn't have thirty other grandchildren. Lord, Buck's brothers and sisters were worse than rabbits. I've never been sorry that I had only one child, because I always felt like having Buck was just about like having a second one. That man never wrote a check in his life. Or filled out an income tax form. Or picked up his dirty drawers off the floor.

All right. So I did retire. Our money was tight, of course. Buck didn't bring in enough from selling Buicks to keep a goose alive, but I had a little savings and I swore and be damned that I was going to take a year off. I had damn well earned it. At first, I enjoyed following the soap operas and staying up for the late movies and having plenty of time to gossip with my girlfriends on the phone. I puttered in the backyard a little bit, slept late, tried to write a song that I was going to send to Loretta Lynn to make a million bucks, but I never finished it. I made a few fancy dinners for Buck, but his hours were so unpredictable that I gave up on that fairly soon. I ran up a skirt (of a decent length) on the sewing machine for Leslie, but she never wore it.

Did my husband stop his philandering? No. We had it out a few times, but arguing with him and listening to his lies was more trouble than it was worth. And still I stayed. Are you there, Dr. Brothers?

It got to me sometimes. Some days I stayed in my robe all day long, pacing and smoking, pacing and smoking, restless as a roach in a skillet. Sometimes I stood at the window and watched the birds pecking at things on the ground and then flying into the distance until they disappeared. I envied those birds so much. Oh, to just be able to pick up and go soaring off till you're nothing but a tiny speck against the sky. Compared with those birds, my life seemed—I don't know—insurmountable, I guess, is the word. I spent a lot of time thinking about things I wanted to do with my life when I was a kid. When I was a teenager I used to talk about becoming a veterinarian. Or a newscaster on the radio. Back then I thought there was nothing I couldn't do. I wondered about Jamie a lot, too, wondered just what direction his life had taken. I spent a lot of time sighing.

For a while, I found something to occupy my time. I started to watch the talk shows, the ones that come on in the daytime that give you all the inside stuff on dysfunctional families. About girls that steal their mama's boyfriends. Or alcoholic lesbian nuns that beat their children. I guess my life seemed bearable by comparison with what these poor people had to put up with. However, I did have a daughter who was like a stranger and, Lord knows, I had a dysfunctional husband, although he seemed to function fine with other women. I had testimony to that fact in the form of lipsticked collars and phone numbers written on bar napkins that turned up when I did the laundry.

After a while I started to tape the damn talk shows. I guess I thought I might want to refer back to them sometime to clear up this or that point. Or maybe I was just trying to get Buck's attention. At any rate, after I filled up the coat closet with VCR tapes, he did complain and I quit taping.

One time Buck got the flu and had to stay home from work. He wallowed in the bed all day long clicking from one TV channel to another while I schlepped orange juice and chicken soup back and forth from the kitchen, smiling all the while, going, "You feeling any better, honey?"

His second day in bed I walked into the bedroom to find him watching that TV like a dog that had something treed. He glanced up at me and said, "Now here's what you ought to be taping, Raylene."

What he was watching was my old classmate, Shirley Jack Crabtree Lazarus, in her gold lamé tights and Property of Jesus sweatshirt doing her Christian aerobics program, a sort of warm-up for her husband's hellfire-and-brimstone program that followed. She was doing leg lifts and quoting Scripture and grinning like a possum all at the same time. I gave Buck a couple of whacks with a pillow and walked out of the room.

"Well, she *is* built good," he said, but he didn't have the nerve to say anything else because he knew I was not fond of Shirley Jack in the least and, of course, he didn't want to run the risk of losing his maidservant.

Then, when New Year's Eve rolled around, I took off my clothes and looked in the full-length mirror in my bedroom and I looked a long time. I said out loud to the person I saw, "Well, I'm here, but who invited you?" My body had gone to droop city. Ever since I was a kid, I had always been an active person, even athletic. It always made me proud when strangers took me and Leslie for sisters, and I think she got a kick out of it too. Secretly, of course. A few years before, Dot and I had been running a mile or so down at the high school stadium every evening, plus I had always bowled off and on with Dot and a bunch of girls I went to high school with. But standing there in front of that mirror that evening, what I saw was that the defeat that I had sort of got used to seeing on my face had slid down to my arms and legs. And worse, I saw somebody who accepted defeat as the natural state of things. I had a husband that ran around on me, a kid out of control, a sink full of dirty dishes, ashtrays full of cigarettes, flabby thighs that looked only vaguely familiar to me (Whose *are* they? How'd they *get* there? I'd wonder as I sat soaking in the tub.). I sat down and wrote out some New Year's resolutions.

And I changed. I joined Virginia Scribner's aerobics studio and got in shape. After a month or so, I was going to two sessions a day, once in the morning and once in the evening. I felt great. It seemed like the dishes and the laundry did themselves, and I could zip that vacuum cleaner through the house in minutes flat. I even cut way back on my smoking for the first time since I was a teenager. I figured it would be just a matter of time before Buck noticed the difference in me. I'm glad I didn't hold my breath.

The day I shot my husband started out like any other. I nagged till he got his lazy ass out of bed; I served his usual breakfast—eggs over easy, a hunk of cold Spam, a can of Royal Crown Cola, and a glass of Sal Hepatica on the rocks. I even tied his necktie, didn't get so much as a peck on the cheek for my efforts, and didn't expect one. I told him I would be in Abbeville all day helping Sue Fontenot put up peaches and I would be home by eight that evening. I waved him off to work and cleaned the house a little. I wrote out my recipe for cantaloupe pie, Leslie's favorite, and sent it off to my daughter in Chicago, where she was making an attempt at being the perfect housewife.

Sue called and said could we make it tomorrow because her mother-in-law fell in the tub and broke her hip. I said sure, and went to my workout, ran my beloved Mustang convertible through the car wash, went to pick up some clothes at the cleaners. My hair was a mess and on an impulse I called Oma Phillips to see if she could fit me in at the Ouch of Class, where I had been getting my hair done since way back when Jimmy Carter was president and the T in the name of the place hadn't yet been blown away by a hurricane. Oma said sure, come on over, so I did. I sat down with a *Family Circle* magazine and started reading an article about how to keep your rosebushes from freezing. Like I owned a rosebush. Like freezing was a real problem in Lake Gladys.

My bowling buddy, Renee Clemons, was sitting across the room under a dryer which she turned off as soon as Oma waddled away to answer the phone.

She said, "Raylene. Raylene, I want to tell you something."

"What?" I said, a little shook up by the tone of her voice, because ordinarily old Renee keeps it pretty light.

"Raylene, I think I ought to tell you," she said in a low voice, "Shirley Jack is in town. . . ."

I felt my back stiffen but I said, "Well, so what?"

"Well, let me finish, Raylene," she said, then paused and finished in a rush. "I-saw-her-with-your-husband."

I was speechless for once. When Oma got to me, she couldn't believe how quiet and cooperative I was being. But she didn't mind because she could talk the legs off a stove herself. I didn't utter a peep while she jabbered on and ratted my hair up half a foot, something she had been trying to talk me into for years. I just sat and looked in the mirror while she "gave me a little height," as she put it. Of course, I looked like a damn fool when she got through with me, but I didn't care. I paid my bill and walked out without even saying good-bye. I know Oma must have thought I had lost my mind.

I drove down the street in a daze. I had been surviving Buck's floozies for years, but Shirley Jack was quite a different story. This woman had been a thorn in my side all my life, and, I truly believe, several lifetimes before this one. It started when she got me kicked out of the Campfire Girls for putting a garter snake in her bed. In high school, she got the boys I wanted and won the Poultry Princess Pageant, in which I was second runner-up. ("Oh, Raylene," she said later, ever so sweet, "I think you should've got first runner-up at least.") She wound up marrying another of our high school classmates, the toothpick-chewing, crotch-adjusting, ducktail-combing Leroy Lazarus, who must have appealed to some rebel instincts buried beneath Shirley Jack's pink organza dresses and plastic hair barrettes. Leroy was famous for biting the heads off of chickens, and I figured he and Shirley Jack could spend their lives one-upping each other with evil deeds. Nobody expected very much of this young couple's future, I can tell you. Everybody could just see Leroy as one of these modern husbands that spend all the baby's milk money on heroin, and a lot of us didn't have much trouble imagining Shirley Jack selling herself in the street. But I'll be damned if they didn't leave town, then turn up ten years later on national television as the devil-chasing Dr. Lazarus and his devoted, hymn-belting, leg-lifting wife, Shirley Jack.

Dr. Lazarus had suffered a major setback in recent months when he was arrested with a prostitute in New Orleans, but he was now back on television and more popular than ever. He had pleaded for God's forgiveness on the air and his devoted followers had doubled their donations. That tear-stained face, those shifty eyes—one on heaven and one on the cash register. His wife's exercise spots and elaborate song productions—"I Hear the Lord A-Knockin'" backed by a well-hairsprayed choir of fifty—only increased the popularity of his program. However, his fortunes fell a few months later when, just as some serious IRS problems were turning up for the good doctor, he got arrested again, this time in Baltimore, and this time with two hookers, one of them fourteen years old, the other twelve. He finally got booted off the air.

So I headed home. I was tapping my fingers on the steering wheel to that old song "Do Wah Diddy Diddy" that poured out of the radio while I waited for the light to change. I was just playing with the idea that, hey, maybe Buck was just trying to sell her a car, maybe I should give him the benefit of the doubt, and then I saw Shirley Jack drive by with a big smile on her face. I watched her turn in at a motel.

They didn't even have the decency to drive out to the new Marriott on the interstate where, with all the traveling salesmen milling around, there is a slight possibility that you can check in without being recognized. No, they went to the Val-U-Courts, where the economical accomodations are managed with a firm hand by none other than Miss Ruby LaFourche, who went to school with the twins and who had served Lake Gladys, Louisiana, faithfully for my entire lifetime as an unpaid one-woman clearinghouse for gossip.

I wish you could have seen Shirley Jack (I grit my teeth as I speak the name). She popped out of her little sports car and went skipping—*skipping*—toward cabin number 8 like there was something she was dying to get at in there. Of course, I couldn't imagine what. But I knew who that yellow Buick parked right in front belonged to. And when she knocked on the door, giggling all the while, I knew who that hairy arm that reached out and pulled her inside belonged to. It belonged to the same son of a bitch whose idea of spending a romantic evening with me was watching *Monday Night Football* with a couple of feet of space and a bag of potato chips and a six-pack of Pabst Blue Ribbon between us. As I watched Shirley Jack disappear into the cabin, the thought did occur to me that maybe with other women he's different, maybe if I was a different kind of woman . . . You see how it is? You see how women are? Do you think he would have ever had that concern about me? No, children, I don't believe so.

The thing that really hurt was the way Shirley Jack headed straight for that little love nest cabin like a pissant leaving a burning log, never thinking to look around to see who might be watching. I guess I would have felt better if they had looked like they were sneaking around. Or maybe not.

The light changed and the car behind me began to honk. I pulled into an alley, turned off the ignition, and just sat there staring straight ahead. I felt like I had been punched in the stomach and kicked in the head. At first, I thought I was going to cry, just to see if I still could, but no, it was no crying matter, I decided. I lit up a cigarette and sat there calm as a woman waiting to get her oil checked. Then I turned on the radio to hear the rest of that song because I happen to like it. After a few minutes, I put out the cigarette in the ashtray and eased on down the street like a woman who used to be a quart low but no longer. Doo-wah-diddy-diddy-dum-diddy-doo.

I drove along just as aimless as a goat, figuring my husband wouldn't be home for hours. Or maybe not till the next day. You know how working late and having a drink or two with the boys can keep a fellow out till way past midnight. Oh, the tales that we married women have swallowed down throughout the centuries. I couldn't remember the last time Buck and I had made love in the daytime, much less at high noon. Oh, let's tell it like it was, I couldn't remember the last time Buck and I had made love period. If it had been anybody but Shirley Jack Lazarus, I would have beat the door down and dragged Buck home by the hair of his head, but the idea of facing that woman, the humiliation of her knowing that I *knew* . . . I just couldn't.

I wondered how late he would come in that night. I wondered if he would think to call home. Sometimes, as a result of my nagging, he did. These calls from his "poker games" were always the same:

"Raylene?"

"Buck, it's way past midnight. You get your ass home."

"Pretty soon, pretty soon, we're gonna play another hand or two."

"Buck, you've got to work tomorrow. . . ."

"Yeah, I'll be there pretty soon," he would say, and then just to give himself an out, he always added, "Probably."

And he would hang up. By the time he did get home and shower and dress and go to work looking fresh as a daisy, I would be a wreck from pacing and smoking and fuming all night long. So many times it happened.

It was barely noon. I went home. I did not slam the door or tear up the venetian blinds. I didn't cry. I sat on the couch and smoked a few cigarettes. The phone rang and I just let it ring and ring and ring while I sat there thinking about all of Buck's little betrayals.

Over the years I had got used to Buck's—what should I call it?—lack of integrity, I guess. Or lack of consideration. He was never a cruel or mean-spirited man, but, I'm here to tell you, it was not very often that he thought of Raylene's feelings before his own. The first time I felt betrayed by Buck was right after the first meal I cooked following our honeymoon trip to Galveston. When it came time to do the dishes, I stood at the sink alone, up to my armpits in soapsuds, while Buck watched TV. I was fit to be tied. Now, mind you, this was after we had completed a series of five premarital counseling sessions at the First Methodist Church—my mother-in-law's idea. (One of her many.) At our last session, the chinless and hairless Reverend Blossom toyed with his rimless glasses and asked Buck what he had learned during these sessions.

"Well-l-l," my husband-to-be drawled, while he squeezed my moist little hand in his big rough one. "I guess it would be the importance of sharing."

And he was not being insincere or sarcastic. He was just being Buck. And unfortunately, he remained Buck all through our married life. In the waning days of our marriage, when Buck bedded down with Poison Ivy Lefever, the merry widow of Lake Gladys, I'm sure he worried more about escaping with his life than he did about doing me dirt. I didn't count.

I wonder how long I sat there on my couch that day. More than an hour, I know. Well, I know it wasn't too much past two o'clock—checkout time at the Val-U-Courts—when the door opened and in walked Buck. I froze. I made a split-second decision on how I was going to handle myself in this situation. I was going to keep on sitting on my couch, legs crossed, leaning back on Maw Turner's afghan, casually maintaining the attitude of a mama lion who had just polished off one gazelle but wouldn't mind another. There were things I needed to say and I would say them. I would not yell.

At the sight of me in my lioness mode, Buck froze too.

"Raylene! I thought you went to Sue's!"

"I changed my mind, Buck."

A second later, Shirley Jack bounced into view and I made another split-second decision. I decided to modify the original plan. I *would* yell.

Oh, God, I'm talking silly here, but what happened that day was not funny in the least. Not then. Not now.

I shot my husband.

But let me see if I can explain how it happened. As I said, I did raise my voice at the sight of the lovable, vivacious, bouncy, carrot-topped Shirley Jack. In fact, I raised it to the roof. I was in such a state at the time that I don't really remember my exact words but I think it's safe to say that the expression *"Get out!"* was used, and I believe I was even so ungracious as to use the word "bitch" in place of her Christian name. It doesn't matter what words were used. What matters is that she refused to budge, said she just dropped by to visit with me, and even said my new hairstyle was real cute. (This last remark was accompanied by a smirk, but I will admit she was on pretty solid ground there.) What also matters is that Buck stood right beside her—you couldn't have got a straw between 'em—and acted like he was embarrassed by my rude behavior to our "houseguest."

"Why, *Raylene!*" he said, with sort of a pained expression and the kind of sharp intake of air that mothers of young children usually follow up with "Why, I'd be *ashamed.*" Of course, he skipped the part about being ashamed. If he hadn't, he would have gotten shot a lot sooner. I guess he was pretty surprised, though, because aside from the rolling-pin incident the year before, Buck was not used to seeing me in a rage. It was not my style. My style as a wife and mother and all-around southern belle, which was taught to me by Miss Viola, was strongly laced with the "boys will be boys" philosophy. Miss Viola had this thing about the importance of a woman maintaining her dignity at all costs, and the kind of feminine dignity I was brought up to admire did not include raising one's voice, especially in the presence of company. And it certainly did not include whipping out a Smith & Wesson .38 to encourage the absence of company. Which is exactly what I did on that unforgettable day, and believe me, of the three of us, nobody was more surprised than I.

You know how you're always reading in the papers about murderers who say they have no memory of pulling the trigger? Well, believe it. Not only do I have no memory of pulling the trigger, I can't remember reaching into the drawer of the umbrella stand and taking the damn pistol out. But I did it. No excuses. All I know is that one second I was hollering at the top of my lungs and the next second I was waving the damn gun over my head and yelling something to the effect that it would be a real good idea if Shirley Jack vacated the premises right away if she didn't want an ass full of lead. Oh, I was in a state.

Well, Shirley Jack looked horrified and who could blame her? At that time in my life I had never had a gun pulled on me personally, but I have now had that experience—details later—and I can assure you it is not a pleasant one. I never should have done it and I want to take this opportunity to tell the world that I truly do regret it.

For Buck's part, he was bouncing around from one foot to the other and saying, *"Raylene!* Good God-a-mighty! Give me that thing!"

He reached out to take it away from me and . . .

(I have to stop pacing and sit down and steady my nerves a little bit. Just talking about this makes my hands shake.)

All right. I am going to tell the facts right now, and this will be the last time in my life that I am ever going to refer to this incident. I am closing the book on it. What happened is, I jumped back and pointed the pistol at Buck. Or I pointed it in his general direction. My hand was shaking so bad I would have been hard-pressed to hit the broad side of a preacher's wife.

Well, being as she was out of the line of fire, Shirley Jack took the opportunity to observe, "Well, Buck, this is what comes from her watching all them talk shows."

Well, I like to have died. I gasped and stammered and stuttered and finally all I could say was, "You told her about my *talk shows?*"

Oh, it seems so silly now, but at that moment, it just seemed like the last shingle on the barn. I could just see Buck Turner and Shirley Jack Lazarus in bed at the Val-U-Courts, sharing a postadultery cigarette and giggling over his silly wife taping talk shows because she didn't have any damn thing else to do.

As I stared at Buck in disbelief, Shirley Jack made a grab for the gun and we struggled over it for a couple of seconds. What I remember is, one, Buck stepping forward with his hand raised like he was going to whack me upside the head; and two, me shrinking back in horror because striking me was one thing Buck had never done; and three, the gun going off, and four, Buck falling over backward. I hope never to hear that kind of a scream from a man again in my life. Nor from a woman, for that matter. The shooting of a human being is not like you see forty times a day on television, people. It's not a casual thing. Did I do it on purpose? I honestly and sincerely do not believe I did. However, I will have to say that at the time it happened I was never angrier with Buck in my life, and it was indeed my finger that was on the trigger. And of course I was the idiot that got the gun out in the first place. I curse the day that Buck brought it home from his daddy's pawnshop, but I do claim the responsibility for the shooting.

I stood there with that .38 shaking in my hand and my hair rising of its own accord about three inches higher than Oma Phillips had ever dreamed possible. Meanwhile, Shirley Jack screamed nonstop a stream of words that no preacher's wife in the world ought to know. I threw the gun as far as I could and it knocked the telephone off a table before landing with a clatter under Buck's La-Z-Boy recliner. I watched in a daze as Shirley Jack dropped to her knees beside my husband. I felt a big surge of relief to see his legs twitching and his hands slapping the floor. Maybe he wasn't dead. Maybe he wouldn't die. Maybe I hadn't killed my husband. Maybe I was not a murderer and this would all pass and I would just keep on being me, gossiping on the phone with Dot and vacuuming and watching the birds and spraying X-15 on the bathroom walls to keep the mildew down and going to my aerobics class and getting my hair fixed at the Ouch of Class.

Shirley Jack looked up at me and screamed, "You've *killed* him!" She called me a few nice names, and then said the thing that made me grab my purse and run out the door and change my life forever. She said, "We were gonna get *married,* you bitch!"

I jumped into the Mustang and spun out of the driveway at about a hundred miles per. One minute I was racing down Maple Street and the next minute I was waiting at a red light, chewing my lips and thinking, since Dot was at work, I just might drive down to Abbeville, try to locate Sue and cry on her shoulder for a while, and then come home and go to the police station. Well, it so happened that my old algebra teacher from the ninth grade, Miss Norma Newton, eighty-five if she was a day, picked that minute to run slam-bang into a truck from the phone company, blocking the turnoff to the Abbeville highway. So I just heaved a big what-the-hell sigh and headed north instead. (If you're reading this, Miss Norma, thank you, and if I ever get back home, I'm going to bring you a box of those chocolate turtles that you love and take you out to the Duck Inn for a chicken-fried steak. I promise.) So I headed out in the direction of Shreveport, never meaning to go that far, because it's more than two hundred miles. I was just driving. And bawling like a baby.

In Opelousas, I stopped at the Dixie Dog Drive-In and had a beer and a smoke. I sat there watching an old woman about the size of Miss Viola browsing through a trash can. She dived so deep into it I could see daylight between her tennis shoes and the ground. I got out of the car and gave her a dollar.

She thanked me and said it was a hard life for a woman.

I said, "It sure is."

She leaned against the trash can while she stuffed her findings into a big plastic Sears bag. When she noticed me watching her, she straightened up and said, "They sing about stouthearted men, but I'll tell you what, I believe it takes a stouter heart to be a woman."

I said, "It sure does."

She looked at my eyes, all red and swollen up. She looked like she wanted to chat for a while, but she had enough sense to see that I wasn't in the mood. "You got troubles too, don't you, honey?" she said, real solemn-like.

I said, "Yes'm, I do," and got back in my car and drove off. I stopped on the north side of town and gassed up and just kept going.

I read somewhere that when you're driving on a freeway and realize all of a sudden that you don't recall anything of the landscape from the last ten miles or so, it's because of a type of self-hypnosis. If that's true, I was hypnotized for about thirty miles. I turned on the radio and that old Beatles song that starts out "The day breaks, your mind aches" blared out at me like it was a personal and confidential message with my name on it. Sometimes I sang along with the radio and sometimes I turned it off for a few minutes so I could clear out my head for thinking purposes. But as far as being aware of my surroundings, I might as well have been in my backyard tying up tomato plants.

I thought about the first time I saw Buck, the all-American jock, standing on stage to welcome me and the rest of the newcomers to Southwestern State's freshman orientation program. Buck was the president of the student body. At the time, I thought this respect that his peers gave him said something positive about the boy's intellectual capacities. See what a naive little country girl I was? I sat on the front row in my little white go-go boots, trying to catch his eye. Oh, he was something to look at, a god in a little cow college full of dirt farmers. He had made a name for himself riding brahma bulls in the mid-South rodeo circuit, and always wore a cowboy hat and cowboy boots around the campus so people wouldn't forget he was from Texas. Everybody called him "the buckaroo" because of this getup he wore.

Those college days, brief as they were—I barely finished out my first semester—were not something I usually dwelled on. Nick's drowning had thrown me into a mental tailspin that summer after high school. I felt like my life was over and there was no reason to go on. And then there was Jamie's disappearance to be dealt with, on top of the twins' suicide and my daddy running off with Tammy Crack. I used to go for days at a time without sleeping. If I had a nickel for every tear I cried during that time, I could buy me a trip to the moon. Going to college the following fall was out of the question. I was just too much of a mess. After a year of grieving and moping, the way I dealt with the pain finally was by carousing and acting a fool with half the boys in Lake Gladys and running around the country in the Corvette my granddaddy had bought for me to cheer me up. I used to walk into that Howdy Club over in New Iberia (with my driver's license doctored up to say I was twenty-one) and the guys would go, "Here she *is!*"

So then, a year later, I did start college. I was a popular girl on the campus, but I had zeroed in on Buck the rodeo star. He was tall, athletic, cute, a little silly, a little childish, a little stupid—all the traits I admired in young men at the time. I set out to get him, and a few days into the school year, I did catch the boy's eye when he saw me drive down Fraternity Row one afternoon in the Corvette. Of course, I was grinning and waving and doing everything but standing up and hollering "Yoo-hoo." Pretty soon, Buck started paying a lot of attention to me, which young men have a tendency to do when they think the girl is rich. It didn't hurt that I had a whole wardrobe of fuzzy sweaters or that I spent half the day in the student union, keeping my eyes peeled for him. I spent the rest of my time hitting the honky-tonks or sometimes a fais-dodo with first one boy, then another, or pressing cold spoons to my neck to treat the hickies. Every once in a while I'd go to class just for the sake of appearances, always scanning the hallways for Buck, who, before I really knew him, was my idea of the big romance, being the big man on campus that he was and from Texas and everything.

I guess my ideas about romance were learned from my grand-mother, who picked up a lot of tips from reading confession maga-zines. She raised me to be a firm believer in miracles and love at first sight and love everlasting (or, as I said, miracles). One thing she used to tell me was that before a girl was married she had to kiss her man to hold him, and afterward she had to hold him to kiss him. When Buck started asking me out, I did give him plenty of kisses (and a few other things) and I did hold him. Meanwhile I was having my doubts. Could I really live with a guy whose favorite movie was *Dr. Goldfoot and the Bikini Machine?* Or who thought the Roman Catholic church was storing up arms to take over the world? But he had the cutest little buns. And was so popular. And sort of harmless.

I remember walking down the aisle that day we got married just before Christmas. There he was in a tux standing at the altar, all eyes and Adam's apple, his smile so innocent and sweet. And here I came, smiling even more sweetly and thinking to myself, *Well,* I wonder how long *this* is gonna last. I remember saying "I do," tears of joy standing in my eyes, while all the time I was thinking, I give it three years max.

But, I admit there were a few stars in my eyes along with the tears. He was the big man on campus, remember. Plus there was the prospect of all the neat presents we would get, and most of my friends were getting married too. I kept thinking about the barbecues we would all have together. I kept picturing myself cheering in the stands at the rodeo, the buckaroo's bride. Oh, maybe it would work. Maybe I'd have a lifetime of nothing but fun, fun, fun. You never know.

And to be honest, I must admit I didn't have much to complain about in the romance department. At first, Buck went at lovemaking like he had just got home from ten years of hard time in the penitentiary. Well, so did I for that matter. But, let's face it, after twenty some-odd years of marriage, a man's heart doesn't skip a beat when he sees his wife silhouetted against the window in a negligee, although if I do say so myself, I've managed to avoid that thick-all-over look that creeps up on a lot of people after they reach a certain age. It's my metabolism, and the aerobics didn't hurt. Buck, on the other hand, had put on a few pounds, especially around the middle, but not enough to discourage the attentions of women like Shirley Jack. Of course, the standards for men in the looks department are a damn sight lower anyway, aren't they, gals? It's not fair, but what is?

I drove all over the map that day I left Lake Gladys. I kept turning off the northbound freeway to go west a little ways on this country road or east on that one and on and on. Ten minutes didn't go by that I didn't think about turning south again and facing the music, so to speak. I prayed and prayed and prayed that Buck wasn't dead. I prayed out loud and I sent up silent prayers and I even tried it once in my pidgin French. But I couldn't turn around. I just couldn't. Well, anyway, I didn't. After a couple of hours on the road, I called home from a pay phone and got a busy signal. I called again and it was busy again. After about the fourth call, I remembered knocking the telephone off its table.

As I drove along I considered the possibilities. Okay, if Buck was dead, what chance did I have in a courtroom with Shirley Jack as the only witness? Slim to none. And if he was alive, she was still there at my house giving aid and comfort to her fiancé. I drove on.

By the time I got to Alexandria, it was dark and I headed west on a little pockmarked blacktop road. Little ramshackle dirt farms flew past in the night while I kept flipping the radio on and off, on and off. On to hear something that might simmer down the boiling stew in my head, and off because all the songs on the radio were about the same damn thing—love and marriage, love and marriage, love and marriage.

After meandering around all night in the middle of nowhere, I pulled off the road beside a cow pasture to stretch my legs. I leaned against the car and smoked a cigarette under the stars, feeling more alone than ever before in my life. Except for the steady chirping of the crickets, the night was quiet and not a single car passed on this deserted road. When I looked at my watch I was surprised to see that it was after two. I wasn't particularly sleepy, but I decided to stretch out and try to take a nap in the front seat of the car. I didn't doze off right away, but when I finally drifted off, I slept till the sun came up.

two

I propped myself up and looked in the rearview mirror. My hair was sticking out every whichaway and one of my eyes was stuck at half-mast. I thought, Well, hello, honey, I haven't seen you around since *The Night of the Living Dead.*

"Knock-knock. Anybody home?" I said out loud to this exhausted woman, but my humor was wasted on that bleak face. I studied myself for several minutes and then sat up and said, Okay, it's time to quit acting a fool. You can't blame your behavior on this "state of shock" bullshit any longer. Gotta go back.

I decided to find my way back to the freeway and head south toward Lake Gladys. I turned on the ignition, heaved a big sigh, and set off down the road. I was just coming up on Highway 49 when I saw way off in the distance a tiny somebody walking along the right-hand side of the blacktop. As I got closer, the tiny somebody became life-size, about my size in fact, only a little chubbier. What really got my attention was this long, long mane of straight hair she had. It was the color of old gold and hung down way past her knees, almost to her ankles.

Now I don't usually pick up hitchhikers and I'll tell you why. I learned my lesson once way back before I was married when Dot Struthers and I were out one day tooling around and acting fools in her daddy's pickup. We stopped to lend a hand to what we thought was a nun having car trouble out on the Abbeville highway. Turned out that under the habit was a fellow that had just broken out of the penitentiary. But, boy, when Dot swung into action, which was about one-tenth of a second after he pulled a little bitty penknife on us, that man didn't know what hit him. She grabbed a tire iron that she always kept under the seat and she carried on so, cussing a blue streak and banging him over the head, that I almost felt sorry for him. When we got him to the sheriff's office, I think he was looking forward to relaxing in his nice, safe cell again.

So. I'm usually real cautious about hitchhikers. But the fact is this woman wasn't hitching. She had her hands full of these little purple Johnny-jump-ups that she had picked along the roadside and didn't seem to be too concerned about getting a ride or anything else. However, I could see this was somebody with a destination in mind. She was walking down that highway in a real businesslike way, pickin' em up and puttin' 'em down, but she was dressed in a party-time muumuu of every color in the rainbow. She didn't take her eyes off the ground as I passed, but for some reason, I couldn't help but watch her in the rearview mirror. Then she did lift her eyes and my left foot went to the brake in a sort of reflex action. Many times since that day, I have wondered what my life would have been like if I had not stopped.

I was whizzing along at such a speed that I had gone about half the length of a football field before the Mustang finally shuddered to a full stop in a shower of roadside pea gravel. I threw the car into reverse and watched my passenger-to-be grow bigger and bigger in the rearview mirror till finally she looked up and smiled in a way that made me suddenly understand why smiling is sometimes called "beaming." I felt warmed and, let's not mince words, it was a feeling I needed that day.

I leaned over to the passenger side and my own smile came in such an easy way that I felt a little twinge of surprise. I didn't know I had it in me that particular day.

"Where you going?" I hollered.

She hollered back like she had known me a hundred years. "Graceland, darlin'!" It was the kind of voice that puts you in mind of smoke-filled honky-tonks. I could tell this was a woman who had done some living and had had her share of laughs, too.

"Hmm, Graceland," I said, and gazed out across the fields. Graceland was a long ways from where we were. Several hundred miles. And here she came high-stepping toward the car, holding out that silly-looking muumuu with one hand while, with the other, she shooed away a swarm of bumblebees as cheerfully as if they were butterflies.

"Get in," I said.

She hopped into the car like a teenager though she looked to be about my age, which is real close to forty and I'm not going to say from which side. She sank back into the cushions with a grateful sigh like a traveling saleswoman who had reached home at last. But first she took both her hands and flipped that long, long mane of hair off her neck to where it snaked across the backseat and halfway across the trunk.

"Well, thank the Lord," she said. "You're here, darlin'."

I said, "You sound like you were expecting me."

"I was," she said. "I knew you were on your way. I had a picture of a blue Mustang convertible in my mind when I woke up this morning, sweetheart. I was visiting my sister back in Vidalia and I just lit out after breakfast. I must've walked a couple of miles."

And after saying that, she did seem a little out of breath, but she leaned over and, just for a second, touched my hand on the steering wheel. "So how you doing now, baby?" she asked, sassy but soft, like a night nurse just coming on duty in the intensive care unit.

"I'm doing all right," I said, "for a woman that's running away from home."

"Well, I could tell you that you should have done it a long time ago. But that wouldn't be right. You're doing what you have to do

40

and you're doing it when you have to do it, darlin'," she said, like she was reciting the price of eggs.

Well, Lord! How much did she know? I whipped my head around to see what was behind those words, but her eyes, fastened on the spot where the highway met the sky, said all was right with the world. And speaking of which, people, I want to tell you about this woman's eyes before I go any further. They were big and flat and glossy like the button eyes of the Marie Antoinette doll that used to sit on Miss Viola's crocheted bedspread, but, Lord, they contained more human life than any eyes I ever saw. They never stopped moving, didn't miss a thing. Brown eyes. Big. Gobs of mascara, eyeliner, shadow, the works. She must have got up way before daylight to make 'em up.

She continued, "Now, baby, you've done your time with him . . . what's his name? Bart?"

"Buck," I said, a little mystified, but only a little because I had already sensed that this wasn't just any old roadrunner I was dealing with.

"Yeah, Buck. I knew I was getting a B."

Some people might have got cold chills or whatever from this woman. But not me. Not the granddaughter of Miss Viola Keating. I knew somehow that she knew what I knew, but I had to find out just how up-to-date her information was.

"And what's my name?" I asked.

"You'll have to tell me, dear. It's not something I can turn on and off."

"My name's Raylene," I said.

"Lord, no wonder I didn't pick up on your name," she said. "Well, I'm Carlotta," she said with a big, toothy smile.

And then after a couple of seconds, I said, "That's Raylene Stout." Two seconds. That's how long it took me to decide I didn't want to use Buck's name as my own any longer, and I never have since that day. I guess what I had in mind was becoming a stouthearted woman. I'm still learning.

Carlotta looked at me and nodded. "Stout," she said. "It suits you." We zoomed on down the road like two old friends out for a day in the country, and her hair rode the wind like the tail of a racehorse. I unloaded on Carlotta. I told her the story of me and Buck, from A to Z, much more of the historical information than I have given you here but I don't want to repeat all that stuff at this time because, frankly, at this stage in my life, it's not the fascinating subject it used to be, this story about a husband who strayed and a wife who drilled him with a .38 and flew the coop. However, the way Carlotta set her face to the task of listening, you would have thought she was hearing some kind of beautiful but sad music drifting across a peaceful lake on a summer evening. At first I thought I would lie, or at least not tell the whole story of what happened the day before, but lying to Carlotta was not an option. Those eyes! I told her everything. When I finally got myself wound down, she said, "Is that all?"

I said, "That's it. Isn't that enough?"

"Call him," she said.

I said, "Well, I tried but the phone's off the—"

"Call him," she said.

I pulled over at an Exxon station sitting out in front of a cotton field and called home.

"Hello?"

It was Buck! He sounded strong as a horse! It took my breath clean away. I was struck speechless. There were things I wanted to say, of course. "I'm sorry," for one. But when my mouth formed to make the words, I thought, Wait a second, *I'm* sorry? I wanted to ask about him and Shirley Jack, I wanted to cuss and holler and rant and rave, but I knew if I opened my mouth at all I wouldn't say anything but "I'm sorry."

"Hello?" he said again.

I hung up and noticed that I was hanging on to the pay phone for dear life. I was shaking like a leaf from head to toe.

So then we're driving along, me and Carlotta, and suddenly everything seems so laid back and *pleasurable,* the way the countryside can be when you know you're only passing through and don't have to stay there. I kept reaching over and touching Carlotta's arm and screaming, "He's alive!"

The first time I said it she smiled and said, "I know what you mean."

And she did know. He's alive, as in he's not dead and my conscience is clear, not as in he's not dead and I've still got a husband.

"It's all for the best," she said with a wise look.

I said, "Well . . ."

She looked impatient. She said, "So you lost a man. So what? Would your life have been perfect if he hadn't played around?"

"Well, no," I said.

"Right, honey," she said. "Let's look at it this way. Most people expect to get more out of marriage than there is in it to begin with. I mean, when has anything else been perfect in your life? Don't you think you ought to be used to a less-than-perfect life? You've had one all along and you've always got along okay, haven't you?"

I sort of shrugged. "Well, I guess," I said.

"What you need is to learn to accept, Raylene, just accept. Life is just a toss of the dice, sweetheart. Take it a day at a time and scratch where it itches and if it don't itch, don't scratch. Life is what it is, baby."

We rode on in silence a little while, but an easy silence, which Carlotta broke here and there by humming little snatches of "Graceland." The subject put me in mind of Elvis and the Wall of Fame in my grandmother's house. On that wall hung a collection of photographs of the twins posed with celebrities. It's a real mixed group—everybody famous or semifamous who's ever been within a hundred miles of Lake Gladys, from Billy Graham to Minnie Pearl. The photos all look very similar, except for the person in the middle. Always, the celebrity is smiling for the camera and flanked by the twins, who are either baring their teeth in a high-wattage smile or delivering a well-puckered kiss to the celebrity's cheeks, depending on just how attractive the celebrity is. Right in the center of this group of fifty-some-odd photos, there's the King.

He's very young in the picture and very handsome and he looks a little uncomfortable being kissed by these two matching thirtyish bleached blonds that he never laid eyes on before. This picture was taken in the mid-fifties, when I was just a toddler and Elvis was the opening act for a Webb Pierce show at the Municipal Auditorium in Abbeville. I grew up seeing that picture hanging dead-center on the wall at the big house, surrounded by pictures of C&W stars like Little Jimmy Dickens and Faron Young and everybody that ever tapped a foot on the *Cajun Jamboree* down at WLGA—Clifton Chenier, Dewey Balfa, Boozoo Chavis—they're all up there. There was a picture of me on the Wall of Fame too. Not anywhere near the center, but on the edge next to Zack the Knife, a local disc jockey in the early sixties. My picture was taken when I was about twelve and had just sung "Lavender Blue Dilly Dilly" on the local radio station on some long-forgotten Saturday morning show. The twins are kissing me, but they don't look near as joyous as they do in the picture of Elvis. When I was a kid I took it for granted that kissing me wasn't that big of a thrill for the twins and that my natural place was on the outskirts of the Wall of Fame with Zack the Knife, who left town under a cloud after embezzling some money from the radio station. When I think about it now, it makes me sad that I felt that way.

While we rolled toward Memphis, I bent Carlotta's ear about the Wall of Fame which led to the topic of the twins which led to talking about everybody else in my family.

I told her about the time the twins incorporated the twist into their stage act and cartwheels into their twist and were laid up in twin hospital beds for a week, and Carlotta didn't just laugh, she erupted, and didn't just slap her thigh, but bent over and gave her ankles a slap for good measure.

I told her about the judge's concern that I get an education, and how he even went so far as to pay for my college education, such as it was. I told her about his remark, when I dropped out to marry the buckaroo from Texas, that ignorance was tolerated in Louisiana, but it was celebrated in Texas. Carlotta listened to all this babbling and nodded just as solemnly as an owl.

She really perked up when I told her about Miss Viola's claim that she was born with a veil over her face, which made her privy to a lot of insights and specialized knowledge that most of us don't have. I mentioned the broom-behind-the-door business and Carlotta looked like she needed a pencil and paper to take notes with.

"Oh, yeah," she said while I explained the whole thing. "I see. I see, sweetheart."

I came to the subject of Jamie, and Carlotta slowly straightened up and sat with her hands clasped in her lap. While I talked her eyes were glued to me and never wavered, hardly blinked. I got to the part about him leaving home and that was the end of the story. Well, after a few seconds of a silence you could cut with a knife, she said, "You'll see Jamie again, darlin'. He's okay. He has friends. He lives near the ocean, darling."

I felt like I had to touch her. I touched her hand. I said, "Thank you, Carlotta." For the first time all day I began to feel breezes and smell the new-mown grass and notice the beauty of the countryside flowing by, the spreading shade trees, some sleek and gentle horses watching us from behind a wooden fence. Carlotta pointed out a palomino bolting across a pasture and a little bitty colt tottering along behind.

"Looky there," she said. "Just look at that."

We both gaped in wonder like we'd never seen a horse before.

A few miles down the road I said to Carlotta, "So. Graceland, huh?"

She answered by singing in a high soprano, "I'm goin' to Graceland, Graceland, in Memphis, Tennessee."

She had rings on every finger and moved her hands around in the air like a hula dancer.

"Well, so am I, honey," I said, and floorboarded that Mustang for all it was worth.

December 20

My hormones kicked in this morning. The doctor said it would happen gradually, but with me nothing ever goes according to plan. Plus last night's full moon was in Aries, which means: Hey! Full steam ahead, Jamie! Damn those torpedoes! Life's too short!

I had dozed off about two after the nightly revelry had died down a little and then I woke up with a start a little while later to the sound of a firecracker/a car backfiring/a gunshot—one's never sure in this posh neighborhood. Really, the Mission is not looking too prosperous these days. Sometimes you have to crawl over the bodies to get in your front door. One doesn't really think about it too much. Well, hell, I don't think about it a bit. Certainly not the danger aspect. In my own house, aka the Hole in the Wall, I've got strangers sleeping on the floor every night and none of these guys was sent over by the Social Register. Maybe the alumni register at San Quentin. I'm being sarcastic. Actually, most of them are just poor guys from Mexico and points south doing the best they can.

This morning the dozen or so nervous bodies sprawled over the floor of my abode continued snoring. Usually their snoring is just white noise to me, as soothing as a waterfall, representing, as it does, money in the bank, but I couldn't get back to sleep this morning. I closed my eyes and tried to meditate, concentrating on my breathing (I've worn out my mantra which cost me three hundred dollars ten years ago during my transcendental meditation period.) That didn't work, so I concentrated on the little plastic Jesus night-light in the kitchen visible from my bed, but that didn't work either. Something was happening—percolating—in my body, in my head. I had the feeling that teeny tiny little people were at war in my bloodstream, a la *Fantastic Voyage*. I kept picturing a minuscule Raquel Welch barking orders, sweeping the hair from her eyes and executing fancy footwork to evade teeny tiny little villains, all within the confines of my tired and flaccid veins. At daylight, the guys on the floor began to stir. Big Victor crawled out of his sleeping bag, lumbered to a standing position, and padded off to the kitchen to make coffee.

He poked his head into the little sheet-tent I rigged up over my bed last week and saw I was awake. "You want coffee, Jamie?"

I said, "Yeah, coffee sounds like a good idea."

He said, "You sound funny."

I put my hand to my throat which felt sort of constricted. I said, "Yeah, I do, don't I?" And I did sound funny.

Well, I swung my feet over the side of the bed and sang along with a car radio that was blaring from the street.

"By the time we got to Woodstock we were half a million strong." I didn't sound like Joni Mitchell, but I was an octave or so higher than the Crosby, Stills and Nash version. Big Victor just stared.

I said, "It's the hormones. They've kicked in."

B.V. looked blank and I tried to translate, but couldn't think how to say hormones in Spanish.

A few hours later, I was just vegetating and getting a little sun at the Twenty-fourth Street BART plaza, where a little old lady dressed all in candy-apple red was rendering a cappella a song, of, presumably, her own composition, titled "Please Release Me from My Sins," sung to the tune of "Release Me." She ripped into the number with a gusto that would have sent Engelbert Humperdinck whimpering to his dressing room in ignominious defeat. She used a red bullhorn to starch her thin quavery voice into a hard-edged vibrato that walloped the eardrums of everyone within the radius of two blocks. The old lady was part of a large contingent of *Testigos de Jehovah,* led by a handsome, young Latino evangelist dressed in a white prom tux generously embellished with satin. He held a white Bible aloft and bided his time waiting for his elderly colleague to wind up her number. I was taking a well-earned breather after cleaning up the shambles left by last night's paying guests. Well, at least I made a stab at it. It's the bathroom that brings tears of exasperation to my eyes. Why, oh why, do they insist on discarding used toilet paper in the wastebasket? Big Victor, who is becoming a regular, explained to me that that's how it's done in Mexico, but I explained right back that we're about five hundred miles north of the border and when in Rome . . .

I'll buy a magic marker and write a sign in *español* to tape over the toilet and hope for the best. My humble ambition for the present is to rent a one-bedroom apartment that would give me my own space with a door between me and the "dormitory" as I would call it. However, since we all sleep in the same room now, at least I can keep an eye on them from my little corner cot in the interest of discouraging arson, homicide, etc. Of course, my guests have a tendency to keep an eye on me too. I'm sure they don't see gals like me every day back in Tampico and Chihuahua, but overall, I must say, these guys have been more respectful than not since I started this business last year. Or maybe it's more like awe than respect. Of course, I guess it behooves them to remain in my good graces since there aren't many two-dollar sleeping spaces to be had in San Francisco.

I had to get out of the house for a few minutes just to assure myself that there was a world outside the dark confines of the Hole in the Wall. I left Big Victor in charge of the pot of beans bubbling on the stove and the two Salvadoreans with whom he was arguing politics. I threw everybody else out and no one will be readmitted till eight o'clock tonight. Them's the rules. I'm going to start enforcing them a little better. One of these days.

It was the first sunny day in the Mission in weeks, and a Saturday on top of it. Everybody was out. Teenage girls with Cleopatra eyes pushed babies in strollers, followed by gangly adolescent fathers sporting 49er jackets and attitude. Weather-beaten men without homes clustered in corners and hashed over matters of life and death and spare change. A little Mexican girl with fine, silky eyebrows weaved through the thicket of people, her arms full of roses for sale. Draped over a bench was an older Anglo man, cadaverous and comatose, a fedora clamped over his head, for all the world like Bill Burroughs after a night in a bed full of Morroccan street urchins. A long thin stream of urine marked the distance between his lanky body and the gutter, but it barely rated a glance from passersby. Hey, we live here. We're not from the 'burbs.

In the midst of all this, up stepped the regal Aquanetta. The tall and bosomy Aquanetta. More pneumatic than a Russ Meyer starlet. Resplendent in spikes and red velveteen pedal pushers. Her breasts—no, at forty-four inches, let's call them knockers—spilling luxuriously out of a skimpy and clingy sweater of purest white angora, she appeared oblivious to the stares and whistles she generated. She is a woman in the business of knockin' 'em dead. Faster, pussycat! Kill! Kill!

My own newly installed bosoms are so modestly sized and discreetly covered that A. didn't even notice them. Or comment on them, which for her is the same thing. It was a kick to see her. I've missed her a lot and we made a big production of hugging and cooing and air-kissing (don't want to muss that makeup!). After six months, she's back from Europe; where she toured with a revival of *La Cage aux Folles*. It was a high-class company she tells me. At length. Princess Margaret came to see the show in London, and in Rome the cast somehow managed to get an audience with the pope. ("My dear, it was high camp!" she confided about the latter thrill.) In Paris, she got her picture taken with Johnny Somebody, who is the Elvis of France, according to A., and in Monte Carlo, Princess Stephanie was like one of the gang, even sharing makeup tips with the chorus girls.

Finally, when I managed to get a couple of words in edgewise, some whiny complaint about my financial status, A. clapped a professionally manicured hand to her forehead and brayed in her earthy contralto, "Girl! Your voice! Your hormones have finally kicked in! Say something else!"

She was oblivious to the heads turning in her direction. I looked around with elaborate nonchalance, like Jack Benny in drag. When I recovered my equilibrium, I gasped, "Please, Aquanetta, we're not on Polk Street." However, she not only shrugged off my remark, but blew a noisy kiss at a passing policeman who had thrown a curious look her way.

Then she said, "Merry Christmas, darling," and reached into a bag from the Conspicuous Consumer gift shop on Castro where you can't buy a greeting card for less than five bucks.

"Close your eyes now, Dagmar," she said, using my Halloween name. But I didn't, because this was Aquanetta I was dealing with and it's best to stay alert. She pulled out a package wrapped in gold foil and tied with a silver ribbon and plopped it into my hands. I remembered telling Aquanetta before her trip, "No Christmas presents this year."

She readily agreed as I was sure she would since she didn't get me a thing last year, nor did she thank me properly for the boxed set of Jean Naté that I got her. I even gave a little dinner party for her birthday last year and all I got for my trouble was a few sarcastic remarks about the cauliflower centerpiece which seemed like a good idea at the time. However, I will admit that on the rare occasions when she has money, she's not loath to part with it.

I unwrapped the gift on the spot. It's this book I'm writing in. A beautiful thing, with a simulated malachite cover and full of blank pages. It's a lovely present, something I need. I do want to begin recording my life again because next year will be a pivotal one—pivotal, but quiet, I hope. I'm delighted at A.'s completely unexpected display of generosity (there's no predicting the old gal).

I haven't kept a diary since Key West and I chucked that one out the window of a moving train in Alabama, the better to start anew when I got to L.A. The Blue Horse binder I used as my New York journal rests somewhere at the bottom of the Hudson River.

"I hope you hate it so I can keep it," said the ever-gracious Aquanetta.

"I love it," said I.

"I was afraid you would," she said, and walked away after inviting me to her comeback performance at Esta Noche on New Year's Eve. In her heels, she went clicking through the plaza, dividing the crowd like a sporty little motorboat parting the water.

The lady with the bullhorn wound up her number and a few intrepid souls clapped. I stuck Aquanetta's gift under my arm to free up my hands. Music lover that I am, I joined the scattered applause and won a smile and a nod from the singer. I clapped all the harder.

three

I've always had a thing about that Mississippi Bridge between West Memphis and Memphis. To see, way down below, that wide, wide ribbon of muddy water so powerful that it cuts the whole United States in two, and there you are way up above, zooming along with nothing between you and the river but a lot of air and a few steel girders. Memphis off in the distance looks like the promised land. I won't say that the sight of it makes you feel removed from all your worries, but it would take a real hard-core sourpuss not to feel the tug of at least a few new possibilities. I could see Carlotta was feeling the same way by the way her eyes were dancing all around.

"Isn't that river something?" I said, like I was showing off something new and expensive that I'd just bought after saving up all my money for a long time. We rolled into downtown Memphis, and at the first red light, Carlotta hollered to an old fellow sitting at a bus stop.

"Where's Graceland, sweetheart?"

He sauntered over to the car with his lips all bunched up and his eyes on the ground like he was deep in thought, the way these old fellows do when they're about to tell you how to get somewhere. He told us it was about twenty minutes away and started reeling off a list of directions that I lost track of after about ten seconds.

"You getting that, Carlotta?" I asked.

She answered me with a quick nod and kept her ear cocked toward the old man. Then she hollered, "Oh, aren't you a darling!" and thanked him and off we went.

"Turn right here, hang a left at the next light, stay in the left lane because you'll have to turn again . . ."

She rattled off the directions like she was reading cue cards and pretty soon we turned into a big four-lane highway lined with franchise hamburger joints and taco stands and used car lots and motels.

"Elvis Presley Boulevard," Carlotta hollered. "Can Graceland be far behind?"

As we got on down the road a ways, we passed several Elvis souvenir shops which Carlotta dismissed with a wave of her hand.

"Let's wait. Those places can wait till after we've seen"—singing her song again—"Graceland, Graceland in Memphis, Tennessee."

And that was fine with me, but ten seconds after we made that agreement, we cruised past a place called the Elvis Emporium and Carlotta took one look, then another, then yelled, "Stop! Stop, baby! Now!"

This place looked a whole lot like the others to me, a low white stucco building with Elvis mementos all but spilling out the windows, a wooden Indian-type Elvis in a white jumpsuit standing outside the front door.

"Well, I thought we were gonna wait," I said, a little frazzled.

"No, honey," she said, waving her arms back and forth in a hysterical way. "No. No. No. No, trust me. Stop this machine, baby. We are being called into the Elvis Emporium. Not just me and not just you. Both of us."

So we stopped. It felt good to get out of the car after driving for several hours. After I stretched like a cat to straighten out the kinks in my back, I had to scurry to catch up with Carlotta. She was heading toward the door of the Elvis Emporium like a woman on important business.

That store! There wasn't a square foot of wall or floor space free of Elvis. Elvis place mats, Elvis refrigerator magnets, Elvis stationery. I'm here to tell you they even had vibrators for women in an Elvis motif (in three sizes, people: Love Me Tender, All Shook Up, and Don't Be Cruel!). We nosed around a few minutes and Carlotta pondered buying a sunburst clock that pictured Elvis knocking 'em dead in Las Vegas, but she made a face and put it back on the wall after checking out the price. A few touristy-looking married couples wandered around the place and a cheerful fat lady stood at the cash register by the door, but I didn't see a soul who looked able to make any kind of serious impact on my life and I figured that Carlotta's ESP has gotten short-circuited this time. We came to a little glassed-in booth at the back of the store, where you could make a videotape of yourself singing along to your favorite Elvis song. Well, it sounded like a good idea to me and talking Carlotta into it took me about two seconds. We decided on "Burning Love," punched the appropriate buttons, and positioned ourselves in front of the camera. My singing voice will never win any prizes, but growing up around the twins, I learned to fall into a pretty good harmony without too much of a strain. And Carlotta was no slouch in the vocalizing department either. She put her arm around my shoulder, leaned back, and cut loose as soon as the light on the camera went on. Boy howdy! By the time we got through with that song, we had opened up a whole new window on rock and roll. We collapsed in each other's arms like a couple of giggling schoolgirls, and when we looked up, we saw two guys peering at us through the window of the soundproof booth. These fellows were watching us the way you watch a couple of monkeys dance a tango. With their mouths sort of open, sort of "Well, what next?" Kind of rattled me. But not Carlotta. No sir. Old Carlotta lit up like a neon sign at the sight of these guys and went bustling out the door of the booth.

Just glowing all over, Miss Congeniality said, "Did y'all want to make a video?"

"No, ma'am," said the older half of the pair. "We were just admiring your singing talent."

Carlotta said, "Our singing talent? You couldn't hear us out here, could you?"

"We didn't have to hear. We could tell by looking that you ladies are uncommonly talented," this same fellow said, but not smart-alecky if you can imagine saying that in a non-smart-alecky way. He was a wiry little man somewhere close to the age of me and Carlotta, sort of battered and nervous-looking, which I soon chalked up to what he did for a living, which was get shot out of a cannon. You see, this guy, Wally, and his buddy, Eddie, worked in a circus, Carlotta found out in short order. It wasn't five minutes before she had the story of Wally's life, though it didn't come spilling out of him like the jackpot on a slot machine the way mine did. At least, not till Carlotta got him cranked up. After a mere five minutes Carlotta and Wally were as solid as a rock. When it developed that the fellows had not yet seen Graceland, it felt only natural and right to invite them along. It also seemed natural and right when Carlotta and Wally slid together into the backseat of the Mustang, which left me up front with Eddie. Eddie was a sweet kid barely out of his teens, a farm boy from Iowa, with a funny haircut, a crew cut on the right side of his head and shoulder length on the left, and furthermore his hair was dark brown on the right and platinum blond on the left. His eyebrows didn't match either. He reminded me of the kids my daughter used to hang out with. But, still, he seemed just as green and simple as a bowlful of apples, and just about as silent. As I drove on down Elvis Presley Boulevard toward Graceland, it occurred to me that Carlotta must have been only half right about the Elvis Emporium. I mean it was clear there had been something there for her (I looked in the rearview mirror and those two were holding hands!), but, as nice and gentle and handsome (well, handsome on one side and pretty on the other) as Eddie was, I really doubted that he was going to make much of a difference in my life. I was wrong.

When I saw those wrought iron gates with the musical notes on them, they looked as familiar to me as the Eiffel Tower or anything else I had seen in pictures all my life. After all, Graceland is a registered National Historic Place, as they told us at the Visitor Center, where I damn near turned my purse inside out to find sixteen dollars for the Platinum Tour Pass, which allows you to see everything. After I got the money together, all I had left was about fifteen cents and a credit card, which was probably maxed out, but I figured I would worry about that later. You don't go to Graceland every day.

We stepped in the front door of Elvis's mansion and got shuffled into groups. Ours included Japanese tourists, blue-haired ladies in print dresses, green-haired kids in leather, a couple of nuns, and leading the pack, a pretty teenage girl with rosy cheeks and a peppermint-striped dress who welcomed us to the group with a big smile and a big "How're y'all?"

Her name, she said, was Stephanie and she was here to point out the areas of interest in the home of the immortal king of rock 'n' roll. She was full of information and wouldn't let us walk a step till she had recited about ten minutes worth of it. Graceland, she told us, comprised fourteen acres and the lovely umpteen-room home we were standing in, all of which Elvis bought in 1957 from a local physician for one hundred thousand dollars. While the ladies in print dresses cooed and chirped about what a steal that would be these days, I was thinking, gee, this place reminds me of the big house—because, like Elvis, Miss Viola liked her acres of creamy carpeting and her mirrored walls.

Eddie looked a little lost so I nudged him and said, "Eddie, you better shut up, or you're gonna drown out everything this girl's trying to tell us about Graceland."

Now Eddie had barely uttered a peep since we left the Elvis Emporium, but it took him a few moments to figure out I was just pulling his leg. I don't believe people joked around too much on that farm where he came from. But finally he did react to my silly prattle with a smile.

I kept on. "Now you and me are gonna have to chaperone that pair back there," I said, with a nod toward Carlotta and Wally. "Last thing I need is for my friend to get pregnant at Graceland."

Well, that struck him as pretty humorous and he laughed and stuck to me like glue the rest of the day, even venturing a comment now and then like "Ooh" and "Wow" as Stephanie rattled off her spiel.

She said, "We want you to see Graceland just as if Elvis himself had invited you over," and explained that this was why the souvenir shops and commercialism connected to Graceland were all confined to one side of Elvis Presley Boulevard. This brought some rude remarks and snickering from the leather kids, but Stephanie moved right along.

"Now this is the Jungle Room," she said as we came to a big room with animal heads on the wall and giant-size furniture covered with fur.

"What do you think of this?" Stephanie directed her question to Eddie, the only young man in the bunch that didn't have a ring through his nose.

"Wow," he said, craning his neck at the ceiling where the grass green shag carpeting matched the floor. Stephanie showed her teeth in a big friendly smile.

"Elvis bought all the Jungle Room furnishings during one thirty-minute visit to a Memphis furniture store," Stephanie informed us like it was something she had just found out herself and couldn't wait to get off her chest. I remember thinking she would be a good girlfriend to gossip with on the phone.

"The acoustics in the Jungle Room are perfect," she said. "They are so perfect that Elvis actually recorded eight hits on his last album right here in this room!" It was all she could do to contain herself.

And on the tour went. Trudge. Giggle. Trudge. Gasp. Trudge, trudge, trudge. To the yellow-and-blue TV room, where three identical televisions were lined up so Elvis could catch all three networks at once. One of the kids in leather, whose head was shaved slick as an egg, asked if this was where Elvis shot the television screens out with a pistol whenever he didn't like a show. Stephanie kind of shrugged the question off and continued with her spiel, telling us Elvis had fourteen television sets in the house. She had to clap her hands to get the group back together after a couple of the kids got down on their hands and knees to look for bullet holes in the wall.

Carlotta left Wally on his own long enough to sidle up to me. "How you doin', sweetheart?" she said.

"How am I doin'?" I said. "How are *you* doin'? As if I didn't know. What'd you do, put a spell on that man?"

She batted her eyes at me in a real comical way, and said, "I believe he put one on me, honey." And she scooted back to Wally.

Then we all trooped into the Trophy Room, which was in a low building beside the main house. The walls glittered with 150 gold and platinum records, a sight which brought another heartfelt "Wow" from Eddie.

This room also featured a lot of faceless mannequins wearing costumes from Elvis's movies and concerts. The kids in leather were snickering and making rude remarks about how slim all the mannequins were, but Stephanie ignored them and rattled off names of the movies where this and that outfit came from. Eddie and I were just taking a closer look at the convict outfit Elvis wore in *Jailhouse Rock* when we heard Stephanie holler, "Don't do that! *Please!*"

The kid with no hair had grabbed Elvis's cowboy hat from *Flaming Star* and tried it on. When Stephanie hollered, he looked around at her with a sort of surly look and took off running, still wearing the hat. I thought poor Stephanie was going to burst out crying, and when Wally lit out after the kid I was right behind him, with a security guard, an older fellow with a limp, bringing up the rear. We chased the kid through the long hallway of the Trophy Room and into the Jungle Room, where Wally tripped over a footstool and fell sprawling. But I kept going. In the living room, the kid jumped across the ten-foot coffee table and I jumped right along behind him. I caught up with him right at the front door, grabbed the hat off his head, and he kept on going. When I sauntered back into the Jungle Room with my prize twirling on my finger, Wally was still on the floor, where Carlotta was down on her knees playing Florence Nightingale. He had damaged his foot pretty bad and hopscotched around the rest of the tour, supported by Carlotta and Eddie. I placed the cowboy hat back on the dummy's head and bowed to the applause from everybody except the remaining leather kids, who mumbled and muttered and wandered off from the group till the security guard rounded them up and brought them back. Wally was full of compliments about my little sprint and so was Eddie, who made a big show of clapping me on the back and saying how quick and peppy I was. Wow, wow, wow. Raylene, the wonder woman, built for speed—that sort of thing.

He said, "We could use you in the circus."

I said, "Well, that's a good idea. I am in the market for a job."

Of course, I was just running my mouth, and didn't think anymore about his remark. However, when we rejoined our group and the tour got under way again, I noticed Eddie and Wally putting their heads together, and Carlotta putting in her two cents worth, too. But before I had a chance to wade through the crowd to find out what they were discussing, Stephanie had rounded everybody up and headed them out the door to the Meditation Garden. Here we stood in a little plot of land surrounded by shrubbery and religious statues not far from the swimming pool. After Stephanie pointed out the large bronze slabs that marked the graves of Elvis, his parents, and his maternal grandmother, she tactfully shut up. I felt quite sobered by the scene, especially since I was standing next to a woman who told me, between sobs, that she was from Tupelo, Mississippi, where Elvis was born, and she considered him family. The woman broke away from the crowd to stand at the foot of Elvis's grave. She closed her eyes and tilted her head toward heaven. But after a few minutes of this dramatic posture, she opened her eyes and looked around her like a woman that's been in a coma for a couple of years. Then, I'll swear and be damned if she didn't leap over Elvis's final resting place like a prima ballerina!

She landed by my side and whispered in my ear, "Elvis is not dead."

I said, "Ma'am?"

"I said Elvis is not dead!"

I shuffled and squirmed and shifted my purse around and said, "Oh, is that so?"

She hollered, *"Elvis lives! Elvis walks the earth! I know it!"*

Well, Stephanie showed a grasp of diplomacy beyond her years, and just said in a real soothing way, "That's right, ladies, the King will never die," and hustled us out of the Meditation Garden and into the little record store called EP's LPs. I started to shuffle through bins containing hundreds of the King's offerings. Then I noticed Carlotta and Wally deep in conversation in a corner of the room.

After a few minutes, she came over to me and said, "Raylene, we need to talk, honey. About your future, darlin'. About our future, mine and yours."

She jerked her thumb in the direction of Eddie. "That kid likes you and he's in a position to get you a job, sweetheart."

"A job?" I said. "You mean in the circus?"

She nodded. "Yeah. In the circus, darlin'."

Well, I burst out laughing, but stopped when I saw how serious she looked.

I said, "Well, Carlotta, my future is in Lake Gladys, Louisiana, the same place I experienced my past. And that's where I'm heading for as soon as we get out of here."

Even as I heard my words hit the air, they didn't have the ring of truth, not even to me. I knew that being as I didn't have a change of clothing with me, if for no other reason, the logical thing for me to do was to get on home and face my problems and get a divorce or beat the shit out of Buck or whatever. But I didn't. I joined the circus.

January 1

So I've got a new year to work with. Good. The old one about did me in. I made one resolution last year and I hereby make it again: All I want is to acquire a new and exciting and different set of genitalia, but don't worry, pretty soon I'll be able to pay for it. It took me lo, these many years to save the money and I intend to go through with it for sure this year. It was a year ago today that I bundled up all my male clothing for the Salvation Army and I started my hormone treatments last April, so there's no turning back now. What would I do with these tits?

Last night, I went to Mona's for dinner with her, Preacher Woman, and Sparkle Plenty. Good food and conversation. I'm wearing a push-up bra, the better to exhibit my new acquisitions. The girls are envious and full of questions about the surgical procedure. Preacher Woman plans to get breasts, big ones like Aquanetta's, but she intends to leave the stuff "down in Jerusalem" the way the Lord made it. "Best of both worlds," she calls it, but personally, I think it seems a rather schizy arrangement. However, that's the dichotomy that Aquanetta also has opted for.

Conversation is light till Sparkle brings up a mutual friend, Al, who is in the process of dying. Subject: Is it okay to commit suicide if you have a terminal disease? My answer: Yes. Sparkle argued that, no, you have to ride the whole thing out or else God sends you back for another go-around, and probably not in some delightful, fragrant vacation spot. We thrashed over the pros and cons of the subject till everyone was thoroughly sick of it. I can barely rememeber the seventies, when you could get through a whole evening and the closest you would come to a life-or-death discussion would be just how much transcendental medication it was safe to take before going out to the disco. We smoked a little of Mona's homegrown, drank champagne, and piled into the car. Destination: Esta Noche, where Preacher Woman and Sparkle are famous show biz icons—famous along Sixteenth Street, at least the stretch between Mission and Valencia. The place is packed to the rafters. And rockin', too. Latin men look so handsome in the dark. And there were more than a few that I wouldn't mind seeing in broad daylight. We had to practically fight our way in.

Speaking of fighting, mere minutes before midnight, we witnessed the most marvelous spectacle: an altercation straight out of *Destry Rides Again* between two of the most cat-clawed and foul-mouthed and least inhibited drag queens that San Francisco can boast: the formidable Aquanetta and her archrival for the spotlight, the white-garbed, titian-tressed temptress, Chili Seven. It started with the tuba-voiced Chili bitching to her cronies about the fit of her new dress, that it, in her words, concealed the most alluring contours of her derriere.

Aquanetta, still bristling from insults—both real and imagined, I'm sure—delivered by the acid-tongued Chili earlier in the evening, couldn't resist a comment, and not the sotto voce kind.

"Contours?" she drawled, investing the word with a couple of extra syllables and more than a soupçon of venom. While her own coterie of friends tittered (oh, yes, including me. I'm just a natural team player), A. continued, "Lay her on her belly, and you could play a game of checkers on that ass."

After warily checking for the fiery Chili's response and getting none, she upped the ante, blithely disregarding the "still waters run deep" theory.

"Or Monopoly! All day and all night! With a board full of hotels!"

That did it. In a flash, the wild-eyed Chili jumped on A.'s back and shoved her face into the Singapore Sling she had been languidly nursing. Bad move, Chili. Aquanetta whirled around to deliver what I believe is called a haymaker in the direction of Chili's heavily rouged jaw. The blow connected but not before Chili grabbed the front of Aquanetta's dress and ripped it down the middle, sending sequins flying. Both parties landed several powerful punches and a number of pithy insults found their targets as well. Then, upsy-daisy, the crowd was treated to the spectacle of Chili's high heels flailing the air and a flash of red panties.

Aquanetta straddled her and slugged her in the jaw. Just as the clock struck twelve, Chili's's open hand emerged from somewhere and gave A. a resounding slap to her cheek that involved Chili's two-inch-long nails. As the new year bonged in, Ooky, the manager of the bar, jumped in and told the girls in his charmingly personalized vernacular to "calm your horses down." Wound up and hysterical as she was (those gals get emotional down there at Esta Noche, sometimes), Chili reacted with an equally resounding slap to his handsome twelve-o'clock-shadowed cheek and, consequently, she starts the new year as an unemployed drag queen. These gals!

Aquanetta swaggered away from the scene of conflict rolling from one side to the other on her high heels. On the way to join our group, she shot a look at the haughty and silent Estrelita, who I guess had given her a disapproving look.

Aquanetta snarled at her. "You makin' a statement?"

As poor Estrelita shrank into the crowd, I grabbed Aquanetta's hand and drew her in.

"Girl, you're losin' it," I said quietly.

She announced, if hoarsely, for all to hear, "I am not losing it. I'm winnin' tonight, honey. I'm the undefeated champion." Then turning to me, she hissed, "Did you see the look on her face? Like, 'Hey, is that shit I smell or what?' It was just a, you know, a shit-smelly look."

"Oh, Aquanetta, that's just how Estrelita is."

"Well, that's true," she said. "She's just got a shit-smelly face, God bless 'er." She hooked a finger into the collar of Carlitos, the cute new bartender from L.A., and said, "Gimme a gin 'n' tonic, will ya?"

And the next thing I knew she had hoisted herself to the top of the bar and slid right across with all the casual agility of Cyd Charisse, landing in a tango posture that required some bending and vogueing on the part of Carlitos, who quickly got into the spirit of things and forgot about serving drinks for a good ten minutes.

What is it about a good catfight that is so emotionally satisfying when you're not involved yourself? I don't know, but I must say the high spirits engendered by this energetic conflict were contagious and I went home feeling all was right with the world. Every year should have such an auspicious beginning!

four

If you have ever wondered, or even if you have never wondered, what it feels like to get shot out of a cannon, I am going to tell you right now. It feels scary, yes, squatting inside that long iron cylinder, waiting for that deafening split-second that will send you winging, but, people, most of all, it feels lonely. Imagine, if you will, a woman in her middle years, from Lake Gladys, Louisiana, recently split from her jackass of a husband, trying ever so hard to organize her mind and go on with her life. There she is, poised with her knees catching a tear that dribbles off her chin and waiting, waiting, waiting, while the ringmaster runs his silly mouth.

"Ladies and gentlemen and children of all ages, it gives me great pleasure, blah, blah blah . . ."

Oh, the thoughts that can run through a woman's head as she waits to get shot out of a cannon. Am I truly nuts or is this just a temporary thing? Did I remember to turn off the coffeepot? Oh, and by the way, why was I born?

Inside this tube, which smells of metal mixed with sweat and tears, my eyes sting with the latter, trying to focus on the circle of light above me. All I can really see are the lights and part of the silvery rigging for the trapeze people with a backdrop of mud-colored tenting. Let me put it this way: think about the situation you were in—the filing job, the impossible love affair, the Turkish art movie—where the only thought that hammered on your brain was, What am I doing here? Now multiply that emotion by ten thousand if you want to get a remote idea of how Raylene Stout, a God-fearing American housewife only one week before, felt the night of her debut as Raylene the Bullet Woman.

However, learning the routine was a big help in getting my mind off my problems. In the early morning the big top smelled like horses and Bengal tigers, mixed with a dash of frying bacon that drifted over from the mess tent. After I tried my stunt a few times, it was, I must say, sort of fun. No, let's get clear here, it was about the most damn fun I've ever had. Of course, there was always that minute of darkness inside the cannon when I thought, Raylene Stout, you are truly nuts, but then, *boom,* and I was released. And, people, you don't know what release means till you've been shot out of a cannon.

But that first night, when I had to do it for real, in front of an audience, I was petrified. I had to call Dot for moral support beforehand.

"Long distance for Dot Struthers." (I called person-to-person; I wasn't about to pay for ten minutes of update on her mother's gall bladder.)

I said, "Hello, Dot, it's me," and she let out a yell that had me holding the receiver out at arm's length. I told her how I was (fine), where I was (North Platte, Nebraska), why I hadn't called before (because I knew damn well she'd open her big mouth to Buck, although I believe I phrased it a little more tactfully than that), what I was doing (rubbing olive oil on my shoulders in preparation for getting shot out of a cannon). This last piece of information was followed by several moments of dead silence.

Finally, she said. "Raylene, I'll swear and be damned, you do not have sense enough to pour piss out of a boot. You come on home."

Then she proceeded to fill me in on the local news. Buck was okay, but calling her three times a day to see if she had heard anything and he had finally reported my disappearance to the police that very day. Shirley Jack was still in town visiting her mother, she said, and if I wanted to keep my husband, I'd better get on back and take care of business. Well, I exploded. I told her that hands which had touched Shirley Jack were not worthy to touch yours truly, that to the best of my knowledge they planned to get married, and that I didn't want to hear another word about making up with Buck. I told her to please call off the cops and to expect a check from me in the mail—proceeds from the sale of the Mustang, which I had left, spattered with my tears, in Memphis on a used car lot run by a man named Honest Al. I told her I would call again soon and I gave her instructions about who to see at the bank to pay off the remaining two payments on my house. There was no way I was leaving that responsibility to Buck. I told her if she was my friend she would wish me luck in my new life and she did, but she didn't sound happy about it. So much for moral support. I hung up the phone and cried. Across the fairgrounds, a calliope was playing "Alexander's Ragtime Band." The song had such a jaunty beat that for a minute I felt like a kid at the circus, and then I remembered I was the damn circus. I dragged myself over to the big top to limber up for the show.

Carlotta's enthusiasm for joining the circus that day at Graceland was contagious. It didn't take her long to convince me that this was just the change of scenery that I needed. And remember Eddie? Well, it turned out that he did have a big influence on my life. This kid swung a lot of weight at the circus, the kind of weight that comes from sleeping with the boss. The clout he had with the circus's owner, Mr. Rosetti, or "Frankie" as Eddie and only Eddie called him, was a matter of public record and all he had to do was mention that he had a couple of friends who needed jobs and Carlotta and I were on the payroll. Of course, in my case, it didn't hurt that Wally was out of commission for a while with his injury, and no one else had been trained to replace him. Eddie's job was selling tickets to the Gallery of Oddities out on the midway. I spent a lot of time visiting with him at his booth, where he sat dressed in a curious outfit that consisted of a yellow chiffon evening gown on the left and a tux on the right. It was Eddie who convinced me I'd look like a new woman with blond hair and it was he who dyed it a color called Sunset Strip Blond for me. I looked in the mirror when he finished his work and liked myself as a blond. I did look like a stouter-hearted woman than the mousy-haired Raylene Turner.

Wally had broken his foot, which was now in a cast, and, really, he was such a sweet man that I liked the idea of helping him out while he convalesced. Of course, it took a little time for him to convince me that I could do it. Then, when Sally the Elephant Girl, who made elephants tap-dance, lent me a cute pink outfit, very sexy, very brief, all sequins and spangles, I was all set. Plus, let's face it, it was a job that paid money, which I needed. Wally and I met in the big top every morning about eight and went through the routine. Carlotta stood behind him the whole time observing and making suggestions. These two were like Siamese twins. I never saw the like. I worked hard, and in just a few days I had it down more or less.

So my time came when we got to North Platte. Wally was waiting for me alone outside the big top before the show began. Madam Carlotta, as she was now known, was busy telling fortunes on the midway, and I felt the absence of her good-natured encouragement and concern on this, my big night. Wally was all soothing words and compliments as he walked me to the float I had to ride on in the parade that started the show. As soon as the lights went down at the end of the parade, I jumped down and ran to take my position behind the cannon, where we waited for my introduction. I kept my eyes on the ground, where the pink satin slippers that Sally had lent me kicked up little clouds of sawdust every time I moved my feet. Wally took my hand and helped me up the three rungs of the stepladder at the mouth of the cannon. When the cannon went off finally and I hit the air my eyes were wide open. You know what I was thinking as I went flying across the tent? Not that there was a lot of time to get philosophical, but I had an image in my mind of the poor twins, how they would have loved the attention! I fell into the net without looking like too much of a klutz and it was over. The applause! The cheering! Yeah, the twins would have loved it, and I have to admit I didn't exactly hide my head in shame. I must have been a sight, bowing, grinning, blowing kisses. It sure beat running a hardware store, I'll tell you!

On our last evening in North Platte, we didn't have a show. Everyone was scurrying around the fairgrounds pulling up stakes and packing their belongings, getting ready for an overnight trip to Billings, Montana. I was barbecuing some pork chops outside the modified trailer that I shared with a woman known only as Alice from Dallas. I say the trailer was modified because certain things like the bed and the doorways had to be widened, and the toilet reinforced, to accommodate her girth and weight of some 850 pounds (and that's all she weighed despite the tasteful sign on the midway that depicted her in a gold lamé bikini as Alice from Dallas, Tons o' Fun). To accommodate Alice's seven-foot height (seven and a half in her custom-made, steel-reinforced wedgies), the ceiling on that trailer was so damn high that sometimes we had to stop on the highway and let air out of the tires to clear an underpass.

Alice was a good friend of Wally's (how good, we'll get to later) and she took me in as a favor to him. I paid her a rent of forty dollars a week for sharing her custom-made mobile home, which was a castle compared to most of the little trailers and vans in the company. I slept on a green velvet couch in her living room and did way more than my share of the housework, as Alice was not the nimblest thing in the world. Nor was she the most industrious. ("My strong points are supervisin' and lovin'," she always said.) However, I didn't mind the housework as I had the place to myself most of the time, except for Alice's bedroom, where she reigned supreme, entertaining a steady stream of men friends.

While I tended to my pork chops on this night in North Platte, I was enjoying an intellectual conversation with some Italian trapeze artists about the different languages animals speak in different countries, according to the comic books. For instance, here in the United

States, dogs say "Bow-wow!" in comic books, right? Well, in Italy they go "Bau-bau!" I forget the Italian for "moo" but cows, too, speak another language overseas, I believe. Cats, however, seem to stick pretty much to "meow" wherever they might roam. Fascinating stuff. (You'd think it was fascinating too, gals, if you had downed a couple of white zinfandels and were getting all this attention from these fellows dressed in tights!) So there we are in the twilight and in walks this real handsome fellow, all cheekbones and flashing teeth and curly hair. I could see the resemblance between him and these Italian guys. He just suddenly materialized, and I do believe he materialized smiling, from behind a cheap purple tapestry of *The Last Supper* that was flapping on a clothesline strung between two trailers. (The tapestry was owned by Woolly Wanda, bearded lady and born-again Christian, that I had become quite chummy with.) Well, conversation stopped. Finally, his brother Angelo stammered his name, which was Armando, and the other two brothers hollered it. Armando strolled over ever so casually—oh, he was something! On the way he grabbed an airborne orange out of the half dozen that Kiko the clown was juggling. After all the hugging and backslapping died down, somebody thought to introduce little old me and durned if he didn't grab my right hand and kiss it! These Italians! I want to ask you gals out there: Has anybody ever kissed your hand? In a serious way, I mean. And if so, was the kisser a handsome Italian a decade or two younger than you with thighs so powerful and convex his pants could hardly contain them? Not like these old sunken, shrunken, saggy shanks like some of your husbands get around on. (Just teasin'!) Well, if you haven't had that experience, you couldn't possibly know how my whole body damn near turned to jelly. You should be so lucky, ladies.

I heard myself saying something like, "Yes, I'm new here. And I love the circus. Isn't it a beautiful night?" Small talk, you know, very casual, but you can bet there was this other little voice in the back of my mind, going, "You're cute. I'm lonely. If you look at me cross-eyed, I'm liable to sink my teeth into you like a big old terrapin and not let go till it thunders."

Before I had a chance to do anything rash, Alice from Dallas bawled Armando's name out her window. Armando's attention was diverted and I was left to fuss over my cooking and recover myself as best as I could. When Armando walked into Alice's trailer with a big box of chocolates under his arm, I made some feeble attempts to continue my conversation with his brothers but they huddled together jabbering in Italian and all but poking each other's eyes out with their hand gestures.

Let me tell you something right here, ladies: Men like fat women. Nobody I've ever met proved that basic fact of life better than Alice from Dallas. For a woman that tipped the scales at 850 pounds, she had the lightest wardrobe you ever saw. I don't think she had a thing to wear that weighed more than a handful of marshmallows, except for her jewelry. Most of her outfits consisted of string bikinis overlaid with a veil or two. She spent her days, both off-duty and at work in the Gallery of Oddities, wallowing around on her satin sheets, never far away from food, a twelve-pound turkey here, a few packages of Oreos there, and the occasional man.

When Woolly Wanda came out to take her things off the clothesline, I lent her a hand. She was one of these tall, skinny women that wear earrings down to their shoulders. Redder-than-red lipstick. Glamorous, you know.

"Wanda," I said, "Talk to me. We haven't dished the dirt all week and I know you must have plenty stored up. I know how you bearded women are."

She smiled. Wanda had this smile like some next-door neighbor you really didn't know very well, who had brought some potato salad over to your house following a death in the family. And who had a stubborn case of constipation on top of it. Kind of sweet, kind of sad, kind of strained. She said we'd have to talk quick because Dr. Lazarus was coming on the TV in a couple of minutes.

Dr. Lazarus! There was no escaping him. You can run but you can't hide. But I had a double-pronged reaction to Wanda's remark:

First, I said, "Wanda, don't tell me that horse's ass is back on TV."

"Why, Raylene!" she said, or more like "Whyyyyyy, Rayyyyy-Leeeeeeeeeene." She was from Mobile and every word came out like

70

molasses on a cold winter morning. You would think I had slapped her, the way she put her hand to the curlers on her cheek (she kept her beard real nice; it wasn't really woolly at all). "You ought not to say that," she said, and she explained that the good doctor was making a guest appearance on another preacher's program. She said she couldn't wait till he had his own show again.

Then, I said, "Well, let's watch him," because, as you can imagine, I was pretty curious as to whether Sister Shirley Jack would be appearing to warble her usual number. Wanda flipped on the TV and we settled down in front of it. Her eyes never flickered from that thing while she massaged an ointment into her beard, her ginseng and Mentholatum treatment that she kept in a coffee can in the refrigerator.

I said, "If you knew what I know about Dr. Lazarus . . ."

She said, "Shh," and kept silent till Dr. Lazarus finished reading a scripture that proved once and for all that a woman's place is in the home. During a commercial, I commenced to give her some highlights of Dr. Lazarus's younger days: how he grew up on my street; how he once poisoned and dismembered my neighbor's kitten; how he knocked up not only a simple-minded girl named Roselle, but her mother as well; how his own mother lives on welfare to this day while Dr. Lazarus flies around the country in a private plane. In short, Dr. Lazarus was not very nice. Then or now.

She just kept rubbing her ointment into her face with a bored expression until finally she said, "Oh, I know a lot of people are coming down on him pretty hard since he got arrested with those women."

"Those children," I clarified.

She ignored me and went on, "But you know what I say, Raylene? I say, judge not that you be not judged. That's what the Lord said, Raylene."

Now, I believe in telling the truth whenever possible for the plain and simple reason that the truth is usually more interesting than lies, and when I get started I just keep going. So I wound up telling Wanda all about Shirley Jack and my husband. Still, she sat there like a rock and ignored me and by the time the program came on, Wanda had me feeling like the fount of all blasphemy, so I shut up and watched.

Ordinarily, Dr. Lazarus, all blow-dried and shiny-suited, would come on to the rapturous songs of heavenly choirs, do fifteen minutes of a hellfire-and-brimstone routine, then introduce his lovely wife's solo. (Yes, I've watched the program many times, I admit. Boredom and curiosity are a powerful combination.)

Well, on this night, when the time came for Shirley Jack's solo, Dr. Lazarus said, "Brethren, tonight I want to beseech your prayers for your sister and my dearly beloved wife, Shirley Jack Lazarus. She's out there watchin' tonight and she was mighty disappointed that she couldn't be here tonight, but she's still a little under the weather. . . ."

I turned to Wanda and said, "She's under my husband is where she is!"

"And I tell you, Raylene," she said, "let him who is without sin cast the first stone."

"Well, one sin I'm not guilty of is adultery, so I'll cast all the stones I please," I said.

"But, Raylene, have you not committed adultery in your heart?"

"Not enough to tell about it," I said.

"Why were you looking at Armando Ghilotto like that?" she said in a teasing way. "I was watching you out my window. You can't keep secrets in a circus. Your face is too open and honest to tell lies like that, Raylene."

"Maybe I ought to grow a beard," I said. "But he is a pretty man, isn't he?"

Well, that question—or let's call it an observation because nobody would question Armando's looks—was all the encouragement Wanda needed to fill me in on the facts of his life. A year ago, she said, Armando was the headliner of the circus, the star performer of the Flying Ghilottos. Then, just as his career seemed to be in high gear, he was offered more money than he could refuse to join another team of aerialists at Ringling, Barnum and Bailey, leaving his brothers behind with the tacky bus-'n'-truck Rosetti Circus. However, the brothers carried on without Armando, and kept building their reputation with youngest brother Guido moving into the triple-somersault spotlight. As it turned out, Armando was not happy with the new team at the bigger circus, and after months of rumors of his return, now he was back.

"Well, that's nice," I said when she stopped to catch her breath.

"Nice? Is that all you can say?"

I moved toward the door as it was getting to be time to be pulling out for Billings. "That's all I can say," I said, and turned around to give Wanda's beard a little tug. "Right now, all I've got on my mind is being the best bullet woman I possibly can." And I wasn't lying. Not really.

January 6

New person in my life. Paco. Well, well, well. I met him today in Dolores Park, where he was selling *mota*. It's the kind of informal occupation he seems well suited for. He has that casual way of floating around like he is something light and fluffy being propelled by the wind. How light and fluffy he actually is remains to be seen. He's one of these kids you see drifting, with their eyes groundward, from one corner of the park to the other, their heads wired for sound. Somehow this one manages to wear the headphones as well as one of those leather Lindbergh caps with the earflaps from Kaplan's surplus store. The pockets in their 49er jackets are always full, a few packets on the right, a few on the left. The packets are these little bitty Ziploc baggies like MDA used to come in during my druggie period in New York back in the seventies when everybody was still alive. Ten bucks apiece for two, maybe three, joints worth of sinsemilla grown by somebody's uncle in Mendocino. Or so they tell their customers. Actually it is more likely to be "flavor of the week" from down at the bus station. If you get busted, the stuff doesn't weigh enough to constitute a felony so the risk is minimal. In the right pocket, the real stuff is kept for hip city folk and in the left the packets are about 99 and 44/100 percent oregano for bridge 'n' tunnel innocents.

I know about the oregano because Paco told me himself in his sweet, resonant voice (not girlish sweet, but boyish sweet) over a glass of cognac at my kitchen table after I made a purchase from him. He told me several innocuous little secrets about himself—the stories behind his tattoos, the brother who's in prison, that sort of thing. It's a method of ingratiation called disarming with candor. It works. In fact, I'm quite taken with him, dear diary. He says (chuckle, chuckle) that with some of those thriftstore yuppies it's hard to tell who's hip and who's faking it, and if he has any doubt about which category a customer fits into, he generally figures them for assholes, reaches into his left pocket, gives 'em the oregano and blows 'em off. That's why I was pleased to learn that the stuff he sold me today was strictly from the right pocket, or "good shit," as we hip city folk say here on the barricades. On the other hand, it didn't take a genius to look at me this morning and see that this gal was hardly concerned about shaking the dust from the hinterlands off her four-inch see-through spikes made of Lucite. No, indeed. Hip City Folk 'R' Us. Furthermore, any fool could have looked at me and surmised that if I set one toenail outside the city limits of San Francisco in the getup I was wearing, I'd probably be tarred and feathered and burned at the stake. No, after dancing and boozing all night at the annual Drag Queen's Night Out Ball, I looked like HCF defined this morning, though, God knows, I have felt often enough that my natural habitat was the asshole pocket of life. I was wearing this gauzy pink harem-girl outfit that made me look like a cross between a Hare Krishna and a hundred-pound wad of cotton candy. This fetching little ensemble was topped off by the honey blond Corrine Calvet wig that Aquanetta gave me because it was getting a little ratty by her standards but not by mine. A decidedly whory look enhanced by the fact that the hair-by-hair electrolysis job on my face is still not complete (I keep breaking my appointments, due to a low threshold for teeth-grinding agony) and a person who is sharp-eyed and/or unkind would not be at any great pains to detect more than a hint of five o'clock shadow. When I staggered past the park on my way home and my kohl-streaked eyes spied Paco, I had to stop and collect myself; he was so much what I liked from a strictly physical point of view—the wiry body, the jawline, the moves, the merciless black eyes—that I heard myself make an "Oof!" sound like someone had landed a blow to my solar plexus. As I got closer, I wasn't disappointed, and when he growled *"Mota?"* out of the side of his mouth, I muttered "Yeah," trying not to look straight at him. (You hear so many stories about plainclothes cops and hidden cameras in Dolores Park.) I strolled on past Paco for a ways while I rummaged surreptitiously in my purse. Then I wheeled around and passed him again. He reached into the all-important right-hand pocket. I didn't slacken my pace in the least as my ten and his dope exchanged places in a gesture so quick and smooth as to outfox the steeliest-eyed vice cop. Continuing on my way, I became aware in a few minutes that he was following me. On Mission Street, I stopped at the first shop window, which happened to belong to a children's clothing store, and pretended to peruse the contents while he caught up with me.

"Hey," he said when he reached me, "Your name Jamie?"

I almost collapsed. He knew my name! Like a bashful little lamb in a Corrine Calvet wig, I nodded and managed to croak, "How'd you know?" (My voice is not that reliable yet. I can sing like a girl and I can sing like a frog.)

He said one of his buddies in the park told him who I was and that I rented out floor space for sleeping purposes. He said he was between apartments and needed a place to bed down till he got organized. Well! I managed to tear my eyes away from the first communion dresses long enough to assure him that I could easily accommodate another warm body. Come into my parlor, said the spider to the illegal alien. Okay, so he's a homeless drug dealer of iffy citizenship status (he says he's from Vera Cruz, but, uh, that was a long time ago) and he says "You know what I mean?" much too often and the gimlet-eyed looks he garnered from not one, but two, policemen as we walked to my house implied a former acquaintance if not an arrest. ("Fuckin' cops, you know what I mean?" he muttered in my ear, but didn't elaborate.)

No, he does not sound like the most commendable candidate for the Young Republican Club, but let's get real: he's barely over twenty and, let's face it, most people—and I'm no exception—find twenty-year-olds the world's easiest to forgive for even the most heinous transgressions, especially when they're cute. And Paco definitely is. When you're that cute, ordinary people—yes, the much maligned beings that are supposedly so ruthless according to the ten o'clock news and history books and Jackie Collins novels—are likely to forgive darn near anything that doesn't permanently maim them and they will even offer up forbearing smiles and benevolent wishes as you walk out the door. At least that's how I am.

As I write this, he sits cross-legged on a blanket on the floor, playing poker and joking with a couple of guys from Guadalajara. Occasionally he looks up at me to share in their laughter and I smile back, understanding one word in five of the rapid-fire Spanish he uses with the Mexican guys.

And the cats seem to approve of him: Eustacia rubs against him and purrs, while Tamsin, usually so aloof, keeps leaping into his lap. It's an unusually quiet night in the Mission and a full moon smiles through my window. Only seven bachelors showed up tonight and that's fine with me, after last night's rough 'n' tumble full house, when somebody tried to flush a Miller Lite carton down the toilet. Big Victor and I were up half the night working plumbing wonders with a plunger and a coat hanger. But everything's fine now and a couple of the guys have already hit the sack, though it's only ten o'clock. The thick, sensuous smell of patchouli incense wafts across the room, Paco's contribution to the atmosphere. He unloaded a dozen little checker-sized cones of the stuff from an inside pocket and presented it to me as a gift. I, of course, was so taken aback by his generosity that when the time came to pass the hat (or, more exactly, the coffee can) for the nightly rent, I strode right past him. Which I think is just what he had in mind, but no matter. Big Victor is curled up on the couch, engrossed in a Mexican romance novel published in a comic book format. I'm relaxing in bed, where the horoscope in the *Examiner* lies open. Under Aquarius, it says, "Recognize your own limitations and concentrate on getting the job done." Ho-hum. I try my rising sign, Pisces. "Be open to change on the home front," it says. That's a little better. I fold the paper and throw it to the floor, while a loud burst of laughter from the poker players fills the room.

five

I got used to my new circus life pretty fast but Carlotta took to it like a cat to a goldfish. People smiled and shook their heads at the sound of her cackle rising in the night. Two days after we joined the troupe everybody knew her name and, you'd best believe, she knew theirs. And she didn't know the word *inconvenient*. For instance, if that rusted-out shell of a trailer she shared with Wally had been a horse, somebody would have shot it a long time ago. Everytime we got to a new town, I held my breath till I saw that Carlotta had arrived all in one piece. And there wasn't enough room in that thing to change your mind. However, to see Carlotta sprawled in a camp chair outside their door, plunging her head into a bucket of soapy water, and to notice that her smile didn't even go away underwater, now that's a happy woman.

One day I was watching her while she went through this daily ritual.

I said, "Carlotta, let me snip off these split ends right here."

Well, you would have thought I had suggested snipping off her nose the way she froze up and hugged that long rope of hair to herself.

"No!" she said.

"Right here," I said, pointing to the very tail end of her mane, where a few frizzled little hairs poked out.

"I said no, Raylene," she said, and the lady was not kidding.

I guess I must have looked a little upset, a little hurt at the sharp way she spoke to me, because this wasn't like Carlotta. So she laid her hand on my arm and switched to a softer tone.

"Darlin'," she said, "I'm gonna tell you something because you're my friend. You see this hank of hair?" She held her hair up in her two hands. "This is my power in life," she said. "Do you understand, sweetheart?"

I nodded just like I had good sense.

"Everything that makes me special is contained right here," she whispered, and she laid that wet mass of hair to her cheek like it was a full-length mink coat fresh from the store. "This is what gives me the power to see the things I need to see to make my life and other people's lives better. This is my strength, sweetheart. And that's confidential information, you understand."

"Okay, Carlotta," I said. "I see," and changed the subject, but I felt like I was seeing a brand-new side of Carlotta, whose ways were so mysterious to me. For instance, Carlotta could be found any morning at sunrise, sitting cross-legged on the ground outside her trailer chanting to welcome the day. Or so I was told by one of the fellows in charge of feeding the animals. (Lord knows, if the day couldn't get started till I welcomed it in, you'd hear roosters crowing at high noon half the time.)

At times I had tried to pin her down about her life story but she would only use words like "here and there" to say where she was from and words like "every now and then" when I asked if she had ever been married, or sometimes she would sigh and say, "Poor Carlotta. Always a bride, never a bridesmaid," and change the subject. Whatever her story was, there was no doubting that she did have some kind of special power. Over Wally, especially. That man treated her with the tender care some men give their golf clubs or their shootin' irons. "Honey this" and "baby that" and "please" and "excuse me." Always kissin' and a-gropin' and a-lovin'. Now I don't want to get into any steamy sex scenes in this account, especially scenes I didn't participate in. However, I must say, it was the talk of the circus how many times a day their trailer set up a bouncing that threatened to send it into orbit. Not to mention the nights! Of course, some fool wrote Don't Come Knockin' If You See Us Rockin' in the dust on the back of the trailer. Do you think Carlotta got upset when she saw that? Guess again. Our girl just sucked in her cheeks and rolled her eyes, and then laughed till she had to sit down.

Her brand-new career as Madam Carlotta, Mystical Seer, suited her just fine. She had her own little purple tent and the simplest of office equipment, a fold-up table and two fold-up chairs which she scrounged by going on a trailer-to-trailer scavenger hunt. Wally shelled out forty dollars for a crystal ball the size of a basketball at a pawnshop in Lincoln, Nebraska, and Carlotta was in business. The crystal ball was mostly window dressing, as Carlotta specialized in telling fortunes by reading the corns on people's feet, and she did a damn good job of it too. People came from miles around to see her, and on her days off, her new circus friends dropped in and put their feet on the table.

I went to visit her after the matinee our last day in North Platte. She and Wally, it was just something that was meant to be, Carlotta told me while we folded her laundry and packed it away for the trip to Billings.

"It was just one of those very, very rare convergences of certain planetary influences, darlin'," she told me. "Venus was in retrogade that day, which usually means don't bother to put on your makeup or your clean drawers, but Jupiter and Uranus, two very sexy planets, were in convergence and I just happened to be born at the right moment to take the fullest advantage of that happy juncture, sweetheart. Get it?"

"Well, sure," I said. "But when do I get mine?"

Just yakking, didn't mean anything by it. But Carlotta took on the look of a hairdresser passing judgment on a bad perm. Then her face relaxed and she almost smiled when she said, "You'll get yours. There's lots of men around here that would like to give you a tumble, sweetheart."

I said, "I don't know if I'm up for a tumble. Who'd you have in mind anyway?"

"How about Pooch?" she said from behind a towel she was folding.

"Oh, Carlotta," I said, "The human corkscrew? Get serious."

Pooch was one of these spotless fellows with never a hair out of place, but Lord, he was just skin and bones and so ugly he could back a dog off a meat truck. Plus, he never gave this human corkscrew business a rest. He was forever swiveling his head around to due south when his feet were pointing due north or twisting his arms and legs and backbone into the damnedest positions you ever saw. He got standing ovations in the Gallery of Oddities when he stretched his fingers out till they were nine or ten inches long. Actually, he really was something, I must admit.

Much to my relief, Carlotta laughed. She said, "Well, I thought you two might make an interesting pair, the bullet woman and the human corkscrew."

"No thanks," I said, "I like my men with a little meat on 'em."

But Carlotta persisted. She liked to tease. She said he looked a little like Fred Astaire to her.

I said, "Honey, if you and me were riding at sixty miles an hour in a train on a dark and rainy night and Pooch passed us going sixty miles an hour in the other direction, and you said he looked a little like Fred Astaire, I'd just smile and say, 'Carlotta, you're full of shit.'" She laughed and made a remark concerning what else a man might have that he could stretch way out there, but I'm not going to repeat it because it is not my intention to write a vulgar book.

I said, "Carlotta! Pooch is out of the question. Not my type. Period. Besides, Alice from Dallas has got him tied up. Tied up in knots, I imagine. He spends hours at a time with her and I know they're doing more than playing cards back there in her bedroom."

At the mention of Alice's name, Carlotta looked like she'd swallowed a whole cup full of castor oil.

"You don't like Alice?" I asked.

"Bad vibes, darlin'," she said. "I avoid her when I can. I don't even like to walk past her trailer. To tell you the truth, Pooch gives me the willies too. I don't think either one of those people is gonna do me any good, sweetheart."

I said, "So that's why you haven't dropped in to visit me. I thought it was because you were too busy practicing your feminine wiles on Wally."

Carlotta said, well, her man did keep her pretty well occupied as a matter of fact, but she wasn't complaining. Then she narrowed those beautiful eyes of hers and said, "Don't worry, darlin'. There's some romance coming down the pike and it's got Raylene Stout written all over it."

I thanked her for the free information and was just going out the door when she said, "By the way, Raylene. Did you hear me calling you last night?"

"Calling me?" I said. "Well, no. What time?"

"After you went to bed, darlin'. Past midnight," she said. "I was just doing some experimenting. Some mental telepathy. I wanted to see if your mind had quieted down a little."

I said, "Well, I guess my mind is just as much in an uproar as it ever was, because I didn't hear a thing."

She said, "Don't worry. It'll get better, sweetheart."

I said okay, and went back to Alice's trailer.

During the trip to Billings, Alice from Dallas couldn't sleep. She had trouble sleeping quite often, which I guess we all would if we spent the whole day wallowing around on satin sheets and stuffing outselves with pizzas and watermelons and moon pies. From my place in the living room ten feet away, her tossing and turning rocked the trailer like a ship during a typhoon. Before I turned in, she called me back to her room for a wine spodiodi, which turned into several wine spodiodis while we played a card game called Texas, Hold 'Em. Between hands, she would open the curtain behind her and wave and blow a few kisses at none other than Pooch, the human corkscrew, who was driving her Lincoln. With every kiss, Pooch would swivel his head plumb around to the back and grin that googly-eyed grin of his.

"Alice, don't wave at that fool," I told her. "He needs to see where he's going."

"Well, he likes to see where he's been," she said. You could never have the last word with Alice.

A wine spodiodi, being a shot of bourbon mixed with a shot of port wine, is a potent drink, and after we had knocked back a few of them, our tongues were pretty well flapping at both ends. In fact, mine was loosened to the point where I had to ask her just what effect Pooch's unusual flexibility had on his lovemaking, as Pooch was her main, if not exclusive, squeeze that week.

Alice licked her thumb and laid down three tens, or a Dallas-to-Fort Worth, as she called it, because of the thirty miles between the two cities. I folded with a couple of deuces and we had another drink before she deigned to answer my question.

"Well," she said, "You've heard that song 'Twist and Shout,' haven't you?"

I said, "Yeah."

"Well, he does the twistin'," she said, "and I do the shoutin', honey."

You'd be surprised at how very humorous that line sounded coming from a circus fat lady shitfaced on wine spodiodis, hurtling across the prairie at seventy miles per hour. Our laughter bounced off the walls of the trailer as we zipped down the straightaway, busting through dust flurries and tumbleweeds. The state of Nebraska shriveled up and disappeared behind us and we never looked back. Little Wyoming towns with names like Chugwater and Big Horn flew past in the night while Alice gave me advice about men, which, although she was much younger than I, I was glad to get, because, as I mentioned, this woman had a way with men. She told me once, cold sober, that she had had every man in the circus that she had wanted. And I believed her. And knowing her appetites, I doubt if you would have enough guys to make up a basketball team from the ones she had not wanted. She even had Eddie once! And she swore and be damned that he thanked her!

She said, "Yeah, I've had 'em all, Raylene, and I'll tell you what. You don't want to own a single one of 'em." She quadrupled her chin the way she did when she was about to deliver an important rule to live by (which she did several times a day).

"Possess love and you destroy love!" she thundered. "And besides, Raylene, there ain't but one way to keep a man's love in the first place and that's not to return it."

Alice was a cynical woman, much more so than myself, but I was feeling sociable and couldn't nod my head in agreement fast enough.

"Yeah," I said, "I wouldn't trust a one of 'em as far as a cat could spit."

I could see Alice had something to add to that so I waited her out while she knawed a turkey drumstick down to the absolute bone. Then she said, "Except maybe Wally."

Well, I guess I must have stopped in midnod. "Who?"

"Wally," she confirmed, wiping some grease off her chin with a small tablecloth she kept by the bed for use as a napkin.

"What's so different about Wally?"

I left that question hanging in the air while Alice contemplated it for a full minute. Alice could dominate a room as much with her silent contemplations as most people could with a nonstop stream of chatter.

"Well," she said finally, "I believe it's the way he smells."

"Smells?" I said.

"Yeah," she said. She heaved her body around and managed to rise up on one elbow, which was Alice's version of bolting to her feet. "That's what it is. It's a garden smell. He smells like the hole that's left in the ground after you pull a turnip out of it on a wet morning."

"They grow turnips in Dallas?" was all I could think of to say.

Alice's dumpling face grew dark and she fell into another silence, a sorrowful silence, a fat silence, if you will. I was all of a sudden aware of the closeness of our quarters, the smoky air, the stars I could see through the plastic bubble on the roof of the trailer. Then she told me the story of her life, about her childhood on a farm in Alabama, where her stepdaddy thought the fat little girl made an excellent punching bag. She was thirteen when she decided she had had enough of the beatings.

She said, "One night I couldn't sleep. I got up and grabbed the *Farmer's Almanac* off the bedside table."

She opened the book, closed her eyes, and moved her finger over the page. She opened her eyes and saw the word *west* and that was all the encouragement she needed. She packed a few things in a paper sack, a very few things because she didn't have much, tucked it under her arm, and lit out the door, heading west. Good-bye Tuscaloosa.

"Well, where does Dallas enter into the picture?" was what I wanted to know.

"I'm getting to that," she said.

She didn't have any trouble getting a ride when she got out on the highway. She was already over six feet tall and weighed upwards of three hundred pounds, but, picture it, thirteen years old, a virginal smile, walking down the highway after midnight with her thumb out. She wasn't out on the road any more than five minutes when a big old Fruehauf eighteen-wheeler stopped and picked her up. The driver was a guy that introduced himself as Goober (Alice stopped to unleash a fit of giggles at this point). He was a young guy, kind of balding, but not bad looking, a lot of tattoos, naked women tattoos. She and Goober rode all night, roaring right past thousands of acres of Mississippi cotton fields with the windows down and the hot wind blowing in their faces. After they exchanged names they exchanged a lot of looks, but said hardly ten words till they got to Monroe, Louisiana, the next morning and he took her straight to a motel, no questions asked. Of course, if he had asked, Alice told me with a wink, she would have probably said, 'Let's go. Time's a-wastin'.'" They checked into a place called the Sleepy Hollow Motel. As you can imagine, they didn't get much sleeping done in the hollow that night, and after he left a few hours later, Alice never smiled a virginal smile again. Which was fine with her because she was, she said, fed up with farm work and ready to step forward and be a woman.

Goober paid for the motel room and left Alice two ten-dollar bills before he went back to his wife and kids over in Ruston. She took a long hot shower and got dressed and walked down to a Rexall drugstore and spent a dollar on her first tube of lipstick. She smeared that lipstick on her mouth and she was ready for the world. She strolled down to the next corner and dropped into an International House of Pancakes. She sat down at the counter and ordered herself some banana pancakes, which took her about ten seconds to scarf down. Then she ordered some strawberry pancakes, which were just as yummy. Well, then she had to try the blueberry pancakes and the walnut pancakes and the pigs in a blanket. Do you think she was worried about what she would do when her twenty dollars ran out? She never gave it a thought, she said. She said she figured the Lord would provide, which he did. She had put away about forty pancakes and enough pigs in a blanket for a Shriners' banquet when this young fellow sat down next to her. He was quite a sight for a country girl like her. He was a skinny boy about seventeen, even more bruised and battered-looking than she was. He wore earrings and makeup. Alice had never seen the like! As weird as he did look, Alice couldn't forget her country manners and, besides, it felt natural to say hello to him and give him a big smile. He acted like he was grateful to have somebody to talk to. After he had watched her eat a few minutes he said, "One thing I like to see is a girl that likes her pancakes and don't care who knows it."

Well, Alice looked him up and down and told him he had come to the right place because she did indeed love her pancakes. She was a spunky kid, but by george, she didn't have anything on this character sitting next to her who said his name was Chuckie. They exchanged the stories of their lives while they chowed down on pancakes and durned if he wasn't a runaway too. From an army post in Florida where his dad was the commanding officer. Well, guess what? This mascara and earrings stuff wasn't exactly his dad's cup of tea and

Chuckie said his whole life had been a series of battles with his father, but Alice could tell by the way he said it that this kid gave as good as he got, or at least tried to. However, he said that the night before he and his dad had had it out for good. This time the old man had looked under Chuckie's bed and found a dirty magazine with naked people in it, and the naked people weren't women either, if you get my drift. That was the last straw and the old man wiped the floor with the poor kid. Well, late that night Chuckie packed up and took off in his car for parts unknown, but not before stealing a wad of money from his dad and setting fire to the house. When the two of them finished their pancakes, Chuckie whipped out a roll of twenties and paid for her breakfast. This was fortunate because her bill was way higher than the nineteen dollars she had left. After he paid their bills, he turned to Alice and said, "Well, you ready?" and that's all the discussion that took place before they joined up and spent the next year together. They strolled out to his car, an old beat-up Plymouth, and took off. As they rolled away from the IHOP, Alice sort of envisioned the two of them going on a cross-country killing spree like young folks on television, but they didn't. They told jokes and swapped stories till they got to Dallas, which was the next big town, and that's where they stayed. Alice paused in her story at this point to pour herself another drink. She said, "So there you have it, Alice from Dallas."

"Well, that's not the end of the story, Alice. What did you do in Dallas?" I asked.

In not more than two big gulps, she knocked back another wine spodiodi before she shrugged and said, "Hung out, put on some weight, met a clown, joined the circus."

"And what about Chuckie?"

"Oh, he went out to San Francisco. That's him there, the redhead." She pointed to a color photo on the wall.

I moved up close to the picture. "This one? This is a picture of three women!"

Alice exhaled a cloud of cigarette smoke and a cough. "The one in the middle," she said. "The redhead."

The women were dressed to the nines, especially the redhead, who

87

sported green sequins and a pink feather boa. They were posed as the three wise monkeys. The other two women sat slightly back, one with hands over eyes, the other with hands over ears, while the redhead, front and center, leered at the camera with her hands clasped firmly over her crotch. The picture was taken outside in the sunlight in front of a yellow sign that said Esta Noche. In the corner of the photo, it was signed, "See ya in church! Aquanetta."

For lack of any other comment, I said, "Well, my word!"

Alice didn't say anything, but watched me with a sort of deadpan look on her face till she exploded with that loud, braying laugh of hers that always ended in a coughing fit. Well! It's a crazy world, isn't it? But I must say that hearing her story that night made me feel much closer to Alice from Dallas in spite of the uneasy feeling Carlotta had about her. Generally speaking, I have found in my life that the more people reveal about themselves, the easier it is to forgive them for whatever they might do. Later, when I did have something to forgive Alice from Dallas about, I was glad she had told me the story of her life.

February 13

I've got to get it together. I haven't even made a diary entry in over a month. Why not? Well, I've been sleeping a lot, that's why. Today is Friday the thirteenth. It rained all day and there's a leak right over the kitchen table, but I don't dare report it to the landlord, for fear he'll come nosing around. All I need right now is for Mr. Wong to discover my thriving hostelry business. I'm sure there's a law against twenty people sleeping in one room and that's exactly how many guests I bedded down last night.

I guess this is called depression. On the one hand I feel I'm being self-indulgent with all these pitiable feelings about myself. But then, I do have rather weighty matters on my mind. After talking about it and thinking about it for such a long, long time, I have definitely scheduled the operation for April 2, delaying Dr. Katzenbach's original date by one day to avoid April Fool's. And I guess it's the prospect of that all-important surgery that's got me down. There are so many angles to consider. Will I get the money together in time? (I only need about a hundred more bucks.) And what if something goes wrong in the operating room? Am I making the right decision here?

All day long, I lurched around the house in robe and slippers, whining and bitching, as slatternly as Shirley Booth in *Come Back, Little Sheba*. Listened to Beatles marathon on KFRC. Thought about when those songs were new. I was barely sixteen, and freshly arrived in New York. I used to slip into the bars on Christopher Street and sit along the wall and try to be inconspicuous and smile back ever so gratefully if anybody whosoever smiled at me. I looked at people so subjectively, if that's the opposite of looking at people objectively. Everybody I met was a fascinating new entity, and I would fall in love at the drop of a compliment, even when I was hustling in Times Square. Well, hell, I haven't changed that much in that respect. Case in point, one Mexican con-boy named Paco, not that he's been that generous with the compliments.

HE'S HALF MY AGE!!! (I don't care.)

He did tell me last week that for a woman I didn't have too big an ass. If I thought that remark signaled a dawning physical interest in me, my dreams were dashed that very same night.

I had closed down my hotel for wayward boys for the night, thinking to take a well-deserved breather. Well-deserved because the rainy night before was highlighted by a brace of cops raiding the place at 2:00 A.M., arresting a couple of Paco's Dolores Park buddies for drugs and I'm-not-sure-what-all. Then after the cops left, a fight broke out between a couple of my regulars, Alonzo and Antonio, over who got floor space next to the window, and this resulted in the shattering of a crystal vase I had bought in Baccarat nearly twenty years before, practically my only prized possession. In short, I had suffered a night when nothing went right and I felt the need for a little downtime in my luxurious digs. I turned everyone away at the door and told them to come back tomorrow. Except Paco, of course. And, yes, truth to tell, it did occur to me that with just the two of us there for the first time, our platonic relationship just might shift into second gear or even soar into high. I made spaghetti. (Choosing Paul Newman's brand of sauce over Sinatra's, figuring the charity the money went to was probably a more politically correct one.) Paco went out to the Palestinian son 'n' pop store on the corner and bought some red wine, which was a nice touch. However, he came back accompanied by one Chuy, who he said was exhausted from not sleeping for three days. Could he please stay? Please?

The slick and agile Chuy. He has crashed on my floor a time or two before. I know his kind well enough. And I know that look, that hollowed-out look of a speed freak combined with the kind of glossy muscles covered with myriad homemade tattoos that one acquires in a penitentiary.

"I'm sorry, Chuy, but I'm closing down the Hole in the Wall tonight. I need a little rest," I said.

He said, "Hey! Me, too. I need a little rest, too, Jamie. I've got to get some rest. Hey!"

And then Paco took up his case.

"He's tired, Jamie. *Muy cansado*, you know what I mean?"

I was too done in myself to broach an argument with the tireless Paco; I tried to protest but by the time the words were out of my mouth, Chuy had thrust two dollar bills into my outstretched palm, slithered over to the closet, pulled out a couple of blankets, made his bed on the floor, and fallen onto it with a heavy sigh. So with a maidenly shrug, I acquiesced, and a midnight tête-à-tête with my dreamboat was thereby sidetracked.

Oh, hell, I thought, let him stay. He's just going to pass out and I don't recall that he made any trouble here before. So his snores provided background and punctuation for the rather strained conversation that Paco and I made over our meal. Strained, because every subtle attempt I made to steer the talk into a more personal vein seemed to be deliberately parried by Paco and twisted into rather banal cocktail chatter.

E.g., "Oh, Paco, what nice hair you have."

"I go to Supercuts. Do you ever go there? It's only eight dollars. Cheap, you know what I mean? This girl named Izzy always cuts my hair. Can I have some more wine?"

"Oh, Paco, what nice arms you have."

"I used to lift weights. Do you know a good gym in the city? Maybe I'll join Gold's when I get some money, you know what I mean? Can I have some more butter?"

"Oh, Paco, what a nice smile you have."

"I need to get my teeth cleaned. Do you know a good dentist? Is there any more of that spaghetti?"

This is not a literal transcription of what was said—I'm sure I was somewhat more indirect in my compliments, but you get the idea. The chitchat simply didn't catch fire the way I had sort of planned it to. And to add to my annoyance, at the conclusion of the meal, Chuy's snores came to an abrupt halt when Paco pushed himself back from the table with a great scraping of his chair against the floor. Next thing I knew the two of them had gone out for a drink, leaving me with the dirty dishes.

They showed up again at half past two. Half asleep, I stumbled to the door to let them in, then stumbled back to bed. But I couldn't get back to sleep. Lifting my head from the pillow, I could see them in the kitchen, their heads together as if planning a bank heist. My curiosity aroused, I heaved myself out of the sack and strolled ever so casually into the kitchen, as though to get a drink of water.

As I entered, Paco turned around and greeted me with such warmth and enthusiasm—"Jamie! You're up! Have a seat!"—that I thought fleetingly of backtracking into the bedroom and hiding my purse. I love him dearly, but let's face it, the hustler instinct is strong in the boy.

First some preliminary pleasantries:

"You look great in pink, Jamie. *Muy bonita, muy bonita,* you know what I mean?" This from Paco.

I did not look great in my pink flannel nightgown. It is a strictly utilitarian article of clothing, hardly designed for lavish compliments. But I thanked him politely, being too sleepy to make an issue of it.

Then Chuy went on a bit about my attractiveness, and his flattery included a bit of groping in the thigh area until I ducked out of his grasp. He has a regulation Latin handsomeness and there's a certain raw vitality, a ballsiness, that's hard to dismiss but the truth is he's scary to me. He enjoys talking about assault-and-battery cases that have landed him in jail.

"He started it," Chuy always says to explain away these altercations, but his ominous smirk forestalls any sympathy you might be moved to offer.

Finally Paco got down to business. It developed that Chuy had a buddy driving up from L.A. with a trunk full of cocaine, the classic stuff, not the rock the homeboys are dealing in Dolores Park now. Nine hundred bucks would pay for several thousand dollars worth of it if sold at the street price and Paco thought this would make an excellent investment for me (and him).

"No, Paco," I said, "no way," while I regretted for the hundredth time confiding in him that I have at last saved the money for my operation. He begged, wheedled, and ran his fingers down my back, but I held firm, telling him all I needed was another drug bust in this house. Finally, he gave up and he and Chuy went sullenly to bed, all considerations of my c'lure gone with the wind.

Just as I turned out the lights, the sad and shambling Big Victor came knocking, exhausted from having hitchhiked from a job in Fresno. I sighed and let him in, though I did take the precaution of turning off the lights to discourage any more drop-ins. Under his arm, the hulking but harmless B.V. carried a fat candle (green for money) from the voodoo section of Safeway. He lit the candle and dedicated it to the Virgin of Guadalupe, setting it near my bed to provide a little light and a little hope for the replenishment of his wallet, since his quick and clever cohort, Little Victor, had stolen a wad of money from him and gone home to central Mexico. Big V. set a few roses, stolen from the yard of one of my neighbors, around the glass-encased candle and mumbled a prayer in Spanish, oblivious to the sidelong glances of the contemptuous Chuy, who takes a more practical approach to acquiring money. I have overheard the two of them wrangling vocally before. It just seems to be a basic personality conflict—a good versus evil clash of biblical proportions, it would appear to the disinterested bystander, such as myself.

From my bed, I watched Big V. perform his rituals and hoped they would bear fruit. He has been one of my most dependable guests from the very beginning. He coughs up his two bucks with a minimum of coaxing, and has often assisted me in breaking up fights, once taking a gash in the arm from a switchblade for his efforts.

Sometimes I invite him to join me in the kitchen for a cognac and listen to his troubles—he's not getting enough work, his shoes are falling apart, he misses his girlfriend in Mexico, that sort of thing. As he talks, I watch his face in the half-light from the Jesus night light and I am always struck by the utter symmetry of his lips. My blurry impression after a couple of cognacs is that it seems a very truthful mouth, and I usually commiserate with him till the bottle is empty. Then, he thanks me, for either cognac or sympathy or both, and we retire to the bed-sitting-room (the elegant phrase Aquanetta uses to designate the room that's not the bathroom or the kitchen).

The light from the candle threw a flickering shadow on the wall and

Paco and Chuy quietly sawed logs from their pallets by the front window. I made a final trip to the bathroom and stood a moment studying my face in the mirror of the medicine chest. Well, now I know, I thought. He's not interested. I hit myself on the side of the head, a little mild flagellation for a poor sinner who had entertained such foolish aspirations. Shuffling back to my bed, I made a motion to blow out the candle but Victor stopped me, insisting that in order for its magic to work it had to burn all night. He went to the closet and took out one of the twenty polyester-and-acrylic blankets, my initial investment in the hospitality business, and made his bed in the far corner. I checked the locks on the doors and piled into my chaste and lonely crib, with only a fleeting glance and a sigh to indicate that Paco was anywhere in sight. I fell asleep and didn't dream (that red wine renders me dreamless), but awoke with a start when Victor's snoring abruptly shifted gears and went into a higher pitch and decibel level. Apparently, this caused Chuy's foot to shoot out involuntarily, sending Big Victor's candle rolling across the floor and smack against his head.

"Ay!" B.V. hollered in midsnore, and lumbered to a sitting position. *"Mi vela!"* he bawled, grabbing the extinguished candle and setting it upright again before glaring at Chuy, who glared back through slitted eyes.

"Cállate!" Chuy spat back at him.

The venom in Chuy's tone hung in the air till Big Victor uttered a face-saving, "Shut up? Who? Me?"

"I'm talkin' to you, *chato*. Shut up!"

Don't ever underestimate a gentle giant. They all have their boiling points and Big Victor had taken about as much from Chuy as he intended to. He stood up, skidded across the room, and let go with a kick that produced a breeze I could feel in my solitary bed. Chuy retaliated with a healthy swat against Victor's leg, and for a matter of minutes, all hell broke loose, till I managed, swaddled in my gown, to wedge myself between the two combatants.

"Stop it! Stop it! *Stop it!*" I yelled, my hands holding them off while my eyes surveyed the room for wreckage. By this time, Paco was not only fully awake but bouncing around the room in his little black bikini shorts in a very disconcerting way. To me at least.

Taking the initiative in breaking up the fight, he plunged into the fray.

94

"Get outta my way, Jamie!" Paco yelled at me.

"Stop it, Paco," I said. "Don't fuck with me."

They did quiet down, but not before the raging Paco shot c barb that hit the bull's-eye he was aiming for, namely my heart. His eyes, sweeping me over from head to toe, poisoned his quietly uttered words: "Don't worry, Jamie."

With Victor's help, I showed Chuy to the door and made it clear he was not welcome back.

And so it goes on palmy Balmy Alley, aka the boulevard of broken dreams.

six

Miss Viola used to say a gossip was somebody who talked all the time about things that left them speechless. Well, that wasn't the problem with me and Alice from Dallas as we rolled on through the night, playing cards and trading stories. To say that Alice's gossip was mostly of a sexual nature is like saying water is mostly of a wet nature. She had the dirt on everybody in the circus and was not shy about spreading it around, especially the dirt about who was making—or had been making, had ever made, had ever wished or hoped or planned to make—whoopee with whom. Janie who hung from a rope by her teeth had accidentally injured two of the clowns—down there, as they say, and Veronica, who stood on her head and did the splits on the back of a galloping zebra, preferred women when the sun went down. And on and on. I wish I could say I tried to change the subject to something more uplifting, but, hey, you never can tell when you might need this information and I confess that I even told a few spicy stories of my own. That's what those wine spodiodis will do to you.

"What's a woman like you doing in the circus anyway?" Alice asked me at one point. Had her eyes all squinted up like she had caught me red-handed at something. "Why ain't you settled down and married somewhere with some guy that's got a good job and knows how to treat a woman?"

"Alice!" I said, "You told me yourself that the way to destroy love is to possess it, didn't you?"

She said, "Yeah, but you look like the kind that would try to tempt the hand of fate."

I told her that at this point in my life I wasn't ready for a relationship. I meant it too, I thought.

She nodded and said, "Honey, listen to me. There's no such thing as relationships anyway. There's only power struggles."

Since we had plenty of time and wine spodiodis, I told her the story of my life. She listened and shook her head in sympathy and sometimes laughed that too juicy laugh that always ended in wheezing and coughing. All those cigarettes, you know.

"Well," she said, after she had heard the heartbreaking, tear-jerking story of the star-crossed love of Raylene and Buck, "I'll tell you what. You do what Alice from Dallas tells you and you won't be on the losing end of love anymore."

Just being ornery and, let's face it, a little curious, too, I said, in a teasing kind of way, something like, "Now, Alice, I could take your advice a lot more seriously if you hadn't lost Wally to another woman. With all your experience and know-how, how did you happen to lose him to Carlotta?"

Alice failed to see the humor in this. Her face went all red and she had another drink. "I believe that woman's got him bewitched," she said. "I don't know what Wally sees in her. He's not like some of these assholes—he's smart, and a woman needs a smart man every once in a while."

I said, "Well, you've got Mr. Twister bewitched and a few other men besides, so everybody ought to be happy."

She said, "Hmm," but she didn't sound happy.

We had not run out of gossip by a long shot when Mr. Twister slowed down and pulled over to the side of the road.

"What the hell?" said Alice, putting her hands down on the bed for balance and spilling her drink in the process.

She looked out the window behind her and hollered *"Pooch!"* so loud he twisted his head around 180 degrees. She knocked on the window so hard I was afraid it would break. Then, she said, "Ohmygod, look! It's a fire."

And what a fire it was. What must have been a little farmhouse standing a little ways back from the road was nothing but a big, huge ball of fire. There was no question of putting it out. The family who lived in it, a man and a woman and their two little girls, stood paralyzed by the roadside watching their lives go up in flames. It was painful to see their faces and to think about how blank faces look when all the hope has been drained away. I clambered out of the trailer and Alice, with a big display of heaving and grunting, hauled herself out of bed to follow me. By this time, after finishing off six wine spodiodis to each one of mine, she was so drunk she couldn't see through a ladder. Several circus people were already standing around looking helpless, though some were trying to lend a hand. Eddie was there, draping an overcoat over the shoulders of the shivering little girls in their nightgowns. Sally the Elephant Girl had rustled up some coffee from somewhere and was trying to serve it to the little girls' parents. But there was nothing to be done. Alice and I huddled against her trailer and I felt my eyes fill with tears, both from the heat and the miserable situation in front of me. Mr. Twister joined us and kind of smirked and said, "Well, I guess next time they'll know to live where there's a fire department."

Well, I like to have slapped him. I muttered, "You rotten son of a bitch, is that all you can say?" And I walked away. I guess my remark didn't endear me to Pooch, but I was in no mood to worry about it. I found myself walking over to the little family and patting the woman on the shoulder. She looked around at me for just a moment with a haggard look on her face, then moved closer to her husband. I retreated to a group of circus people chattering away in some foreign language, and I stood there smoking a cigarette, but I couldn't tear my eyes away from the catastrophe. After a while, the circus trailers and cars began to pull out and continue on their way. When I noticed Alice heading back inside, I snapped out of my daze and pushed myself away from the car I had been leaning on. By this time, the little family was surrounded by well-meaning neighbors and the smaller of the little girls was asleep on her dad's shoulder. I looked at them one last time and at their little house flaming against the early morning Montana sky and suddenly I felt overwhelmed by the scene. It seemed like such a lonesome place to live and to have your house burn down on top of it. I just laid my forehead in my hand for a moment and let the tears flow. Then I felt a hand on my shoulder. I looked around and it was Armando.

"It's very sad," he said.

Our eyes didn't only meet. They held like they were locked together. Let's not mince words—a connection was made, okay? When I thought about it later, I couldn't remember a time when Buck had ever looked at me in that long and lingering way, even when we were courting, even when we were yelling at each other. Armando's big brown eyes seemed to be as wet as mine and as we studied each other's faces, my thinking capacities seemed to shut down for the moment, except for that one little wistful thought fluttering around in the back of my mind that said, well, Raylene, this is something new. I could hear the other circus people rustling around, getting back into their cars and trailers, chattering away, some of them even laughing, but the sound of them was separate and apart from what was happening in my world at that moment. It was like they were in a faraway room up three floors and down three halls in a big hotel or something.

When Armando spoke, he said in a voice so low I could barely hear him, "Those poor people."

I nodded and repeated his words, then turned away to follow Alice into her trailer.

February 18

My birthday again. Raylene was on my mind all day and I had the very best, most sincere intentions of sending her a card, if not a bottle of Jack Daniel's or something, but I'm still letting things slide. Yesterday, the most productive thing I did all day was watch an old Yvonne De Carlo movie on TV from start to finish. *Buccaneer's Girl.* One of those only-girl-on-a-ship-full-of-men movies, which is my favorite genre, next to women's prison movies. Loved every second of it, too, but, to be perfectly candid, it didn't give me a real feeling of accomplishment. I guess I should be out hobnobbing with shopkeepers and neighborhood layabouts, getting used to my new voice, which seems to be smoothing out quite nicely and, in fact, occasionally ascends into Yma Sumac regions. However, I've got to get used to this new sound myself before I start springing it on other people. So I watch television. And sleep. I did summon the energy this morning to gently admonish Paco re the PG&E bill and his habit of running the furnace while every window in the house is wide open. He re-monstrated so vigorously (Big Victor turned up the heat, why do I always blame him for everything, blah, blah, blah) that I turned over and went back to sleep.

I'm thinking a lot about the future me and about what a very long way I've come from Lake Gladys, Louisiana. What next? Will I go to another town and start all over? And where would I find another town full of grown-ups like San Francisco? I would have to go back to Europe. I guess this should have been all thrashed out during the months of therapy I endured before I could begin the hormone treatments, but what a waste of time that was. Dr. Mahoney with his red face and cigars seemed such an unlikely candidate for gender identity therapist though he did wear a lot of tweed in an effort to look the part. (Those campy jackets with the patches on the elbows! Where do they get them? Do they come from the factory like that? I always picture a long-suffering wife with an English rose complexion smiling wanly as she patiently sews them on and plots murder.) I would always find myself speaking to the good doctor in support group clichés, using words like "trapped" and "dilemma" and could never bring myself to do too much in the way of soul baring. I mean I could tell he didn't want to hear it anyway. Who would? Besides, in my crowd, there's nothing you could say about changing your sex that wouldn't be a cliché. Or as Aquanetta says, "Oh, hey. What's the big deal? Everybody's doing it."

Whatever I did say, Dr. Mahoney just agreed, even going so far as to shake his head and go "Mmm, mmm, mmm" at moments when sympathy seemed appropriate. Which I confess I really didn't mind. However, I felt as though he would be more comfortable discussing politics or carburetors and I didn't want to make him feel uncomfortable or embarrassed. Heavens, no. I sat in the leather chair with my legs crossed demurely and watched the film noir shadows of the venetian blinds on the wall while I fielded his inane questions about my childhood and thought, Who ever heard of an Irish shrink? He seemed so bland and impersonal compared to the social welfare shrink I had years ago in New York—the black-clad, lion-maned, and zaftig Rachel, whose tart-tongued commentaries were always so provocative, if not particularly conducive to psychological insights ("Oh, Jamie, blow it out your fucking shorts! Whose mom did give 'em what they needed? Whose dad did?").

There is one bit of news to report. Aquanetta has wheedled and cajoled the girls at Esta Noche into giving me some business. I'm doing charts for Preacher Woman, the Two Gingers, Sparkle Plenty, and Estrelita, which will net me a hundred bucks, which I can dearly use.

Since I borrowed twenty dollars from Aquanetta last month, she has certainly taken a keen interest in my gainful employment. The plan is I will set up shop in Esta Noche's dressing room periodically and do horoscopes for the girls and whoever. Maybe some tarot cards on the side. Aquanetta planned it all. I could let Big Victor stay for free, she said, in exchange for functioning as my sergeant at arms. He's good at breaking up fights and turning down rowdies at the door. And he keeps a close eye on Paco, which is not a bad idea. Last week that little bastard took ten bucks out of my purse. But what can you do? He does have his good points. On a good night, he might bring in half a dozen of his Dolores Park cronies, which helps a lot to enrich the Hole in the Wall coffers. And, uh, he translates pretty well for the guys that don't speak English. And, well, I can't think of any other good points at the moment. Did I mention that he was nice to look at?

So tonight I cranked out horoscopes, which wasn't difficult after I gave my Salvation Army computer a few whacks to get it going. The activity made me feel productive for the first time in days and bolstered my spirits considerably.

seven

You can have Paris. For me, the most romantic city in the world is Billings, Montana. And my favorite part of the city is the fairgrounds. I guess it's just one of those "eye of the beholder" things. On day one there, I was out of bed like a shot at seven o'clock, and on day one, mind you, I had been on the road practically the whole night before, drinking with Alice from Dallas. But I was up and at 'em, ready to greet the day. Then, after a quick stop at the mess tent for coffee and a light breakfast, I wasted no time scurrying over to the big top. I spied Armando the second I walked into the tent, but busied myself tying (and untying) a shoelace till he showed up at my side. It took Wally and Carlotta half an hour or so to get there, but do you think I complained? Well, in a way. Like this: "Oh, gosh, Armando, Wally's late again. I hate to keep you from your practice." Hee-hee. But keep him I did. We lounged around leaning on the big cannon, talking and laughing about nothing and pretending to watch some clowns practicing a new routine. Then Wally stumbled in, sleep still in his eyes, and I had to go to work. You might think that being a bullet woman would not require a whole lot of practice, that it's sort of a passive thing. Not so. There is a lot to learn. You would be surprised how very important your body's position inside the cannon is. If your backbone or even your foot is skewed slightly to the left, you're likely to hit the air like a foul ball, and if you really go afoul, you can easily miss the net, which is no more than twenty feet wide. Just as important as your physical position, or maybe more so, is your frame of mind. The more you empty your mind of everything except your upcoming blast across the tent, the better it will go. Then once you're aloft, your posture has to be streamlined so as to float through the air with the greatest of ease, as they say. Hitting the net the right way is important too, as it can save you a broken neck or twisted ankle. So as you can see, being a bullet woman is serious work, but I loved the early mornings in the big top. Little shafts of sunlight poked through holes and gaps in the tent and lent the proceedings a special mood. Every once in a while the quiet would be cut by a shout from somebody on a trapeze or one of the riggers whose voice would echo across the empty bleachers. Wally was a patient teacher. We had agreed that three good blasts out of the cannon per morning was sufficient practice. If you think that doesn't sound like a lot of practice, then I daresay you've probably never been shot out of a cannon. Believe me, in that business too much practice is worse than not enough. It would take me half an hour of lying like a dead woman on the net before my ears stopped ringing.

But let's look on the bright side. Every flight I took was greeted with applause and shouts of "Bravo" from Armando and his brothers and whoever else was brushing up on their craft at the time. Once, Armando dropped into the net beside me when I was just lying there on my back after a good shot across the arena. Our fingertips touched and I thought, gee, it's funny how sweat smells better on a young man than an old one.

"That was almost perfect!" he said, and went on to offer a tactful suggestion or two on how to land without killing myself.

I'm going to say something now that might make some of you young gals out there lift an eyebrow and that's this: We didn't look at men's bodies when I was coming up. A man was just a thing in a suit and a hat to light your cigarettes. At least in the movies, and that's where I got most of my ideas about what life was supposed to be like. Back then, women's idea of a "dreamboat" was Cary Grant, and do you think Cary Grant had thighs? Or a booty? Not to my knowledge. He had a cleft chin and a smooth line of talk and that was supposed to be enough to keep us young ladies satisfied back then. It's true I married an athlete and it's true we had some pretty good times together bedwise at first, and with the blinds down, I guess I did take a few peeks at him below the neck, but it was within the bonds of holy matrimony, which is different. Different from what? Different from eyeballing a man dressed in white leotards who couldn't walk without rippling from neck to ankles. Yes, children, Armando was built. Never mind that he was, oh, about fifteen years younger; never mind that every other woman in the circus had eyes for him; never mind that, on this particular day, Sally the Elephant Girl, with thighs as hard and slick as the fenders on a Corvette, was flouncing around in cutoffs. I could see she was sending electric charges through every man in the tent, Armando included.

"Carlotta," I said, once we got our heads together.

She cut me off. "You like him," she said. You never had to waste your breath with Carlotta.

"What are my chances?" I asked, watching him turn a double somersault high above the center ring.

Carlotta said, "Let's put it this way, honey. Life is short. And hard. And boring. And you could damn well use a picker upper."

"And what does that mean, Madam Carlotta?"

"It means you've arrived at a time in your life when you'd be foolish not to take chances, sweetheart."

About that time Sally shrieked so loud that elephants less well trained than the two she was working with would have stampeded. Armando had jumped down right next to her just to give her a jolt.

The two of them chased around the center ring like two grade school kids, giggling and pinching each other while the elephants stood by and thought about whatever elephants think about when on break.

I felt old suddenly and lonely as a lost sock. I told Carlotta I thought I had arrived at a time in my life when I was foolish period.

Each time I saw Armando, in the mess tent, under the big top, or just walking across the fairgrounds, he made a big fuss over me like I had just returned from the wars.

But he wasn't one to ignore any woman, I noticed. It wasn't only Sally, Queen of the Pachyderms, who was taken anyway by Marcel the lion tamer. Armando was just a full-of-life guy that liked women, and you don't run up against one of those every day. Right, girls? It wasn't hard to imagine that Armando had more than one or two fillies in his stable, the way he opened doors for women and showered them with compliments, and, in general, behaved the way a man oughta.

One night, I sat looking out the window of Alice's trailer while she polished off a couple of barbecued chickens, washing them down with a six-pack of Dr Peppers. An after-dinner snack. She chattered away about getting a permanent and a whole new look for herself, while I watched Armando's trailer across the way in hopes I would catch him coming or going.

Alice said, "It's funny how a new hairdo can change a girl's whole personality."

I said, "Uh-huh."

The windows of the little silver trailer that Armando shared with one of his brothers seemed to glow with a warmer and happier yellow than any of the other trailers. Music and laughter and loud talk poured out of them, while the moon rested in a notch between two hills. And there I was stuck with Alice.

Alice, a frustrated hairdresser, was telling me I would look a lot better if I would go all the way to platinum blond.

"Uh-huh," I said, not half listening. "Maybe I'll do that."

Then she got around to Carlotta.

"She'd look a lot better with a simple pageboy. She needs to get rid of at least two feet of hair," said Alice, "or maybe a yard."

"No, Alice," I said, "Carlotta's not gonna cut her hair."

Alice said, "Well, she ought to."

"Well, she won't," I said.

"She will sooner or later," Alice said, "if she wants to keep Wally. A woman has to change her look every once in a while if she wants to keep her man interested."

I guess I was just tired of Alice being the world's foremost authority on everything under the sun. I guess I just wanted to shut her up. And that's why I turned to her and said, "Alice, Carlotta has power. Power to keep a man, power to see the future, power to do a lot of different things, and that power is in her hair."

That shut her up all right.

I turned back to the window and put Alice from Dallas out of my mind. After a while I got out the sheets and made my bed on the couch and turned in. If you've got a secret, don't ever tell Raylene Stout.

Now, for a change of subject: Once when we were in high school, my girlfriend Sue Fontenot talked to a ghost. On the phone. It was her grandfather who was crazy about Sue, his only granddaughter, and who had dropped dead of a heart attack just a couple of months before. She told me about it one day as we sat in the bleachers at the football stadium after band practice.

I said, "Sue, you must have dreamed it."

"Raylene," she said, "it was not a dream. And that's why I didn't tell you about it sooner. I knew you wouldn't believe me."

"Well, what did he say?" I asked her.

"He just said he loved me and he was proud of me for getting on the honor roll."

"And then he hung up?"

"He said 'Good-bye, and he hung up.

"Oh," I said.

She said, "Don't tell anybody, okay?"

I said I wouldn't and I didn't till now, and Sue and I never spoke about it again.

Sue, if you're reading this in your Early American living room in Abbeville, I believe you now.

When I went to bed that night in Billings on Alice from Dallas's couch, I fell into a peaceful sleep. A few hours later I woke up. Here's what woke me up: I was lying under a sheet and a light blanket. Suddenly, I felt something like a real big silk scarf was being lifted off the top of the covers. It felt like somebody had just taken this invisible scarf between two fingers right in the middle of the couch and, zip, it was lifted without a sound. There is no question in my mind that I was awake, and, believe me, every detail I'm about to tell you is as clear in my mind as the moonlit night that it happened. I opened my eyes feeling very peaceful, feeling that right there on that couch was a damn good place to be. I remember pulling myself up on my knees and peering out the window at Armando's trailer, where all the lights were out and all was silence. I thought about Carlotta calling me in her mind and how this would be a good time to try that again. I remember trying to make my mind quiet, trying to imagine there was nothing up there between my ears but a big bubble of air.

I settled back on my pillow and looked around the room, which was a combination living room/kitchen. On the wall, Alice had one of those plastic clocks that look like a cat with a pendulum tail. It was pink. The tail was going back and forth, back and forth, tick, tock, tick, tock. I could hear Alice snoring, but only faintly because I had closed the bedroom door before I went to bed. I put my hands behind my head and closed my eyes for a few seconds. When I opened my eyes, there the twins were at the foot of my bed.

You might think I jumped sky high and hollered or had heart palpitations or something, but no, it wasn't that way at all. Not in the least.

"Hi," I said.

"Hi," they said, somehow managing to strike a harmony on just that one word, the way they used to sing. Then they looked at me a long time while I looked at them in the moonlight. They were so beautiful, absolutely at their best, and I can't tell you the look they gave me. It was pure . . . what? Devotion? Warmth? Sincerity? It was a look of love, and somehow the knowledge swept over me that, hey, that feeling had been there all along. I don't mind telling you that I'm dabbing at my eyes right this minute while I remember, but you know what? That night in Billings, nobody got hysterical, and if you knew the twins and me, you would appreciate that. We were never what you would call "stoics." But, no, overlying and underlying the whole scene was a calmness and a peacefulness that just plain went right through me. They looked the way they looked when I was just a little kid, when we would all go to the political stumpings and they would knock the crowd dead with their singing and piano playing. They had their hair again. And how! It was as blond as hair can get and ratted to a fare-thee-well, the way they used to do it for special occasions. They wore identical blue dresses that I remember Miss Viola running up on her old Singer with the foot pedal many years ago. I stared at them the longest time, feeling such a mixture of feelings that it's hard to put my finger on them now. Sadness and wonder were in there, but in the most gentle way.

Then I said, "Y'all look so pretty."

"So do you," they harmonized.

"I've missed y'all so much," I said.

As the words spilled out of my mouth, I realized how very true they were.

"We've missed you, too," they said.

Tick, tock, tick, tock, tick, tock.

"How's Miss Viola?"

"She's fine. She sends her love."

"And the judge?"

"Everybody's fine. Everybody loves you," they said.

Now I know you're probably saying to yourself, the woman was dreaming, and I don't blame you. But no, it was different from a dream. It was more like a new way of being awake. It was like tuning into a radio station that had always been there, but behind a wall of static, and one miraculous night for whatever reason, it came in clear as a bell. I remember thinking how very easy it was to tune in, and wondering how come I had never done it before, but also I was afraid that if I spoke too loud or made a sudden movement, the whole scene would just evaporate, and I wanted it to go on and on.

I said, "Maybe everybody over there loves me. But not over here."

"That's why we came," the twins said.

They opened their hands that had been clasped in front of them and each one of them held out a lemon to me. I sat up and took the lemons in my hands. You know how rare it is to find really good lemons at the grocery store? They're either too hard or too soft? Well, not these. They were so perfectly lemony-colored and felt so good in my hands that I couldn't take my eyes off of them.

"Miss Viola sent them," the twins said.

I nodded. I knew what to do with the lemons.

"Why didn't she come herself?"

"She's busy," the twins said. "She sent us." I nodded again. I understood.

February 24

I am sitting in the very bowels of Esta Noche, the basement dressing room where the drag performers paint and putter and pout when not humbly basking in the glory of stardom onstage. Blazing mirrors reflect wig stands and paint pots and a sequiny swirl of faux femmes coming and going in a cloud of cigarette smoke. It's like the strippers' dressing room in *Lady of Burlesque,* and I'm trying my damnedest to be like Barbara Stanwyck tonight, spitting aphorisms out of the side of my mouth like watermelon seeds and calling people "kid," just trying to fit in with these show biz folk.

I'm sitting in a corner with Preacher Woman. She's an earthy gal, a double Virgo, both sun and moon, but her Gemini rising sign allows a little air to leak into all that cynicism, so she's not totally averse to the notion that her life is predicated by the position of the stars. Or maybe she's just being a good sport.

"Let's take a look at some of the transits," I say, poring over her chart. I purse my lips and narrow my eyes contemplatively.

"Oh, yeah, okay, girl, let's do that." She's got that knitted-brow look too, but the cause has nothing to do with her planetary aspects. What she is concerned about is the amount of eyeliner she can apply without making her eyelids stick together when she blinks. She pencils a liberal amount on, then blinks, then tissues it off, never turning away from the mirror.

"Well, Uranus and Neptune are conjuncting right now in Capricorn, which means—"

"Say what? My *anus?*"

I ignored this very weak joke and continued with my spiel, or tried to.

"Excuse me, Jamie, hand me that powder puff, will ya, darlin'?"

"—which means that they're heading for Aquarius, which is going to affect your tenth house, your career . . ."

"Mmm, is that right, child?" she asks, casting big-eyed sidelong looks at herself in the mirror, practicing smiles and checking her teeth for food particles and whatnot. Yes, I think she's just being a good sport.

I almost backed out of this astrological commitment, much to Aquanetta's exasperation, but I'm sorry, I just haven't been a very public person lately. However, A. won out in the end, as she so often does—I believe indefatigable is the word—and here I am, cradling my chin in my hand and trying to impose some order on the destinies of these gals whose only hard-and-fast rule for living is "Do it now."

Resorting to aphorisms again, I hear myself saying, "Beauty's only skin deep." This chestnut is tossed off in the direction of Preacher Woman, who has abruptly run up to the top of the stairs and stands there peeping at the show through what appears to be a bullet hole in the door. She clatters down the stairs and picks her cigarette out of the ashtray to take a quick puff. I've never seen her out of drag and the idea of Preacher Woman in a business suit, or even referring to her as a "him," is inconceivable if not laughable. She's doing Diana Ross tonight, albeit a slightly plump Miss Ross, and looks pretty in a way that a good caricaturist could draw in a continuous whirl of circles.

"You look fabulous, Preacher Woman," I say, and Aquanetta, seated at my right, quickly agrees, "Faaaabulous!"

Preacher Woman thanks us and says the worst part is waiting to be called on stage. I can understand what she means. The standing up in front of everybody and performing can't be any more nervous-making than sitting in the basement with these showgirls whose flinty eyes and unsolicited suggestions have triggered enough flop sweat on Preacher Woman's forehead to wilt two powder puffs, going on three.

"Just a little more blusher right here, Preacher Woman."

"Is that all the bigger your tits'll get?"

"The lipstick's too light. Try the cocksucker red."

Aquanetta sits in the center of the room holding court with the dour Estrelita and the Two Gingers, who perform as a duo. She is drinking a martini, adjusting a neckline here, a hemline there, tossing out zingers to anyone who will stand still for them. She is having a field day ribbing Ginger Who Looks Just Like Connie Chung about the the older gentleman who has been sending her flowers and buying her drinks. A. makes a rude remark about the liver spots on his hands.

Ginger, it must be said, is just as direct and a great deal saucier than the famous newscaster she resembles. She smears on lipstick at the mirror before delivering her retort: "Honey, when a man's got a million bucks and a ten-inch dick, those liver spots look just like freckles." This announcement is punctuated, in the absence of a rim shot, with a sharp click as she reholsters her lipstick.

"Wasn't it Dorothy Parker who said that?" Aquanetta inquires of the big-haired and bubble-headed other Ginger, known among the cognoscenti as Ginger Who Fell to Earth. Ginger II obligingly delivers the giggle which is her stock reaction to most situations.

And on and on it goes while I chitchat nervously and watch the dishers and dishees like a spectator at a tennis match. Then, somebody hollers down the stairs.

"Aquanetta! You're on!"

She takes a deep breath, then another. I walk to the top of the stairs with her and watch as she fairly flies into the crowd. She smiles radiantly between hellos and kisses as, teetering on her spikes, she threads her way through the throngs of guys. The emcee, the towering Virginia Slim, delivers a few appropriate lines about our favorite diva fresh from a sellout tour of Europe. Virginia's spiel winds up with ". . . and here she is, one hundred sixty pounds of raging, white-hot funk, the fabulous . . . *Aquanetta!*"

And she's on. Her number is one that she unearthed from her archives of drag music of the twentieth century. Namely, one "Teach Me, Tiger" by April Stevens, a pop record from the early sixties that features a lot of easy-to-lip-synch heavy breathing and lyrics simple enough that one is hardly likely to forget them, even while executing the splits onstage at the Esta Noche.

> *"Teach me tiger*
> *How to love you*
> *Wah wah wah wah wah."*

Outfitted in a skintight sheath in tiger stripes, she's at the top of her form. She's clearly enjoying the attention. Clearly.

> *"Teach me tiger, how to tease you,*
> *Wah, wah, wah, wah, wah.*
> *Tiger, Tiger, I wanta squeeze you,*
> *Wah, wah, wah, wah, wah."*

Nice round of applause, if a few decibels short of deafening. Aquanetta jackknifes her body into several very stagey bows and looks past the lights.

From my station at the dressing-room door, I recognize a few dim faces above the hands colliding loudly in the dark. I spot a whole contingent of regulars from the Hole in the Wall, the result of Aquanetta handing out free passes the night before. They are whistling and stomping near the back of the bar, and I wave. Looks like they all came out, Paco, Big Victor, those two hot little brothers from Oaxaca, that whole gang of roofers from down on the peninsula who stay every time they're in town. Aquanetta strikes a final pose, bares her teeth in a final snarling smile, jumps down from the stage, and kisses her way to the back. I go to meet her.

First, Paco grabs Aquanetta by the waist and gives her a big smacky kiss on the cheek, and then turning to me, he delivers a similar display of exuberant affection, rather to my surprise.

"Jamie," he says. "Can we talk?"

I glance at Big Victor. "Well, sure. What about?"

Paco also glances at Big Victor. "In private," he says.

Taking my elbow, he steers me out the front door and onto the sidewalk. His eyes dart up and down the street, while he nervously rakes his fingers through his hair. Gathering his thoughts, I guess.

After a somewhat strained pause, I say, "You look good." Which he does.

"Thanks. Uh, Jamie?"

Then the little bastard makes a wheedling last-ditch effort toward getting my money again. The dope deal was weighing heavily on the boy's mind.

"No, Paco," I say. My eyes fix on the window of the Sincere Café next door, and I automatically clutch my purse a little closer to my bosom.

He, too, suddenly becomes inordinately interested in the window of the Sincere Café, while I take on the mien of a rather crotchety ole schoolmarm.

"Paco, listen. I thought you understood. I do have some money saved. I also have surgery scheduled for one month from today and I need every cent of that money. . . ." I repeated this information several times in several different ways while he remained stonily staring at a man slurping wonton soup inside the café.

"Paco, look at me."

He looks at me briefly, then back at the fascinating tableau of a man and his wonton.

"Paco, I cannot give you the money."

"Not give, lend, you know what I mean?"

"Paco, I cannot lend you the money."

I walk away, but I can't help glancing back at him. He spits angrily at the ground and mutters *"Chingada"* before stalking down Sixteenth Street.

eight

I don't know whether I blinked my eyes or took too deep a breath or what, but just as suddenly as they appeared, the twins were gone. I wish I could tell you they dissolved into the moonlight or something, but, no, just, zip, they were gone. For a minute or two, I sat there with the lemons in my hand, trying to tune into that same station, thinking I could make them come back, but something told me it was no use. I got up and tiptoed over to the drawer where Alice kept her spoons and forks and, quieter than the mice that called her trailer home, I took out a big tablespoon. Then I found a pencil and paper. I drew a figure eight lying on its side and wrote "Raylene" in one circle and "Armando" in the other. I slipped into some jeans and a T-shirt and snuck out the door.

Such a night! Just dark enough, just light enough. The trailers and trucks and tents all sat there in the silvery moonlight and whispered, "Do it, Raylene." The Montana version of a springtime wind hit me in the face and sent shivers down to my toes. I scoped out the grounds to make sure nobody saw me. I slunk over to Armando's trailer and stood still as a post for a moment. Silent night, magic night, not even a peep from the animals.

You don't crawl under a trailer. You get down in a push-up position and scrunch your way forward on your elbows. And if you're a middle-aged woman in tight jeans holding two juicy lemons, a flimsy piece of notebook paper, and an oversized tablespoon from a fat lady's kitchen, you've, well, got your hands full. But I made my way to the geographic center of Armando's trailer and started digging. Quietly. After I had a hole big as a teapot, I stopped and thought, well, maybe they go in separate holes. Then I thought, no, that wouldn't make sense. So I laid the lemons in the hole, side by side, separated by the piece of paper that carried the name of me and you-know-who. I looked at them for a long minute and then lowered my head to kiss each one of them before I covered them with the loose dirt, which I patted down into a neat little grave. Then I scrunched my way out, went back to Alice's, and slept like an organized woman.

Well, the results weren't long in coming. I went to the mess tent the next morning after just a few hours of sleep. I sat down and had some coffee and eggs with a Hungarian juggler named Ivo. He was one of these talkative guys with bad teeth and a breath that would knock a buzzard off a shit wagon. But nice. He was telling me all about the time he smuggled his little dog, Simone, out of Poland. (Don't ask me how we got off on that subject.) Actually, it was a story that did pretty well capture my attention, the picture of Ivo walking across the border, or waddling, I guess, in an overcoat with poor Simone pressed between his skinny thighs. However, it wasn't such an interesting story that my heart didn't stop when Armando appeared out of nowhere. He was dressed in sweats and breathing hard, just finished with his morning run. It so happened that Ivo and I were sitting next to a table where two of the sexiest women in the whole circus, a couple of talent-free hootchy-cootchy dancers, Jeanette and Twyla, sat swinging their legs and plotting their next seductions. Well, I might as well have been the only woman in the tent. Armando trotted over to my table and said something that would have made a lesser woman choke on her coffee:

"Raylene! I was just thinking about you!" Loud, too.

It's not my style to be coy, but as soon as he said this, I thought about something Miss Viola used to say. She always said there wasn't but two things that brought people trouble. One was saying yes too soon and the other was not saying no fast enough.

I turned to Armando in slow motion sort of, acting like it was all I could do to tear myself away from this fascinating story Ivo was laying on me.

I said, "Why, Armando, how nice to see you."

Like Miz Astor, you know. (Out of the corner of my eye, I could see the two floozies at the next table freeze, thinking to pick up some pointers on how to be high-class, or at least how to fake it, I guess.)

Armando sank into a chair beside me. He was watching me, like Superman doing this X-ray vision thing, and it was all I could do to maintain myself. But I did. I was still doing the Miz Astor number, because Ivo hadn't got down to the punch line of his story yet. So when he finally did get to the part where Simone barked, I got a chance to favor Armando with one of my glances. Well, let's call it one of my lingering glances. Thank you, Miss Viola.

Armando walked me to the big top for my morning practice session, all but throwing his coat over puddles for me. He grasped my elbow, ever so gently, you know, and whispered sweet nothings in my ear. Such manners.

Here's a news flash for all you fellows out there: Women like good manners! And don't go telling me you've got good manners, but you just don't use 'em. We want you to open those doors for us and send us some flowers too. And I'm not talking about this one-perfect-rose bullshit, either. We want a whole bouquet, don't we, girls? A box of Russell Stover's cream centers wouldn't hurt.

You know what? Armando did bring me flowers that day. He knocked on Alice's door after lunch and presented me with a fistful of little violets just like Dagwood or somebody in a cartoon. He complimented me on my form and grace and so forth and so on that I had so ably demonstrated that very morning. With my nose in the violets, I fluttered my eyelashes and generally acted like he was talking about a performance of *Swan Lake* instead of getting shot out of a cannon three times.

After the matinee, he asked me to go for a walk, so we went for a walk. He asked me to go for a ride, so we went for a ride. He asked me to give him a kiss, so I gave the poor boy a kiss. And then another. And then another. This was up on top of Ole Smoky or someplace like that where the local teenagers parked to make out. In the dusk, the city of Billings was a blanket of twinkling lights spread out in the distance.

"Raylene. Raylene, darling." Kiss, kiss. (You know these Italians!)

"Yes, Armando?" Kiss, kiss. (And you know us hot-blooded gals from south Louisiana!)

He said, "You're like no one else."

Well, I couldn't argue with that, especially with my tongue tied up in a bowknot with his the way it was.

And on and on it went. Now bear in mind that I was a couple of decades out of practice with this kind of stuff, but I'm here to tell you it's like riding a bicycle. You sure don't need to waste your money on night school to relearn it.

We went back for the evening show and everything about the circus had a brand-new layer of color and charm and excitement. When my fanfare began, I ditched the cigarette I was smoking and pranced into the spotlight, holding my arms this way and that and executing a couple of pirouettes, not the least bit unaware of the attention I was getting from Armando warming up on the trapeze above the center ring. I won't say that self-confidence was the main emotion I felt as I squatted inside the cannon that night. Let's face it, under the best of circumstances, the prospect of gunpowder exploding under your behind is hard on a gal's nerves. However, a little smile curled the corners of my lips as I waited in the dark. Then, *boom.* Up, up, and away. When I reached the top of my arc and was falling into the net, I showed off a little. Sort of posing like somebody in the Olympics as I landed. The applause! For a second I thought about the twins again, and for the first time, it was crystal clear to me why they had always yearned for applause and built their world around that yearning. I understood, too, that their failings in the mothering department came from nothing but their ignorance, and that's forgivable. I felt like I had closed a door that had been standing ajar for a long time. Which was just as well, because I did have something else real important on my mind. Or somebody, that is.

Have you ever actually had a roll in the hay? You know how delightful and picturesque it looks in the movies. Well, just try it. You'll be picking straws out of every nook and cranny you've got for hours afterward. But just because Raylene Stout claims it's an overrated pleasure doesn't mean you should turn the experience down if it's ever offered to you. It happened between the matinee and the evening show when Armando invited me for a stroll. It was such a sunny afternoon, a little breezy, but just enough to encourage one to snuggle up next to one's warm-blooded, athletic Italian admirer as one strolled across the fairgrounds with nothing on one's mind but thoughts of doing what comes naturally. Everyone was out in the sun. We waved at Carlotta and Wally, who sat playing cards and drinking beer. We got involved for a minute in a game of Frisbee with some clowns. Even Alice from Dallas was taking the sun, reclining on an industrial-strength chaise lounge and entertaining a few men with her stories. Nice day. We ended up in the corner of the fairgrounds where the animals were quartered. We visited my monkey friends, and then we took a few minutes to pet the elephants. That is, I petted the elephants while Armando had a brief and quiet conversation behind my back with the guy in charge of feeding the animals. It was a conversation that started out with "Jerry, don't you need to take a break?" and ended up "See you later, Jerry." In seconds this guy made himself scarce, leaving us alone with the animals, who didn't look surprised to see him go. Armando, quick as a flash, pushed and pulled and threw several bales of hay together to form a nifty little four-wall bedroom with the sky for a ceiling. Not a haystack, exactly, but close enough.

I would be lying if I said I protested right away. I would not be telling the whole truth if I didn't mention that, in fact, I seem to recall clapping my little hands together in delight. Hee-hee. However, after a while, when things started moving a little too fast for me, I said, "Armando! Not now!"

Armando said, "Why not?"

I said, "Because it's almost time to get ready for the show."

He said, "Don't be silly," which is a phrase that, when whispered with an Italian accent into a feminine ear, sounds very much like, "Oh, you beautiful doll. You tear my heart out when you tease me this way."

"Not now," I whimpered.

"Not now?" he said. "Raylene!" And he went into a spiel, which did not sound exactly unrehearsed, about some African pygmies who lived deep in the jungle and whose language had only two words to designate time—"now" and "not now."

"Hmm," I said, and started peeling off my nylons. Then, Armando took over the job, while a giraffe peeked over a bale of hay.

March 22

Up at the crack of dawn to tiptoe past a gaggle of snoring Mexicans and wait in front of the house for Aquanetta. She roars up in her muffler-impaired Volks and we're off to the Marina while the city sleeps. A. won a day trip for two to the Farallon Islands in a bar raffle, and has chosen me to accompany her, nature lover that I am. Well, I did sign a save-the-whale petition once when Greenpeace came knocking.

Aquanetta drives with one hand and tugs at the cowl collar of her nautical-looking sweater with the other. She tells me it's new, or at least newly acquired, and allegedly worn by Sterling Hayden in its pre-flea-market incarnation. She tries the bill of her baseball cap at several angles.

"Would I look more jaunty and fun-loving with the bill in back, darling?"

At the pier, some forty outdoorsy-looking people are milling around waiting to board a squarish vessel that will take us out to sea. At first, in our parkas and jeans, we blend in with the well-bundled-up bird-watchers from central casting, but, no, A. will not be overlooked. She snags some old duffer with hair in all the wrong places by his flanneled sleeve and orders him to take our picture.

"I've been here ten years and this is the first wholesome thing I've done," she yells for the edification of a group of onlookers, who smile and titter self-consciously while I cringe. We board the boat and the trip starts off fine. The cityscape recedes as we glide beneath the Golden Gate Bridge. There's the Cliff House, there's the windmill, there's Land's End. Leaning on the rail, A. and I take in long drafts of the salt air and I'm glad I came. I'm glad I'm alive. For the first fifteen minutes. Then I experience what Harry, our genial young tour guide, calls "gastric awareness." Do I ever. The boat is doing a bucking bronco number above the water and my stomach doesn't take long to catch the rhythm. First, I go to the toilet and drop gratefully to the hopper without a second to spare. Spasms of shit shoot out of me while I cling desperately to the handles on the wall and lift my eyes to God. Then I go sit in the stern, the boat's "center of gravity," according to the Hush-Puppied and crew-cut Harry. His feminine counterpart, a strapping six-footer, big as a tank and sweet as a rose, is right behind me in her wide-load Levi's reminiscent of the grotesquely oversize kind displayed in store windows as an advertising joke. Then seconds later, I see her hanging over the back of the vessel heaving her guts into the bay. I sit there quietly and take deep breaths and "scan the horizon" as the guide has recommended—not focusing on anything close. (A. comes up to me occasionally and with my eyes on the clouds, I grunt replies to her inane remarks about my iron constitution.) After a few minutes I tell myself, "Boy, I sure am glad that's over." Then seconds later, I run to the back of the boat to heave and wipe my mouth and think about the underrated pleasures of dry land, such as its immobility. And I'm thinking about the Vietnamese boat people out there all those months on those little dinghys being tossed about with no possibility of coming to land. And the Haitians that were, well, in the same boat. And the people on the *Titanic* singing "Nearer My God to Thee."

A. strolls over to tell me she's bored with the endless seascape, says she feels like she's watching *L'Avventura.* I tell her *Last Year at Marienbad* was a laff riot by comparison, then I lean over the rail to heave again. When I sit down again beside A., I become aware that she's squirming and twisting her rings around, signs that all is not well. I ask her if she's sick, too.

She says, well, yes, in a manner of speaking. Meaning what, I ask. She falls uncharacteristically silent before exhaling a big dramatic Aquanetta sigh and says she got tested last week. I grab her hand and sit there with my eyes scanning the horizon of her face. But you got tested years ago, I say. You came up negative, didn't you? True, she says, but this time she came up positive and she doesn't want to talk about it, she just wanted me to know, just wanted to tell somebody. We sit there several minutes, just a couple of pretty gals holding hands, my mind scanning the horizon of my life, thinking how my knees gave out and I landed in a heap on the floor the first time I got this particular piece of news from a friend. Actually it was somebody I barely knew. That seems like such a long time ago. Soon I have to get up and heave again, and then again and again over the next four hours. I'm annoyed at the people around me who are eating sandwiches and drinking coffee like nothing is happening. Or maybe, like me, they're just all cried out. I feel as if there were a certain number of tears alloted to me and I've spent 'em and all I'm left with is a dull ache that won't go away. So many people have disappeared that I stopped counting long ago. So many that the gay papers have taken to printing obituaries under the sting-reduced heading of Transitions.

Somebody sights a whale. There's a couple of them surfacing in the distance. Big fucking deal. I heave again.

We finally get to the damned islands and cut the damned engines, but we don't get off the damned boat. I manage to scarf down a banana and a couple of vanilla wafers that A. has scrounged somewhere. The large female tour guide is back in commission again and, her robust singsongy voice restored to its former heartiness, she's pointing out this and that species of bird, almost all of them in the endangered category. Harry's voice floats across occasionally from the other end of the boat, where he lectures to his own group. Words like "extinct" and expressions like "vanish from the face of the earth" float across the deck, now eerily silent without the hum of the motor. Dozens of seals sun themselves on the craggy rocks of the islands and bark at the gawking tourists. Scrawny pelicans cling to guano-splattered boulders and cast jaundiced eyes at the slim pickings beneath their feet. After a camera-clicking hour of coasting around the islands, we head for home. Drowsy from mal-de-mer pills, I can hear A. entertaining a group of ski-booted Stanford students she has been chatting up.

"As we say good-bye to the Farallon Islands . . . ," she intones in best Robin Leach fashion as we head away and the students laugh politely, but the best I can muster is a perfunctory grimace-grin that I aim in her direction, hoping she'll get the message: There's nobody who can hold a candle to you, my dear crazy friend. Nobody in the world.

It takes forever, but we finally reach the Golden Gate again. On the concrete underpinnings where the bridge joins the shore, someone has written in letters three feet high, Sailor, Would You Wipe Your Mother Out with a Nuclear Bomb? Don't Serve on Nuclear-Powered Ships! Aquanetta and her giggling coterie fall silent, whether from contemplation of the unpleasant graffito or simple ennui, I don't know. As we cruise past the beach at Land's End, one of the students tries his own Robin Leach style to announce, "To your right, you can observe the homo sapien, a terrestrial mammal with extremely interesting mating habits." He is talking about the few intrepid nudists who look like ants in the distance (it's not a sunny day). I move up beside A. at the rail and we crane our necks to check out the bodies. After a moment of eyeballing, she leans over to me and says in a confidential tone, "They're almost extinct, you know." All I can do is nod.

She asks me about Al's funeral, which I attended yesterday.

"The preacher was terrible," I said. "All this yadda-yadda-yadda about streets paved with gold. The music was okay."

"Live?"

"Taped. Stuff Al picked out himself."

"Classical?"

"No. Just stuff he liked. I don't remember what exactly. Well, there was a Dolly Parton song."

"Oh, dear," sighed Aquanetta, looking out to sea.

We pull in at five-thirty and my urge to kiss the angry and malignant, but oh-so-solid, planet beneath my feet is almost irresistible. A. shifts her rattletrap Volks into low to climb Divisadero Street and pats me on the knee.

"Well," she says, trying to salvage the day, "the old gal got to see her whales and her sea lions, didn't she? They really do have very interesting habits and mating cycles and so forth, don't they?"

"I'd rather watch them on television," says I.

We drive on in silence till she says, "Well, at least now the hapless Aquanetta can stop putting all her money into that retirement fund." She eyes me sharply before continuing. "That's hapless, honey. Not hopeless. Not helpless. Not scared shitless. In fact," she says, "I figure I can afford a once-in-a-lifetime spree down at the Foxy Lady Boutique."

I tell her, "Well, that's seeing the glass half-full," and what else is there to do but laugh as she floorboards the Volks through a yellow light at Market. She pulls up in front of my house and I turn to tell her good-bye or thanks or something, but the words won't come.

"Just one thing, Jamie," she says.

"What?"

"About my funeral?"

"Yeah?"

"No Dolly Parton."

I am not a big hugger, but I lean over and give Aquanetta the most sincere hug of my life. I get out wearily and stand at my door and watch her chug away, then come to a screeching halt. She throws the VW into reverse and backtracks to my front door. She rolls the window down and hollers, "And no Willie Nelson, either!"

As she drives away, I can hear her cackling all the way down Balmy Alley. Then I drag myself inside and collapse on the bed.

nine

That afternoon in the hay was the first of our "stolen moments," mine and Armando's. I kept sleeping on Alice's couch and Armando stayed on with his brother, Guido, who, by the way, seemed to like me an awful lot too. (Be careful where you bury those lemons, girls!) Sleeping space—or "sleeping with" space—was not easy to come by in the circus, but we found plenty of time to be together, me and Armando. In Bozeman, Montana, I started getting up early to run with him— up by the big top, down by a stream, over a fence, under a weeping willow tree, pant, pant, pant. Only a couple of miles, but that was enough to make me the most light-headed and lighthearted person in the circus, especially when you factor in what I was already feeling— being in love, that is, and I'm sorry for you if you don't know what that feels like.

In Missoula, I quit smoking. Cold turkey. Because Armando asked me to.

In Boise, we held hands as we lay on our backs in the grass, picking out shapes in the clouds. I discovered a new talent in myself: being quiet. I told Armando about it.

"I've never been the kind to stay quiet for long," I told him. "I guess I've always been afraid I'd miss out on some fun somewhere. But this is kind of nice."

He knew exactly what I was talking about, which was so often the case with Armando. He told me he meditated twice a day just to quiet his own mind down and he would teach me. So he did, and, for sure, it was something new. It was a challenge to sit still in the morning for twenty minutes and then again in the evening and just be. It took me a week or so to even begin to dam up the river of trivia that ordinarily overflows the banks of my tired old mind. But after a while I found it was happening. And then one morning, sitting cross-legged on the floor of Armando's trailer, blinking as I came out of my trance and without giving it a thought, I put my hands together and prayed a silent prayer. I prayed that I would, just for that day (I didn't want to be too greedy), live a life of peace and harmony that would touch the people around me (especially Armando!) with love and understanding. I said amen and got up and went about my day feeling so refreshed and mellow that Alice from Dallas accused me of taking dope. I found myself thinking about Miss Viola a lot in those days, thinking that at last I had tapped into her religious streak that had nothing to do with Bible thumping and hymn singing and hate thy neighbor, but everything to do with being a kind and gentle person. I got in the habit of calling my daughter once a week and it seemed like we laughed more together and shared more than ever before. She got a kick out of telling her friends about her mom's new job and I filled her in on every detail.

And then there was Buck to be dealt with. When Buck crossed my mind now, the image I saw was just a middle-aged bumbler who popped his collar buttons down at the car lot laughing at jokes he had heard before a million times just to be agreeable, who knew his dreams didn't have the chance of a snowball in hell, and who campaigned for the presidency of the Rotary Club like it was the United Nations, just because he needed some little symbol of his own worth. So he screwed around a little. Let him who is without sin . . . you know? So he screwed around with Shirley Jack, well, that's where the picture began to fade out, and I would think about something else. Fast.

Alice from Dallas had a birthday party on our last night in Idaho Falls. She wouldn't reveal her age, which I reckoned to be in the midthirties, but it's hard to tell about a woman as large as Alice. Everyone gathered outside Alice's trailer to drink her wine spodiodis and wish her health. I had never seen Alice so full of life and hospitality. She was bustling around and ducking the paper lanterns we had strung up and pouring drinks and kissing people and joining in songs and kicking up her heels like a woman six hundred pounds lighter.

"Happy birthday, Alice," I told her, and she could see that I truly wished her well.

"Thank you, honey," she gushed, and grabbed me in a big bear hug with a loud jangle of amber necklaces that she wore for bracelets, gifts from a Russian sword swallower. I hugged back as best I could, but as you can imagine, getting your arms around Alice was a day's work. She gave Armando a hug too and looked us over good.

She told him, "You sure got her all mellowed out and don't she look pretty?"

I must admit I did look pretty good that night; let's not mince words: I looked like a million bucks all scrubbed and shining and in love and decked out in a tight red dress I got in Kansas City. I had had something on my mind for several days, something I wanted to talk about with Armando. And besides, as we all know, love is like cheap champagne. You have to shake it up every now and then or it'll go flat on you. I guess that's why, that night in Idaho Falls, I decided to tell Armando my age.

"Honey," I said, after the party, when we were walking by the banks of the Snake River. (By this time we were well into the honey stage.)

"Yes?"

"Honey, I want to talk about something."

"What's that?"

"Well," I said. "You know I'm older than you."

"So?" he shrugged. A smart woman would have shrugged right back and pointed out how the moon reflected in the rippling waters of the river. But not me.

I told him my age. I said it in a way that begged something and challenged something at the same time.

"You look much younger," he said. I don't know if he shrugged again, because I had averted my eyes like the bashful little thing I am at heart; however, there was a shrug in his voice. I think.

"Well," I said, "That's how old I am and I just wanted to tell you."

"Why?" he asked.

"Well, I want everything to be clear between us and I want you to know that I'm definitely an older woman, as they say."

"So?" he asked.

"So does it make any difference to you?"

"No," he said. "Why should it?"

"Because you're what? Twenty-five?"

He looked insulted, drew himself up, and said, "Twenty-six!"

We laughed, and kept walking. He was throwing stones in the river. I was racking my brain for a way to recover what I may have lost. You know men. They say they don't care about something, but they do. And like cheap champagne, if you shake love up too much, it'll blow up in your face.

Pretty soon I heard myself go, "Armando?"

"Yeah?"

To my credit, I want to state right here that I did pause a long time to reconsider whether I should go on. To my discredit, I have to say that instead of stuffing a fist in my mouth, I did in fact go on.

"Armando, I want to tell you something else," I said, warming up to tell the biggest and stupidest lie I ever told.

"What's that?"

"Well, Armando. Honey. I'm not what I appear to be. I mean, getting shot out of a cannon and sleeping on Alice's couch and all. Actually, I do have some money. Money my grandfather left, quite a bit in fact."

Later in the solitude of Alice's trailer:

"*Why?*" I yelled it loud enough to wake the dead.

"That's what I want to know," said Alice, and she bellowed "*Why?*" loud enough to wake a rock.

"I did it simply because I'm an asshole," I said. I tried to explain it. To myself as much as to Alice. I said, "I guess I thought that I had weakened my position by telling him my age. So, I told him I was also rich to sort of even things out. Does that make sense?"

"Oh, I guess," said Alice. "Sort of. It would make perfect sense to an asshole."

I said, "I just wanted to make sure I hadn't damaged our relationship."

"Oh, please," said Alice. "Raylene, I told you there's only power struggles. And when you resort to lying," she said, "you're giving up power." She could have been a four-star general in another life.

I went to bed and squirmed and sighed and turned and tossed and got up again. I went to the door of the trailer and looked out at the treetops that were stirring with the whisper of a gentle breeze. Seemed like they were saying, "S-s-silly, s-s-silly, s-s-silly," as I stood there feeling miserable, feeling restless. Across the way I could see a light in Woolly Wanda's trailer, so I gathered my robe around me and trudged over there. She was fully dressed and seated in her recliner in front of the TV, where she was watching one of her religious programs. I waited for a commercial break and counted the various pictures of Jesus in the room. When I got up to about six or seven, I noticed, on top of the fridge, a familiar-looking hat, a green velvet job with a little feather in it.

"What's the human corkscrew been doing here?" I asked as soon as an ad for a gospel record, *God's Greatest Hits* or something, began to roll.

"Pooch?" she asked, still pretty absorbed in the TV.

I set the hat on my head and said, "How many human corkscrews do you know?"

She said, well, he sometimes, uh, dropped by to watch the gospel programs with her.

"*Pooch?*" I said.

She sort of let her body relax and leaned back into her chair, making a real effort to look casual. "Oh, sure," she said. "He's a big Shirley Jack Lazarus fan."

I squinted my eyes at her and said, "Now Wanda, you and me both know Shirley Jack hasn't been on the air in a month of Sundays. . . ."

"Well, you never know when she might turn up again though. I keep hearing all these rumors that Shirley Jack's coming back. . . ."

I squinted at her some more from this angle and that angle and told her Alice from Dallas would make mincemeat of her is she wasn't careful. I never could resist teasing the bearded lady about men.

She threw a pillow at me and said, "Raylene Stout, you need to brush up on your Bible. I would recommend Ecclesiastes, especially the third chapter where it firmly states, 'Be not curious in unnecessary matters.' If you'd get right with the Lord, your mind would be cleansed of such foul thoughts."

I told her that if the Lord cleared out every foul thought I had that night, my mind would be as empty as my pocketbook, which led to the subject of my financial status and recent lies told thereof. After I finished the recital of my foolishness, Wanda said, "Now tell me again why you thought you needed to tell Armando this lie about having all this money?"

I told her, "Well, to sort of balance the scales. I wanted him to think that, hey, the woman's old, but at least she's rich."

She said, "Raylene, a false balance is an abomination to the Lord. That's what it says in Proverbs."

I said, "What the hell does that mean?"

"It means the truth shall make you free," she said.

When I left Wanda that night, she was standing in the doorway of her trailer, waving her arms around and quoting Scripture, most of which had to do with lying versus telling the truth.

"Raylene?" she called to me in the dark.

"Yeah?" I hollered back.

"It's better to have a little with righteousness than great revenues without right." Her voice floated on the wind.

"Okay," I called.

"That's from Proverbs, too," she added.

I said, "Okay, thanks," and stepped up my pace the better to get out of earshot.

I went back to bed and it took me a long time to get to sleep.

March 28

I succumbed to the entreaties of Aquanetta and accompanied her to a potluck thrown by our chicks-with-dicks support group, the Halfway Hussies.

Luckily, Big Victor got in last night from his construction job in San Jose so I left him in charge. I say luckily because leaving the house in the charge of the reliable and prudent Paco for an entire evening is always a teeth-grinding, fingernail-gnawing arrangement for me to make. When Big Victor is here, I can depend on him to maintain some semblance of order; If Paco is stoned on weed, which he often is, he has a tendency to throw open the doors to the whole neighborhood. At two dollars a night, the accommodations should be well within the reach of the most destitute panhandler, but the actual asking for money is my job because it does serious damage to Paco's dignity. The boy is not what you would call responsible.

I did take the precaution of unplugging the phone and jamming it into my purse, since he hasn't paid me yet for last month's eighty dollars worth of calls to Mexico.

So off we went, Aquanetta and I, in her Volkswagen to the home of our hostess, Bettina. Mona opened the program with a demonstration of a dozen or so hairstyles that can be built around your basic Jewish flip. Then Ginger Who Fell to Earth took the podium and presented a giggly monologue about makeup tips till the ever vigilant Bettina clapped her hands sharply and yelled, "Refreshments!"

I stood by the table, and chomped on carrots dipped in ranch sauce, and listened to Aquanetta hold court, yakking about her plans to premiere her own show at Esta Noche tomorrow night. Out of the corner of my eye, I spotted Joe, the highway engineer, who never misses one of these events and usually brings his wife. He's crazy for pillbox hats and wears them with a rubber band beneath his chin. And those long black Olive Oyl skirts! He's also sort of crazy for me for some reason, but when I saw him bearing down on me, I scooted a little closer to the venerable Daphne Lynn, who looks like the Three Stooges and Dame Edith Sitwell rolled into one. Her social skills, at best rudimentary, are still vastly superior to those of Joe, who, since I'm a fella on paper, thinks it's okay to pinch my tits and discuss them at length and demonstrate their bounce for his mousy, horn-rimmed wife, who always trails him around the room. I leaned toward Daphne Lynn and murmured, "Nice earrings."

She slowly turned and gave me an appraising look as if to say, "Are you serious?" (Understandable since said earrings were a complicated arrangement of a map of Texas and a myriad of highlights of the Lone Star state—the Alamo, oil wells, longhorn steers, etc.) She gazed at me long enough to make me squirm before she said, "Name pop female vocalists from the fifties with alliterative names."

I didn't blink an eye as Daphne Lynn and I had spent twenty minutes at our last meeting naming all the states of the union that end in *a*. The time before that, the subject was tongue twisters and I learned to say, "She sits in her silly silk slip and sips Schlitz." Daphne Lynn pushes the outer envelope of small talk.

"Alliterative?" I said. "Like Joni James?"

"Very good," she nodded. "And the singing rage, Miss Patti Page," she added, to prime the pump.

"Well, there was Gogi Grant," I offered.

"And don't forget Kitty Kallen. Nor her nibs, Miss Georgia Gibbs."

"Doris Day?"

"Good," she pronounced. "How did I forget Doris?"

I was on a roll. "Lotte Lenya," I offered.

Daphne Lynn scowled and shook her head negatively. "Pop, honey, pop."

She rejected Mary Martin and Marilyn Monroe as being not strictly fifties and not really a vocalist, respectively. She grudgingly accepted Marian Marlowe of *The Arthur Godfrey Show,* but only if I would accept Doris Drew, who, she claimed, sang on Tennessee Ernie Ford's television show. She launched into a lengthy explanation of what "pop vocalist" means in the lexicon of Daphne Lynn.

Finally, Bettina clapped her hands again and introduced our guest speaker Toni, nee Tony, who, no shrinking violet, took a spoon and clanged it against a glass to take center stage.

Gender-confirmation surgery, she told us, freed her after a lifetime of entrapment in a body that was now just an ironic memory. She went on at length with generalities we already knew such as the operation takes less than three hours and costs upwards of twenty thousand dollars and don't expect your insurance to cover it. She went under the knife two months ago and just last week had sex for the first time as a woman. In a very fancy suite at the Mark Hopkins, if we must know, with the man who paid for her surgery, "a married man very prominent in San Francisco society," she breathlessly confided to a dozen of the biggest blabbermouths in the city.

"I was just dying to try ole Susie out," she said, speaking of her newly created personal private place, "and she worked just fine, thank you." She went on to elaborate about the feeling of pure exhilaration she got last week when a platoon of construction workers honored her sashay through the Financial District with a chorus of wolf whistles. I got the impression that her sugar daddy's generosity is unlikely to be rewarded with strict fidelity; especially when Toni espied, out the window, a well-built man in bicycle shorts and delivered a wolf whistle so loud and shrill the wineglasses hummed in protest. Of course, Aquanetta took that as her cue to holler, "Wake up, little Susie!"

When Toni wound up her spiel, Bettina got up and declared her intention to go to Tangier, where she can get the surgery for five thousand dollars, and asked if anyone else was interested in case she could arrange a package deal, but she got no takers. The girls mostly just looked at one another and made faces, which is not surprising as only a couple of them besides me actually intend to go all the way with the surgery.

I was relieved when Aquanetta sidled up to me and muttered, "Let's go. I can't take another minute of this." A little support goes a long way with me when you're talking about groups.

She dropped me off at the Hole in the Wall around one, after promising to drop by and cut my hair in the morning. Exhausted, I waved her off and staggered into my humble refuge.

ten

Alice from Dallas, so impossible to overlook, was a natural target for gossip. The story that the women in the circus liked so much was that Alice kept a pot of aphrodisiac stew bubbling on her stove at all times and that explained her success with men. Not so, ladies. In the first place, Alice wouldn't have known how to turn on the stove to heat up a love potion. Or anything else. When Mr. Rosetti hired Alice away from another circus, he agreed in writing to supply her chow, because I saw the contract. I can also vouch for the fact that there was rarely a thirty-minute period in the day when Fabio from the mess tent was not sliding through the door of that trailer with some steaming dish or other. Even when Alice was on duty in the Gallery of Oddities, this fellow was apt to slip into her bedroom to leave a surprise offering of a few barbecued chickens or a couple of apple pies. Fabio, who was the circus's official good-luck dwarf, considered feeding Alice his full-time job and it was a job he took seriously: "Would you like some of this, Alice? Would you like some of that, Alice?" And when the answer was yes, which it usually was, he would go tearing off to the mess tent to return minutes later burdened down with whatever Alice's heart desired. Like most of the men, Fabio adored her, and yes, small as he was, and big as she was, there were days when Alice shut the door of her bedroom and invited him to stay awhile, much to his delight. No, this gal had no need of love potions. There is just something, I decided, about a woman of that size that men see as an irresistible challenge, like Mount Everest is to mountain climbers. Alice from Dallas was the Everest of women, except this challenge was a soft and easy and sweet-smelling one.

So I'm sure you will understand why, although Armando and Alice claimed to be just friends, I tended to keep a close eye on the two of them together whenever he would come over for a card game or something. And I have to say that in Cheyenne, Wyoming, when the two of them were invited to appear on a local TV talk show one afternoon between the matinee and evening performance, I felt more than a little nervous. Why? Because they would be together for probably hours while I chewed my fingernails down to the quick trying to do that thing I have so little talent for: waiting. In fact, I snuck over to Eddie's ticket booth to see if he could swing a little weight with Mr. Rosetti.

"Eddie," I said, "I need a favor."

"Oh, yeah? What's that?" says he.

"Why can't I get on that talk show too?" I whined.

Well, at this, Eddie clapped his hand to his forehead. "Oh, God," he said, "not you, too." Then he rattled off ten or twelve names of people who had made the same request—Sally the Elephant Girl, Woolly Wanda, a bunch of clowns, they all wanted a little airtime. All I wanted, I told him, was to keep an eye on my property. But he said, sorry, Frankie wouldn't budge on this one. He had been invited to bring only his top few acts and he had chosen them very carefully to get the maximum amount of publicity. I walked away disappointed.

Alice's TV had been on the blink ever since she threw it at Pooch for calling her, in a moment of passion, by Judy the Juggler's name. I decided to drop in on Woolly Wanda to catch the talk show and visit awhile. By this time, I had got to the point where I would just open Wanda's door a crack and holler "Yoo-hoo, it's me!" and walk right on in like a neighbor in a sitcom on TV. That's how chummy we were. On the other hand, there were not very many who got turned away from the sociable Wanda's door. She was the ambassador of goodwill of the circus, always sitting there in her recliner beside a TV tray that held a Bible and an assortment of what she called "snackettes." Everybody knew what they were getting into when they went to Wanda's— sermons and Ritz crackers topped with little globs of some kind of cheese product—and most people chose to stay away. But not me. I had told Wanda right up front, "Now, look here, Wanda, you can save all the souls you want to, but do it when I'm not around," and she got my drift. I've always found that I get along with people a lot better if I level with them from day one. So since Wanda and I were straight on the religion business, we were able to get past that and let our hair down about various other things, not the least of which was men, being as Wanda had, number one, more experience with them than you might expect for a holy roller like her, and, number two, a powerful curiosity about her idol, Dr. Lazarus, about whom I happened to have a wealth of information, none of it pleasant, which I was only too willing to share. So we were pretty close, Wanda and me, and that's why, when I walked into her trailer this particular day, I only gasped at what I saw, instead of falling out in a dead faint like some of her acquaintances would have done. Have you ever seen a human corkscrew make love to a bearded lady? Any decent person would have taken one look at these two a-going at it like a couple of weasels and backed out the door. But, I'm sorry, yours truly had to make sure it wasn't a mirage or something there in the rumpled sheets of Woolly Wanda's bed. And it wasn't, folks. No, it was real life, my poor eyes decided once they bounced back into their sockets. I stood there a few seconds till these two characters slowed down enough for Wanda to holler "Raylene!" and for Pooch to swivel his head around backward and say something original along the lines of "Don't you know how to knock?"

All I could think to say was "Excuse me," and I was out the door like a flash, slamming it behind me and hotfooting it back to my own cozy home in Alice's trailer. Those two! Together! Well, I had to sit down on Alice's couch to think about this. Wanda and her Bible-thumping ways and Pooch the human corkscrew, who called Alice from Dallas his dimpled darling and his fleshy flame. I looked at Alice's cat clock and saw that it was time for the talk show and I flipped on the TV and twisted every knob the damn thing had, but it was no use. There's not a TV in the world that could survive a toss across the room by the likes of Alice from Dallas. I put on a bright green sweater over my jeans (only sighing a tiny bit at the thought of how Buck used to call this particular color "Raylene green"; it's true, it is my color). It so happened that just across the street from the fairgrounds and not more than a hundred yards from Alice's trailer, there was a little bar, a cute little stucco place called the Watering Hole. So I strolled over there and walked through the swinging door like I owned the place. There were a few people at the bar and several others at little fold-up card tables scattered around the low-ceilinged room. I waved at a couple of tent riggers from the circus and settled down on a barstool held together with black electrical tape in front of the TV, which was already tuned to the right channel, and there was Alice being interviewed. She was reclining on a mattress atop a flatbed truck, since she was too wide to get through the door of the studio. The interviewer, this young, handsome fellow, was like somebody you would see in *People* magazine that's successful and comfortable with it. Like one of these lawyers that write best-sellers in the subway on the way to work. He fawned over her like he was talking to a major celebrity and that suited Alice just fine. She answered his dumb questions like they were smart questions, placing a plump hand to her throat and batting her eyes in deep thought first. Ahhhh, yes, she loved working in the circus. Welll, no, it wasn't easy buying clothes for a gal her size. Noooo, she had never been married, but yessss, there was somebody special in her life at the present time. It seemed to me like those sexy eyes of hers kind of darted to a position off camera before she answered that last question, but, I'll admit, I could have been wrong about that, uptight as I was. I ordered a peppermint schnapps with a beer chaser. After Alice's interview, it was Armando's turn. He entered the camera range in a most dramatic way, executing a series of back flips clear across the length of the flatbed truck and causing my heart to stop when he came within inches of falling off. His interview was brief and to the point. Yes, he came from an old circus family; yes, he practiced every day, and no, he had never fallen from the trapeze during an actual performance. And was he married? Uh-uh. And was there somebody special in his life right now? Uh-huh (blush blush). My heart just melted. A commercial came on and then the end of the show. By this time, the two riggers were sitting on either side of me at the bar, joking and carrying on, but it took them awhile to snap me out of my little mood. Of course, I was feeling better quite a while before I let on; you know how us gals like to pout and sulk, especially when we've got a lusty young man on either side of us trying to cheer us up. However, it wasn't long before we were drinking a toast to our health and trading shoptalk. And then we were drinking a few more toasts to a few other good causes and trading a little more shoptalk. You know how these barroom conversations get more and more fascinating with every drink. After I started seeing double, and, like the song goes, feelin' single, I decided I had to leave, so I did, although I'm not so modest that I'm not going to tell you that one of these rigger guys, Tobias by name, had fallen madly in love with me by this time and wanted to walk me home. The other one, Arnie, was real sweet, but he was one of these heavyset fellows who can't sit on a barstool without his shirt riding up to reveal the crack in his behind. (Dot Struthers, who has a name for everything, calls this common barroom phenomenon BCS, or butt cleavage syndrome.) Not exactly a sight to make a gal's heart skip a beat, so it was all right with me when Arnie took a shine to an older woman sitting on the other side of him. Tobias, on the other hand, was kind of cute, but no, I said, walking me home wouldn't be such a great idea, and he understood since my connection with Armando was not exactly top-secret information.

I went back to Alice's only to find an empty trailer. I sat on my couch-bed for a little while and watched the tail of the cat clock go back and forth, back and forth. The TV show had ended hours ago, and still no Alice. And no Armando. I decided I was hungry and went to the refrigerator. I stood there a long time looking at the sad-looking contents, mostly my stuff since Alice's food was brought in. I sighed and grabbed a carton of eggs, figuring to scramble a couple of them and call it a meal. There were two eggs left and—*splat!*—first thing I did was drop one of them on the floor. That was all I needed to sink down on my couch-bed with my head in my hands. I sat there a few minutes, staring at the egg on the floor, and finally said what the hell and went back to the bar for a few more rounds with the fellows.

Well, I walked back into that bar and it was Raylene, queen of the hop, the way this Tobias and Arnie carried on. Whoopee! She's back! Everybody in the place turned around to look at me. I was up for it, though, drunk as I was. I was grinning from ear to ear and going howdy, howdy, howdy, and you know how it is when you're that damn drunk: everybody grins back at you at first and you get to thinking you're a lot more amusing than you are. I had another beer and then another, and sat there cracking jokes with these fellows and laughing and hooting and slamming my bottle down on the bar. This was one of those cool, dark bars where it's always the same time of day—happy hour—but, mind you, this was a workday. In fact, the Old Milwaukee clock on the wall was telling me I had about forty-five minutes before time to get into my skimpy little bullet woman outfit. Even as tipsy as I was, I was thinking about the time. We're kidding around about this and that and pretty soon old Tobias starts getting at me— "Whatsa matter, Raylene? Armando ain't back yet? You think Alice from Dallas got ahold of him?" He was kidding, but you have to bear in mind that these riggers were as hip to Alice's reputation as I was, so it was sort of like serious kidding.

Well, I had to save face, didn't I? And I was three sheets to the wind, wasn't I? So I said, "I'll tell you what, Tobias. I always say it's better to have loved and lost than to have spent your whole life with the son of a bitch." I about half meant it, too. Alice from Dallas with my man. The very idea! And Tobias, as liquored up as he was, believed me for sure. So much so that he started making little remarks that required putting his lips right up next to my ear and an arm around my waist. Things like, "Mmm, mmm, mmm, that perfume is driving me crazy," or "Come on and have just one more drink, honey." Original stuff, you know. But, as I said, Tobias was not an unattractive man. Rigging tents tends to keep a man in pretty good shape, and he did have a good sense of humor, though I was a little put off by a gold tooth he had right up front. At any rate, when I slid off my stool and announced I was going to get ready for the show, I didn't discourage him too much when he insisted on walking me back to the trailer. It was past sundown by then and it was all I could do to walk a straight line. I figured it wouldn't hurt to have an escort. We walked through the fairgrounds making chitchat. We got to the trailer and I said good night and thanks for a good time and so forth and opened the door. When he suggested he would stick around and make coffee while I changed and then walk me to the big top, I said okay. As lovey-dovey as he was inclined to be, I could tell Tobias was nothing to worry about, and to tell the truth, I was enjoying his company. Not to mention the fact that I was more than a little pissed off at the continued absence of Armando and Alice.

I changed in the bathroom while he fiddled with the coffeemaker. When I came out dressed in my spangles he whistled and held out a cup of coffee with a big smile on his face. I did a little pirouette, just acting a fool, and that's when my foot hit the egg on the floor. Zippp! I made a two-point landing on my behind and the back of my head. If I had been sober, I'm sure it would have been quite painful. Tobias slapped the coffee cup down on the counter and reached out to help me up, but damned if he didn't slip on the egg, too, and fall right on top of me. The whole thing was so ridiculous that we collapsed in giggles and, although I thought I felt a gust of wind like maybe somebody opened the door for a second, it was so quick and I was so drunk I didn't give a single solitary damn.

March 31

I should have known something was up when Paco asked me for a date. Our relationship has been a little strained of late, but at least I think the truth has finally dawned on him: i.e., he ain't getting my money.

Turned out he was taking charge of me in order to deliver me to Esta Noche for a surprise birthday party. After he left in the afternoon, I took the phone off the hook and started getting ready in the middle of the afternoon for our big date. Soaked an hour in bubble bath, shaved my legs and everything else marred by an errant hair, gave myself a long and sensual facial (sensual because at last the electrolysis is complete and my face feels as irresistibly smooth as glass), toweled off and, for a solid hour, stood naked in front of the full-length mirror on the bathroom door. I studied myself, sighed, wiped away a tear or two, pulled my hair back, up, down, this way and that, and at one point, remembering somebody's last words—Flaubert's?—which were spoken to a mirror, I looked deep into my own eyes and said, "Well, old chap, I guess we won't be seeing each other anymore."

I made my face up in layers, thinned the nose, built cheekbones, accomplished miracles. Then I wriggled into the absolutely dazzling dress from Kimberley's Consignment Shoppe, where all the Pacific Heights ladies discard their frocks after one wearing. This midnight blue–sequined sheath once graced the body of Linda Ronstadt in performance at the Kennedy Center, according to the saleslady, and I gloried in the aura of fame and fortune that clung to the garment like a sweet aroma as I adjusted the spaghetti straps. Silver satin pumps, like new and fresh from the Salvation Army, completed the ensemble, and I spent another half hour or so preening and posing prettily and just plain admiring myself in the mirror. I thought I looked rather like a tall, cool Hitchcock blond, the kind that has to be tortured to give up her secrets. At sundown, Paco walked in the front door and did everything but fall in a dead faint on the floor in his appreciation of my staggering beauty. The Corrine Calvet wig sat all forlorn on a wig stand looking downright dowdy next to my own shoulder-length tresses; which had been washed, dried, bleached, styled, thickened, brushed, pampered, and offered up to God as the symbol of my impending feminity. I looked good. I must say Paco went all out. Had borrowed somewhere ("from a friend," he said, and I didn't inquire further) not just a car, but a BMW. A dark blue one which was just a shade away from the color of my dress. He wore a suit, too, black and expensively cut, borrowed from the same friend, and were it not for the little blue bolt of lightning tattooed on his neck (unnervingly close to the jugular) the handsome Paco, with his patent leather hair slicked back, would have looked at home ensconced in a box seat at the San Francisco Opera.

I taped the Closed sign to the front door and Paco took me to dinner at that restaurant that looks like a ship down at China Basin, because once he heard me mention that I had always wanted to eat there. We sat in a romantic corner, but dolled up as we were, hardly went unnoticed in the busy eatery.

We got to Esta Noche at ten and it became clear to me why I was taken to dinner. The usual Saturday night crush was there and everything looked normal except for the huge blowups of me on every wall with the words Happy Birthday, Jamie written across them. At my entrance, everybody clapped, and from the gigantic speakers between which I was sandwiched,

Neil Diamond began to croon soothingly "Girl, You'll Be a Woman Soon." Aquanetta had taken advantage of my absence to sneak into my house and confiscate the big box of photos from under my bed, and pictures of me were strung on the wall from one end of the bar to the other. Every stage of my life from the time I left Lake Gladys was represented: in late adolescence in Paris, seated at Le Coupole, wearing shades and a leather hat and a world-weary look, beside Paolo, who brought me to Europe and of whom I was indeed beginning to weary at the time; a few years later in Barcelona, another snapshot shows me in a similar sidewalk café shot on the Ramblas, this time all smiles with my arm around Alfonso, the one who got away; at eighteen, I'm posed in a wintertime Rockefeller Center, bravely smiling to cover how frightened and alone I really am, carefree ice-skaters providing a colorful background; then, at twenty-something, in Berlin, doing drag for a New Year's Eve party; then, there I am in my middle thirties, looking sort of unisex in long hair and a pantsuit, standing at the entrance of the bed 'n' breakfast that Marty and I ran in Key West, thinking I was set for life. This was about a year before Marty ran off to Costa Rica with the dishwasher and sent me into the free fall that delivered me to L.A. (a city I never quite got the hang of), and finally, San Francisco and back to the hospitality business, however humble. Seeing my life spread out before me in such distinct chapters, I was struck by my lifelong ability to chuck it all and create new beginnings for myself. I wonder if I still have that capacity. I'd better.

My first impression when I realized that this was my life strung from the walls of this packed and sweaty club was that my privacy had been invaded in a most surprising and not altogether pleasant way. However, my second impression was a shrug and a sardonic smile—influenced no doubt by the two martinis at dinner and by Aquanetta's draping an arm around me and saying, "That was all another life, girl." By the time she bounded onto the stage and led the crowd in "Happy Birthday, Sweet Sixteen" in my honor, I was in a nodding and grinning mode, and clapped along with the music as vigorously as anyone.

When I went downstairs to powder my nose, the girls descended on me with hugs and best wishes and presents galore. Except for a hard rubber dildo from the mischievous and tiny Filipina, Chacha Chavez, and a couple of boxes of Summer's Eve douche, the presents were mostly in the clothing line, mostly in the Frederick's of Hollywood style—split-crotch panties, push-up bras, etcetera. Average housewife supplies.

We closed the place down, Paco and me, and driving home he asked me, "Are you nervous?"

"About what?" I asked, so inebriated a six-car smash-up wouldn't have made a dent in my nerves.

"About, you know, the operation," he said.

"Oh, yeah, that. Hmm, I don't know, I don't think so. No."

We went home and slept on separate sides of the room and I fell asleep happy, feeling I've come a long, long way from Lake Gladys, Louisiana.

eleven

After we had a good laugh and a little coffee, and after I went to the bathroom mirror and slapped myself upside the head a few times to where I was almost seeing single again, I jumped into the pineapple gown and hat that I had been issued for the parade inside the tent that started each show. I tugged at the lowcut neckline and the pineapple puffed sleeves, trying my best to cover my bullet woman getup. I straightened the pineapple hat that weighed a ton, and I was ready, or as ready as I would ever be. Tobias walked me to the big top and I slipped in with just a minute to spare. The show was in full swing, the band was playing a medley of Hawaiian songs, and the ring-master was blathering on about a tribute to our fiftieth state. I hopped aboard the first float and took my place as the pineapple princess on a little pedestal overlooking my handmaidens, Jeanette and Twyla, who, in grass skirts, were already competing to see which one could do the most tasteless and vulgar hula. In front of us, Sally's elephants, also dressed in grass skirts, led the procession, shaking their rumps to

"Lovely Hula Hands." Round and round we went and somehow I managed to stand upright and smile and wave and blow kisses. The parade ended and I bounded into the little changing tent, shucked off that sweltering polyester gown, and straightened my sexy spangles. I felt like taking a nap, but the show must go on, and I stood there and took several deep breaths and whimpered a little before off I went again, dragging myself into the big top. In the far ring the tenth clown had just stepped out of a car not big enough for two Louisiana bayou polecats. I lifted my eyes to to way up above the center ring and there *he* was. Armando. The focus of every eye in the tent, at least every feminine eye.

To see Armando doing his work in the air was to see a man with his mind on his business. He might play around during the morning rehearsals but when the people were there, it was different. If he had anything else on his mind except giving them their money's worth, it didn't show. I stood in the shadows a moment and just watched him do what he did so well. I tried to translate the secret language of the eyes that he and his brothers spoke in the air, but it was no use. The word that came to me as I watched him dive and swoop in the air like a beautiful white seagull was *professional.* The second word that occurred to me as I watched him was *idiot,* and I wasn't thinking about Armando; I was thinking about yours truly, Ms. Stout, who was no more steady on her feet than an old worn-out plow mule. When the ringmaster introduced me—"Ladies and gentlemen and children of all ages . . ."—I sucked in my stomach and posed for the people, chin up, chest out, like Gina Lollobrigida in *Trapeze,* before gulping hard and lowering myself into the cold black hole of the cannon's mouth.

To this day I don't know what went wrong. It could have been any one of a number of things: my feet could have been planted less than a hundred percent straight or maybe one of my shoulders was higher than the other or who knows what. And, of course, all that booze I had guzzled didn't exactly do me any good. All I can tell you for sure is that the second I hit the air I knew something was goofy. And two seconds later everybody else in the tent knew it too, because instead of heading straight across the tent for the net, I was veering off to the right.

"Oooooooohhhhh," the audience said as I began to swerve.

"*Ohhhhhhhhhhh!!!!*" they said when they could see I was going to miss the net. And don't think I wasn't aware of what was happening. No sir. Right at the top of my arc, I began to scramble with my arms and legs, like somebody in a *Roadrunner* cartoon, trying to get back on target. It's a wonder the audience didn't take it for a comedy act, but I didn't hear anybody laughing. It's also a wonder that I didn't kill myself, but, believe it or not, half of that bunch of clowns that got out of the minicar managed to rush over to the right spot just in time to catch me, or at least break my fall. After we all collapsed in a heap, the clowns got up and dusted themselves off like it was part of the show. When I started breathing again, I managed to stagger to an upright position and give 'em the Gina Lollobrigida business again, one hand on my hip, the other making a little gesture in the air that said, "There you have it, folks." This time I got a standing ovation, but I barely noticed because by this time Armando had covered the space between his trapeze and his somewhat older girlfriend and he stood before me in all his flashing-eyed glory.

"Raylene! Are you all right?"

I felt like hell from bottom to top, but I said, "Yeah, I'm okay," just before I took a step toward him and fell in the sawdust at his feet. It was only a twisted ankle, but you would have thought I was half-dead the way the audience cheered me as I hopped out of the tent, supported by Armando on one side and Wally on the other. Wally still seemed a little distracted and off his feed, but he arranged to take me back to Alice's trailer on one of the tractors normally used for hauling animal cages around, and Armando went back to finish his show.

"Will I see you later?" I asked him before he left.

He said, "Yeah, sure," but he wouldn't look me straight in the eye and there was nothing I needed more at the time than a good look straight in the eye from Armando.

After Wally dropped me off, I was glad I had the trailer to myself. First, I sat and cried a little. Because of my suspicions, because of Armando's behavior, because I was lonely. Plus my damn ankle was throbbing with pain, but like they say on the bayou, I was hurtin' all over worse than anywheres else. I decided that what I needed was a good long shower. I hobbled into the bathroom and turned the water on as hot as it would go. I stuck my face right up to the spigot and just surrendered every inch of me to the flood, thinking, I guess, that the shower would wash away my worries. And I did feel a little better, maybe by 2 percent, when I turned off the water and stepped out of the stall. I stood in front of the mirror and gave myself the kind of intense look that I had wanted to get from Armando. I examined the little wrinkles at the corners of my eyes to see if they were spreading. They weren't shrinking, that was for sure, and what about those two little lines from my nose to the corners of my mouth? This was not the face of a girl fresh out of school, and I decided it was just as well that Armando had not taken a closer look. A knock at the door interrupted this productive line of thinking and I was so happy to see Carlotta that I gave her a big hug. She said she closed down her tent the minute she got the word about my accident and didn't even take the time to unwind her turban.

"It's the stars, sweetheart," she said. "It's a wonder you didn't kill yourself. You oughta count yourself lucky, darlin'."

"Well," I said, "for some reason, I'm not feeling real lucky tonight."

She said, "I'm serious, Raylene, this would be a real good night to go to bed and pull the covers up over your head and stay there till daylight."

I said, "Lord! That seems a little drastic."

She took my hand and pulled me down to sit beside her on the couch. "You look terrible, darlin'," she said, after giving my face a good once-over.

"Well, you'd look bad too, if you'd had a day like mine. It's not like I didn't get drunk. It's not like I didn't lose my man. It's not like I didn't miss the net and twist my ankle and make an ass of myself."

She said, "Hey, let's back up a little bit, baby. Lost your *man?*"

"To Alice," I said.

At the mention of Alice's name, Carlotta's jaw dropped an inch or so and she gave me a piercing look. She said, "You sure about that, honey?"

"Well, no," I said.

"I didn't think so." She got up and paced back and forth in front of me.

She said, "That woman! You know what? Me and Wally had a falling-out today about that fat lady. He was watching her on that TV show like she was a big movie star or something. Got me upset, honey."

"Oh," I said, "that's how come he was so down in the mouth tonight."

She said, "The whole world is down in the mouth tonight, darlin'. Like I said, it's the stars. Pluto and Jupiter are both in retrograde at the same time. Last time that happened, I lost a job and a husband and fell off a curb and fractured my elbow. It's a day designed for disaster, honey."

She said she was going to take a sleeping pill and wake up to a brand-new tomorrow when the planetary situation would be straightened out. She advised me to do the same and left. I wish I had listened to her now, but you can't change the past. And sometimes I have my doubts about the present and future. The older I get it seems more and more that Carlotta was right: It's all in the stars and there ain't nothing you can do about it, try as you might.

When Alice from Dallas got home, it was well past midnight. When she lumbered through the door, she heaved a big glad-to-be-home sigh, only to confront, laid up on her very own couch, a seething, snarling she-beast from hell. Or Raylene Stout. I bolted to my feet like a woman with two good ankles and a backbone of solid steel.

"Where have you been?" I growled. There was no mistaking my tone of voice, any more than you would mistake a lion's roar for a purr. The question and my attitude, which was hands on hips and fangs bared, set Alice back on her heels for a moment. But only a moment.

"Where have I been?" she repeated after me, just trying to make sure she had the question right. She only knew me in my role of obedient houseguest, and this new facet of my personality took some getting used to, I'm sure.

"You heard me," I said.

She said, "Why, Raylene, you know where I've been. I told you I was going to be on television."

I consulted the cat clock. "Till two A.M.?"

"So?"

"Don't you think you need to explain?"

Well, at this point, Miss Alice had recovered her composure enough to put her own hamlike hands on her own hips and state her case: *"Need? To explain?* Now, you listen to me, missy!" Missy she called me. "This is my trailer," she bellowed, "and I'll come and go as I please. You understand that?"

Now ordinarily, I would have backed down, not out of fear, but just out of an unwillingness to create a scene that would just be too damn tiresome to get over, but with old Pluto and Jupiter both backpedaling at such a rate, hell, I was ready for a little action and damn the consequences. I must say, as your typical gracious southern belle and representing the garden society of Lake Gladys, Louisiana, that bellowing is not my style, but, folks, that night I gave it a good shot.

"Yeah," I hollered at this mammoth woman, "I understand that, and I also understand that you're going and coming with Armando!"

This caught her up short. "Armando?" she said, "Armando? He came back and did the show!"

This caught me up short. Because I knew he did the show, and the clear-eyed way she pointed it out told me she was innocent of any postshow hanky-panky. And probably of the preshow kind, too. However, by this time, I had built up a head of steam that was hard to shut down and I kept on a-sputtering.

Alice stepped closer and sniffed the air. "Raylene, this ain't logic you're talking. This is honky-tonk logic, honey—this is a woman believing whatever she needs to believe, to hell with the facts. If beer could talk, it'd sound a whole lot like you tonight."

"Then where the hell did you go after the show?"

She gave me a grim look and said, "Raylene, I'm not going to continue this until you quiet down."

I repeated the question in a quieter but no more pleasant way.

Alice, not exactly trembling in her boots, ignored me, lit a cigarette, blew a smoke ring, and said, "For your information, I took the evening off from this fleabag circus. Furthermore, I just got back from the offices of the *Wyoming Tribune,* where I was interviewed in depth and at length and, incidentally, treated like a queen."

I knew she was telling the truth. Alice wouldn't stoop to telling me a lie. So why didn't I just say, "Oh," and settle down and act like a halfway civilized woman? Why? Because just about the time she was giving me this news, the door opened and in strolled everybody's favorite human corkscrew.

I said something along the lines of, "Oh, shit, it's you," as opposed to something like, "Why, Pooch, how lovely to see you," and right away he had his dander up. Which was fine because I was ready for him.

He said, "I need to talk to Alice. Alone."

I said, "Fine. I've already said my piece." At that point I was ready to take a walk, because I had no interest in eavesdropping on these people. But, no, Pooch chose to read something into my innocent remark that definitely was not there. In fact, people, I swear to you, it had been such a day that the mating of Pooch and Wanda that afternoon had, if not slipped my mind completely, dropped to about zero point five on the scale of importance.

"I bet you did," he said.

Now those four little one-syllable words, insinuating as they did that I had said something that I had not, were not only rude, but came at a very bad time—just when I needed to spew to high heaven like a volcano that was way overdue. However, first, I got real quiet for a couple of seconds before I said, "Excuse me, Pooch. What did you say?"

He said, "You heard what I said."

I said, "You're right, Pooch. I told Alice everything I know. Everything I've seen. I didn't leave out any of the gory details."

Poor Alice didn't know what the hell was going on. "What is all this about?" she said.

Teeth gritted, eyes slitted, I shot the walking pipe cleaner a look. "This is something between me and Pooch," I said.

"Well, I'm afraid you're going to have to tell me what exactly is going on between you and Pooch," said Alice in a voice that wasn't very loud but clearly promised to huff and puff and blow the house down if she didn't get the right answer.

I was too agitated, though, to much care about Alice from Dallas. I said, "Well, maybe you ought to take that up with Pooch. I'm going for a walk." And I did, forgetting all about my ankle till it hit the ground and the pain shot right through me.

I'm not a big door-slammer, but that night I made an exception. Wham! The trailer vibrated behind me as I limped off in my housecoat across the fairgrounds. A cool breeze rustled my hair and sort of blew some sense my way. Got me to thinking, Now who exactly am I mad at? Alice? No, I was satisfied that she hadn't been fooling around with Armando. Pooch? No, it irritated me just to look at him but he wasn't worth losing my temper over. Armando? Bingo. He was clear on the Alice charges, but what the hell was with him anyway? Yesterday, he called me his little tomato; today, he drops me like a hot potato.

Behind me I could hear the sounds, only slightly muffled, of Alice exploding and Pooch coming back at her with, "Now, honey, this," and "Now, honey, that." A little ways ahead of me I could see Armando's cheery little silver trailer and hear Italian rock 'n' roll even at this late, late hour. I strolled in that direction, figuring I would just knock on the door and take the bull by the horns, but I lost my nerve when I looked in the window and saw him playing cards with a couple of his brothers and Fabio, Alice's gofer. It looked like a serious game, poker chips piled up to their chins, and everybody, including the non-smoking Armando, chewing on cigars. It didn't look like ladies' night, so being the sensitive and tactful and cowardly person I can be in such a situation, I wandered on.

I sat on a tractor seat near the animal cages and gazed at the moon like a turtle on a log. After a while, I headed back to Alice's trailer. The night had simmered down, radios off, lights out everywhere, but as I got closer to my lodgings, I could still hear Alice holding forth about something or other.

With my hand on the doorknob, I heard her go, "You hear me?" just like she didn't have her volume turned up to window-rattling levels.

Pooch muttered something which I didn't quite get, but for sure it was along the lines of, "Yeah, baby, I hear you." That's how humble his tone was. I'll say this for Alice from Dallas: she could have given lessons in how to put men in their places. Women, too, for that matter. It was not my intention to eavesdrop, or to get crossways with Alice in any way whatsoever when she was in such a state, but the fact is, as I walked through the door I couldn't help but hear her lay down the law to him:

"Tonight, Pooch, you hear me? You take care of this *tonight*. And I mean it."

Neither one of them looked glad to see me as I limped over to the couch.

"You feel better now?" Alice asked me in that short way she used when she didn't give a damn if you liked her or not, which was most of the time.

I said, "Yeah, I'm all right," and dropped to the couch like a dead woman.

"Good," she said and turned back to the human corkscrew. She said, "Pooch, get outta here. I'm sick of looking at you," and he left without a word, closing the door behind him with a soft touch like he was at church.

She gathered up a couple of pizzas that Fabio had left on the counter and stomped back to her room without another word.

April 7

A raspy whisper hit my ears and, at about the same time, I became aware of the unmistakable smell of a hospital room. Medicine and crepe-soled shoes.

"Is he awake?" the voice said. "I mean, is *she* awake?"

I opened my eyes slightly and for a moment lay very still, watching dust motes dance in the few feeble shafts of sunlight penetrating the blinds. I took in my surroundings, just gittin' the lay of the land, as Mae West used to say: the pitcher of water at my bedside, the plastic straw in the glass beside it bent at a forty-five-degree angle, one of those dark green plastic-and-chrome chairs that some factory somewhere turns out exclusively for hospitals, a *Vanity Fair* and a bio of Katherine Anne Porter I had brought with me . . .

I turned my head to face the two nurses, sat up and gave them a smile of utter confidence, of feminine confidence, if you will.

"Yes," I said, "she is awake."

twelve

I fell asleep and dreamed about home. About a hot day out on the bayou in my grandfather's pirogue so light and swift that he always claimed it could float on a heavy dew. Me and the judge, fishing, joking, laughing in the shade of the big cypress tree with the boards that Jamie and I nailed to the trunk to make a ladder. Then my cork started bobbing up and down among the water hyacinths and I pulled my cane pole up with a jerk. But it wouldn't budge. "Judge," I said, "help me." We both wrestled with the pole. We jostled and twisted it this way and that and finally something shook loose and up popped my catch—*whoosh!* Nick Tarkington, withered and wrinkled and deadly white, eyes blazing, mouth wide open in a bloodcurdling scream . . . My eyes flew open and I bolted upright to a sitting position. I was awake but Nick's scream kept coming. Then, as my brain began to click into position, it dawned on me that, oh, hell, it was only Alice. This woman rarely believed in turning down the volume, especially when she was taking her pleasure. And that night she was taking her pleasure, make no mistake. In the weeks I had spent with her, I had got familiar, much more familiar than I wanted, with the various yelps, shouts, and downright screams that meant Alice was making love. This gal believed in whooping when she made whoopee. However, what I was hearing tonight was enough to make me wonder if I had ever really enjoyed the physical side of love myself. Somebody had the fat lady going, and to make this account as truthful as possible, I'm going to have to admit to feeling a little twinge of envy as I sat there in my lonely and somewhat shaky bed that night. I shook my head and wondered, Who has she got in there now? Mr. Twister, the human corkscrew? I remembered what she had told me about the twistin' and the shoutin', and she was sure enough catching up on her shoutin'.

"Oh, yes. Oh, honey. Oh, baby. Oh, darling. Oh, oh, oh, oh, Ohhhhhhhhh. *Ohhhhhhhhhhhh!*"

All of a sudden, Alice's shouts seemed to take on a different tone—strangled, breathless, panicky. I got panicky myself. What was going on in there? Just as I got to my feet, the noises turned into these sharp, frantic little gasping sounds.

"Alice? Alice? Baby?" It was Pooch. No mistaking that thin, wheezy little voice. If a snake could talk . . .

I got to the door and shot through it just in time to see Alice depart this life. Her head flopped back on the bed while Pooch and I hollered in unison, *"Alice!"* But she was gone. I stood there paralyzed with horror and watched her eyes roll back in her head, her hands clutching her huge bosom. Herman, kneeling naked between her legs, clasped his hands together like he was praying and tried one last time to rouse her.

"Alice!" he screamed while I stood there with my hand over my mouth. He grabbed at her wrist with one hand and slapped her face with the other. *"Alice!"*

I felt Alice's spirit leave that room as surely as I feel the air conditioner's steady breeze in this motel room right this minute. It didn't happen the second she looked dead. I think she hovered above the bed a few moments while she got her bearings, but, boy, when Alice from

Dallas took her leave from this earth, she knew where she was going and she was outta here. In an instant, the air in the room turned ice cold and the two candles on either side of the bed sputtered cut. There might have even been a rustling sound but I don't want to testify to that because the whole thing happened so damn fast.

"She's gone, Pooch," I said, and noticed that he was still visible in his nakedness, all too visible, people, despite the fact the candles had gone out. In fact, the whole room seemed to be bathed in a golden kind of glow which shook me up once I became aware of it. Didn't I see the candles go out with my very eyes? Where was this weird light coming from?

You know what it was? It was hair. Yard-long lengths of thick, fiery, blond hair draped across the headboard of the bed, curled up on the floor, even pinned to the wall like some kind of trophy. Hair that blazed in the night as bright as lightning bugs in a moonless Louisiana swamp. And you know who it belonged to, don't you? Sure you do.

I gasped as the whole story broke over me at once and it took a few seconds of sputtering before I was able to spit out what I needed to say in order to believe.

"It's Carlotta's hair."

"I did it for Alice," he said.

Now, mind you, here I am talking to a naked man in the hours before dawn and not a man I ever would have chosen to see naked, I can assure you, but I am rooted to the spot. We're separated only by the humongous hump of Alice's body.

"You cut off her hair," I whispered, while a dull memory of something Carlotta said swept over me: *I'm going to take a sleeping pill.*

"Alice asked me to do it."

A flood of thoughts tumbled through my head as I stood there shaking my head and wringing my hands. Thoughts about guilt and blame. I knew who told Alice Carlotta's secret in the first place. I wheeled around and threw my housecoat over the thigh-length T-shirt I was wearing, but before I could get to the front door, I felt Pooch's hands around my waist. His bony fingers stretched when I pulled away from him.

"Oh, no you don't," he said, and wrapped a bony leg around and around and around me like a cat-o'-nine-tails.

I grabbed that cat clock off the wall and beaned that sucker so hard he went to the floor in sections like a deck of cards dropped from a stepladder. For good measure, I kicked him in the last place that a man likes to be kicked and lit out into the night without looking back. I limped toward Carlotta's trailer with tears springing to my eyes for so many reasons I had lost track of the count. The Cheyenne dawn was just coming up purple and a gray cloud drifted across the fading moon. I looked up at the stars that were being swallowed up by the morning and wondered which ones were Jupiter and Pluto.

"You sons of bitches," I sniffled, and shook my fist at the sky.

Wally's trailer was parked on the opposite side of the field from Alice's, which was probably Carlotta's idea, and I was out of breath before I got halfway there. I paused for just a moment to lift my ankle and waggle it to scatter the pain around a little bit if not relieve it, and that's when I heard the wail. And such a wail it was. It was a wail that traveled the length of the fairgrounds and split the early morning silence like an ax through a post. I hopped on ahead while lights flicked on and noses emerged from trailer doors all around me. The sight that greeted me at Carlotta's place shook me up as bad or worse than what I had just left behind at Alice's. While Wally moaned in the most sympathetic way possible, Carlotta dashed around him in their tiny space, boo-hoo-hooing in a hysterical fit. In her hand, she held a little plastic hand mirror, which she looked into again and again, shrieking louder and louder each time. And she looked different. So different I don't know if I would have recognized her in the street. Her hair, hacked off as it was, no more than a couple of inches from her head, had turned a dingy, mousy color and stuck straight out in a porcupine fashion. But that wasn't all. Something had slipped out of her eyes, something like fire, and what was left reminded me of wet ashes.

Wally started smacking his palm with his fist. His only remark when he turned and saw me was, "If I ever find out who did it . . . !"

"I know who did it," I said, my voice and hands trembling.

Wally and Carlotta both froze and stared at me.

"The human corkscrew did it," I said.

Wally jumped to his feet like he'd been stuck with a cattle prod. "I'll *kill* him!" he roared.

"And he did it at the request of Alice from Dallas," I said, wanting to get the whole story out as soon as possible.

Carlotta tugged at what was left of her hair and screamed, "I knew she was involved in this one way or the other. I'll kill her. I'll kill her."

I said, "That won't be necessary."

"Meaning what?" said Carlotta.

"Meaning she's dead."

"Dead?" said Carlotta, not believing me.

"Dead?" said Wally in a softer tone, not wanting to believe me.

"Dead," I said, nodding at Carlotta and then Wally and then Carlotta again.

I sat on the side of the bed and explained how she died, or tried my durnedest, and since Carlotta was the last person in the world I would have ever attempted to lie to, I had to confess that it was me that planted the seeds of mischief in Alice's head. Carlotta stood and gawked at my teary face while I poured out my miserable story. I wish I could say that my friend rewarded my truthfulness by taking the news in a philosophical way. No such luck. She raved, she ranted, she hissed and screeched and moaned and steam shot out of her ears. I had never seen her or any other living being in such a state and I hope I never do again.

"How *could* you? How *could* you?" was the refrain she kept coming back to while I stared at my hands in my lap and Wally rushed around cussing and looking for his gun. When he found it and we heard the sharp little clicks that meant he was loading it, Carlotta and I both shut up and paid attention.

"No, Wally," she said, lowering her voice for the first time since I got there.

"Yes, Carlotta," he said with a steely sound that sent Carlotta's hand flying to her throat so fast it made me realize it was probably the first time he had ever dared to cross her. By this time, I was a little too intimidated to argue with anybody, but I did manage to cast a no vote in this little venture. Wally paid no more attention to my opinion than Carlotta's, and before we could say another word, he was striding out that door like a man on a mission. Carlotta followed a few paces behind going "Wally! *Wally!*" and I followed her, limping along in the most miserable way and keeping my mouth shut for once, except for the occasional moan. I caught up with them at the door of Alice's bedroom. The three of us stood there in silence and surveyed the scene. After a long and awkward few moments, I took a step forward and pulled a sheet over the large and pathetic body of Alice from Dallas. Pooch was nowhere in sight, of course.

After another moment, Wally said, "God rest her soul," and I said, "Amen," while Carlotta stared at the body like you stare at a fender bender when you're out for a drive in the country. Too bad, but you'll get over it. Then Wally wheeled around and headed out the front door. He looked everywhere. In the mess tent, in the big top, in the trucks and trailers of everybody known to be Pooch's friend. The whole circus was in an uproar by the time somebody suggested checking Woolly Wanda's place. And, no, folks, that somebody was not Raylene Stout. Even the animals were braying and neighing and trumpeting and roaring by the time Wally threw open Wanda's door. For my part, I had given up the chase not long after it began, sore as my ankle was, and wandered back to my tractor seat by the monkey cages, where I hung my head and wondered how it would feel to plunge into a river somewhere and drift out of consciousness while the water closed over my head for the last time. I stayed there till I heard the commotion that meant the jig was up for the midnight barber. I lifted my head and listened to the shouting and buzzing across the way, and for a moment, I leaned back with a sigh and figured I would be better off staying where I was till the whole business was cleared up. Then it occurred to me that maybe Armando was part of the bustling crowd of curious onlookers to this little drama, so down I scooted from my perch, squarely into a large mound of horse droppings which, when I look back, must have been an omen of some kind.

Wally found Pooch in Wanda's kitchen in the cabinet under the sink. The poor human corkscrew was coiled around the plumbing in such a way that it took three men to unwind and remove him. While Wanda stood by weeping into her beard, several men brought Pooch to his feet to face the staring and glaring and gun-wielding Wally.

"Put the gun down, Wally," said Carlotta, who was beginning to sound calm and rational again, and whose sheared head, by this time, had returned to a normal look by means of a purple turban.

"Put the gun down, Wally," said Woolly Wanda, who put her hands together in prayer and didn't sound the least bit calm and rational.

"Put the gun down, Wally," I heard Armando's voice flat and strong from across a sea of heads.

I guess it was because I felt a certain amount of responsibility, or call it guilt if you will, for this whole sorry mess, that I didn't even have to think it over before I moved up by Wally's side and said, "Wally, give me the gun."

To my surprise he handed it over. Or tried to. I would like a see a slow-mo instant replay of exactly how this gun—or pistol actually—changed hands as I stepped forward like some kind of no-nonsense policewoman to take possession of it. Just as my hand closed over its handle, my weak ankle collapsed and, *blam!,* the damn weapon went off and sent a bullet straight into Wanda's kitchen wall, narrowly missing her favorite picture of Jesus, the one where he opens and closes his eyes as you move your head up and down. While everybody ducked for cover, I lost my grasp for a second and the gun went falling to the floor. The way the human corkscrew threw an arm out and snagged that pistol in midair was enough to put the fear of God into a lawyer. He was like a rattlesnake striking, the way he shot that other arm out and grabbed me around the waist before anybody knew what was happening.

"Let her go, Pooch," said Carlotta, still the clear, hard voice of reason.

"Let her go, Pooch!" wailed Woolly Wanda, dropping to her knees and all but foaming at the mouth.

Then Armando said, "Let her go, Pooch," or at least that's what he started to say. Before he got to the third word of that little sentence, Pooch took aim and got off a shot that hit Armando in the toe of his shoe, sending him hopping around on one foot with a look of pure amazement.

In the stillness that followed, Pooch said, "I hate to break up this little party but I've got some business out of town." Then he twisted my arm behind my back till I hollered and he dragged me off toward Alice's red Lincoln parked not far from Wanda's trailer. Wanda pulled out all the stops at this point, scooting along behind us and babbling away, trying to talk some sense into Pooch, telling him that this thing had gone way too far already, and of course she was right. How much prison time can a man get for cutting off a woman's hair, even if the charge includes breaking and entering? It's true that Alice was gone, but there's not a jury in the world that would convict a man of loving a woman to death, especially one that weighed more than a Jeep and smoked three packs of unfiltered Camels a day. However, now, as Wanda pointed out, a kidnapping charge would put a different face on everything. The law would hunt him down and nothing would ever be the same again. Even as distraught and shrill as Wanda was, Pooch barely noticed her, so intent he was on shoving me into the car, fishing the keys out of his pocket, and getting on the road. Seeing that her words were lost on him, she stood at the driver's window and screamed at me, "Raylene! Raylene, don't let him do this!"

I hollered back at her, "Get a grip, Wanda. I don't have much say-so in this deal."

That jolted her back to reality for an instant, long enough to turn toward the trailer and holler "Armando!" like that was another alternative to handling the situation.

I rolled my window down and yelled, "Wanda, you shut up! He's already shot Armando once."

"I don't care. If he loved you, he'd come after you," she sobbed, just as Pooch turned on the ignition. "If it wasn't just your money he was after, he'd come and get you."

Now this was plainly the raving of a hysterical woman and I didn't pay any more attention to it than the man in the moon. Pooch threw the Lincoln into first gear and I looked back for my last glimpse of the circus: a motley gang of people grouped around Wanda's trailer looking about as dazed as I felt. I looked in vain for Armando's handsome face. My heart withered to the size of a walnut as I hunkered down in the plush seat of Alice's Lincoln.

April 20

In the last week, as I have shyly and then more boldly ventured out of my house as the post-op Jamie, there seems to be a subtle difference in the way people relate to me. They seem to be friendlier, more sincere, calmer. Or maybe it's just me. It must be just me. I'm sure it's just me. Today I took a long walk, wound up at the Purple Heart Thrift Store way down at Mission and Duboce. I wandered around, looked at a used record rack but decided it wasn't worth the marked price of two bucks, checked out some shoes, finally got an ancient Laura Nyro record for fifty cents. On the way back home, walking down Capp Street, I found I was *strolling!* Usually I'm rushing out to get whatever I need, and then beating a quick retreat to the safety of my home. But this afternoon, my feet seemed to fall, of their own accord, into a languid side-to-side pattern not so conducive to speed and I found myself noticing the splashy colors of the old Victorians, identifying (or trying to identify) the birds in the trees, stealing peeks at the shirtless Latino boys working on their cars, acting coy when they eyeballed me. I got home to find Paco and three of the regulars sitting at the kitchen table, playing cards and drinking beer. The news that Jamie is now *una mujer auténtica* has, unsurprisingly, been well dissemininated among my clientele and has been the subject of much discussion and—how shall I put it?—light banter. As in: "Jamie, show us your poo-seee!" But jokingly. I must say that what has been rather unexpected is the way my regulars have handled this situation. Now that the status of my gender has emerged from the twilight zone, I'm a little taken aback at the aplomb with which these street guys view it. However, on the other hand, for all practical purposes, I've been a woman all along to them. Furthermore, Big Victor is good at spotting the potential troublemakers who couldn't handle sleeping in the same room with a woman. He weeds them out with a guttural *"Completo"* at the quickly slammed front door, and that's that. I still sleep on my solitary cot in the corner overlooking a room carpeted by sleeping male bodies. I still stretch out my hand for the nightly two bucks from each of them, a businesslike look etched across my features. I still get up in the morning and serve the rice and beans and send the men on their way. And, if I opt to sleep in after a late night (or if I just don't feel like getting up), I can depend on B.V. to empty the place out. I've forgone the possibility of romance (or sex or both) many times in the interest of maintaining the respect necessary to run a place like this efficiently. So that's it, they respect me. Sort of. I think. Aquanetta called in the evening to report that a picture with Marie Windsor—our favorite gun moll—is scheduled to be on Channel 7 at some ungodly hour of the night which is completely out of the question given my hostel situation. I hung up to watch that cultural high watermark of live television, *Police, Camera, Action!,* which had half a dozen of the bachelors clustered around the set to observe iron-jawed-'n'-fisted policemen breaking into unsuspecting people's homes to arrest and handcuff them and drag them out to be stuffed into patrol cars and carted off. I'll admit to a perverse fascination with the program and even more so since they have been shooting in San Francisco this month and the landscapes are familiar. I keep waiting for it to be set in one of the upscale neighborhoods, where I know the truly big-time scams take place. And I keep wondering why the cops depicted here are so much more clear-eyed and reasonable than the foul-mouthed variety who liven up the evenings at the Hole in the Wall from time to time. Tonight's star arrestee, a feisty old grandmother who lives over on Bryant Street and bakes brownies full of *mota* for the homeboys, gives the camera the finger and the bachelors erupt in cheers and laughter.

thirteen

Pooch hot-wired a Toyota in a sleeping Cheyenne neighborhood and never took his right hand off that gun. As we glided down the street like a couple on their way to factory jobs, I looked back at Alice's candy-apple red Lincoln with its big balloony white sidewalls and felt a bunch of different kinds of regret. I regretted my big mouth, the trouble I had caused Carlotta. I regretted that as bothersome as she could be sometimes, I would never again lay eyes on Alice from Dallas. My regrets concerning Armando were like a big black cloud hanging over all these other sorrows. Could I have been so wrong about his feelings for me? Would I ever see him again? And, by the way, what the hell did Pooch have in mind for me? No, my mind did not rest easy as I looked back at Alice's car gleaming under the streetlights in a row of colorless law-abiding station wagons. That Lincoln, which Alice had won in a poker game in Confidence, Iowa, many years before, and had never ridden in because she was too damn fat, seemed, at that moment, to be the bright and shining symbol of the circus for me. The sure knowledge that I was leaving that part of my life behind and entering something new and bleak and threatening swept over my limp body like an ill wind that blows no good. I got a new grip on the armrest and with all the high spirits of a turnip, I turned to face the long gray streets of Cheyenne.

Pooch was looking a little peaked, I noticed out of the corner of my eye. He worked a wad of gum in his mouth, but mostly seemed to be chewing on his lips while beads of sweat dotted his forehead. Two or three tiny little atoms of sympathy in some out-of-the-way cubbyhole of my brain whispered, "The poor asshole." However, my seething anger far outweighed any hint of warm feelings for the human corkscrew. Not to mention the fear that felt like a fish flopping around in my stomach. I never had been much impressed with Pooch's brand of sanity. He was the kind that would never look when he could leer, never talk when he could hiss, never smile when he could shoot a chill up your spine with that alligator grin. Neither of us said a word, even during the hot-wiring operation, until we were well into Colorado, which, once you catch Interstate 25 in Cheyenne and blink twice, you're in.

"Where you taking me?" I asked when I saw a sign that said Denver 50 Miles.

"Shut up."

"Let me go, Pooch. You made your getaway. You don't need me anymore."

"Shut up, bitch," he said, and we kept cruising along in the shadow of the Rockies.

We drove all day and what little conversation we exchanged was so pathetic on my part and so rude and vulgar and threatening and hateful and evil on Pooch's part that I've blocked out most of it in my memory. But, here's a for instance just to give you a flavor. After we had been on the road several hours during which time he had pulled over two or three times to relieve himself against the back tires, I spoke up and said, "Pooch, could we please stop at the next rest room?"

"Rest room?" His snake eyes flew open like I had suggested a detour into the fiery jaws of hell.

I squinted into the sun and spoke as calmly as I could. "Rest room, Pooch, I need to use the rest room."

"Rest room?"

"Pooch, please, I really do need to go."

"Well, what do you need to do, Raylene?"

"I told you, Pooch, I need to use the rest room."

"Well, I mean do you need to take a leak or a dump?"

Did I mention that whenever the human corkscrew got off a humorous line such as that one his lips would retract in a hideous grin to reveal several more pointy canine teeth than the average human being is entitled to?

Looking straight ahead out the windshield I said, "I need to urinate, Pooch."

He said, "Well, hell, I've been urinating all day, Raylene, and you don't see me tying up rest room facilities."

I bet we went fifty miles before that son of a bitch finally did pull over, but not before I was reduced to tears and the car shook with the human corkscrew's sadistic laughter. I'm sorry to disappoint anyone who thought this was going to be one of those stories about a woman falling in love with her kidnapper, but maybe next time. We gassed up at the station where he stopped and later he pulled over at a roadside Dairy Queen and jumped out and ordered a couple of burgers. Other than that, it was a day of hard driving and the beautiful scenery flowing past might as well have been some picturesque beer commercial on TV for all the attention we gave it. A light rain started to fall right at the Utah state line and just outside of Crescent Junction, the bottoms dropped out of the clouds. It began to rain pitchforks and yearlings and the windshield wipers were no help at all against the flood. We pulled off the road and took shelter from the lashing rain under a tree. After a few minutes, the rain let up enough for Pooch to head the car toward a neon sign some ways down the road.

A motel. Oh, Lord, I thought, please, not that. The Fiesta Courts, it was called, a group of little stucco cabins in turquoise and pink. The office of the place had a little sheltered front porch where, from their rocking chairs, a man and a woman about my age observed the rain with contented smiles. They seemed to be a living advertisement for their warm accommodations. As our headlights struck them, their smiles seemed to grow even broader and I remember thinking something like, Huh? Life can be like that?

Pooch turned off the ignition and turned to me.

"I'm gonna get a room," he said.

I didn't answer.

"You ain't gonna holler, are you?"

I shook my head no.

"You know I'd kill you, don't you?"

"Yeah, I know," I said, without looking at him.

The carefree couple got up from their rocking chairs and ushered Pooch into the office. He rented a room and they followed him out to the porch where the lady, who had a sweet, open, sort of Patsy Cline-ish face, waggled her fingers at me with a shy smile. I waggled my fingers back at her with a sickly smile till Pooch got back in the car.

I walked into that motel room like a woman entering a prison cell, scared and lonely but resigned to her fate. To my surprise, and Pooch's too, I think, the room he had rented had two double beds. He sat me down on the one next to the bathroom, pointed a finger at me, and said, "Stay!" Which I did. I sat there running my fingers through the tangles of my hair while Pooch poked around doing man stuff: slapping and cussing at the air conditioner, ripping the sanitary band off the commode, taking a loud and splashy piss.

Now, mind you, when I left the circus, I didn't depart with a carload of matched luggage and trunks and hatboxes. No, I had a classy jeans-and-T-shirt outfit that I had thrown on during Wally's manhunt. Accessorized by a dirty pair of tennies and a spunky attitude that was getting less spunky by the minute. Playing it light, I said, "You know what, Pooch? If I had me a toothbrush and some toothpaste and a hairbrush and a bottle of shampoo, it would make a big difference in my life right now."

"Is that right?" he said with a big ugly leer.

"That's right," I said, kind of casually, putting my hands on my knees to keep them from knocking together.

He dropped onto the bed beside me and put his hand on my knee and his face right up next to mine.

"We've got some business to take care of first," he said.

Oh, Lord. My stomach turned. Everything else trembled.

"What kind of business?" I said with my eyes on the neon sign in the great outdoors where life was a fiesta and motel proprietors rocked happily on porches.

"Just how much money have you got, Raylene?"

"Money?" squeaked the former bullet woman, whose weekly paycheck was due that very day in a two-bit circus five hundred miles to the northeast. "Pooch, I don't have a dime. Look!" I pulled my pockets inside out to reveal nothing but a few shreds of lint. "If I had known you were gonna kidnap me, I would've brought my purse."

If I thought this last remark was going to bring a chuckle from the human corkscrew, I should have saved my breath. He grabbed my arm and twisted it up behind my back in a way that knocked the breath out of me as much from surprise as from pain.

"You know what I mean," he said.

"Pooch, stop, you're hurting me," I pleaded with tears springing to my eyes. By this time, what was left of my spunk you could have swept under the rug. He let me go as suddenly as he grabbed me and what he had to say next came out in such a rush that it took a few seconds for his words to register in the worn-out lump of pizza dough I was using for a brain.

"Everybody knows about that rich husband you left down in Louisiana."

Well! My rich husband. Any other time this would have been the occasion for knee slapping and roars of laughter, but the fact that the human corkscrew had chosen to emphasize his words by squeezing my thighs with his bony fingers put a check on my sense of humor.

"Pooch, I don't know what you're talking about."

He grabbed me around the waist and pulled me to him, moving one of his hands up over my breasts.

He went, "Oh, you don't know what I'm talking about?" and slid the hand down my stomach and into my jeans. At that point my adrenaline kicked in and after a little struggle I managed to catch him off balance and twist out of his grasp. I jumped to my feet and headed for the door, but I was no match for the human corkscrew. He shot one of those tentacle-arms of his out and snagged me by a belt loop and I bounced back to square one, on the bed beside him. First thing I knew, he had a knee between my thighs and was all over me again.

"Wait, Pooch. Wait just a minute."

"Wait? What for?"

I said, "We need to talk."

He said, "Yeah, we sure do," but he didn't stop what he was doing, which involved his hands and the upper part of my body and not much imagination.

"Pooch," I said, but he paid me no mind.

"Pooch!"

"You talking to me?" he said into my neck, where he nuzzled like we were a couple of honeymooners.

"*Pooch!*" I hollered, and then I flat-out screamed a scream so long and loud that I never would have dreamed I had it in me. And from the way he jumped to attention, it came as a bit of a surprise to him, too.

"Jesus, woman, pipe down," he said, those snake eyes glaring out from under those thin, colorless, little snake eyebrows.

I took advantage of the sudden silence to get to my feet in a semi-dignified way and face him.

"Pooch," I said, "about my money. I guess what you're talking about is what you heard Wanda say."

He said, "Wanda?" like this was a name he had never heard before.

"Woolly Wanda," I said, trying to inhale and exhale in the casual way of a woman discussing mutual acquaintances with a friend. "You heard that remark she made about Armando. That maybe he was interested only in my money."

"Oh, yeah," he sneered, "she did say that, didn't she?"

"Well, you know Wanda," I said. "Sometimes she talks crazy. Everybody knows that."

He said, "What everybody knows is just what I said. That you left a shit-load of money back there in Louisiana."

Then he pounced, grabbed my hair, jerked me down to the bed again, where he yelled in my ear. "You think you can keep a secret like that in a circus? Don't lie to me, bitch!"

And as soon as he said it, I knew he was telling the truth. It was only logical, now that I thought about it, that the story of my alleged wealth should have spread all over the circus. Why, I told three people myself and as Miss Viola used to say, a secret is something that's either not worth keeping or too good to keep. So there I was, folks, not exactly in the best position to engage in heavy thinking, sprawled back on my elbows with the hair of my head held firmly in the hand of the human corkscrew whose free hand was beginning to wander again.

Playing for time, I said, "Pooch, I want to talk."

By this time his hands were crawling up my thighs in a spider-like way that, from the look on his face, must have struck him as mighty amusing. However, spurred by a big dose of desperation, I mastered my nerves enough to speak with an authority that got his attention.

"Stop it, Pooch. Stop it *right now* or I'm gonna scream."

And guess what? He did. When Raylene Stout puts that steel into her sweet little voice, they sit up and take notice. I bounded up from the bed again and perched on an armchair of orange plastic a yard away.

"All right, Pooch, I'm gonna tell you the truth," I said. "You're right. My husband does have a little money."

He said, "A lot, I heard."

"Well," I said, "that depends. A lot to one fellow is a little to another."

He stretched out that long neck of his till he was close enough to lick my nose.

"How much we talkin'?" he said.

"Oh, I don't know," I said, eyeing the ceiling, "Hundred thou, I guess."

He drew that buzzard neck of his back in and nodded several

times. His glittery little eyes darted around the room and I could see he was doing some heavy thinking.

"What's his phone number?" he hissed at me.

"Whose?" I said, just because I was beginning to feel a tiny bit feisty again.

"What's his phone number?" he roared, and lunged at me just enough to make me jump halfway out of my skin. It took me a few moments to remember the phone number that had been mine for decades but I managed to stammer it out, thinking that, gee, it would be kind of nice to hear Buck's voice along about now. Pooch scribbled the number down on the phone directory cover and dialed it. He let it ring a long time before he hung up.

He said, "He's probably out with some other woman."

I said, "You're right, and I'd be out with some other man right now if I wasn't locked up here with you." After I had collected myself enough, I rambled on, thinking that as long as I kept the idiot talking he might keep his mitts off the lush body of the bullet woman.

"Pooch," I said, "I want to talk seriously. You know what? My husband would kill you if you harmed a hair on my head. That's the truth."

That was something I said without benefit of thought, a reflex action of the tongue, but you know what? As soon as I said it, I realized that it was indeed the truth, and the tear ducts that had been working overtime that whole day once again sprang into action as a vision of the buckaroo crossed my mind. I pictured him in the kitchen opening a can of Chef Boy-ar-dee spaghetti and slicing cheese for a grilled-cheese-and-sardine sandwich, his standard meal for my canasta nights with Dot and the girls. Some ball game would be blaring on the TV, caravans of ants making off with everything that wasn't nailed down, dirty dishes stacked to the ceiling. In my mental picture of him, a mournful look on his poor, lonesome face told his whole history. . . .

"Yeah, Pooch," I said, "my husband would cut you up into little pieces and use you for fishing bait."

"Oh, would he now?" said Pooch. The raw malice in his voice joined forces with my natural insecurity to send another picture floating through my head: Buck and Shirley Jack laughing and dancing in slow motion at a fais-dodo on Main Street while Cajun fiddlers smiled down at the middle-aged but oh-so-spry lovers from the bandstand.

"He'd track you down to the ends of the earth," I said, realizing I might be exaggerating just a little.

Pooch sighed in a heavy, dramatic way. "So how come he hasn't tracked you down, Raylene?"

Well, this question required some fast thinking, but I managed to come up with something about a trial separation, about Buck's dreadful temper and Mafia connections.

"Look, Pooch," I said, "I'm not looking for trouble. All I want is for you to let me go."

He said, "All I want is to get me some money."

I said, "All I'm saying, Pooch, is my husband is a dangerous man. I got into this mess against my will, but I don't want to see harm come to you or anybody else and if you think Buck wouldn't harm you . . ."

"Go to bed," he said, and jerked the covers down on the bed away from the door.

So I did. Fully clothed and with a troubled mind. Pooch dialed the number I gave him a few more times but there was no answer and finally he turned out the lights and collapsed on the other bed. I lay awake a long time listening for the regular breathing that would tell me he was asleep, but I never heard it. As exhausted as I was and with the blessed relief that came from knowing there was three feet of space between our beds, I fell into a dreamless sleep and didn't wake till daylight, when Pooch shook my shoulder.

"Get up," he said, "we're getting out of here."

"Where we going?"

"Get *up!*" he yelled.

April 28

Early this morning, Aquanetta and Paco helped me box up a lot of junk—books, records, knickknacks—things that have languished in my closet for years, and A. drove me down to the new flea market on South Van Ness and dropped me off before continuing on to her volunteer job with the AIDS hot line. By midafternoon, I had cleared forty-two dollars, which should have been the happy end of that story. However . . .

I was actually singing (quietly) as I came around the corner of my block with the money stashed in the red purse with the shoulder strap. I was walking along, my eyes on the sidewalk, my mind on things I needed to do to prepare for a probable full house tonight because Saturdays are generally busy. I got home and there on the steps sat Chuy.

"Oh, hi Chuy," I said, a little startled, because my regulars know the rule about not showing up till eight o'clock, and Chuy has bedded down enough here lately to qualify as a regular.

"Hi, Jamie."

"You're a little early," I said, taking a handful of bills out of the mail-box. "I don't open up till eight, you know."

"I know the rules," he said, watching me as I put the key in the door.

When he asked if he could come in for a drink of water, it caught me unawares. For a second, I considered telling him I would bring a drink to the door, but then, I figured that was a little ridiculous.

"All right," I said after a moment, "but you can't stay. I've got to get this place straightened up."

We walked inside and I sat on the couch opening bills and ignoring— or pretending to ignore—Chuy, who proceeded into the kitchen, where he got a drink from the tap. I gave the phone bill a once-over-lightly, and then, when I noticed Chuy standing in the kitchen doorway, a twice-over-lightly.

"Where you from, Jamie?" he said.

"All over," I said.

"You look a lot like a girl I used to know in Vegas," he said. "You ever been to Vegas?"

"No, I've never been to Vegas."

"This girl was a hooker. You ever been a hooker?"

"No," I said, refusing to look at him.

He laughed and wheezed and coughed and finally dropped down beside me on the couch.

I looked at him finally. "Really, Chuy, you've got to go. I've got a lot of work to do."

"Yeah, I know, I know," he said, "I'm gonna go. How does it feel to be a woman now, Jamie?" He punctuated this last sentence with a grab at my crotch that was quite painful.

I slapped him hard. He slapped me across the side of the head with a force that was not softened by a huge skull ring he wore on his middle finger. He lunged at my crotch again and began kneading me like bread dough. "Show it to me, Jamie. I just wanna see, okay?"

As stunned as I was, I could only stare at him and say, "Stop, Chuy."

Before he could respond, we heard a key in the door and Paco walked in. I jumped to my feet and said, "Okay, Chuy, you have to leave now."

Paco strolled in with a playful smirk. "Don't let me break anything up."

I said, "Get him out of here, Paco."

"What's going on?" he said.

Chuy said, "Jamie wants to try out that new thing she's got. Isn't that right, Jamie?"

I said, "I want you to leave now."

Chuy said, "She's just saying that."

"Paco, make him leave," I said, in a very level tone, knowing as I said it that his wiry arms were no match for Chuy's penitentiary muscles.

Chuy narrowed his eyes at Paco and said, "Yeah, Paco, make me leave."

Paco mumbled, "I don't want to get involved in this."

I said, "I want you to get involved, Paco. I want you to make him leave."

After a moment or two of glances being exchanged among the three of us, Chuy sprang up from the couch and put an arm around Paco.

He said, "Let's go get a beer, little buddy."

I stood there speechless as the two of them walked out the front door. They were going down the steps when I went to the doorway and called Paco's name very sharply. He turned around and walked back to me with a sheepish look.

I said, "Paco, I want that key back. I don't want you to have a key to my house."

He gave me the key and walked away with Chuy.

fourteen

We drove. And drove. I sat as close to the passenger window as possible and observed the sights as we crossed Nevada. Scrub brush and vultures and sun, lots of sun. Highway 50 is no scenic wonderland in the best of times, I have found out since then; however, when you're traveling in the company of an unattractive man singing "Let's Spend the Night Together" at the same time he's chewing gum with his front teeth, the landscape takes on a charm and grace that makes you drink it in like the nectar of the gods. A couple of times I closed my eyes and tried to meditate but it was no use; first, Armando would pop into my brain and refuse to leave, and then the ever witty Pooch would make a grab at my knee and holler, "Wake up, Raylene!" with a high-pitched giggle. Oh, such wit.

Whatever grief Pooch felt for the late Alice was kept well under wraps, believe me. He stopped at several pay phones but still there was no answer at Buck's end and I wavered between worry and relief. I dozed off and on and watched the sun go down. Mostly I just listened to the wind as we zipped past networks of white lights that represented towns like Ely and Reno. I was just to the point where I was beginning to think, well, I feel sort of normal, I guess, and I'll survive this, when we rolled past Sacramento on the freeway and Pooch flipped on the radio. All of sudden, the car was full of good ole Wolfman Jack's peppy voice just as loud and clear as I used to hear it on Nick's car radio in high school. He was saying something about his wedding anniversary. After all these years, he said, he and Wolfwoman were just as much in love as ever and he was spinnin' some of her favorite Jerry Lee Lewis golden oldies to show how much he cared. Now, *this* was normal, it occurred to me as I sat there cold as a popsicle—Wolfman Jack and Wolfwoman. Nick and I would have been like that, still in love and treating each other nice after being married a hundred years. What was not normal was what I was seeing out of the corner of my eye—a leering, sneering, jeering human corkscrew twisting his pelvis around to an inhuman degree to the tune of "Whole Lot of Shakin' Goin' On." And, of course, when that number finally came to an end, I just loved it a few minutes later when he began singing along with the radio and grabbing my knee each time he said, "Goodness gracious! Great balls of fire!" Made me feel real special. Oh, I don't want to talk about it.

The dawn was coming up when we got to the Bay Bridge on the east side of San Francisco. Something began to stir inside me as the tires on the Toyota went *kerplunk, kerplunk, kerplunk* crossing the long, long stretch of concrete over the San Francisco Bay. This was the end of the continent, we couldn't go any farther west than this. What now? Off to the right, every light in the downtown high-rises seemed to be turned on and twinkling a welcome. I rolled my window down, and the air felt sort of welcoming too, so cool and thick. I started grabbing big handfuls of it till Pooch told me to close the window and stop acting a fool. I sat up and, in spite of my fatigue and worry, I looked around and said more to myself than to Pooch, "San Francisco. I've always wanted to see San Francisco."

Pooch said, "Well, I'm glad I could be of service. Welcome to San Francisco."

We rolled down empty streets whose names sounded sort of familiar to me—Market, Mission—and once pulled up at a red light next to a cruising police car.

"Don't even think it," said Pooch as his hand went to the gun in his shirt.

Pooch parked the car on Mission Street and checked us into a seedy red brick hotel while I stood beside him and read the hand-lettered signs on the wall behind the desk clerk. *In God We Trust, Everybody Else Pays Cash. No Visitors. No Radios After 10 P.M.* No Cooking. You Break, You Pay. Extra Towel, One Dollar. Something told me not to be too disappointed if I didn't find free mints on my pillow. We trudged up to our deluxe accommodations on the third floor. One double bed, one straight-backed wooden chair, a sink against the wall, and a unisex bathroom down the hall. I peeled back a flesh-colored Band-Aid stuck to the middle of the door and found it was covering what appeared to be a bullet hole. Pooch sat on the bed and picked up the phone. Again, he got no answer.

I stood at the sink and examined my dirty face in the mirror above it. I was thinking about Armando, wondering if he was worried about me, wondering if that whole affair was a product of my imagination, when my eyes lighted on the double bed which I had been trying to ignore. The sight of it had a powerful effect on me. I threw up. Just ducked my head into the lavatory and threw up everything but my socks.

"Jesus!" said the sympathetic Mr. Twister, whose nose was out of joint to begin with judging from the way he had slammed down the phone receiver. I gave him a sour look and got back to the business at hand. By the time I finished and washed my face and dried it, Pooch had kicked off his shoes and made himself at home on the bed.

"Get some rest," he said in a way that was almost gentle.

I sat down on the chair.

"Lay down!" he said in a way that was not gentle at all.

I was too weak and exhausted to argue. I did lie down and the bed felt good to my aching body. Pooch didn't say a word or make a move toward me and I dozed off to the rustling of a newspaper he had picked up in the lobby. I slept for hours and when I woke up it was dark out. I could hear Pooch punching numbers into the telephone.

"Hello?" I heard him say. "I need to speak to Buck."

April 29

Big Victor was delighted to hear of Paco's new persona non grata status and insisted on taking Aquanetta and me to an early dinner at La Rondalla to celebrate. There's nothing quite so relaxing and rejuvenating as an evening out at someone else's expense, and B. V., bless him, made it clear that he was picking up the tab. He's flush these days, having worked two solid weeks pouring concrete and laying tile in a big South City project.

Settled into the corner of a booth in the dimly lit restaurant, I began to let go of my jangled feelings and before I finished my second margarita, was beginning to nod my head and murmur, "Uh-huh, that's right," to B. V.'s various putdowns of his nemesis, Paco. E.g., Paco steals food from me, makes too much noise, has questionable friends. B. V. says I should have kicked him out a long time ago.

By the time the chili *rellenos* arrived, I was having a hard time concentrating on the conversation, though my input was not missed, I'm sure, since Aquanetta was there to take up any slack. I was more absorbed in the rollicking Mexican music from the jukebox and the shifting lights of the restaurant's year-round Christmas decorations. On the way home, Big Victor bought a seven-dollar case of Burgie and the party continued. B. V. settled himself in front of the television while A. and I repaired to the kitchen.

After chugging a couple of Burgies, Aquanetta said, "We need to talk."

She is getting very impatient for me to lose my virginity. She sat at the kitchen table and ticked off the virtues of each new arrival as the guys came straggling in. This one had a beautiful smile and that one had a saucy derriere. She even saw sex-symbol possibilities in Big Victor, citing (loudly and within earshot of B. V.) the "big nose, big hose" theory of anatomy. She entertained the troops, telling fortunes with a deck of Bicycle playing cards, until one Javier showed up. When he walked into the kitchen to see what was going on, A. looked at me and said, "All right, here we go." Javier is tall, dark, handsome, strong, silent, and straight. He works construction with a firm in Daly City that asks no questions about immigration status and has been a perfect gentleman the few times he has stayed in my establishment, which means he comes, goes, and starts no fights. He comes from Zacatecas and more than that I do not know, because, as I said, he is silent. In minutes, A. had him seated across the table and was laying out his future. "Oh, my goodness!" she said, looking at the cards; then, to make sure he got the message, she slapped her forehead and said, *"Ay, caramba!"* Javier, it seemed, was in for some awfully good luck. And very soon. The kind of good luck that involves a beautiful blond enchantress, an American citizen who's mighty horny and, furthermore, is a distinct possibility for romance, marriage, and green card. A. saw Javier meeting said enchantress in a dark and smoky setting, very much like, hmm, Esta Noche. It just so happened that she had on her person, lodged right between her breasts, to be specific, a free pass for Saturday night and she would be delighted if he would be her guest at this most *divertido* of San Francisco nightspots. Javier took the pass (silently but cheerfully) and stuck it in his thin and well-worn wallet and it wasn't at all clear that he understood what the hell A. was talking about. A. had to leave to do her show and, after throwing a multitude of kisses around the room, dragged me out to the front porch.

"That's him," she said. *"Señor Correcto."*

"Oh, I don't know, Aquanetta. He's never shown much interest in me."

"Well, hell," she said, with a disdainful look at my flannel muumuu, "look at you! What do you expect? You're not gonna set anybody's heart a-pounding dressed like ole Mother Hubbard."

I explained that, under the circumstances, I did not believe it was in my best interest to present myself to my overnight guests as a short-fused sex bomb. I mentioned Chuy and a few others whose emotions were best left untampered with. But she wasn't listening. She wouldn't leave till she got my promise to show up Saturday night at the club.

fifteen

A cockroach the size of my thumb came crawling out from behind the medicine chest and scuttled across the wall like he was late for an appointment. The insect disappeared into a crack in the wallpaper while I lowered myself onto the rickety chair and almost but not quite suppressed a moan of envy at his freedom. I sat there at attention, my back flat against hard wooden slats and my hands on my knees while the degenerate Mr. Twister made contact with a man and a world that had not so long ago served me as a life, and not such a bad one, compared to my present setting. He had the phone receiver squished up so close that his bat-wing ear flattened against his head. I could picture Buck's earnest and relatively innocent face (relative to Pooch's) yawning as he identified himself over the two thousand miles of telephone line to this evil person perched on the side of the bed like a vulture on a hanging tree. And I could picture me too if I had been there in Lake Gladys on this late Saturday night. I'd probably still be up, probably puttering around the house, pickin' up 'n' puttin' up, making lists, doing a load of wash, while the TV flickered in the background. I would be taking my cozy little routine for granted, maybe wishing I was somewhere else leading a life with a little excitement in it, a litt'e adventure. . . . People never know when they're well off, do they?

Pooch raised his voice to make sure I heard his next worlds.

"Well, this is an old friend of his. Could I speak to him, *ma'am?*"

I would like to say that I ignored it, that that one word didn't close around my heart like a fist. But my tongue would rot off if I told a lie that big. Of course, I told myself, female doesn't equal floozy, and I tried to picture Dot dropping by to borrow a late-night cup of sugar and just happening to pick up the phone. Nope, not likely. Well, there was Maw Turner. She sometimes took a break from her coupon clipping long enough for Paw Turner to chauffeur her over for a white-glove inspection. But, no, they would long since be back on the road to Beaumont by this time, Maw fretting about her Chihuahuas every mile of the way. (She has three of them and their lives are just one endless yapping contest.) That left the floozies. And that most particularly left a certain well-known preacher's wife.

Buck came on the line.

Pooch said, "Uh, Buck, you don't know me, but I've got some news for you about your wife."

Just to irritate me, he twisted his head around clockwise and then counterclockwise, sneering the whole time. "Oh, yeah, yeah, she's all right. Doing fine, in fact. Lookin' good." The son of a bitch winked at me.

Tension that I didn't even know was there dropped away from my neck and shoulders. Buck was concerned about my well-being or at least paying lip service to concern. No, he was too dumb for lip service. He cared.

"But, what I called to tell you, Buck, is—"

I bolted to my feet and shrieked, "Buck, I'm in San—"

Before I could name the city Pooch backhanded me across the face so damn hard I dropped to the floor. He pulled his gun out and held it on me while he spoke again, words that made me realize just how much television this sorry bastard had watched in his time.

"If you want to see her alive again, Buck, I can arrange it. For a price."

He named the price and my mouth flew open in disbelief. Fifty thousand bucks! Lord! I'm sure Buck must have gasped too, at the very least, because he was a man who had never seen a hundred dollars altogether at one time, mainly because I never had allowed it. When it came to money, Buck was about as responsible as a cat in heat. Pooch told him to get the money together and he would get in touch with him later. He hung up the phone and sat there wringing his hands, stretching those fingers out to inhuman lengths.

After a bit, I said, "Pooch, I've got to get into the bathroom and take a shower."

His eyes darted around a little bit more while he mulled my request over.

He said, "Just a shower and that's all?"

At this point, I put a little vinegar into my voice because suddenly the whole situation seemed so intolerable to me: the man, the room, the world, my smelly armpits.

I said, "I don't know, Pooch. I might take a dump, too. I'm playing it by ear."

He hemmed and hawed till we were both satisfied that he was the man in charge; then I grabbed up soap and towel and padded two doors down the hall that reeked of many a cigar smoked over many a year. At first I thought he was going to follow me, but he grabbed the straight-backed chair and brought it out into the hallway. He sat there and smoked a cigarette with one hand and fondled the pistol inside his shirt with the other. Oh, really, he thought he was Jack Palance or somebody.

I guess because we were on the third floor Pooch figured there was no danger of me climbing out a window. Silly man. I peed and turned on the shower and headed straight for the window that looked out on a dark alley. This hotel, like everything else in San Francisco, was a hundred years old and it took me several minutes to get the paint-encrusted window open, but by george, I did, finally, and Raylene Stout was a free woman. Sorta.

There was a ledge less than a foot wide and I inched along it, praying between gulps, and thinking about how much more fun this situation is when viewed on *I Love Lucy* from the comfort and safety of your living room. I heard a police siren off in the distance and, much closer, a glass bottle crashing to the sidewalk. Some drunk in the alley, I figured, but I didn't dare look down. In a minute or two, or after six eternities, depending on who was keeping time, I reached the corner of the building, where down below a green canvas awning stretched over the front door of the hotel like God's own trampoline. A piece of cake for the bullet woman, I said to myself, and hunkered down for the jump. Then, no, I decided. I straightened up and thought about that bad ankle. Several people loitered on the sidewalk and I thought about yelling. Then I thought about Pooch. Then I jumped. I made a fine landing on the awning, bounced up, came back down again on the canvas, grasped a pole, and slid to the ground. I half expected applause, but the people on the sidewalk didn't look as if my daring feat was anything out of the ordinary, and after a glance in my direction, they went back to passing around a bottle wrapped in a paper bag. After I made sure I was all in one piece, I laughed out of sheer relief. The laugh was cut short by a gunshot whistling past my ear. I looked up and there was Pooch leaning out a third-story window. Surely a warning shot, I thought in midstride, but I didn't slow down to find out.

The stretch of Mission Street where I found myself reminded me of something Miss Viola always said about cities: that they were just big towns full of millions of people being lonesome together. The sidewalk near the hotel was thronged with people who looked like so many scarecrows and not happy ones either, though they staggered around joking and hooting and cackling like they were having the time of their lives. I thought again of Lake Gladys and the warm safety of my little home. I wondered where Armando was. I wondered if he was thinking of me. I was traveling too fast to see much more of the street than a blur of color, but I could tell I hadn't landed on Park Avenue. I sidestepped a puddle of vomit and managed to avoid the grasp of a bearded man who actually said, "Hubba hubba" as I whizzed past. The fresh smell of a misty rain was beginning to complete with the stench of urine as I ducked into the doorway of a porno bookstore and peeked back in the direction I came from. No sign of Pooch. I could see the awning of my rescue down the street and I knew that any second his scrawny frame would come crashing through the hotel's front door. I jumped over a poor man in a tattered overcoat lying on the concrete and set off again at a gallop. The rain was coming down now directly into my face, and I couldn't tell the water from the tears. Out of the crowd a face appeared that didn't strike me as fearsome, an old lady wearing house slippers and a blue stocking cap and a satisfied smile. She reminded me of the old lady in Opelousas who gave me the inspiration for my new name. I tugged at her elbow to get her attention.

"Ma'am, can you tell me where to find a policeman?"

She shrieked to high heaven and slapped my hand away.

"Help!" she hollered. "Help! They've landed again, they've landed again."

Well, it was a little embarrassing and would have been more so, but for all the attention the old lady's outburst got from the people milling around, she might as well have been humming "The Old Rugged Cross." At least I didn't have to give an explanation to curious onlookers about a case of mistaken identity. I wouldn't have had time anyway. Pooch was coming. I could see his green hat bobbing above the crowd halfway down the block. I took off again. I took a left on Sixteenth Street and trotted off in a new direction. Everything within sight seemed like a threat to me. The blackened doorways of storefronts were just hiding places for God-knows-what and even the neon signs outside the bars and liquor stores seemed to be warning me against dangers I had never considered before. I thought of ducking into one of the bars and getting help or at least I could hide behind a jukebox or something if Pooch stuck his head in the door. Then, remembering the old lady in the stocking cap, I thought, well, no, and just kept jogging along. However, by the time I reached the middle of the block, I was panting and crying and my bad ankle was beginning to set up a protest by sending little hints of pain that promised to grow into the real thing any minute. Then I saw the big yellow sign over the doorway of a bar in the middle of the block. ESTA NOCHE in all caps. I remember thinking, hmm, why does that ring a bell? Then, because I was so weary, I thought, what the hell, and turned into the swinging door. On my way in, I glanced at a poster taped to the door. It was advertising a show and the name *Aquanetta* leaped up and hit me right between the eyes. Oh, God. Clickety-click-click-click. Things started falling into place in my head. Alice from Dallas. This was the place in the picture on Alice's wall. She did say her friend was in San Francisco. And he did sign his name *Aquanetta,* not an easy name to forget. As miserable as I was, I felt a surge of joy go right through me to know there was someone in this town whose name I knew besides Pooch. Suddenly, I realized how terribly lonely I had been those last few days.

Inside Esta Noche was a different world from the the one San Francisco had shown me so far. A tidal wave of sound damn near knocked me down the instant I stepped through the door. Way down at the far end of the room a spotlight shone on a beautiful and dramatic-looking brunet with her hair all slicked back. She was dressed in a green satin gown and singing some song in Spanish that sounded just as dramatic as she looked, and she was singing it loud too, mind you. Her voice, bursting out of a refrigerator-sized speaker to my right, lifted a few wisps of the wet hair on that side of my head. As I stood there inside the door, trying to pull myself together, a young Latin guy sat counting a pile of greenbacks in a little glassed-in booth to my left. There was a sign that said four dollars admission but I just strolled on in like a woman who had all her marbles, one who didn't have a pistol-packing madman hot on her trail, and nobody stopped me. My stroll turned into a shuffle once I got inside because people were packed elbow to elbow in the place, making a flashy striding entrance out of the question, which was just as well considering my bedraggled state. The room was pretty dark and everybody's attention was focused on the singer, who, by this time I had figured out, was only moving her lips to a recorded song. After a few minutes, I looked around and noticed that almost all the people in this crowded room were men. Mostly good-looking Latin men. Even, it didn't take me long to figure out, the woman on the stage and a handful of other people in party gowns and high heels were of the male gender. Well! I was thinking, how about this? My first gay bar and complete with drag queens just like the ones they're always trotting out on the daytime talk shows. What a break! Pooch would never look for me here. If he did poke his head in the door, I would be mighty surprised if he stayed. Now where's Aquanetta? I edged deeper into the crowd and managed to get a couple of six-foot she-males with hair out to here and up to there between me and the doorway. I must have looked a sight, dripping wet, hair all stringy, eyes all swollen from crying. Not at my most glamorous, for sure, but the woman on the stage was literally bending over backward to reach the climax of her song and no one paid me a bit of mind. I was standing there trying to catch my breath, thinking what to do next, when somebody grabbed me around the waist. I screamed, but nobody heard me over the dramatic diva's song, which was basically a long series of screams, broken up by sighs, gulps, and sobs. Next thing I knew a redheaded woman (or whatever) with a bosom you could set a drink on was yelling directly in my ear, going, "Where have you *been?* You look like *hell!*"

I almost collapsed in her arms when I realized she was the one who had grabbed me, and not Pooch. I considered her question a moment (I must have looked real stupid) and stammered something about, well, I'd been out in the rain. She grabbed my arm and pushed her way through the crowd, dragging me after her. She led me to a corner of the barroom and through a door.

"Aquanetta?" I said, but she couldn't hear me over the music. She pulled the door shut behind us and proceeded down a flight of stairs.

I tried again. "Aquanetta?"

"God! That outfit! Come on," she said, pulling me along.

Downstairs in the dressing room, she practically threw me into a chair in front of a mirror. She started pacing up and down. A few of the bar's performers stood around half-dressed, smoking and gossiping, but she ignored them completely.

"Where have you *been?* You look like a fucking drowned rat!" she yelled at me.

I just stared at her, thinking she was nuts, but she kept pacing and yelling.

"I called Mona! I called Jackie!" she hollered. "Half the town's looking for you!"

When she stopped to catch her breath, I said, "Who's Mona? Who's Jackie?"

She halted in midpace. She leaned down and peered into my face. Then she peered at my face in the mirror, which was surrounded by lightbulbs, just like dressing-room mirrors in the movies. Tired as I was, I just sat there like a statue.

She said, *"You're* not Dagmar!"

"Oh my God," she said. "Who are you?"

"My name is Raylene Stout. Are you Aquanetta?"

She sank into the chair next to mine and clapped her hands to her face and peered out at me between her long green fingernails. "My name is Aquanetta," she said. "I'm so sorry. Jesus! You're not even a drag queen, are you?"

"No," I said, "I'm just a woman."

"Oh, my God, one of those," she said, shaking her head. She examined me from every angle before she grabbed a dainty and almost naked little Oriental person by the elbow and said, "Ginger, look at this. Does she remind you of Dagmar or what?"

Ginger, busily getting ready for the show, glanced my way and said, hmm, yeah, I did look a lot like Dagmar, and she went back to winding duct tape around her crotch or his crotch or whatever. Aquanetta asked me what I'd like to drink and she sent one of the performers, a guy in a tux, upstairs to get bourbon and Cokes for us both. I told Aquanetta I needed to get in touch with the police.

"What for?" she asked with a sour look that I presumed stood for her impression of the local police.

She moved closer to me while the story of my life, at least the most recent part, tumbled out of me. I started with the circus and told her about seeing her picture on Alice from Dallas's wall. Aquanetta listened, her jaw clamped shut, her eyes like saucers, the lacquered nails of one hand to her lips. When I told her about Alice's death, a look of such sadness passed across her face that she looked like another person, a much younger one who had seen a lot of trouble. By the time I got to the part about the evil Pooch, I was bawling and Aquanetta was passing me one Kleenex after another. I talked and talked and talked till I was out of breath. I told her about Buck, about Armando, about Carlotta, about everybody. Before I finished relating the adventures of Raylene Stout, we had polished off a total of five bourbon and Cokes apiece, and, as you can imagine, were feeling pretty darn chummy.

Aquanetta threw the empty Kleenex box into the wastebasket and said, "Don't worry, Raylene, everything's gonna be all right now."

And, tipsy as I was, it did seem like things were working out just fine or at least not too bad.

May 3

So I went to Esta Noche to give romance a chance. I spent a couple of hours getting ready and gave Big Victor a free night's lodging in return for minding the store. My plan to arrive at the club fashionably late was enhanced by the arrival, as I was walking out the door, of none other than the noble Paco, looking too much like Eddie Cantor not to be loaded on speed. Chuy, he said, had gone south one step ahead of the law—something about a drive-by shooting. While the glaring Big Victor stood behind me with his arms crossed, Paco begged to stay the night as the homeless shelter was full. I said no. He said please. I said no. He said please again. I said no again. He said he wanted to talk to me. I said I'd rather not. The back-and-forth went on for some fifteen minutes or so, till I told him to come talk to me some other time, as B. V. stolidly stood his ground.

I drove to Esta Noche in Aquanetta's car, which she, glorying in her role of romantic catalyst, had lent me for the evening. The place was packed as usual for a Saturday night and I entered the fray with head held high, keeping an eye peeled for Aquanetta and (discreetly) for Javier. Neither of them was in sight. A new girl was onstage performing, with the elaborate hand gestures of the novice drag queen, that old disco standard, "I Will Survive."

"So will I," I muttered to myself, and made my way to the door that led down to the dressing room, but the cramped and feather-festooned den of femininity was empty except for the Two Gingers.

"Where's Aquanetta?" I asked the usually loquacious Ginger Who Looks Like Connie Chung.

"Gone," she said, her terseness owing to a fishnet-stocking repair job that commanded her attention.

"Where?" I asked.

"I don't know," she said impatiently, her hands and teeth hopelessly ensnared in a mesh of thread and fishnet.

As I turned to leave, the other one, Ginger Who Fell to Earth, teetered past on her three-inch platforms and piped up, "Hey, Aquanetta's pissed at you, Dagmar."

"How come?"

"You stood up a blind date or something, right?"

"I was late," I said. "Did he show?"

"He was here for a while, but I think the place freaked him out a little bit and he split."

"Hmm, too bad. Where'd Aquanetta go?"

"I don't know. She left with some woman."

"What woman?"

"Some woman I didn't know."

"What'd she look like?"

"She looked a lot like you as a matter of fact," said GWFTE, pulling a ruby out of her navel with a healthy *fwump!*

I couldn't think of anyone Aquanetta knew who resembled me. I went upstairs, got a drink, watched the show, and went home manless. I was in bed before last call, all alone except for you, Dear Diary. As Joni Mitchell used to say, it was just a false alarm. Another one.

sixteen

Aquanetta had me going. I had kept my mouth shut for so long that I was making up for lost time. She asked me where I was from and I told her, feeling a little twinge of homesickness, a little touch of pride. She made a face at the word *Louisiana* and said she had been in New Orleans only last year.

"The humidity!" she hollered. "Plus every time you turn around, somebody's playing 'When the Saints Go Marching In.' "

That pretty well put both my homesickness and my pride in perspective and I thought, well, yeah, here I am in San Francisco . . . the Golden Gate Bridge, Chinatown, Fisherman's Wharf. *Pooch.*

But, you know, that last little old thought, unpleasant as it was, drifted over my head for only a moment like a smoke ring and then started breaking up into little wispy puffs as I looked around me at Aquanetta and her sequin-happy crew. The smell of lipstick, powder, 'n' paint, and, from the corner of the room, the moans of a king-size drag queen being crammed into an ironclad corset were so real, so *there,*

I began to feel part of the world again. Pooch? The desert? Just a recent nightmare. At one point in the evening I did try to call the police on the bar phone upstairs, but since I wasn't in immediate danger the 911 operator directed me to another number. I dialed that one, but after twenty minutes on hold, I gave up and went back to my bourbon and Coke. I could sense that Pooch was gone anyway, probably already across the state line. And I guess I was right. I never heard from the son of a bitch again.

When Aquanetta suggested we get out for a breath of fresh air, I bolted to my feet and said, "Good idea!" with nary a thought of any danger lurking in the dark. When we emerged into the night air, everything had that fresh look and smell that cities get at night after a good rain. The neon signs that had seemed so threatening a couple of hours before were bold and cheery splashes of color in the dark that made you think, gee, I never knew green could be so . . . *green.* I sauntered beside Aquanetta, who was on her turf, make no mistake. The sights she pointed out to me were mostly the street people. She knew all their names—that's Dolores, that's little Henry, that's so-and-so, she said as we passed doorway campsites—and she delivered capsule histories of some of them. This one used to be a Disney animator or a drummer for Jimi Hendrix, and that one just got out of jail, and this one deals coke, and so on.

They knew her too. "Hi Aquanetta." "How's it goin', Aquanetta?" They all brightened up at the sight of this gum-chewing redhead strutting their way, even the ones that weren't so harmless looking. I remember one snaggle-toothed guy with a hunting knife on his belt and a scar that started on his cheek and disappeared into his shirt. He lurched forward from some black hole in the wall, and I was ready to run.

He said, "Hey, Aquanetta, you got a cigarette?"

"Of course, darling, do I look like a nonsmoker?" she said, fumbling in her purse without batting an eye.

For her part, Aquanetta was the queen of the night out for an image-polishing stroll among the peons. Regal, you know, but checking up on the welfare of her subjects.

"Hello darling." "How's that leg?" "Did you ever find your dog?" She paused every few steps for brief exchanges and greetings, and I stood behind her giving curt little nods to this one and that one like the lady-in-waiting who's just along for the promenade.

When Aquanetta suggested we hit the International House of Pancakes in memory of Alice from Dallas, I suddenly remembered how very hungry I was and all but hugged her in my flurry of agreement. Then I remembered something else.

"Aquanetta," I said, "I don't have a cent."

She waved my worries away with a don't-be-silly gesture and stopped at a pay phone. She called a taxi and soon we were hurtling across hill and dale in the backseat of a cab the color of an egg yolk. I sat up, all agog at the looks of this wonderful city I had landed in. I wanted to memorize every cupola and chunk of gingerbread on every Victorian castle; I took mental notes on the names of the grand hotels and restaurants and promised myself I'd know them from the inside some day; I read the street names out loud—Van Ness, Geary, Pacific—and tried to learn them by heart so that when I was an old woman I could look back and say, why, sure, honey, I knew San Francisco.

Aquanetta, on the other hand, leaned back and stretched out in a luxurious and leisurely heap, and sprayed herself in odd places with that perfume that looks like Giorgio but isn't. After she got all settled, she turned to me.

"So what do you do now, Raylene? You going back to your husband?"

I said, "My *husband?*" Without thinking, I laughed a laugh that was like a bark.

"Well, you do have one," she said. "I mean you're not divorced."

I said, "Not yet."

Well, at this remark, Aquanetta sat up and said, "Don't."

"Don't?" I said. "Don't what?"

"Don't get a divorce."

By this time I was sort of used to Aquanetta's habit of dispensing advice. Mind you, she had already recommended unsolicited remedies for my split ends and my ragged nails, not to mention a book about Zen Buddhism that would clear up all my questions about life in the here and now as well as the hereafter. ("I adore Buddhists, darling, because they won't cut your throat if you don't want to be one, too," she said.) However, in view of the fact that the only information I had thus far given her about my husband was that he was a confirmed and habitual skirt chaser, I must say this last bit of advice came out of left field.

"Why on earth not?" I asked, like a divorce was something I had already decided upon and set a deadline for. Actually, even in the most high-pressured, hot-blooded throes of my romance with Armando, when divorce seemed the most logical next step in my life, the idea of it was just something that simmered on the back burner of my mind, something that could be put off indefinitely as long as I was not revving up for another go at the gold ring of matrimony. The truth was that thinking about a divorce meant thinking about Buck and thinking about Buck meant thinking about other people of the feminine persuasion who did not exactly contribute to my peace of mind.

Aquanetta crossed her arms and lifted her chin and took on the faraway look of a person about to deliver some important, well-thought-out philosophy of life, or at least some important philosophical tidbit.

"It's not worth it. One husband's like another."

"But I'm in love, Aquanetta."

"The acrobat?"

"Aerialist," I corrected her, and feeling self-conscious about how highfalutin the word sounded, I put my hand on my hip and lifted my chin and repeated the word in a snooty way and laughed. But Aquanetta ignored me. With her eyes all squinched up, she chewed her thumb, obviously deep in thought.

"Go back to the husband," she said.

"But, Aquanetta, you don't know the whole story!"

"Sure I do. You'd be surprised how many times I've heard that story. Woman marries man, man chases skirts, woman leaves man, woman marries other man, other man chases skirts and the whole damn thing starts all over again. One husband's like another in the long run."

I said, "Hmm," and looked out the window, thinking the spirit of Alice from Dallas was alive and well in that taxicab. We stopped at a red light and a well-built young man crossed the street in front of us, moving the way a lot of well-built young men move. Like he had a system of tiny bed-springs where the rest of us have bones. The thought of Armando flooded my exhausted mind so suddenly that I was surprised how the idea of him crowded everything else out of my head.

"No, I'm really in love, Aquanetta."

"I know. With the aerialist."

I nodded in a stupid way. "With Armando," I said.

I couldn't really see Armando with some other woman. Not so soon anyway. Even considering the cool attitude he had been showing toward me. I knew he was out there somewhere, worried about me, wondering if I was worried about him. I tried to think where he would be, but the names of the podunk towns on the circus's schedule slipped my mind at the moment. I would have to look at a map to jog my memory.

Aquanetta said, "Look, Raylene, let's get a grip here. Number one, you're broke."

"Yeah, that's true," I said, and suddenly it struck me that, hey, lack of money is indeed a problem. After all I had been through, being without money had been the least of my worries. Like they say, everything's relative.

"So call your husband," said Aquanetta. "Tell him you're okay, set his mind at ease. And tell him to wire you some money."

We turned into Lombard, a long, flat street full of motels that could have been in any town in the USA and there at the end of it was the International House of Pancakes. We stopped in front and Aquanetta gave the driver a handful of ones with barely a glance. She led me to a turquoise-colored booth, mumbling all the while about husbands and ignoring the curious looks we got from the clientele, who appeared to be cast members from some wholesome family sitcom just taking a break for a few flapjacks. We looked over the menu and debated the merits of banana versus strawberry pancakes. Finally we got a towering stack of every variety, and over this pile of pancakes that would have done justice to Alice from Dallas, Aquanetta put my life into focus for me. First, there was the issue of money: I needed some. Second, Buck was undoubtedly worried sick about me and I owed it to him to tell him I was out of danger now. Sitting in the safety of this cozy haven of fast food, the truth of this statement struck me like a whip. Suddenly, I could see Buck pacing, fretting, even whimpering in our shadowy little house. I laid my fork aside and jumped up to use the pay phone on the wall, but it was out of order. I sat down again and Aquanetta kept ticking off my problems like I had never left: third, I needed a place to sleep, she said. She took a sip of water and swished it around in her mouth while she watched a mother trying to quiet a squalling baby in a high chair.

She said, "Kids! Ugh. Now where was I?"

"I need a place to sleep," I said.

She said, well, she was between apartments herself and was staying at a friend's house. She and the friend were not on the best of terms right now—something about whose turn it was to take out the garbage—and it wouldn't be a good idea for her to bring home a guest. However, she did have this friend, Dagmar. . . .

I said, "Dagmar? The one that looks like me?"

"The same," said Aquanetta. Dagmar, she said, rented out floor space in her house for two dollars a person.

"Two dollars?" I said. It seemed like a lot of money at the time.

"I'll lend you two bucks," she said.

Well, okay, that sounded fine to me, I said.

Aquanetta smiled and said, "Now you understand this place of Dagmar's is nothing fancy. We're not talking about the Hyatt Regency here. We're talking about one big room with sleeping bodies strewn from one end to the other."

Well, that was okay, I said, feeling only a little uneasy. Without a cent I was not exactly in a position to be choosy about sleeping arrangements. In fact, filled to the brim with pancakes and bourbon as I was, sleeping anywhere at all seemed like a luxurious pleasure. Besides, I was curious to see this Dagmar that looked like me.

But Aquanetta went on. "Now I should tell you," she said, "that the sleeping bodies will most likely be all men."

Well, that caught me up short. "Oh," I said.

"But it'll be all right," she said. "After all, Dagmar's there too."

I said, "Well, yeah, but Dagmar is a . . . I mean Dagmar's not a real woman, is she?"

"Oh, yes, my dear. Dagmar is an authentic female. She didn't used to be, but she is now."

Aquanetta's eyes glittered with mischief as she watched for the reaction of the swamp woman from Louisiana, a reaction which amounted to a blank look and another, "Oh."

Aquanetta said, "Is that all right then? I mean, we've got to deposit you someplace. And it's just for tonight. Just till your husband can wire you some money."

I said, "You've sure got a lot of confidence in my husband, but yeah, it'll be okay I guess."

"Fine," she said. "You can call your hubby from Dagmar's place."

She polished off the last of the pancakes and we walked out on Lombard Street, where Aquanetta hailed a cab with an earsplitting whistle. On the way to Dagmar's place, she named each neighborhood we passed through—the Marina, Pacific Heights, the Western Addition, and so forth—and pointed out famous people's homes in the voice of a weary elevator operator announcing the floors. Cruising through the Tenderloin, we counted bodies sleeping in doorways.

Aquanetta said, "It's just like Calcutta, darling, except everybody's got a gun."

Soon, we were back where we started from, I noticed, as we rolled past Esta Noche in the darkness. We rolled down the streets, mostly empty except for some newspapers flying in the wind. Inside the cab, I felt so safe and cozy that I leaned my head back for a few moments and closed my eyes and latched on to a thought that hovered right behind my eyes: *I'm okay, Carlotta, I'm okay.* I knew that somewhere Carlotta was worried about me, and I didn't want that because I knew that I had caused her way too much trouble already. *I'm okay, Carlotta, don't worry.* I kept holding on to that thought till we turned down a street so narrow it was more like an alley.

"This is it," Aquanetta said to the driver, pointing to a tiny house, old and battered and badly in need of paint.

"Your new home," she said to me, "at least for what's left of this night."

She escorted me to the door and rang the bell. Then she rang again, tapping her foot like a woman in line at the bank. Finally the door was opened by a big, bleary-eyed guy, beefy and brown, in sweatpants and nothing else. Aquanetta spoke in a stage whisper, "Oh, hi, Victor. I've got a guest for you."

Victor, slack jawed and heavy lidded, pointed to me and said, "Her?"

"Yeah. Her," said Aquanetta as she brushed past Victor and stepped over sleeping bodies to reach a cot in the corner of the room. Victor staggered to a couch in the middle of the room, dropped onto it, and rolled up in a blanket.

"Dagmar!" she whispered, sitting on the cot and grabbing the foot of the person asleep on it. "Dagmar!" Wake up, dear."

Dagmar moaned and after a few moments reached the eyes-open stage. She lifted her head from the pillow just long enough to identify the intruder. Then she sank back and said, "Oh, it's you."

After some back-and-forth about a blind date that didn't pan out, Aquanetta grabbed her foot again to keep her from drifting off. "Dagmar, I've got a guest for you."

"Good," came the drowsy reply. "Two bucks. Blankets in the closet."

"Okay," said Aquanetta, closing Dagmar's lifeless fingers around a couple of dollar bills. "Here's the money, darling. Now you be nice to my friend. She's a female guest, Dagmar. You'll like her. She's from Louisiana. Her name's Raylene."

"Huh?"

"I said my friend here is from Louisiana and her name is Raylene."

After a long silence, I saw Dagmar's head rise again. Then I saw the silhouette of her thin figure sit up in the bed.

"All right?" Aquanetta said, getting to her feet.

"Yeah, all right," Dagmar said after a bit.

I edged into the house from where I had been standing in the doorway. Dagmar seemed to be watching me as she sat up an inch at a time and pulled on a robe over her nightgown.

"You sure it's okay?" I said, a little flipped out at the sight of eight or nine men wrapped in blankets and snoring on the floor.

"Yeah," said Dagmar. "Oh yeah," she said, walking toward me in the dark. She came and stood in front of me and looked me in the eye in such a direct way that I started squirming and yakking like a damn fool. I said, why, Aquanetta was right. She sure did look a lot like me. She sure did. Well, well, well. Same kind of nose and chin and blah, blah, blah, why, we could be sisters! All this time Dagmar was watching me like I was something pitiful which I guess I pretty much was.

"How about cousins?" she said.

I shifted from one foot to the other and back again and tried to absorb what she had just said. Well, yeah, why not cousins?

Then Dagmar said, "Hi, Raylene," in such a simple and sympathetic way I had to stop my bullshitting and assess the situation.

Well, I had my mouth set for catching flies. I looked at the woman with the scraggly fresh-out-of-bed hair and said, "Hi."

Aquanetta looked surprised but kept silent when Dagmar took both my hands in hers and said, "How's everything in Lake Gladys?"

Well, there was a split second when those words, that voice (though, Lord knows, much changed), and that face all came together in a very neat and clean way and my right hand flew out of Dagmar's grasp and clapped itself over my mouth to hold in a holler. The kind of holler I'm talking about would be hard to describe. Shock? Joy? Even horror? All I know was that it was raring to jump out of my throat and it was all I could do to contain it.

"It's Jamie," Jamie said quietly.

"I know," I said even more quietly from behind my hand, and then something happened that I had never experienced in all my adventures and misadventures and trials and tribulations: my knees gave out on me. They just turned to water, and plop, first thing I knew, my behind was crashing into the floor. I tried to stagger to my feet, then, what the hell, sat down again, like a rag doll somebody threw in a corner. From way down in the bottom of my lungs or somewhere, my voice came rising up to a place where it could find release at last.

"*Jamie!*" I yelled.

The bodies on the floor stirred and mumbled and a couple of the men rose up on their elbows. Aquanetta didn't know what the hell was going on and said so, but nobody paid any attention to her as Jamie sank to the floor beside me. I looked at this blond bombshell a long time and my voice went all quavery when I whispered, "I sure am glad I'm sitting down."

"Me, too," this new person whispered back.

Naturally there were a million and one things to say but I didn't say a word and neither did Jamie. For a while. All I could put forth was this dry little laugh and Jamie matched it and pretty soon we were hysterical with laughter—real, unforced laughter. There was some crying to do too, but that came later, when it was catching-up time. We talked until well past daylight. Jamie had seen hard times that made my kidnapping escapade seem like an excursion in the park. Sleeping in train stations and under bridges in first one country, then another, and being without friends. But, of course, the real story Jamie had to get off his chest, excuse me, her chest, was the sex change. She said it was something that had been in the back of her mind her entire life. She said that in the days when the twins used to dress us in matching outfits, she felt jealous that I was the one who got to wear the dresses. Well, I was just floored. I always thought I knew Jamie so well. (However, now that we were on the subject, I did recall that when we used to play Tarzan and Jane, it didn't bother Jamie to let me take the Tarzan part.) Aquanetta hung around to witness all the true confessions and wouldn't leave until I got on the phone and got squared away with my husband.

"Call him," she said, "and I'll go home and leave you two alone. The poor man must be frantic."

So I called Buck. Didn't even call collect. Jamie insisted she wanted to pay for the call.

And a woman answered.

"Hello?"

It was a real perky hello. Especially for that hour in the morning. Shirley Jack Lazarus has made a career out of being perky. I waited a few seconds, opened my mouth, and then waited a few seconds more, while I experienced what they call a slow burn.

Finally, in a real flat voice, I said, "Is Buck there?"

Shirley waited her own few seconds, probably deciding whether to keep on with the perky routine. Then, after deciding that, yes, perkiness had served her well throughout the years, she chirped, "Yes he is. Just a minute, please."

"Who is it?" I could hear him saying in the background.

"I'm not sure," was her sweet little answer.

When he came on the line I said, "Buck, I'm all right" through clenched teeth while I glared at Aquanetta.

"Raylene? Is that you? Are you really all right?"

"Yes, I'm really all right, Buck."

"Well, thank God," he said, and laughed a nervous little laugh.

I said, "Yeah, thank God."

"Well, where *are* you? I've been worried to death. They've got the FBI out looking for you all over the country."

"I'm in San Francisco, Buck." And then, ready to wind this conversation up, I said, "Listen, Buck, I need you to send me some money."

"Some *money?*" he said, like why on earth would I need anything like *that?*

"I'm broke, Buck. I'm completely broke and I'm staying with my cousin Jamie in San Francisco."

"Who?"

"Jamie. My cousin. I've told you about Jamie a million times. Get a pencil. I'm gonna give you the address."

He fumbled around for five or ten minutes looking for a pencil. (I could just imagine what that house looked like.) After I gave him the address, I said, "Now, Buck, I want you to go down to Security Savings. I've got a little better than nine hundred dollars in there and you'll find the passbook on the top shelf in the bedroom inside a book called *Secrets* by Danielle Steel—ha, ha, ha, yeah, I know, very funny. Ida LeBlanc is the teller down there and I'll call her and tell her to let you have the money."

Well, he wanted to know how come he didn't know about this savings account and I told him if he had known about it he would have spent it already on his women and that shut him up. Then he wanted to know where the rest of my money was.

I said, "What money? That's all the money I've got in the world, Buck."

"What about that fifty thousand?" he wanted to know like he was asking where I put the peanut butter.

I think I have already mentioned in passing that the man I married was not a genius. I lived with Buck for all those years and just sort of adapted to the fact that he didn't have sense enough to come in out of the rain, but I must say the lack of intellectual stimulation did make it a lot easier to leave him. It's not the heat, it's the stupidity.

"Buck! Now tell me, where would I get fifty thousand dollars?"

"Well, that's how much that fella was asking for last night. Where'd he get the notion we had that much money?"

I wish they would invent a telephone line that you could slap people through. So you could just reach out and punch someone.

"Buck," I said, "I lied to the son of a bitch because I thought he was gonna kill me. I told him you had a lot of money. Can you understand that? Is that too tough for you? Am I talking too fast for you?"

"Oh," he said.

Sometimes Buck could be so thickheaded it took my breath away.

"Buck, are you gonna do what I said? I need that money and I need it now."

He said he would and then he said, "Raylene?"

"What?"

"I sure am glad you're all right. You don't know what I've been through."

I gave him what I believe is called a pregnant little pause, as you can imagine. "You don't know what I've been through either, Buck."

Of course, the pregnant pause was wasted on Buck. He said, "I was so afraid you were dead or hurt or something. Did that guy hurt you?"

"No, I'm okay, Buck, I'm really okay. The only thing I need is for you to send me the money. All right?"

As I hung up, I managed a tight little smile for Jamie and Aquanetta, but it would have slipped away if I hadn't grabbed the coffeepot and put my two remaining ounces of energy to work pouring a cup of coffee.

May 9

Listening to Raylene entertain the troops, one would think she has been here a year instead of a week. She knows all their names and they lounge all over the kitchen while she fries up eggs in the morning to augment the regular rice and beans (her revenue-increasing idea) and keeps up a steady stream of chatter.

"Gustavo, can you open this jar? Jose, I'm gonna steal that shirt from you."

One thing is obvious. She's good for business, which somehow doesn't surprise me. I haven't had less than a dozen guests a night since she arrived. Several of the guys who deserted out of loyalty to Paco have returned. I've even indulged myself in the luxury of having Big Victor turn away a few of the more rough-'n'-tumble types. Next thing I know we'll be taking reservations and advertising in the *Chronicle*.

The first morning Raylene was here, after Aquanetta and all the guests had gone and we were finally alone, I felt oddly shy all of a sudden. I told her, "I hope this whole gender reassignment thing doesn't freak you out too much or anything."

She said, "Well, no, not really. It's just that I wonder if you know what the hell you've got yourself into. Lord, I'm not sure you know what being a woman entails, Jamie. . . ."

"Well, it's too late now," I said.

She laughed and said, "All right, enough beating around the bush here. I want to get a look at those things," and clamped her eyes firmly on my bosom. She took the neckline of my nightgown in her hands and held it out. She inspected the merchandise and finally shook her head and said, "Umh, umh, umh," like Miss Viola polishing off a lecture to noisy grandchildren. Then we laughed till we had to lean on each other for support, and that was that on that.

Even the Hole in the Wall sleeping arrangements don't faze her. Big Victor, the president of her fan club, dug up a rusty cot for her somewhere and now our two little beds sit side by side in the corner, partitioned off with a thin blanket in a manner reminiscent of *It Happened One Night*. She says it's been so long since she slept in a bedroom of her own she wouldn't know how to act anyway. When I hear her hooting and cackling and carrying on, she seems like the same Raylene that used to stand outside my bedroom window and blow a police whistle till she was red in the face to wake me up on school days. But sometimes, she lets down her guard for a moment and I become aware of a heavy current of melancholy running not too far beneath her antic behavior. One thing is money. The funds her husband promised to send still have not shown up and she hasn't been able to locate that circus which owes her a paycheck. Another thing is her love life. She mentions this Armando from the circus twenty times a day and talks about setting out to find him when she gets her money, but I think it's only talk. She talks about the difference in their ages but she says it's okay because she looks younger than she is. Then she asks me if I agree that she looks younger than she is and I, of course, say yes. And she does look pretty good. She combs the want ads every morning over coffee and talks about getting a job as a store clerk or something and an apartment and settling down here in the Mission near me, at least for a while. But nothing definite is happening for her and I think things have been so indefinite for such a long time that she badly needs some "centering and grounding," to use Aquanetta's phrase. She does need to slow down. But she always did need to do that. At least the house is a lot cleaner as a result of her abundant energy. Sometimes she tells me I'm lazy as a sow, but she jokes about it. Says Miss Viola would turn over in her grave if she could see my kitchen. Yesterday morning she was quiet for a few minutes, her head buried in the newspaper. Her face was so full of something I can only call "cheerful desperation," I had to look away.

Then I blurted out, "You can stay here as long as you like, Raylene. I don't want you to worry about anything."

She said, "I'll get a job. I'll start my life over. People can start their lives over. They do it all the time." Then she folded the paper and glanced very pointedly at my cleavage before saying, "Of course, I guess you'd know more about that than I would, wouldn't you?" and we both pretended to laugh.

seventeen

Stay busy. That's what Dear Abby always advises for the common broken heart. And I guess it's good advice. As good as any. It was easy to stay busy at Jamie's, where Jamie's idea of cleaning house was collecting the beer bottles off the floor to put in the recycle bin. It wasn't a luxury apartment to begin with—I kept thinking about Jackie Gleason's place in *The Honeymooners*—but if it had been, you wouldn't have been able to tell for all the grime. I spent a whole day scrubbing down the kitchen stove, and the bathroom was something I don't even want to talk about right now. Or ever. And I must say that my mind was just as engaged during this time as my body. This rather big change in Jamie was, for sure, food for thought. To begin with, as much as I hid my shock behind good manners and joking (two things that were invented to hide your true feelings behind) . . . listen! That stuff down there between your legs is pretty basic plumbing, and, God knows, I had never known anybody personally who had fooled around with it surgically. Of course, the talk shows on TV trotted out a different transsexual every other day, but this was somebody from Lake Gladys, somebody in my family. Yes, I would be lying if I said the new Jamie didn't come as a large jolt. My closest relative, my oldest friend, the person I had missed and worried over so much . . . that person was no more. It took some getting used to. Those first few days were hard. Sometimes when Jamie would recall something that happened thirty years ago, I would get—just for a second, mind you— a little goose bump or two. Who *was* this sort of slinky blond with the voice as high or higher than mine and how did she know all the secrets of my childhood? But you adjust. Gradually, as we cooked together and argued over what kind of eyeliner was the most waterproof, I began to get used to the idea that I had not lost Jamie, I had just gained a girlfriend.

And then there was Jamie's guesthouse to run. On a quiet night, the house would rock with crazy young guys, usually from Mexico or Central America, doing what crazy young guys on their own do at night—playing cards, drinking beer, watching television, yelling, fighting, arguing in Spanish about God knows what. On a livelier night, a bedraggled mariachi band or a group of Jamie's female impersonator friends might turn up and throw the whole place into confusion. In the daytime, when things did occasionally get so quiet that I might be tempted to engage in a worry session, there was always house cleaning to be done and I threw myself into scrubbing and straightening up the house till I damn near dropped from exhaustion.

One afternoon, Aquanetta brought an old coffee-stained highway atlas over and we sat at the kitchen table and took a good look at Wyoming and the surrounding states. The circus's travel itinerary was no big secret, but it was just something I had never paid much attention to, since one town in the western United States looks pretty much like another—Burger Kings and gas stations in the foreground and purple mountain majesties in the background. Anyway, as I looked at the map, I realized that the names of the towns didn't really ring a bell either. I did recall that Alice from Dallas had mentioned that we would be in Grand Junction, Colorado, soon and she intended to call up an old boyfriend while she was there. So on a what-the-hell basis, I called the sheriff's office in Grand Junction. The sheriff, who sounded like he'd been interrupted in a game of checkers that he was eager to get back to, said, yeah, there had been a circus but it had pulled out last night.

"Well, do you know where the circus was going to next?" I said, knowing I sounded like a fool.

He paused long enough to make sure I knew that he thought I sounded like a fool, too, before he said, "No ma'am, I don't keep up with the circus. That's not my job."

"Thank you." Click.

I laid my finger on the map and ran it along Interstate 70 to see if any of the towns nearby sounded familiar. Green River, Cisco, Parachute—none of them jogged my memory and I threw up my hands. I never had been able to make any sense of Mr. Rosetti's booking schedule. Sometimes we would ride all night and pass through two states to get to the next play date and other times we would stop at the next town. Armando could be in any one of those rectangular and semi-rectangular states or even up in Canada. The only thing I could think to do was wait and visit with Jamie till the circus reached Seattle, where it was going to be part of some big Fourth of July festivities. This would create a nice cooling-off period for both Armando and Carlotta. If things went well, I thought, their grievances against me would fade with time and they would only remember the nice things about me, the endearing qualities (if they could think some up). Jamie said it was a great idea for me to stay with her, that we needed time to get reacquainted and, besides, I was a lot of help around the house. And I did love San Francisco, which, I had already decided, was my favorite city anywhere. I walked for miles in the city with Jamie and sometimes by myself. We shopped in the produce and fish markets on Mission Street and made a sport of keeping the cost of lunch down to a dollar apiece. One whole rainy afternoon we played pinball in a North Beach bar while listening to opera music on the jukebox. Another day, we went out to the Cliff House and watched the seals play on the rocks for hours. I went to the Cinco de Mayo celebration at the Civic Center with a bunch of the guys who regularly stayed at Jamie's and I danced in the sunshine till I collapsed. If a museum was having a free day, we went. If a poetry reading in a coffeehouse was free, there we were. I loved riding the buses all over town and rubbernecking at the window, while Jamie sat on the aisle and pointed out buildings and monuments and bridges.

So I wasn't having a miserable time, but it bothered me a lot that my money didn't arrive from Buck although it didn't surprise me. Knowing Buck, I expected it to take him a couple of days to coordinate his activities until he reached the point where he could actually bring himself to address the envelope, lick the stamp, and mail it. I got in the habit of waiting for the postman every day, sitting on the stoop of the Hole in the Wall, my feet dangling over the pavement. Jamie's place was actually two apartments, one on top of the other, but the abandoned apartment upstairs reminded me of pictures of ghost towns in the Old West, broken windows and tattered curtains and an occasional glimpse of one of Jamie's cats taking a suspicious look at the world outside. Except for the cheery murals of cornfields and street scenes on the fences and garage doors, Balmy Alley would have been a sad little backstreet with a pothole here and clump of grass there; however, on a sunny morning, it could be quite homey with its rickety old houses and secret little patches of green behind spiked fences. However, I didn't have time to lie around all day worrying about the mail. We stayed busy at one thing or another and spent a lot of time just plain catching up. One evening we were standing at the kitchen table, folding fresh-laundered blankets in the quiet before the guests arrived.

"Jamie," I said, "I want to ask you about something."

"Okay."

"All these years you've been away from home. Haven't you ever wanted to go back?"

"Not really," she said.

"Never?"

"Well, maybe at first," she said. "I was scared at first out there on my own. But I met people. People who helped me."

"Why did you run away in the first place?"

Jamie's eyes were sad as she looked out the window.

Finally, she said, "Because I couldn't stand it another minute. In that town. In that house. With my father. The beatings."

She carried some blankets to the closet. When she came back to the table, she said, "That last night was the worst."

I said, "Yes, it was. It was a horrible night. Nick jumping off the bridge . . ."

"Yeah," she said.

I said, "I still think about Nick after all these years."

"Me, too," she said. "It was such a tragic thing. He was such a nice person."

I said, "You know, I've felt sort of guilty all these years. In fact there have been times when I've lost a lot of sleep over the part I might have played in Nick's death. Why did he jump off the bridge? Could I have made a difference?"

"Oh, no," Jamie said. "Oh, *no!*" She studied the floor a moment and seemed to be weighing her words. "No, Raylene," she said, "I'm sure you couldn't have changed what happened."

I said, "But, you know we were on the outs sort of and he did try to make up with me at Dot's party and I sort of behaved like a . . ."

"Oh, no, no, no," she said. "There was a lot of stuff going on in Nick's life. That crazy drunkard he had for a mother for one thing, plus a lot of stress about money for college and so on."

We folded blankets in silence a minute or two. Fold, fold, fold. Then I said, "You know, his mother died not long after Nick did? OD'd on pills and liquor."

"Yeah, you wrote me that," Jamie said.

Jamie had a way, even when she was a little boy (well, how else would you say it?) of just shutting down sometimes. Withdrawing. The old turtle routine. But the old Jamie would always snap out of it in a few minutes and say what was on his mind. We piled the blankets in the closet and the only sound was the siren of a police car careening down Twenty-fourth Street to some terrible crime somewhere. I remember thinking at the time, Jamie has changed. In more ways than one. This new person is a brooder. Not like before. And not like me. At least, when I do brood and there's another person in the room, I sum up my thoughts every once in a while and give voice to them. Just so everybody knows where I stand. It's a technique that comes natural to me and seems to be what people expect of me. I knew Jamie had not said everything on the subject of Nick that she had in her mind, but I knew that when and if the time came that she wanted to share her thoughts, it would have to be her idea. The doorbell rang about that time and Jamie marched over to let in her first guests of the evening, a couple of Mexican teenagers, speckled all over from a house-painting job. I bustled around and found out their names and that, yes, they spoke a little English, and that this was their first time here and that they hailed from Mazatlán and had heard about the place from Big Victor. I showed them where the blankets were and verified the price of the two-buck accommodations. I told them showers were fifty cents extra and showed them the orange crate where the towels were kept. All this should have been taken care of by Jamie, of course, but, I swear, I don't know how she ran this place without me. Jamie's style was to open the door, let 'em in, joke around a bit, and go read a book. If anybody reading this is considering a sex change in hopes of acquiring a more energetic personality, my advice is save your money.

The doorbell began a pretty steady ringing (no one admitted after ten, one of my innovations) and I swooped around playing the hostess with the mostest. As usual, Jamie retired to her corner and pulled back my blanket-curtain, or "walls of Jericho" as Jamie called it, and collapsed on her cot with a thick book by Tolstoy or somebody. To see her glued to that book and turning those pages in such a leisurely way, you would have thought she was all alone in her room on a quiet winter evening. And to see me waltzing to the door and taking care of business, you would have thought, hey, this woman is a born land-lady; no way was she so recently the famous and popular bullet woman, must be a case of mistaken identity.

"Oh, hello, Jose. Hi Juan. It's good to see you. Come in, Arturo. We've missed you. Where have you been? Oh, you went out of town?" And on and on. Of course, sometimes I had to play the bouncer. Like,

"Hi Felix. I told you not to come back here and I meant it. Now go away before I call the cops." (Slam!) This to a guy who had stepped way over the bounds of propriety by breaking through the walls of Jericho and demanding a good-night kiss from both me and Jamie, while copping a feel or two or three or four in the process. Tut-tut. We'll have none of that. However, for the most part, Jamie's guests were a well-behaved lot. Just homesick country boys from south of the border, some of them not even old enough to shave, grateful for a place to lay their weary heads.

One of the regulars, a sad-looking, skinny little boy named Hector from a small town near Guadalajara, had shown up with a guitar slung across his back. With only a little urging from me and a couple of the guys, he agreed to play it. I pulled a kitchen chair into the main room for him and found a few votive candles in a kitchen drawer and lit them for atmosphere. Hector played that guitar like it was something he had invented, and the songs he sang were the saddest I ever heard, though I couldn't understand a word of them. The crowd of some dozen or so guys was quiet and respectful, letting the sad songs sweep over the room, reminding them, I guess, of their families and the lives they had left so far behind. Hector's voice was so clear and so direct, his back straight against the chair and his feet flat on the floor, that even Jamie's attention was drawn to him. She laid her book facedown on the bed and watched. I sat with Big Victor and another guy on the couch which also served as Big Victor's bed, the place of honor for the establishment's sergeant at arms. The others sat on blankets on the floor since there were no chairs except in the kitchen. (Jamie went for the uncluttered look in the interior decoration department for practical reasons: the less furniture, the more sleeping space on the floor.)

Hector sang a bunch of his songs, then sang several more requests, and sometimes the crowd sang along with him. I couldn't sing along in Spanish, of course, but I applauded after each song like Julio Iglesias had dropped in and treated us to a few off-the-cuff numbers. One of the guys brought a big bottle of red wine out of his knapsack and I rustled up a bunch of glasses and jelly jars in the kitchen and began passing them around. In short, the mood was cozy and warm, and it occurred to me that I hadn't felt so comfortable and peaceful since I had left Armando.

It was almost eleven when the doorbell rang. I asked Victor to get it and tell them to come back tomorrow since the deadline for overnighters had come and gone. Victor stayed at the door a few minutes and I heard him arguing in Spanish in the background, but I was focused on Hector, who was singing a song at last that I did recognize, "Ceilito Lindo." Victor was still at the partly open door when Hector wound up his song. I clapped along with everybody else and yelled over my shoulder, "Tomorrow night, Victor. Tell him to come back tomorrow night." This ten o'clock rule was one I wanted to enforce because the first few nights I stayed with Jamie, we had guys straggling in till all hours, or maybe staggering is the word I need. Things came to a head one night—or one morning, actually, as it was five in the A.M.—when Jamie opened the door to a big beer-soaked fellow with his hair in his eyes, who couldn't stand without leaning against something, but somehow found the strength to lunge at a sweet little Guatemalan fellow with a wicked jagged-edged knife. A dispute over a job or a girl or whatever. Jamie bandaged the Guatemalan's wounded arm and Big Victor ushered the Mexican out while I wiped up the blood and hollered, "No more of this shit! Enough already!" And the ten o'clock rule was born.

I was standing at the closet passing out blankets. I could see Big Victor was having some trouble with the person at the door but before I could march over to reinforce his efforts with my loud mouth, he called to Jamie. After the scattered applause for Hector's last song, the room was so quiet that Jamie's bare heels hitting the floor seemed to echo.

"Hi, Paco," she said in a raisin-dry tone of voice.

My ears perked up at the name. Jamie had told me all about this one.

Paco said something I didn't catch and Jamie said, "You haven't heard about our new rule?"

Big Victor left Jamie alone with the newcomer, who argued and joked and wheedled till she gestured for me to come to the door. She turned to me and said, "This is Paco."

"Hi Paco."

I looked him over. He was just a kid, draped in a long, baggy overcoat several sizes too big for him.

"Paco," she said, "Say hello to my cousin Raylene."

"Hello," he said. The smile he gave me was pretty dazzling, full of straight and perfectly white teeth. However, I somehow had the feeling that this smile was offered on a strictly conditional basis, and could be withdrawn without warning.

When I left them, they were still going back and forth about his staying there. I somehow dozed off despite the constant buzz of talk and occasional hoots of laughter from the fellows and I didn't wake until I heard Jamie slip into the bed beside me.

"Raylene," she whispered. "You awake?"

"Yeah."

"Well, I let him stay. Just for tonight."

"Okay."

"He's so full of apologies and everything."

"Okay."

"Plus it's been so boring around here without him."

"Okay."

May 11

Aquanetta dropped by in late afternoon decked out in a rather fetching Dale Evans ensemble, all buckskin and fringe and décolletage, accessorized by a little leather pouch full of Maui Wowie around her waist. She insisted that Raylene try it and of course I required no coaxing. We sat at the kitchen table, where A. rolled a joint in the blink of an eye, passed it around and started rolling another. She was full of news about her new crush, a local rock singer who performs in a clown outfit, which quixotic effect she admires because most rock singers, she said, are such fucking clowns to begin with. She sealed a joint expertly with a flick of her tongue and added, "But he's hot. Hot in the sense that truly not giving a shit is hot."

After a few minutes the radio, which had been playing softly, seemed to bathe the room in reassuring sound; seemed, in our silence, to provide a very necessary soundtrack for our oh-so-relaxed afternoon. Some formerly important Russian official with an unfamiliar name died in Russia today, and a DJ in Berkeley was playing "Back in the USSR" in memoriam. Raylene said the song made her feel real festive. When she suggested a toast to the late Russian, I dug out a bottle of two-dollar André champagne that somehow got overlooked at the last birthday party. I opened it with a grand explosion. Champagne shot to the ceiling and dribbled all over the kitchen while we whooped and hollered and laughed. We sat and talked while the room grew darker. We went over several subjects in depth, e.g., astrology, the best way to make corn bread, a promising new AIDS treatment, the how and why of Michael Bolton's popularity, how to grow longer nails, how not to get audited by the IRS, and, finally, the free square-dance lessons down at the Rawhide.

Aquanetta pulled out a lipstick and languidly began to write something with it on a paper napkin, which she then held up for all to see. It read:

CLOSED
FOR
TONIGHT

By the time A. had the napkin taped to the door, Raylene and I were scrounging through my closet for full-skirted outfits, and minutes later we were folding ourselves and squishing our petticoats into A.'s Volkswagen. We roared down Folsom Street laughing all the way. At a red light, Aquanetta practically dislocated her neck checking out a passel of plaid-shirted homeboys clustered on a corner, smoking this 'n' that. They leered, she leered back, and so did Raylene. The light changed and I hollered, "Go!" as loud as I could, visions of Suddenly, Last Summer dancing in my head. First stop, the Line-Up for margaritas and tons of tortilla chips and salsa. Then we headed down the street to the Rawhide. Aquanetta often says the only important thing she has learned in San Francisco is how to walk into a room. This is something she works at. Heads turned as she opened the swinging doors by pressing her prodigious tits against them (busting through, one might say). She slunk toward the bar, waving cowboys aside, right and left, while Raylene and I followed in her wake, a bouncy entourage of two. The dim lighting lent a coziness to the place that's right in keeping with our mood and the blaring C&W music was the kind that A. claims can make a better person out of you, in this case, a Clint Black two-step called "No Time to Kill." We stood at the bar and drank Coronas—none of that cheap domestic brew for Aquanetta—and if Raylene saw anything unusual in the sight of men dancing together, it certainly didn't show. I said something to the effect that the pee-oh-tee has wiped my memory free of care. Aquanetta reflected a moment on my remark.

"Isn't it the truth? Actually, it's not so much 'I don't remember' as 'Who gives a flyin' fuck?' she said, and pulled Raylene and me onto the dance floor, where we joined a line dance as if we knew what we were doing. Raylene struck up a conversation with a couple of amiable guys from Sacramento ("hayseeds," as A. calls 'em) and they were soon swirling us around the floor in a demonstration of the Cotton-Eyed Joe. A. and I took a break outside to smoke another joint. A. had decided by this time that she liked—no, adored—the hayseeds from Sacramento ("They're so down home," she said) and bought Coronas for them while Raylene and I hit the dance floor again. She moved around doing dance-floor shtick—cheeks sucked in, remote expression, nothing too original. However, when I caught her eye occasionally, she ducked her head and smiled in a dippy way that clearly said, "Just look at us, will ya?" We kept going till she suggested we go outside for a breath of air.

We were sitting on the curb in front of the club and our recent euphoria was beginning to feel a little frazzled around the edges.

"Jamie," she said, watching the traffic, "do you remember when we used to play Pleased or Displeased?"

"Uh-huh," I said.

"Are you pleased or displeased?"

"Displeased."

"What would it take to please you?" she asked mechanically.

"A couple of egg rolls, maybe. Or some pot stickers."

"What else?"

I thought a long time and feeling a surge of generosity, I opted for flattery.

"To be able to adjust to the hassles the way you do. To be able to make the most of bad situations. To maintain a positive attitude. Like you. Are you pleased or displeased?"

"I'm pleased," she said, sounding a little weary. "I'm pleased as hell that you think I'm like that. It pleases me that people don't know how scared and awkward and stupid I really am."

The swinging doors opened behind us and out stumbled Freddy, one of the Sacramento twosome. Like a kind and patient teacher to a tardy pupil, Raylene turned to him and called, "Are you pleased or displeased, Freddy?"

"I'm just as pleased as punch, sugar dumpling. How about you?"

"We're just about that pleased, too," said Raylene. "Right, Jamie?"

"I'm getting there," I said.

Aquanetta dropped us off at home well past two o'clock and we sat at the kitchen table, feeling bleak and exhausted the way one does after nights like this. Over a cup of herbal tea, I surveyed the sparsely furnished wasteland of my castle.

"I need to do a major overhaul on this place. Maybe some drapes would help," I said.

"I need to do a major overhaul on my life," Raylene said. "You know, if I could just get my love life straightened out, I think everything else would fall into place."

"Oh," I said, "is that the secret of successful living?"

She said, "It's no secret, Jamie. I don't have any secrets."

"Oh," I said, feeling a little uneasy at the mention of secrets. Was there something slightly accusatory in her tone? Did she want to thrash out the Nick Tarkington thing? I didn't. I steered the conversation back to interior decoration.

"Forget the drapes, Jamie. Just forget 'em for a while," she said.

In the silence that followed, she appeared, by means of pursing her lips and straightening her skirt, to be composing her thoughts.

"Where," she said, "do you want to be in ten years?"

"What is this? A job interview?" I said, to lighten the mood, but she really wanted to know.

"Just tell me, Jamie."

It struck me as such an odd question outside of a personnel office that I had to think hard to come up with any kind of answer at all. Finally I said, "The where doesn't matter. I just want to be with somebody that needs me."

"And loves you?"

"That, too."

The silence, so unusual in this place, lay all around us till I suggested it was bedtime.

eighteen

If this book ever winds up in a library, they'll probably stack it away in the tall tales section or in the mythology department or something. But I don't care. I have committed myself to telling the truth, and it's not my fault that certain details of my story sound like something dreamed up by some half-crocked romance writer. Besides, let's face it, the truth is a lot more interesting than lies anyway. One of the details I'm talking about is this: the fact that as I came through the door to meet my husband face-to-face for the first time in five months, the radio was playing "our song," which was "Higher and Higher" by Jackie Wilson. I could hear it and I was sort of humming it as I stood with my key in the lock of Jamie's front door. I had just got back from a persimmon-hunting expedition all up and down Twenty-fourth Street, where the Latino produce markets carried a lot of out-of-season stuff imported from God knows where. I wanted to show off for Jamie and the boys by making a persimmon pie, which is the only kind I ever make since all you have to do is heat up persimmon pulp and buttermilk and flour and a couple of other things in a pie plate and it makes its own crust. However, persimmons were nowhere to be found and hadn't been around for months, and so I carried a bagful of limes which I found on sale someplace, and as I opened the door I was just wondering what the hell I was going to do with twenty-four limes. The door swung open, that music hit me full force in the face, and there was Buck sitting on the couch, no one else around. (Jamie had run out to buy cigarettes.)

"Buck!" I hollered, losing my grip on the bag of limes, which went rolling every which way.

My husband stood up, shy as a high school boy on his first date, and I must say, standing there in the early evening light, Buck looked good. Buck's a handsome man when he's standing face-to-face with you across six feet of floor space at six o'clock in the evening. He was dressed neat as a pin in some decent-looking corduroy slacks, and here's what got me: he was wearing this red mohair sweater that I knew he hated and never wore unless I bitched for half an hour first because I happened to like it. (Plus I'd spent $39.95 on it down at Sudy Patterson's little boutique for the "now" man and Miss Sudy would rather die than accept a return. She makes you bring back not only the ticket, but every little tag and piece of paper that ever came near the goddamn sweater, plus the tissue paper, and oh, God, it's just too ridiculous.) I didn't go "Gulp" or swallow my gum and my heart didn't skip a beat or anything, but, hey, as a gesture of *respect,* that sweater was Buck at his best. And it showed his humor, too, because we're telling the truth here and Buck was a man that liked to laugh. One of my favorite things about Buck from the time we were newlyweds was the way he could be sitting all alone in the living room watching some dumb sitcom on TV, not aware that anyone was listening, and from the kitchen or bedroom, I could hear him laughing these belly laughs as loud as if the jokes were just plain hilarious. Okay, so he did that because he wasn't very smart. I don't care. It was just kind of endearing, if you know what I mean. And he laughed at my jokes the very same way, and take note of this, you men out there: Laugh at a woman's jokes and she'll stay with you a lot longer than she ought to.

"Hi, Raylene," he said.

My first impulse was to say something wiseass about the sweater, but then I thought better of it, and I kept my mouth shut for once. And, you know, while I was standing there with my mouth shut it occurred to me that, hey, five months ago the wiseass remark would have prevailed, we would have had a short laugh, and then we would go back to being strangers who wound up by accident in the same bed, the same house, the same planet. What could you call that little veil of silence that fell across my usual routine and blurred the sharper edges of it? Kindness? Maturity? Forgiveness? All of the above? Maybe I had become a better person for all the trouble of the last five months. Maybe Buck had too . . .

Yes, he said, he had the money, but not all of it, because they weren't giving away gas for free, you know.

. . . Or maybe he was still the same old Buck.

After I kind of got myself together, I sat on the couch beside him (separated by two or three feet, please rest assured) and said, "There's one thing I want to say, Buck. Officially. I truly am sorry I shot you. It's the most hideous and ugly thing I ever did and I hope you can forgive me."

He twisted around and scratched his head and looked out the window and said, "Don't worry about it, Raylene. You know me, I can take a lickin' and keep on tickin'."

Words came to my lips but they stayed there; words like, yeah, and you can take a beatin' and keep on cheatin'. But I was still doing the ex-wife thing, thinking about my words before popping off.

What I did say was, "Well, Buck, I didn't mean for you to bring me that money in person. The U.S. mail could've taken care of it just fine."

Buck said, "I know that, Raylene. But you didn't think I was gonna pass up a chance to see you, did you?"

Now, to the unexperienced layman, his words might very well be chalked up to empty flattery. After all, we all know the man's history, don't we? But to the professional ear—and make no mistake, my Buck-translator credentials were current and valid—I knew the man was glad to see me, had worried about me, and did care about me. As he damn well ought to after all the cooking and cleaning I had done for him over the years. And, like I said, he respected me. Any time money or financial transactions came up in a conversation with his buddies, Buck would say, "That's Raylene's department," and I must say, he would take my side in just about any argument as long as it wasn't with him. And that's worth something, isn't it, ladies?

We had a lot to say, of course. But the very first thing he wanted to know, even before I explained to him about my kidnapping, was what the hell the story was with Jamie.

"What do you mean?" I asked, doing my deer-in-the-headlights number. Just acting a fool.

"Well, isn't Jamie supposed to be a, uh, *guy?*"

"Oh, that," I said. "Well, she was but now she's not."

All right, now this is what I mean when I address the subject of Buck's IQ. Most of us, if we were in Buck's shoes at this point, would go, click, click, well, I guess Jamie went to the doctor and got the he stuff changed into she stuff, right? But, no, Buck's comeback, even after giving it some thought, was, "You mean, they raised her as a boy, but she was really a *girl?*"

I did my best to stick to words of one syllable as I explained Jamie's story.

Buck fell *out!* His face went white as he threw his hand up over his heart. He shook his head like he was trying to clear it. *"No!"* he hollered. *"No!"*

In fact I thought he overreacted so much that I got a little annoyed. I said, "Don't you want to hear what happened to *me?*"

"I can't believe it," he said, ignoring me. "I just can't believe it."

"Buck," I said. "What about me? I was kidnapped at gunpoint by a homicidal rapist and dragged screaming across the desert. Wanta hear about it?" I said, embroidering the facts only slightly.

So finally he settled down enough for me to tell my story, and he did seem concerned. He sat up. "Who did it? Who kidnapped you?" he said. "Who *was* this maniac?"

I leaned back and crossed my legs and told the story, using sort of a flashback technique. Well, Mr. Twister kidnapped me from the circus and brought me to San Francisco, where I accidentally met up with Jamie. Well, the reason he kidnapped me was he needed a hostage so as to escape what was shaping up as a lynch mob. Well, he kept me after he escaped because he thought I was rich. Well, he thought I was rich because of this lie I told this guy in the circus. . . .

And about that time, in walks Jamie. Buck, who was just warming up to my story, went stiff.

"Oh, hi, you're back," she said to me.

"Yeah," I said, "I guess y'all met. I was just bringing Buck up-to-date. About everything."

She wandered into the kitchen and Buck watched her out of the corner of his eye till she disappeared around the corner. Then he looked at me and shook his head, but I kept telling my story. I recited my adventures in a sort of cool manner, like all this stuff happened to somebody else a long time ago, and Buck listened the way any back-fence neighbor would have—tightening his eyes in sympathy or nodding to show agreement. When my final flashback hit on the subject of the day I left Lake Gladys, I did, I confess, get a little emotional. Well, if pounding the couch with my fist and even wiping away a teeny-weeny little tearlet from the corner of my eye would qualify as emotional. Surprised myself, even.

Now even with all my translation experience, I had to stop and think when Buck did nothing more than grasp his knees and mutter, "Aw, *Raylene!*" to my sudden outburst, what some might call a tirade. Aw, Raylene? Now what did that mean? Was he embarrassed? Sorry? Pissed off? Fed up?

"Well, what are you gonna do now?" he asked.

"Well, I'm not going home with *you!*" I said, which created a sort of awkward moment, because I realized as soon as the words were out of my mouth that nobody had invited me to go home with him. Oops.

Buck gazed out the window at a ragged black man pushing a creaking and rattling shopping cart along Balmy Alley and didn't let on that he even heard what I said. Now when Buck doesn't let on that he heard, it usually means that he didn't hear. One thing about him, you don't have to translate the expressions on his face, and I must admit I do like that in a man. After the black man halted his cart and sat on the curb to sort through a bag of cans and bottles, Buck turned to me and said, "Well, Raylene, I'm not planning to go back to Lake Gladys myself. I want to try my luck in some other place."

"What about your job?" I asked.

"I quit it. I couldn't stand it anymore."

"What about the house?"

"Well, I rented it out to Peggy Ann and Hoopy," he said, looking at the floor.

Well, my heart sank. Peggy Ann was Buck's baby sister. The rebel sister and the scourge of Maw Turner's life. She was sort of what they call "out there." Thoroughly modern, you know, with the combat boots and the boa constrictor around her neck. And Peggy Ann liked her cocaine, too, I believe. She sang (I'll leave it up to you, Dot, as to whether you want to put that word in quotation marks) in her boyfriend Hoopy's band, Straw Lana, which is a damn silly name for a band, but, Lord, it's ten times better than Anal Warts, which it spells backwards, and which was the band's original name, and which Maw Turner swore and be damned was the direct cause of her first stroke. Peggy Ann's only talent was making her own stage outfits. I especially liked the blouse that featured cutouts for her nipples, as if the damn thing wasn't made out of clear plastic to begin with. I don't claim to know very much about show business, but if pressed, I would have to say that Peggy Ann and Hoopy have some more dues to pay before they sweep the Grammies. Or make enough money to pay rent.

But I didn't say anything. I just kind of nodded and blinked back the tears.

Finally, I asked, "Well, where are you going to go now?"

In true Buck style, he said, well, he wasn't sure. He said he had several places in mind and was taking a good look at San Francisco, too, while he was here.

"What about our stuff, Buck?" I didn't mention Hoopy's .457 Magnum and his habit of using Maw Turner's wig stands for target practice, but it was weighing heavy on my mind.

He said he had taken a moving van to his mother's house and dumped the contents of our house in her garage. "Except the stuff she could use," he said, "which I moved into her house."

I didn't have the heart to ask which stuff that was. I didn't have the heart to think about dealing with the cranky Maw Turner when it came time to reclaim my goods. I didn't have the heart to continue this conversation.

I was glad for the interruption of Jamie bringing out Cokes on a tin tray which she balanced on her head.

She said, "I learned to do this in Bangkok."

Oh, good, I thought, here's something new we can talk about and act like we're just casual people at a tea party.

"Bangkok? Well, my, my, my, is there any place you haven't been?" said the prodigal wife. I displayed my teeth and raised my eyebrows like a nervous hostess diving into a discussion of shoe sales.

That was enough to launch Jamie into a travelogue that included Singapore and Hong Kong in addition to Bangkok. I smoothed out my skirt and threw a couple of warning looks at Buck. He finally caught my meaning and sat up and acted fairly civilized. As Jamie went on, he even began asking all these questions that I'm sure never bothered him before. What kind of weather have they got over there in Bangkok? How many people have they got over there in Hong Kong? It was clear he was making the effort to be sociable, and you know what? I appreciated it. I could tell that Jamie did too. She was real nervous and yakking a mile a minute, trying to cover it. She told a story about losing her wallet at the thieves' market in Hong Kong, and another one about being laid up with a rare tropical disease in Bangkok. Jamie wound up her spiel and without much more than a nod at Buck she went back to the kitchen like there was important work to be done there.

"Have you got that money for me, Buck?" I said, brisk and businesslike, not about to take any nonsense.

He took his wallet out of his back pocket, stiff and wincing like every little movement hurt him in his heart. He took out a roll of bills and looked at it like he was in mourning before handing it to me. I'm sure it was the most money Buck ever had his hands on in his life and I even felt a little pang of sympathy, knowing how he hated to give it up, knowing how he must be thinking about all the beer and floozies that money would buy. Poor fellow.

I sat up on the edge of my seat, licked my thumb, and started counting the bills.

He said, "There's a little over seven hundred dollars there."

Which there was. Seven hundred and twelve dollars. I could have thrown a hissy fit about the missing almost-two-hundred dollars, and in earlier days, you can bet I would have. But not this time. He had already told me he had taken out trip expenses and never mind that it was my money, never mind that he could have mailed it to me, never mind that, if I had got myself worked up into a sweat about it, I could have made him promise to pay it back and spent the rest of my life waiting for him to deliver. No, this was the new Raylene, the one that was learning what the Beatles meant when they said, "Let it be."

I led him to the door. When I finally got him outside, I stood in the doorway and said, "Well, thanks for bringing me the money, Buck. I would have been happier if you had brought me the whole nine hundred dollars but I guess I would have dropped dead from surprise, too. So, I guess it's okay."

"Well, Raylene," he said, "what do you think you're gonna do now?"

I told him I was going to stay with Jamie a little longer and rest up, then maybe rejoin the circus.

He said, "Oh, you like the circus, huh?"

My first impulse was to say that I had never been happier than I was in the circus because that's where I fell in love with Armando. But why do you suppose I bit my tongue and just muttered something about yeah, I did like it quite a bit? Why did I hesitate to tell Buck that there was someone else in my life and in my heart that made me feel like a live woman again for the first time in years? Do you think that I was trying to keep from hurting him? Do you think a man, had the situations been reversed here, do you think any man would have spared my feelings? Let's take a poll, ladies.

I even told him I was sorry that we couldn't put him up for the night but that we were expecting "guests," which, of course, was true.

"Oh, that's all right," he said, "we got a little room out at the Econo Gardens out on One oh one."

We? I thought, watching the streetlights come on and not half paying attention. Who's "we"? But I didn't ask. I didn't care.

May 13

So Buck Turner turns up. In the late afternoon, the doorbell rang and there he was, the buckaroo in person: tallish, dressed rather neatly in sweater and corduroys (though I wasn't wild about the shaggy red sweater, which glowed with a radioactive intensity that would have meant sudden death in a bullring), sandy hair, not bad looking. A healthy bit of paunch, but he gets around nicely without a wheelbarrow, contrary to what Raylene has intimated about his physique. He seemed to do about half of a double take (well, a take, I guess you would call it) at the sight of me and he said, "Oh, hi, I'm looking for Raylene Turner?" When I didn't answer instantaneously, he added, "I thought you were her at first. I'm her husband?"

I actually felt my back stiffen. It was the unexpectedness of it all. It was the man who had thrown my cousin over for Shirley Jack Lazarus. It was the voice—a car salesman's voice, but southern. It was the head-to-toe-and-back-again sweep of his eyes.

As dryly as I could manage, I said, "Oh, you're Buck."

"Yeah, that's me."

I told him Raylene had gone to the grocery store and would be back in a few minutes. When he asked if he could come in and wait, I graciously said, "Well, uh, okay."

Suddenly, realizing he was expecting a Jamie of a different gender, I panicked at the idea of introducing myself, and launched into a steady stream of chatter to divert any questions regarding who I might be. He sat on the couch while I blathered away about how Raylene was out, should be back any minute, and wouldn't she be surprised, etc., etc. While I went through my contortions, he sat so comfortably, so quietly, so smilingly, that he only spurred me on to more insipid inanities: Do you think it's going to rain? Ever been to San Francisco before? Oh, no? Oh, you'll love it. Oh, where are my cigarettes? I thought I had some cigarettes around here, blah, blah, blah. He said he didn't smoke, and I said, well, I did, and he wouldn't mind if I ran out to the corner grocery and bought a pack, would he?

He took advantage of this brief break in my hysterical spiel to say, why no, of course not, and by the way, I sure did look a lot like Raylene. Who was I anyway?

"I'm Jamie," I squeaked as I walked out the door and shut it quietly behind me.

At Garcia's Liquors, I dragged out the purchase of cigarettes for as long as humanly possible (toyed with the idea of switching brands, turned purse inside out to obtain correct change, struck poses in the shoplifting mirror, read Mr. Garcia's palm, admired wallet photos of his grandchildren, etc.). Then I trudged back home and was happy to see that Raylene had returned. I retired quietly to the kitchen but not before catching the look of sheer horror that Buck gave me as I ambled past.

So she had told him.

I slunk out to the back porch and sat there playing with the cats for a few minutes. Then I got out my lipstick and decided to make myself pretty and serve Cokes because, by God, this was my house and I was not gonna hide in it—from anybody. Buck looked at his shoes as I passed out Cokes all around. Then I sat down and started that nervous gabbing again—this time about my travels in the Orient. Raylene seemed a little surprised at my verbosity, but maybe also a little relieved to have a break from holding up her end of what had to be a strained conversation. Buck began to come

241

around. He listened, occasionally asking appropriate questions. After Raylene got her money from him and gave him the bum's rush, we straightened the house a little and got ready for the evening's madhouse. I paused in the scrubbing of a frying pan to ask, "Well, did you explain to him? About me, I mean."

She said, "Oh yeah, sure. Why?"

I said, "I just wondered."

Raylene declared it was high time to wash the windows, and although I was less than enthusiastic about the project, she found vinegar and newspaper and went to work on every window and mirror in the house. I finally joined her at the windows overlooking the street and made a few halfhearted swipes while she hummed something that sounded like "Ruby, Don't Take Your Love to Town" in lieu of talking.

When Paco, looking slick in a new leather jacket, rang the doorbell half an hour before opening time, I was happy to see even him and didn't bother to pretend otherwise. I opened the door with a flourish and said, "Come in!"

He looked a little mystified at my high spirits. "You're in a good mood. Much better than usual. You know what I mean?" This he said with a sense of wonder, and not without good reason, as he has so rarely been on the receiving end of my more lighthearted humors of late. It's my way of punishing him for past transgressions.

He strolled in, giving the place considered nods of approval, as if making an inspection tour. "The house looks good," he said. And it does, rather. At the insistence of Raylene and Aquanetta a couple of days before, I broke open a box of ancient souvenirs and we spent an afternoon utilizing the contents in a frenzy of redecoration. Or make that decoration, as redecoration implies that the place was decorated to begin with. On the previously bare walls we put up a couple of travel posters picturing sunny, idyllic views of Morocco and Mykonos. From somewhere, Aquanetta dug up a tacky calendar depicting the Golden Gate Bridge and taped it to a kitchen wall. And a red shawl from Turkey is draped over the back of the couch neatly covering a couple of places where the cotton stuffing peeks out. Aquanetta wanted to distribute a few little artifacts and curios—fake pre-Columbian statuettes, fake Fabergé eggs, fake Lladro figurines—around the place, but I drew the line at displaying anything that would fit easily into a pocket. However, the place does look somewhat more colorful, somewhat more fit for human habitation, somewhat less like the Tijuana drunk tank.

"You know what, Jamie? *Sabes qué?*" Paco turned to me with narrowed eyes, "You got good taste. *Sabor muy buena.* You know what you need? You need some money. You know what I mean? I bet you could make this place look like *un palacio.* You know what I mean?"

Oh, sniff, sniff, could that be the vapors of a pie-in-the-sky scheme I smell drifting down the pike? Or possibly the fumes of a felony?

"What've you got, Paco? Another dope deal?"

"Oh, Jamie . . ."

"Oh, Paco. What is it this time?"

Although Raylene was in the kitchen banging pots and pans around, he moved his head up next to mine and said, "Can I talk to you alone?"

Felony, I decided. We went out on the front porch and sat on the steps. The hard-jawed Paco took my hand and said, "Yeah, Jamie, it's dope."

I didn't reply. In any way, shape or form.

"You remember Chuy," he said.

Again, I chose to remain silent. In fact, I began to think of my face as something made of granite, something impervious and oblivious to the sands of time as well as to the slings and arrows of the present. He seemed to be searching my face for a reaction, but I wasn't playing along.

"Jamie, you are not listening to me," he pleaded. "This is a really, really big deal. You know what I mean? I know you don't want to get mixed up with no dope, but this is a lot of money we're talking about. A lot, Jamie."

I bit. "How much?"

He inched a little closer. "Jamie. We're talking eighty thousand, maybe a hundred thousand dollars. You know what I mean? It's stuff that Chuy brought up from San Diego."

"For an investment of how much?" Just curious.

"About two thousand," he whispered, while I watched Anita disappear (by degrees) around the corner.

"Boy, you never stop, do you?" I said. But I was vaguely, and almost unconsciously, translating one hundred thousand dollars into goods and services, the way one does when a large sum of money is mentioned. I added,

"Paco, you could spend that money real fast in San Francisco. Maybe a year. Maybe two."

Paco's face tightened defiantly. He said, "No. I will not be stupid. I know how to spend that money. In Veracruz, where my godmother lives. I will be ready for life, Jamie. You know what I mean? Ready for life. *Lista para la vida.*"

I said, "And what about my part of the profits, Paco?"

He said, "Everything's fifty-fifty. You gimme the money and I do the action, take the danger. You know what I mean? Fifty-fifty."

"What would you do with fifty thousand dollars in Mexico?" I asked him.

He leaned back all dreamy-eyed and expansive, the way one gets when asked how one would dispose of a large sum of money.

He said, "I will give my mother some money. Maybe she will buy a house. And I will give some to my godmother. I will start a business. Maybe I will have a little fruit store where you can buy *melónes* y *melocotónes*. I will be the boss."

I thought about Paco's life here in *El Norte*. A life on the edge in every way, no concern beyond the next meal or the next bed or the next immigration officer. That kind of life takes place on an urban battleground, and the battle is just to remain standing, just to keep your wits about you. Which Paco did very well. So what if the urban guerrilla has to break a few of the white man's laws to survive? I thought of stories Paco had told me about his childhood in Mexico, about him and his uncle pushing a dead car twelve miles into town in the rain, about a scar he showed me on his toe, which was bitten by a rat while he slept on a pile of straw in a barn. Certain planetary dues had been extracted, it seemed to me. In fact, I thought it would be fine if a lot of money dropped into his lap, but count me out.

"I'm sorry, Paco, but I just can't."

"But, Jamie-eee, it's the chance of a lifetime, you know what I mean?"

To begin with, I told him, he must be nuts if he thought I would enter into any kind of a deal whatsoever with the vile and wicked Chuy.

"No, no, no, Jamie. I deal with Chuy. You don't have to see him, don't have to talk to him!"

I told him to save his breath because even if all other systems were go, I still didn't have the money.

"Maybe Raylene?" he asked hopefully.

"Nope," I said, trying for a tone that would put a lid on the conversation. It was a tone I found myself using quite frequently with Paco, a tone that had gained some authority with repetition. He cocked his head and looked so dejected that I put a hand on his knee and said, "Don't worry, Paco. Somebody will come along with some money."

After a while he said, "You're right, Jamie, I will get the money somewhere. From somebody. You know what I mean?"

"Yes, I know what you mean."

"Maybe one of your guests?"

My rueful smile became a rueful laugh as I tried to picture one of my street urchins ponying up a couple of thou. Paco laughed too, in a staccato burst, but said, "You never know. *Nunca sabes. Nunca sabes.*"

"That's right," I said, opening the door for the night's first group of bachelors, "You never know. *Nunca sabes.*"

nineteen

I didn't sleep so well the night after Buck's visit. I tossed and turned and thought, not about me and Buck and all our years together, but about what my life would have been if I had never met Buck, about how it was going to be without Buck, about the weight one person can add to another person's life for better or worse. I took a walk the next day all by myself. The day was bright and cool in that San Francisco way and I set out a little after noon strolling along with no thought as to where I was going, except to try to stick to streets that were reasonably flat, which is not the easiest thing to do in that city. One of these walks where you try to set your mind in order, at least temporarily, by means of looking at scenery, breathing in the new and breathing out the old. I wandered up South Van Ness, where the classy-looking Victorian homes and gas stations and fast-food joints are all jumbled together in a scatterbrained way that's sort of cheerful if you allow it to be, and sort of depressing if you don't. I took a right at Market and browsed through the vegetable stalls at the Civic

Center Plaza and daydreamed about living on a little produce farm somewhere with Armando. Early to bed, early to rise. Oh, yes, a straw-hatted Armando, leaning on a rake, dabbing the sweat from his brow with a handkerchief as I skip out the screen door with an ice-cold pitcher of lemonade for him . . . oh, my!

So, I traipsed on down Market Street, past the hordes of tourists and homeless people, the apple-cheeked young people in suits who work in the financial district, the bicycle messengers, the rich, the poor, the haughty, the humble, till I got to the Ferry Building, where I stopped to catch my breath. I sat on the dock and breathed in the salty air and watched two skinny little boys throw a Frisbee back and forth in a little patch of green.

My life would work out, it dawned on me. How could it not? Just a matter of putting one foot in front of the other. Why had I been so tied up in knots lately? It was Buck. Buck had been the issue, I realized. And now he, I realized suddenly, was a nonissue. So that's what my rambling little walk was all about. I had a little money now. I would simply go to Seattle in July, make up with Armando, maybe resume my bullet woman duties . . . or maybe not. I would just let it happen, whatever was in store for me. I remembered something Aquanetta had said about worry: that it should not be confused with preparation.

With my mind a clean slate, I wandered on down the waterfront till I got to Fisherman's Wharf. The place was crammed with people in vacation outfits and attitudes. I edged my way into a crowd surrounding a juggler, a young man dressed all in black-and-white polka dots. To look at him, you would have thought this young man was playing out his life's ambition this very moment, just keeping a half dozen apples in the air. I thought, that's how I want to be. That's just how I want my life to be. I want to keep any number of apples in the air and I want to be *there* while it's happening and never lose my smile. It dawned on me that lately my life was more tied up with the past and the future than the right now. When the juggler's girlfriend passed the hat, I gave her a dollar, and started to drift off with the rest of the people. A feeling in the back of my legs told me my walk was over. I caught a Van Ness bus and headed back to the Mission. My seatmate was a growly old lady in a platinum blond wig, who had thirty-seven grandchildren and a charm bracelet representing the birth of each and every one, which she proceeded to show me. By the time I got home I had oohed and aahed till I was out of breath. I was pretty well all in as I trudged up the steps of Jamie's house, but my day was far from over.

I am not a hysterical woman, though I suppose, as a woman who shot her husband in the heat of passion, I have to qualify that remark by saying I reserve the right to a little healthy bucking and snorting when provoked to the end of my patience. Or taken by rude surprise. Which was the case when I walked into Jamie's house the day after Buck's visit, closed the door behind me, and confronted on the coffee table three feet away . . . an *armadillo.* Well, what could I do but scream? Bloody murder! I jerked that door open and ran outside, then peeked through the crack and hollered for Jamie. And here she came, sauntering up in her flip-flops.

"Good *Lord,* Raylene!"

"Tell me that thing's not alive, Jamie."

"It's a *purse,* Raylene," she said, like, ha, ha, silly *you.*

"Oh," I said, and eased back inside. "Whose?"

Jamie cocked her head in the direction of the kitchen. "Hers," she said.

There, sitting at the table in the cutest little sailor dress I've seen in recent years—in fact, the only little sailor dress I've seen in recent years—sat that beloved star of the airwaves and revival tents, Ms. Shirley Jack Lazarus. Looking at me through eyes narrowed against a thin stream of cigarette smoke that she was hissing out. Had her hair dyed the color of a Sunkist orange and ratted to the size and shape of a bowling ball. She sat behind a glass of iced tea which was about as big as she was and showed her teeth in a way that didn't really remind me too much of a smile. We stared at each other for a few seconds, and I'll have to give her credit for not flinching. When she didn't say anything, I figured it was my move.

"Shirley Jack, what the fuck are you doing in my house?" I asked politely.

"I *love* those earrings!" she squealed, talking about the green dice earrings that Aquanetta had given me.

I encouraged her to vacate the premises by promising to kick her ass up between her shoulders unless she was gone by the time I counted to ten.

"You look great, Raylene. Seriously!"

I said, "Are we having the same conversation here?" I shot a look at Jamie, who leaned against the counter and did a hand-on-chin innocent bystander routine. "Jamie," I said, "does this sound like two people engaging in a little social chitchat?"

Jamie said, "Uh . . ."

Shirley Jack giggled as only she can giggle and said, "Now, Raylene, you stop that right now. Why, I'd be *ashamed.*"

The *boldness* of the woman! When I think back from where I am now, I have to admit that Shirley Jack was not an unworthy opponent. We're talking about a woman here with plenty of nerve.

"Ashamed?" I said. "*You* would be ashamed? I don't think so, Shirley Jack. I don't think you know what the word means."

She took the manner of a patient and good-natured grammar school teacher whose unruly students had finally pushed her just a little too far. "Now, Raylene, I want you to sit down right here beside me because we need to talk." And she said it just so brisk and businesslike, patting the table beside her, that I found myself sinking into the chair. In a grudging way, mind you.

"Jamie, could I have a glass of that tea?" I said, because my mouth felt a little cottony all of a sudden. Jamie said, "Sure," and not a word was spoken by anyone as she walked to the refrigerator, filled a glass with ice cubes, poured the tea, and set the glass before me. You would have thought the survival of this small group depended on my getting that life-preserving glass of tea.

I took a long drink of tea, zeroed in on Shirley Jack, and thought to myself, Okay let's deal with the *right now.*

I said, not in the friendliest of tones, "All right, let's talk."

Shirley Jack seemed to settle herself a little more comfortably in her chair, recrossed her legs, took another sip of tea. No hurry.

"Don't this beat all?" she said, shaking her head and making a sad little smile at the corners of her mouth.

"What exactly?" I said.

"Well, *this!*" she said, opening her arms, her palms up. "I mean us three classmates meeting up again after all these years, and"—she gave Jamie a long look—"the circumstances."

My back went up at the idea of this woman describing us as being any kind of her "mates," but I didn't see any point in pursuing the subject.

"What circumstances are we talking about here?"

"Well," she said, "I mean . . . isn't Jamie the prettiest thing? Just as pretty as a picture." She sniffed so prim and proper I wanted to reach across the table and help myself to a handful of her Sunkist hair.

I said, "Is that why you came over here, Shirley Jack? To get a good look at my cousin?"

"Well," she said, "I'll have to admit, this is sort of new to me, and, yes, I was curious when, ah, when Buck told me about Jamie. Well, after *all*, we were classmates." That word again. "We were *buddies!*"

Well, I had to gasp at that one. "No, Shirley Jack, you and Jamie were not buddies. Ever."

Jamie had tuned out. She sat all glassy-eyed and smoked one of Shirley Jack's cigarettes and I had the feeling I was all alone with the famous preacher's wife.

"Oh, Raylene!" She leaned in to be closer to both of us and said, "You know what? It takes all kinds. That's what I always say. It takes all kinds. And I think that's just fine. Just *fine,*" she hastened to assure us, even going so far as to reach over and pat Jamie's hand. "And doesn't she look fabulous?"

She went on for a while about Jamie's good taste in her clothing and makeup and whatnot while my hands clenched and unclenched around my glass of tea, which I pretended was Shirley Jack's white (and slightly crepey, I was happy to note) throat.

Tuckered out as I was from my afternoon ramble, and seeing as Jamie was not the least bit interested in holding up her third of the conversation (in fact, she seemed to be there in body only), I had very little energy to deal with Shirley Jack and decided to cut this meeting short. She was just winding down a story about how chummy she was with this gay hairdresser who worked on her television show ("Why, he's just like anybody else!") when I cut in and said, "All right, Shirley Jack, you've had a good look at Jamie and you ought to be satisfied. We've got work to do here and I think it's about time for you to leave."

"Wait just a minute, Raylene," she wheedled.

I stood up to terminate the interview. "You put that armadillo under your arm and you get out of here."

She said, "Raylene, will you please stop it. I want to talk to *you*. It's you I really came to see."

I said, "We don't have anything to talk about, Shirley Jack."

"Oh, yes, we do," she said.

"What?"

"We need to talk about a divorce," she said.

Why is divorce such a dramatic word or am I showing my age here? All I know is it hung in the air a second or two like something alive and kicking before I said, "Well, Shirley Jack, I believe that's between me and Buck, don't you?"

At this, Shirley Jack sat a little straighter in her chair, and if I had had any doubts about her status as a hard-nosed businesswoman, she erased them with a look like a laser beam.

"Raylene," she said like she was being real patient with me though I damn well didn't deserve it, "Raylene, let's talk woman to woman here."

I told her that was fine with me but make it snappy because I was a busy woman and I didn't have time for a stupid woman.

"Raylene, there's not but one thing I'm here for. I want to see Buck get out of this marriage as soon as possible and with a fair settlement."

I said, "A fair settlement? I'm not going to discuss any settlement with you! Why isn't Buck talking to me about this?"

She said, "I'll tell you why. Because you can pull the wool over Buck's eyes a lot easier than you can mine, honey." Just a-spittin', just like a cat.

I want to record here that upon the completion of this last sentence, the woman reached across the table to a box of toothpicks, grabbed one, shoved it into her mouth between a couple of front teeth and never took her eyes off of my face. Just for the record.

You know the expression "saved by the bell"? Well, I'll swear and be damned, the doorbell that rang at just that moment was all that saved Shirley Jack from a face full of Lipton's orange pekoe over ice. My fingers unclenched from around the glass and I watched Jamie get up and answer the door like perhaps I was expecting a package or something.

It was Paco. He came bursting into the room like the vice squad was in hot pursuit. He slammed the door behind him and leaned against it, all panting and pop-eyed.

"They're after me!" he said.

"Oh, God, what now?" said Jamie.

"Sshhhhh . . ." Paco put his finger to his lips.

Jamie crossed her arms and stood there in a very grim attitude. Paco gave her such a woebegone look that she began to soften and then he put his hands to his face and collapsed in laughter. I tiptoed to the kitchen doorway, with Shirley Jack right behind me.

"Just testing, just testing," he said, and he came dancing into the room, kissing Jamie's cheek and twirling her around to the window, where he pointed out a beat-up Plymouth he had just bought for fifty dollars down.

"My own car! My own wheels!" he yelled.

Then he pulled a bottle of champagne from the folds of his overcoat and announced it was his birthday and that he had a job as night clerk at a hotel a few blocks away. Not a very nice hotel, I assumed, from the face Jamie made. But Paco was excited about it and went on about being paid under the table and being able to sleep all day in his own room in the hotel. Looking on the bright side. While Jamie padded off to get glasses, Paco sang under his breath and threw his coat over a hook behind the door. I was just wondering how much celebrating had already taken place when he caught sight of me and this strange woman watching him from the doorway.

"Raylene! Baby!" he hollered. He kissed me on the cheek with a loud smack and whirled me around to where I was facing Shirley Jack. It was the look on her face—sort of a "Well, now, what's this?" look—that spurred me into action.

I yelled, "Paco! *Baby!* I've *missed* you!"

I pulled him closer and laid a rather serious kiss on his lips and managed to whirl him around to where Shirley Jack couldn't see the look on his face which translated to "What the hell's going on here?" Understandable since I had barely spoken half a dozen words to him before this. I hugged his upper arm and gazed at him with pure mouthwatering lust. And I must say it didn't take Paco long to recover his cool; I think this kid was used to being admired.

"And who's this?" he said, clasping his hands behind his back and nodding at Shirley Jack in a kind of debonair way.

Before I could say this is nobody you want to meet, my classmate and buddy had stepped forward with a *curtsy,* mind you, and introduced herself with the sweetest little old Bayou Country smile you ever did see. Still like a cat, but one that had just lapped up a fresh bowl of half-'n-half.

"My name is Shirley Jack. Shirley Jack Lazarus," she said with just the quickest glance from under those modest black spider eyelashes to see if the name meant anything to him.

Which it did, I'm afraid. Paco's eyes flew open and he swept them over Mrs. Lazarus from head to toe. Caught off guard, he rattled off a few sentences in Spanish which any fool could have interpreted as something along the lines of "Not the one and only! Not my idol! Not my heart's desire!" When he calmed down enough to express himself in English, he told her he had *loved* her shows, both the *Gospel Jubilee* and her exercise program, *Kickin' Back with Shirley Jack;* that he used to watch her and Dr. Lazarus every day on a station out of El Paso; that once Dr. Lazarus had cured a neighbor of his in Mexico of—how you say?—athlete's foot, and on and on. Shirley Jack hung on his every compliment; had that fierce little red mouth drawn up into a cooing little bow like a society lady at the Beaux Arts Ball. Every now and again I would feel her glittery little eyes lighting on me to make sure I appreciated the fruits that stardom had dropped into her deserving lap. For my part, I was still making with the adoring looks while Jamie poured champagne all around. Our prima donna of the airwaves looked from me to Jamie and back again and said, "Y'all know who he re- minds me of? A little?"

"Who?" we asked in unison.

"Nick," she whispered. "Nick Tarkington."

Jamie shrugged, but I was quick to agree. "Oh, yes," I said. "That's what I've always thought, too. He's just like Nick." And I took the opportunity to give Paco's ear a little bite.

"Around the eyes," she said.

I looked at Paco's eyes and said, "Yeah, you're right. Around the eyes. Just like Nick."

I think it was at that moment Shirley Jack picked her next con- quest: Paco. As soon as she took one good slug of champagne, I said, "Shirley Jack, that's enough champagne for a woman of the cloth. I hate to rush you off, but we have work to do here." I had had just about as much of her as I could stand, and Paco's fawning over her celebrity status didn't make her any easier to stomach.

"Well, I guess I know when I'm not wanted," she said, giving a perfect imitation, for Paco's benefit, of a gracious celebrity lady tak- ing her leave of a rude and overbearing autograph hound, and, to my relief, she did get up and make as if to leave. After a few pleasantries which included a gentle pat on Paco's smiling face, and, believe it or not, air kisses for me and Jamie, she stopped at the door and said to me, "Well, I'll see you later, Raylene. We'll talk." A very pointed look she gave me.

I didn't say a word, but the second that door closed, I bolted for the broom in the corner. Jamie saw me and let out a whoop as she pulled out a drawer and grabbed a fork. I rushed to the front door, up- ended the broom, and slapped a wet dish towel over the straw. When

Jamie plunged the fork in, I hugged her and we both cackled. I felt so clever I all but danced a jig.

"*Qué pasa?*" Paco wanted to know. Should I smile or not, his face was saying over the top of a champagne glass.

"It's an old family custom," Jamie said, which must have been all the explanation Paco needed, judging from the way he went back to guzzling champagne. Then he said, "Why you don't like Shirley Jack, Raylene? She's a nice lady, a pretty lady. You know what I mean?"

I was just about to say something about her staying out on 101 to steer clear of the vice squad when Paco's words stopped me in mid-wisecrack. I started to set him straight, then decided what the hell, if he thinks she's pretty, okay, that's fine. But, I'll tell you what. If Paco had not made that remark I could tell the entire story of my life without mentioning Shirley Jack's looks, although, like it or not (and I do not), Shirley Jack Lazarus is an important supporting character who cannot be ignored (as much as I'd like to). It is not, in fact, my habit to be too hard on other women's looks because, number one, don't think I haven't overheard mean-spirited remarks about my own looks that hurt my feelings, and number two, I think women who knock other women for their lack of beauty probably go to hell when they die because women suffer enough here on earth from the way men put them down.

All right, having said all that, just let me say this: when we talk about Shirley Jack, we are not talking about a pretty woman. I know I already said she won a beauty contest, took the world of television gospel by storm, stole every boyfriend and husband I ever had practically, and captured little Paco's heart, but trust me, in the beauty department, Shirley Jack is not about to run Elizabeth Taylor out of business. First of all, it's not that hard for a girl to win a beauty contest in Lake Gladys, Louisiana (especially with the likes of me as the competition); there's enough beauty contests to go around in the state of Louisiana so that nearly everybody wins once, plus I wouldn't call the Poultry Princess a top-of-the-line beauty contest, since looks counted second to creative use of chicken feathers. All right, and about being a TV star—think about it—can it be that tough? I'm surprised that some talent scout from Hollywood hasn't discovered me by now. I feel like I've got as much going for me as some of them you see up there. Which brings us to the man-stealing issue, and this is for you men out there, because I know you women don't have to be told the following fact—are you ready? Okay: A woman does not—I repeat, does not—have to be pretty to steal another woman's man. All she's got to be is available. And unscrupulous. (You young, inexperenced girls might do well to write that down someplace where you see it several times a day. Like maybe the palm of your hand.) And as for Paco, he was just at that age when even the tackiest, and I do mean the tackiest, stars are dazzling. Plus, as it became clear soon enough, the fact that a TV star might have some money was never too far from Paco's thoughts.

It was Paco who found the gold cigarette lighter Shirley Jack left behind on the kitchen table. He picked it and threw it up in the air a couple of times.

"It's nice," he said. "You know what I mean? I guess she'll be back for this pretty soon."

"No, she won't," Jamie said, shaking her head.

Paco asked where she was staying and I told him.

He said, "I'll take it to her. I'll take it to the Econo Gardens. I've got a friend that works out there."

Jamie and I couldn't think of a good reason why he shouldn't take the lighter to her, and we didn't try very hard, so Paco, after a little more champagne and a lot more chatter, left in his new car with the lighter.

May 15

There's lots to tell, dear diary. I slept in today while Raylene took off with a couple of the boys from Veracruz to dance in the *Carnavál* parade. I deserved the rest. Big Victor's birthday party, which I had reluctantly agreed to, went till almost four o'clock this morning. Music, tequila, copious amounts of *mota* that somebody brought up from Oaxaca, one fistfight, one broken window, a few speckles of blood on the wall. Raylene was up and at 'em at seven, cleared my bachelors out, and left me blessedly alone. For maybe two hours. Then Aquanetta showed up at the door in one of her leather-'n-lace split-up-the-side ensembles, the very thing for early morning wear in the Mission. She was frantic to be brought up-to-date on Raylene's life, having gotten just the skimpiest details on the phone the night before while I was cradling the phone to my ear and mixing margaritas at the same time.

"I want the complete and uncensored account," she announced this morning, while I staggered around trying to make coffee. "What'd he look like?"

"Who?"

"The *husband!*"

"Oh, all right. Not bad looking at all, actually."

"What'd she look like?"

"Who?"

"Shirley Jack!"

"Oh, you know what Shirley Jack looks like. Like a petite Robert Mitchum with lipstick. You must have seen her on TV while you were flipping channels sometime."

An hour and a pot of coffee later we were still dissecting Raylene's husband and his paramour when the doorbell rang again. Paco this time, gleaming smile, looking gorgeous in jeans and a new red corduroy shirt, wanting to take us for a spin in his new car. Aquanetta jumped up from the table and spilled her coffee, so effusive was her greeting.

"Paco! Darling!"

She couldn't be more favorably disposed toward Paco these days and the reason is simple. She owes her new Tuesday night show at Esta Noche, "Aquanetta's Follies," to Paco's influence with Ooky, the bar manager. She had nagged Ooky for months to let her present her own show, but to no avail until Paco, Ooky's newest crush, offered to help her out with a little pillow talk. The three of us slid into the front seat, me in the middle, as the big-hair look that A. currently sports could block the driver's vision. Paco went into a long explanation of the car's funky smell, something involving brake fluid and dog puke. He peeled rubber halfway down Balmy Alley, and said he wanted to drive out to the beach, just wanted to see how fast he could make it. He couldn't stop talking about Shirley Jack.

"She *likes* me, Jamie. You know what I mean?"

Aquanetta, of course, cut through the hubris in her usual fashion; "You gonna fuck 'er?"

"No! Yuk! *No me gusta las mujures!*"

"Then what difference does it make whether she likes you?" I asked.

Paco cruised a couple of telephone repairmen at the corner as he turned it on two wheels and said, "Think about it, Jamie."

I thought about it and said, "Oh. I see."

"Tell me," said Aquanetta.

"Paco needs two thousand dollars. For a top-secret project. He thinks Shirley Jack's good for it."

"Not unless he fucks her," Aquanetta said.

Paco went into his "yuk" routine again, trying for a laugh, but Aquanetta pressed onward. "You wouldn't do it for two thousand dollars? Hell, for two grand, I'd fuck 'er and do 'er hair."

That got Paco's attention. "Really? Really? Oh, I don't think so. Not me."

"She's funny. She kissed me on the cheek. She kissed me *here* one time," he said, pointing to his lower lip. "She fooled around and joked. And her husband? He was there! In the same room! He saw everything. He don't care! You know what I mean? He don't care!"

A. was intent on a faraway cargo ship that just hove into view as we came over a hill, but I hastened to set Paco straight. "No, Paco," I said. "That was not Shirley Jack's husband. The man you saw at the Econo Gardens happened to be Raylene's husband."

Paco said, "Huh? What? Raylene's husband? No. Raylene's husband is Dr. Lazarus? No!"

He held his head tilted toward me as if waiting for reassurance on this weighty matter.

"No, Paco," I said, speaking directly into his ear. "Raylene's husband is not Dr. Lazarus. Raylene's husband is named Buck. Buck is the person you met at the Econo Gardens."

Paco slammed on his brakes at a red light and leaned forward on the steering wheel. He looked annoyed.

"Look, Jamie, I *know* Dr. Lazarus. I've seen him on television many, many times. *Muchas veces.* You know what I mean?" He lifted his chin with a fine show of indignation.

Aquanetta and I exchanged looks while somewhere off in the distance a foghorn mooed its lonely warning. Before either of us could speak, Paco continued, "I met the guy named Buck, too," he said. "You mean that's Raylene's husband? The guy at the Econo Gardens?"

I said, "Well, ex-husband is more like it."

Paco said, "Oh," and twisted around in his seat while he mumbled to himself in Spanish. "I didn't know that. He's a nice guy, Buck. You know what I mean? I think he's much nicer than Dr. Lazarus."

"I wouldn't be at all surprised," I said vaguely, while trying to figure out the Econo Gardens scenario.

Paco went on wide-eyed as if imparting vital information. "Dr. Lazarus is not like he is on TV, you know what I mean?"

Aquanetta leaned across me to inquire, "Didn't he speak in tongues, darling?"

Paco said, "No. He speaks very plain. Very clear. *Muy claro*. You know what I mean? Shirley Jack, I'll give you one more chance. Shirley Jack, this is my last offer. Shirley Jack, you're ruining us."

Seeing he had our undivided attention, Paco downshifted into second and huddled over the steering wheel kamikaze-style as he roared the final couple of blocks to the beach.

"Well, where does Buck fit in with all this?" I asked when we came to a stop with a general shuddering all around of both car and passengers.

"Excuse me?" Paco cocked an eyebrow at me, pretending to keep one eye on the cargo ship, silently sliding toward points oriental.

Aquanetta, brisk as only she can be brisk, took charge.

"Okay," she said. "Let's take it from the top, Paco. You went to the Econo Gardens to take back Shirley Jack's lighter, right?

"Right."

"You knocked on the door and she opened it, right?"

"No," said Paco. "First, I went to see my friend Oscar. He's from El Paso. He works in the office at the Econo Gardens. Old friend of mine."

"Okay. So you said hello, how are you, to your friend Oscar, he told you what room she was in, you knocked on her door and she opened it, right?"

Paco looked at A. very levelly as she spoke and waited quietly for her to finish before saying softly, "No, Aquanetta, that's not right. That's wrong."

I said, "Tell us what happened, Paco. In your own words."

"Thank you," he said, and arranged himself into a comfortable story-telling position and leaned against the car door. "Okay," he said. "I drive to the Econo Gardens, right?"

"Right," said Aquanetta.

"In my new car, right?"

"Right," said A.

"I go into the office and talk to my friend, Oscar, right?"

"Right."

"We talk about long time, no see. He hugs me. He's very happy to see me. You know what I mean? My brother played on the same soccer team with Oscar in El Paso, right?"

A. and I nod dully.

"Okay. Oscar gives me a cup of coffee, asks me about my brother. Is Franco okay? Oh, he's married? Got a kid already? Wow. Stuff like that. You know what I mean? So we're talking, me and Oscar, and this guy walks in the office. Oscar says, 'Hi Buck,' and this guy says, 'Hi Oscar,' and he says hi to me too. Very friendly guy. You know what I mean? Oscar says, 'This is my friend, Paco, Buck,' and me and Buck shake hands and say how ya doin' and all that. Then, Oscar goes, 'Hey, Buck, when you going to Alaska?' "

"Alaska?" I said.

"Alaska?" Aquanetta said.

"Yeah. Alaska," Paco said. "Oscar goes, 'You need somebody to help you drive, don't you, Buck? Take Paco. Paco wants to go to Alaska.' This is how Oscar is. Always bullshitting. You know what I mean? So I say, no way, not me, I'm not going to Alaska."

"Alaska?" I said again.

"Alaska?" A. said again.

"Yeah. Alaska," Paco said again.

The day was fairly warm on the usually windswept beach and Aquanetta suggested we get out of the car and walk on the sand. She kept her high heels on and resembled some kind of big awkward bird pulling them out of the sand as she ambled merrily along. The three of us walked along with our heads close together, or as close as A.'s coiffure would allow, while Paco continued his account of the doings at the Econo Gardens. He said that Buck, after a few minutes of chitchat and kidding with Oscar, bought a candy bar and left in his car.

Then Oscar lowered his voice to a confidential tone and said, "Hey, guess who's staying here, man? You won't believe it!"

Paco pretended to think hard and then snapped his fingers. "Shirley Jack Lazarus!" he said.

"How'd you know, man?"

"She's a friend of mine, man."

"No shit, man?"

"Sure, man, that's what I'm doing here. I came to see Shirley Jack. You know what I mean?"

"You gonna see her old man, too? Dr. Lazarus?"

"He's here too?"

"Just got in an hour ago."

Paco asked for the room number, but Oscar looked uneasy, said he had promised Shirley Jack not to tell anyone. However, just about that time, the door of the office opened and in breezed Ms. Lazarus in a silky pink bathrobe and apparently nothing else, holding an unlighted cigarette. She asked Oscar for a light, called him honey. Then Paco, who had been sitting behind a potted palm, bobbed up and lit her cigarette with a flourish and an "At your service, madam."

She was surprised to see him, very happy, remembered his name.

"Come on down for a visit," she said, taking his hand and pulling him out the door before he had a chance say yea or nay. Paco was feeling somewhat nervous at the prospect of meeting up with her husband, and if Dr. Lazarus was not in evidence, he was even more nervous at the prospect of being alone in a motel room with Shirley Jack clad in a bathrobe *solamente*. However, looking back at Oscar, who was grinning and winking, he followed her as a face-saving maneuver, scuffling along, wishing he had mailed her the lighter. With Paco in tow, she opened the door to her room to reveal Dr. Lazarus, who was in midpace and midsentence as if he had not stopped pacing and talking the whole time she was out of the room.

"Who's this?" he growled.

Shirley Jack introduced Paco as simply "one of my best San Francisco friends," obviously goading the good reverend to a show of temperament. However, Dr. L. apparently found it in his best interest to remain calm, and told Paco that he was glad to meet him, but he needed to speak alone with his wife. Which was fine with Paco, who would have fled out the door had not the reverend's wife caught him by the shirttails. She insisted that Paco stay, pushed him into a cushioned chair, on the arm of which she perched herself to smoke and fondle her San Francisco friend while the reverend ranted.

Paco said, "It was like on television. You know what I mean? He was *preaching* to Shirley Jack. Yelling. But she don't care. She was too busy with me. She hug. She kiss. She pinch. She squeeze. She mess my hair. You know what I mean? And he don't do nothing. Just holler. But not about me."

The upshot of Paco's story was that Dr. Lazarus was concerned about one thing: the fact that Shirley Jack was running around all over the country with Buck, a married man. But Dr. L's problem made little or no impression on Paco. He had his own agenda.

"She likes me!" he exulted as we slogged through the sand. When that made zero impression on Aquanetta and me, he added, "And she's rich."

Aquanetta said, "Well, if she's so rich, why is she holing up at the Econo Gardens? There are better places to lie low in San Francisco. In fact, there's none quite as bad."

"Yeah," I said, "and why did she and Buck drive across the country on Raylene's money? Why didn't they just fly if she's all that flush? And why is she interested in Buck's divorce settlement?"

But these practical and logical questions were of no interest to Paco, who fell silent as he squatted and picked up sand dollars, cleaning them off on his sleeve, pocketing a few of the more perfect ones and sending the ragged ones skimming across the water. Aquanetta plopped to the ground and drew her knees up to her chest as she looked out over the water. She closed her eyes, breathed deeply, and muttered something about negative ions. I settled back on my elbows and wondered at the vastness of the watery world in front of me. Something about the back of Paco's smooth brown neck as he dug with a stick in the sand made him seem younger to me than ever before. At that moment, it was easy to write off his bad points as understandable little foibles, his cruelties as temporary deviations from the norm. Preoccupied by such thoughts, I was caught quite by surprise by his next words.

"Dr. Lazarus wants to see you, Jamie."

"I beg your pardon?" I said.

Aquanetta said, "He said, dear, that Dr. Lazarus—"

"I know what he said. I mean, uh, so Shirley Jack wasted no time in telling him about me, I'm sure. I'm sure they got a big kick out of that."

Paco said, "Yeah. She said, 'Paco is a good friend of Jamie's,' and Dr. Lazarus, he laughed, he said, 'Oh yeah? How good?' He said he was coming to see you. He said he didn't believe Shirley Jack. Said he had to see for himself."

"Well, tell him I charge admission," I said, as the same wind that had seemed so refreshing a moment before spattered my face with sand.

Paco said, "He said he never saw a girl that used to be a boy. He said he remembered you from many years ago."

"Yeah, I remember him too," I said sharply.

Paco stood up and brushed off his knees. "He said—"

I said, "Paco, I don't care what he said. Please don't tell me what he said. You don't even have to mention Dr. Lazarus again to me. And that goes for little Miss Shirley Jack, too."

"Look at that ship," said Aquanetta dreamily, shielding her eyes and looking out to sea, where the ship was just a dot on the horizon. "Don't you wish you were on it?"

"It's a cargo ship, Aquanetta," I said, my good humor officially terminated for the day.

She hoisted herself upward, teetered on those heels a moment, and began trudging up the beach. We piled into the car and got back on the road somewhat jerkily owing to Paco's lack of proficiency with the straight shift. Aquanetta fiddled with the radio dial till she got to the Spanish station where Paco hollered *"Aquí!,"* and we went racing down the coast to a snappy *norteño.*

Back at the Hole in the Wall, Aquanetta and I jumped out of the car and headed for the crowds lining Twenty-fourth Street, while Paco roared away to work. The *Carnavál* parade seemed to have started on time for once and we had missed the first few minutes of it. Standing in the third row of spectators, A. and I craned our necks to see what had already passed: a couple of politicians waving from convertibles, a brass band of little girls dressed in purple and gold; a group of sexy dancers in Aztec-flavored outfits; no Raylene. Swinging our hips to the beat of a passing group of percussionists, we inched forward, managing to insinuate ourselves into a position where, although we were still not on the front line, at least we were standing behind relatively short people. Watching a pushcart vendor wend his way through the crowd, I was only vaguely aware of a mass of orange hair in front of me. Then, I heard it speak. Or whine.

"I'm *hungry*, Buck. Buy me something."

With a great deal of coquettish indecision, Shirley Jack fingered every chocolate bar and bag of chips on the cart, finally choosing a box of lemon drops.

I whispered to Aquanetta, "That's her, that's Shirley Jack."

After a sharp intake of breath, Aquanetta fairly brayed, "You're kidding! And *that's* Buck?"

At the sound of her voice they both turned around. Well, all I could do was smile and make introductions and inane "small world" remarks. Buck, looking rather glum in a Hawaiian shirt, nodded and smiled nervously. His inamorata, after squealing my name loud enough to turn heads a block away, settled back and stuffed her face with lemon drops while she regarded Aquanetta dubiously. However, in all fairness, I will admit my friend's lace-up-the-side outfit was probably a design seldom seen on the evangelical circuit. We made small talk consisting mostly of Shirley Jack's complaints that Buck never took her anywhere. Finally, he said, "Aw, put a lid on it, Shirley Jack," and, with a pout, she turned back to the parade to watch a guy dressed as Uncle Sam walk by on stilts. I got the impression the honeymoon was over. The tension was relieved somewhat when Aquanetta pointed down the street and hollered, "There she is!"

Yes, indeed, it was Ms. Raylene Stout a-struttin', wearin' nuttin' but a button and a bow. Or very little more. Grinning deliriously, she pranced along in the very first row of a group of samba dancers. Waving her hands and shaking her behind, she acknowledged every whistle from the crowd as if it were directed to her alone.

"Where did she get that *outfit*?" Aquanetta asked enviously.

"She's gonna catch her death of cold," Shirley Jack offered sullenly, while Buck followed Raylene's advance with a look of sheer delight.

As she approached our corner, Raylene performed a cartwheel. Then, beaming at the applause she got, she did another one, coming to a standing halt face-to-face with Buck.

"Hi, honey!" he hollered impulsively.

Raylene, looking surprised but still not able to wipe away her smile, stammered, "Oh, hi!"

The band accompanying her group launched into a song with a fast staccato beat and Raylene, catching the rhythm with her shoulders, moved backward into the line of dancers. Or started to. First, I saw Shirley Jack's dainty hand flick outward, and then, Raylene, six feet away, fell on her ass. The lemon drops. It happened so quickly and her guilt was so obvious I couldn't contain myself. I was livid.

"You little bitch! You did that on purpose!" I yelled, while Buck turned to Shirley Jack to shout more or less the same words.

And she slapped him. And I slapped her. Aquanetta looked on with ill-concealed delight, along with several dozen strangers. Two male dancers helped Raylene up and she was off again, unbowed and unhurt, oblivious to the drama in our little group.

Holding her cheek, Shirley Jack looked at me in disbelief. "You *hit* me," she said. "You *morphodite!* You *hit* me!"

"You fucking well had it coming!" was the best retort I could come up with. I could hear some silly wag in the background laughing and saying, "Hit the bitch again," and I almost took him up on it.

Drawing herself up to her full five feet zero, Shirley Jack said, "Let me tell you something, you . . ." She sputtered and caught her breath. "If your cousin hadn't been shaking her naked ass in the middle of the street like the whore of Babylon . . ."

I snarled, "Don't call my cousin a whore, you . . ."

While I paused, trying to think of a name bad enough, Buck quite surprised me when he stepped between us, going practically nose to nose with Shirley Jack. He said, "Don't you call my wife a whore!"

With that, Shirley Jack's eyes narrowed and her mouth clapped shut. She stared him down for several seconds before squeaking, "Your wife, huh?"

Thrusting her nose in the air, she turned on her heel and parted, to the applause of several rowdy bystanders. I couldn't think what to say. Buck turned again to the parade but clearly the zest had gone out of the occasion. I looked to Aquanetta for guidance. She suggested we go up the street to Café Boheme for coffee. It seemed right to ask Buck to join us, so I did. He looked from me to Aquanetta and back again.

"Okay," he said, then smiled in a tentative way. "All right. Yeah, let's do that."

twenty

A couple of days went by after Shirley Jack's visit and she didn't come back. I can't say that she and Buck slipped my mind completely, but I did get busy job hunting, thinking I might make a little money doing something or other at least till I went back to the circus.

Then she called. The phone rang at two o'clock in the morning and it happened to be one of those rare times when we had our bachelors all settled in and bedded down and snoring by midnight. I might as well have been alone in the room for all the attention the ringing phone got from the others. I climbed over Jamie and several bachelors to answer it.

"Is this Raylene?" Drunk. The preacher's wife was drunk. I know drunk when I hear drunk. There's a real wide gap between drunk and perky.

"Yes it is." I can sound pretty unperky myself when I'm fresh out of bed at two o'clock in the morning.

Pause, pause, pause on her end. "Shirley Jack? Shirley Jack, is that you?" I said, not exactly holding out the hand of friendship.

"Yeah," she said. "Yeah." Then she said it one more time, like she was gathering her thoughts. I could hear music in the background. Some kind of C&W. Fairly loud, too. I could picture her in that little sailor dress standing at a pay phone in some dark and smoky bar.

Before she could say another word I cut her off. "Shirley Jack, let me tell you something. Number one, don't call me at two o'clock in the morning. Number two, don't call me when you're drunk. Number three, don't call me period." And I hung up and went back to bed.

Two minutes later the phone rang again. I bounded out of bed, mad this time, and reached the phone in one giant step.

"Shirley Jack?" I said.

"Yeah?"

"What do you want?"

"Is Buck there?"

I didn't answer.

"Raylene? Is Buck there?"

"No!"

She said, "That son of a bitch!" And she hung up.

I went back to bed, picking my way through the bachelors in the dark, almost breaking a leg as I stumbled over one guy who woke with a yelp that set up a temporary stir in the room. Safe again under the covers, I couldn't sleep. Where *was* Buck? Just curious, you know. Jamie had told me that he was planning to go to Alaska. And not necessarily with Shirley Jack. Did he take off already? I couldn't help but wonder what was going on in that glorious romance of the century. I thrashed around and pounded my pillow and tried to doze off, but it was one of those nights when my brain, so sluggish in the daytime, was as lively as a sack of cats.

It seemed like no one I knew these days had a stable and rooted life. I thought about Dot, how smart she was, how dependable, how her life—going to work, taking care of her folks, eating, sleeping, playing bridge, bowling, going to church, talking on the phone—how it made sense.

Then there was me and Armando and Jamie and Aquanetta and Paco and Buck and Shirley Jack and several other people I had come to know in San Francisco. I wondered where all of us sort of drifting people would be in a year's time, or in ten years' time. I looked out the window at the few dim stars that were visible through the buildings and the treetops and wondered just what the hell the planets were up to right now, what kind of gyrations they were putting themselves through to create so much turmoil down here in our world. I missed Carlotta suddenly, wondered what she was doing tonight, how her hair was coming along, how she and Wally were getting along. What advice would she give me now?

I got up at six and went down to the corner to get a paper while the coffee perked. I sat and looked over the news till one by one the bachelors got up and staggered into the kitchen. I felt energetic and really on my toes the way you do some mornings when you have only had a couple of hours sleep. While I stood at the stove frying up eggs, I got into a long conversation with one of the new boys, a Salvadorean named Carlos, about the chances of his ever returning to the coffee plantation in his country that he left five years ago.

"But why would you even want to return?" I said.

"It's my home!"

"But, Carlos," I said, "it's so dangerous. They've killed so many of your relatives. They've burned your house. . . ."

"But this country is not my *home,*" he said. "And things change."

I drank some coffee and thought about it. "But there's such a thing as starting over, Carlos. Or maybe not. Maybe you're right, Carlos."

He said, "I know I'm right."

I said, "I know you're young." And we left it at that, but as I served up the eggs and beans, I began to get the straw-hatted picture of Armando again. Maybe I'd wear a peasant blouse as I brought that lemonade out. And some of those flat-heeled sandals with the straps that crisscross your ankles.

There I was at my age, mooning about oatmeal cookies and picket fences like a high school sophomore. When I stopped to think about it, it struck me as kind of funny because when I was really in high school, nothing was more boring to me than the idea of "home." Like Carlos said, things change.

I was still in my dreamy early morning mood when Dr. Lazarus paid the social call that Jamie had warned me was on the agenda. A few of the more slow-moving and/or sociable bachelors were still gathered around the television when the doorbell rang about ten times in a row. That silly Paco, I thought, since he had promised to drop by and give me a lift to the grocery store. Since I was standing at the stove, whipping up a huge batch of fudge that I had promised Big Victor, I asked Carlos to answer the door. He went padding off and busy as I was with the constant stirring that fudge requires, I barely heard the front door open and close. I was throwing every bit of body English I could muster behind that wooden spoon, hell-bent on making fudge for once that didn't come out as sloppy as cake batter.

Out of the corner of my eye, I saw Carlos standing in the kitchen doorway.

"Raylene?" he said, stopping in the doorway just short of the fresh-mopped floor.

"Yeah?" I growled. I was all charm and graciousness, wiping my hair out of my eyes with the back of my hand, getting fudge on my face. I looked around and right behind sturdy little Carlos, Dr. Leroy Lazarus himself loomed in the doorway. There he was, wrapped in gray sharkskin from neck to ankle, grinning that twinkly grin so beloved to televangelism fans throughout the United States and Canada and Latin America.

"Raylene!" he hollered, and came striding lickety-split across the kitchen floor, fresh mopped or not. While he hugged me from behind, I just said, "Hi, Leroy," and kept stirring while I explained I was in the middle of something I couldn't interrupt and would he mind standing in the doorway since I had just mopped.

"Go right ahead, go right ahead, Raylene," he said, ever so gracious, and kept hugging.

Somebody turned off the TV and the guys watched from the other room as I twisted to one side, the better to get Leroy's hands off my behind, where they had come to rest after this oh-so-affectionate hug. I suggested again that he retreat to the doorway since the floor was wet and he did, nodding to the curious bachelors as he walked.

"Dr. *Lazarus?*" said Antonio, one of our regular bachelors, a faithful and committed couch potato, who always sat in front of the television from the time he got to Jamie's till bedtime. The voice he used to identify Shirley Jack's husband implied that the messiah was here at last and walking among us.

"Yep, that's me!" said Leroy Lazarus, and he got off a quick salute to Antonio. I wasn't sure whether the other bachelors recognized our visitor as a television celebrity or were just in some sort of awe at his presence, because this was something that Dr. Lazarus did have—presence. Or maybe what he had, it occurred to me as I noted the shiny reddish hair (much shinier and fuller and healthier-looking than I remembered), shiny eyes, shiny teeth (much more even and white than I remembered), shiny suit, and shiny shoes, could be called "sparkle." And sparkle, as any preacher or politician or used car salesman can tell you, can carry you a long way in life. Whatever he had, he did know how to use it, and the bachelors, not always the most reverent bunch, trained their respectful gazes on the good doctor like they were waiting for instructions from above.

I introduced Dr. Lazarus to the fellows and he swooped down on them in a flurry of handshakes and howdy-do's. A certain full-of-shitness had always had the upper hand in Leroy's personality, but today he outdid himself in the grinning and glad-handing department. He even autographed a book of matches for Antonio, not that Antonio had requested it. After he made his way around the group, Leroy turned to me and stopped short like he was surprised to see me standing there watching his routine.

"Look at this blond!" he said. "Look at this gorgeous blond. You make a mighty fine blond, Raylene. Ain't she something, boys?"

The guys tittered and shuffled their feet, all of a sudden shy in the presence of this celebrated holy man.

"Raylene! How many years? How many years has it been?" He

said, "Boys, I used to know this ole gal when she was the hopscotch champion of Lake Gladys, Louisiana."

The bachelors all looked at one another and smiled, wondering, I'm sure, what the hell kind of sport hopscotch was.

"Raylene, you look like a million bucks! You can tell when a woman's right with the Lord. Look at that face, boys, not a wrinkle on it." He leaned in a little closer. "Well, maybe if you held her down and put a magnifying glass up to her eyes, you might count a few crow's-feet, but overall, you look darn good, Raylene. Now how long has it been?"

Well, hell, what did I care how long it had been? But you know what? As much as I hate to, I have to admit that this constant explosion of gassy energy that Dr. Lazarus used for a personality put me a little off balance. I could have and probably should have said something along the lines of "Not long enough," which would not have been untrue nor improper considering the way this person I had never had any use for had barged into the house uninvited. However, rattled by the hurricane force of his nature, I just stood there over my pot of fudge, sort of hiding behind a thoughtful expression that anybody would have taken for a woman counting up the years. Before I could mumble some number, Leroy exploded again.

"Raylene! We've got to talk! We need to get down to brass tacks!" He looked around at the bachelors and sort of stage-whispered to me: "You reckon we could get a little privacy here?"

I told the bachelors I'd see them later, since it was past time for them to be gone anyway. I pointed to the coffeemaker on the counter near Leroy and invited him to pour himself a cup. He went on a few minutes about what a "mighty pretty place" San Francisco was, then stood poised with his coffee cup halfway to his lips like somebody seized by a sudden thought.

"Where's Jamie?" he hollered like he was addressing me from the pulpit. Then he lowered his voice to a confidential tone. "Is it true what Shirley Jack tells me about Jamie? Now tell me she's kiddin', Raylene."

Instead of answering, I glanced over my shoulder at the walls of

Jericho behind which Jamie lay, probably wide awake. Leroy slapped his thigh and hollered, "Now this I've gotta see! This I've *gotta* see! Where is he anyway? I mean, where is *she* anyway? Is she here?"

Yuk-yuk. He laughed till he choked and I waited him out, stirring like crazy. He sputtered to a halt when he noticed I wasn't laughing.

I turned my face toward him and lowered my voice several notches. I said, "Is that why you came here? So you could make fun of my cousin?"

"Why naw, naw, naw, naw," he said. "You know me better than that, Raylene." His eyes darted around the room like he was doing some real heavy thinking.

I said, "Oh, do I?"

He dropped the subject and dove headlong into a new one: his wife and my husband. "I think it's a shame and a disgrace, Raylene," he said, winding up a few introductory remarks that got him so agitated he was wiping his face with a silk handkerchief that he pulled from his breast pocket. The whiff of Old Spice that came drifting across to me, the pinkie ring—oh, this was class.

"Well, that's something I don't know a thing about, Leroy. That's something I don't *care* a thing about. That's something that happened a long time. It's history to me, same as my so-called husband."

He said, "Well, *I* care about it, Raylene, and I'll tell you why." He spoke with so much preacher-force that I turned and looked at him leaning against the doorframe. He squinted his eyes like he was really going to give me the lowdown this time. "My marriage is money in the bank to me," he said. "It took me a long time to work up to where me and Shirley Jack are now in the evangelism business, and I don't intend to let her wreck everything we've slaved for."

I didn't mention any part he might have played in wrecking their business. I just said, "Well, I think that's a mighty romantic reason for wanting your wife back, Leroy, but you're on your own. I'm afraid I've washed my hands of Buck and Shirley Jack both."

"Does that mean you're getting a divorce?"

I shrugged. "Well, yeah, I guess that would be the logical next step. It's not something we've discussed so far, me and Buck, but I do know that I don't want to be married to him anymore."

"Well," he said, "I'm not finished being married to Shirley Jack yet. I'm not gonna kid you, Raylene. You and me have known each other too long. Shirley Jack is a star. And don't think she don't like being a star, 'cause she does."

"I wasn't denying that," I said.

"And she wants to keep on being a star, you'd best believe."

I said, "I believe it."

"And the only way she's gonna keep on being a star is by keeping on being the wife of Dr. Leroy Lazarus."

"So?" I said. I turned off the stove and started searching in the cabinet for a platter to pour my mixture into. I was getting ready to whisk up his now empty coffee cup, tell him it was real nice to see him, and show him the front door.

"So you can divorce Buck, Raylene, but Shirley Jack is not about to mess up her good thing by parting from me. Why, she wouldn't be leaving just me, she'd be leaving fifty million adoring fans."

"Why is she doing this then?" I asked out of simple curiousity.

"Why is she running around all over the country with a married man? Raylene, I'm gonna level with you. Shirley Jack thinks she stands to gain some money if you divorce your husband."

"Well, she doesn't," I said.

"Don't underestimate Shirley Jack, Raylene. Just because she's not officially married to Buck don't mean she can't get her hands on whatever money he brings out of a divorce."

"There's no money, Leroy. When Buck and I get divorced, the financial settlement is going to be real easy to take care of, due to the lack of finances."

He gave me that squint again. Seemed like he was looking first into my left eye, then my right, then back to my left, and so on. Seemed like he was telling me that if there was the tiniest trace of a lie in my eyes he was damn well going to find it. "Well, that ain't what Shirley Jack thinks," he said.

"Well, I don't care what Shirley Jack thinks," I said.

"What about the house?"

I didn't answer till I finished pouring the steaming fudge into a big fish-shaped platter that I found way up on the top shelf of the cabinet.

"Leroy, if Shirley Jack can get Buck's sister out of that house, I'll give her half of it. However, I've got a question or two of my own for you."

"Shoot," he said. "You know me. My life's an open book."

"All right," I said. "What I want to know is this. Let's say I did have a little money. No, for the sake of argument, let's say I had a lot of money."

"All right," he said, and nodded.

"Leroy, what the hell difference would it make to Shirley Jack if there was money to be had from mine and Buck's divorce? All that money y'all have brought in over the years? That big old mansion in Houston that I've seen on TV? That private plane you come to Lake Gladys in? All those people out in television land that send you their Social Security checks every month?"

He looked down at the floor, frowned, crossed his arms, and said, "Well . . . all right, Raylene, I'll tell you. You may have heard about a little trouble I had down in Baltimore last fall?"

I nodded. The whole world knew about the Baltimore business, which involved the good doctor and the kiddy hookers.

"It was a nasty business. A setup all the way, of course."

"Of course," I said, and he looked up quick to check my face for signs of sarcasm, but he found nothing there except a general look of distaste, which I'm sure television evangelists get used to when they venture into the real world.

"Well, Raylene, I don't know if you've ever had any experience with bloodsucking lawyers. . . ."

"No," I said, "my experience with lawyers has been mighty sparse, I'm happy to say."

If he took offense, he was too wound up in what he was saying to show it. He slammed his fist into his hand. "Damn. They'll nickel-

and-dime you to death, Raylene. Always keep your nose clean so that you don't have to deal with 'em. That's my advice to you."

"Thank you," I said. "But, Leroy, I can't believe you can't afford to pay your lawyers. I mean all that money rolling in . . ."

"Well, there's been other setbacks, Raylene, just between you and me and the toaster," he said. We overextended ourselves on Shirley Jack's aerobics studio chain and my tour of South America last year didn't pay off the way we planned. Lord, those people are close with their money down there. Even the Christians, and believe me, you have to beat the bushes to find 'em down there. And then we had a little trouble with a bookkeeper dipping into the till and . . . The fact is, Raylene, Born Again Enterprises has been operating in the red for a long time now and I can understand Shirley Jack perking up at the whiff of some easy money . . . but what she don't realize is that we could pull ourselves out of this slump eventually if she'd just come on home and behave like a natural woman and wife."

The doorbell rang and when Jamie hollered "I'll get it!" from somewhere in the other room, I could see this part of our conversation was over.

Paco burst into the house, all bright-eyed and breathless. Having his own wheels for the first time had given the boy a new lease on life, it seemed like. Sure gave him a happy disposition.

"Hi, Raylene! Are you ready?" he said, and then stopped short at the sight of Dr. Lazarus.

"Oh! Hi!" he said. He looked a little puzzled and waited for Leroy to make the next move.

"Well, look who's here," said Leroy in such a hearty and friendly way that Paco's tense shoulders relaxed. Then he noticed that Leroy was talking to Jamie, who stood behind him.

"Hi, Leroy," Jamie said, just as level and noncommittal as you please.

"Well, well, well," said Dr. Lazarus.

"Well, well, well," Jamie echoed, not batting an eye.

"You've changed a lot since I saw you last, Jamie."

"Haven't we all?" she said.

Leroy fidgeted with his silk handkerchief. "Well, it's great to see you looking so good and all," he said.

"Really?" Jamie said as if surprised to hear such a remark, but not too surprised.

"Yeah, really," said Leroy. "Come on over here and let me get a good look at you, Jamie."

Jamie stepped in front of Paco and stood there with a hands-on-hips, challenging look. She wore her old regular blue chenille bathrobe, which never had struck me as the least bit sexy before, but today she had wrapped and tied it in such a way as to be kind of low-cut and curve-hugging. Even fresh out of bed, makeup free, and with her hair combed only with her fingers, Jamie managed to put forth an attitude that said, "I'm looking good," and that's enough to convince most men. (Take note, girls. That information comes in real handy sometimes.)

Leroy said, "My, my, my. I'll tell you what, Jamie. You make a mighty good-looking woman." Then he turned to me for confirmation. "Don't he, Raylene—I mean, don't she, Raylene?"

I said, "Yes, she does," trying to sound as unemotional and uninvolved and icy cool as Jamie.

Leroy went on, "In fact, it's been such a long time since I saw you, Jamie, I have a hard time remembering what you used to look like as a . . . you know, as a boy. Lord, how long *has* it been?"

Jamie shrugged.

Leroy sat there with his mouth open as if unsure what came next. His eyes flitted from Jamie to me to Paco and back to Jamie. Finally he said, "At the class party? At Dot Struthers's place on the river? Remember, Jamie?"

"Oh, yeah, that's right," Jamie said, and smoothed the hair at the back of her head.

Leroy said, "Remember, Jamie? It was the night Nick drowned. Nick Tarkington? Remember? You were there, weren't you?"

When Jamie didn't reply right away, he said, "That was a long time ago, Jamie. Yes, it was. It's really been a long time since I last saw you. . . ."

His voice drifted off before his eyes lighted on Paco. "Howdy, Paco! You know, Jamie, speaking of Nick, Shirley Jack thinks Paco looks a lot like him." Before Jamie had a chance to answer, he went on. "How you been, Paco? How's that car? Is it still running? You keeping it full of gas? You seen Shirley Jack today?"

While Paco grinned and answered his questions (fine, fine, yes, yes, and no), Leroy turned his attention to me, threw his hands up, and said, "Well, Raylene, what do you think? A man like me's got a wife like Shirley Jack . . . she's a handful, I tell you!"

I said, "I don't doubt it."

"She's a handful, ain't she, Paco?"

Paco smiled, halted, smiled again. "She's a . . . a *what?* Handful?"

But Leroy had turned his attention back to me. "It's all about money, Raylene. She don't care for Buck. I really don't think she does. Maybe she did at first, but now she ain't after nothing but some easy money."

I said, "Well, Leroy, if she's looking to get money out of me, you tell her she's just pissing up a rope."

He turned his attention to Paco again, since Jamie had disappeared into the bathroom. "What're we gonna do about these women, Paco? Ain't they somethin'? You don't have a wife, do you, Paco?"

Paco said no, he didn't.

"Well, take my advice, son, and just stay free from the bonds of holy matrimony. You'll be a lot better off. Ain't that right, Raylene?"

"I guess so," I said, not that I was worried about Paco's committing matrimony. "It doesn't seem to work out for too many people these days, that's for sure," I said, just because I am a person that would rather talk than keep her mouth shut.

"That's right," said Leroy. "And in the long run, all they want from you, Paco, is security. *Security.* That's spelled m-o-n-e-y, son. I tell you what. If I wrote my wife a check right this minute for, say, twenty thousand dollars, she'd follow me home like a meek little lamb and this whole love affair of hers would be a thing of the past."

Up to this part of the conversation, Paco had been in a grinning and shuffling mode, but the mention of large amounts of money can get the attention of the best of us.

He moved closer to Leroy and said, "Yeah, women. They need a lot of money, huh?"

Leroy said, "That's right, Paco, and the more they get, the more they want." He began stuffing his handkerchief back into his pocket a millimeter at a time, which was fine, since I was just about to tell him I had no more time to visit and would he please leave and not let the doorknob hit him in the ass.

But before I could open my mouth, Paco was telling Leroy something about a rattle in a wheel bearing of his car, then the two of them were heading for the door to look at the car.

"Hey, Paco," I hollered at his back, "you're supposed to be taking me to Safeway."

"Yeah, I know," he said. "I'll be right back."

They were gone for an hour.

Late, late that night, I got another call from Shirley Jack. Same honkytonk music, same drunken voice, different subject.

"Raylene, is that you, honey?"

Honey, she called me.

"Yeah."

"Is Paco there?" she said.

"Paco?" I hollered. (I had been having such a nice dream about me and Armando cavorting on a beach with snow white sand and turquoise water.)

"Yes, Paco," she said in a surly way (or in a typical Shirley Jack way, that is).

"No!" I hollered, and slammed down the phone.

May 17

I'm Paco's confidante all of a sudden. I guess he thinks that because I'm from Louisiana just like Shirley Jack, I can explain her. I can't. However, he is bursting with positive energy lately. He dropped by this morning just after I gave up on fixing the leak in the kitchen faucet. I gave up on fixing the one in the bathtub yesterday. The toilet has developed the jiggle-handle-after-you-flush syndrome and the light switch in the kitchen is broken. The house is falling apart all of a sudden and I just don't care. Maybe it's time to get a new place.

Paco drops by with gifts in hand now. Proud to be working. A six-pack of Bud today.

"Why she's calling me, Jamie? She called me at work last night. Three times. She was drunk too. Fucked up. You know what I mean?"

"What did she say?"

"She says she expects to see me again."

"She *expects* to see you again?"

"No, no. She said she *hoped* to see me again. I get confused. It's the same in Spanish. *Esperar*. Means expect, means hope, means wait, too. It means three words. You know what I mean? She says she want to run away with me," he chortled.

"Run away? From what? From whom? From Leroy? From Buck?"

"She don't know where Buck's at. She says she don't give a shit. You know what I mean? But he's got the car. She don't have no car now. She called me to bring her Kentucky Fried Chicken yesterday."

"And you went?"

"*Sí, señorita,*" he said with a grin.

"And you got away alive?"

"I told her I had a date."

"So where's Leroy?"

"Dr. Lazarus? He don't stay at the Econo Gardens."

The faucet dripped. Paco smirked. I waited.

"He stays somewhere else," he said, suddenly worrying the thorns of the tiny cactus in the middle of the table.

"Where, Paco?"

"It's a secret."

"Where, Paco?"

He said, "He's at the Purvis! Don't tell nobody."

"The Perverse Hotel? Where you work? My, what a coincidence."

"Yeah, we're friends. You know what I mean?"

For a moment, I did wonder what he meant. But then, no, I decided, not Dr. Lazarus. Robbery, arson, rape, murder, maybe, but not messing with pretty young boys.

"Well, you know how to pick 'em," I said.

"Don't tell nobody, okay? He don't want Shirley Jack or Raylene or you or nobody to know."

"Well, I don't blame him," I said. The Purvis Hotel is perhaps half a step up from the Hole in the Wall as a chic San Francisco hostel. I guess they do have beds there, though they are usually rented by the hour.

"He comes down to the desk, talks to me a lot. Very friendly. I send Isabelita up to see him. He likes Isabelita. You know Isabelita? Always hanging out in front of the dirty-book store?"

"Oh yes, she's delightful. I love her hot pants outfit with the heart-shaped appliqué over the crotch. She makes Aquanetta look like a nun."

"Oh, he likes Aquanetta too," said Paco.

"Aquanetta? How does Dr. Lazarus know Aquanetta?"

"She came to the hotel to visit me last night. Dr. Lazarus likes her *tetas grandes*. He pinched Aquanetta on the ass. He thinks she is a real *muchacha*. I don't tell him the truth. You know what I mean?" Paco threw his hands up in the air and then down on his knees. Roaring with laughter, I believe, is the expression.

"He says he will take Aquanetta to Houston and she can sing on his new television *programa*." That was the cue for both of us to roar with laughter.

"Oh, God, what a pair they'd make," I said. "It sounds like poor Shirley Jack has been left behind. She really doesn't know where Buck is?"

"No! He's gone. She don't know where. Maybe to Alaska. You know what I mean?"

"No, he's not in Alaska," I said. "He called today from a pay phone downtown."

"What did he say?" Paco loves gossip.

"He wanted to talk to Raylene, said he wanted to tell her good-bye."

"What else?"

"Nothing." I do not bestow confidences upon Paco. Might as well shout them from the highest steeple.

"Well, I guess they both want to run away."

"Well," I said, "where does *she* want to run away to? She's not so keen on Alaska, is she?"

"Oh, she wants to go to many different places. New Mexico, Canada, Australia."

"And she wants you to go with her?"

"She *likes* me, Jamie! I told you!"

"Does she know you're gay?"

"No! I don't have to tell her everything!"

"Of course you do, Paco."

"Por qué?"

"Because she wants you to fuck her, Paco. She is hoping you will fuck her. She is expecting you to fuck her. She is waiting for you to fuck her."

He shrugged. "She don't have enough money." He put a clownish frown on his face and said, "Too bad, Shirley Jack. It is very sad. I am very sorry."

"You and Chuy are still looking for that two thousand dollars?"

"What two thousand dollars?" he grinned.

twenty-**o**ne

The Hole in the Wall could wreck my nerves sometimes, I must say. Especially in the mornings when all I wanted to do was herd 'em up and head 'em out. I got pretty efficient at sending the bachelors on their way in the early A.M. And it was not just a matter of standing beside the front door and telling them good-bye and see you tonight. No, think of it. A dozen or so snoring, snorting, farting, goofing, giggling, belching, chattering guys, juveniles for the most part, sprawled from one corner of the room to the other, and very few of them eager to rise and shine and be outside before eight. Some of them, of course, had short-term jobs lined up—painting, construction, roofing, hauling trash, and so forth—and these guys were oftentimes up at daybreak and gone before I woke up. But most of the other fellows were not what you would call self-starters, and getting the worst ones going was like pulling an ox out of a ditch. That was my self-appointed job ('cause Jamie just plain didn't *care*)—to get 'em up, fed, and out the door in order that I might salvage from the remaining hours of the day some kind of life of my own. So there I'd be as the sun came up over Garcia's Liquors down at the corner: Ms. Stout with her tail up and stinger out, hollering, cussing, joking, and delivering ultimatums.

"Jose, you see this pitcher of ice water over your head? I'm giving you ten seconds to get up off of that damn floor. Ten . . . nine . . . eight . . ."

"Hector! (Rap, rap, rap.) You turn that shower off this minute if you expect to come back here tonight. You know the three-minute rule and don't tell me you don't."

While I got things percolating, Jamie was usually laid up in bed like a big old sack of potatoes. The longer I stayed at the Hole in the Wall, the easier it was to see the blood connection between Jamie and her father, who I'm sure was the laziest man in Lake Gladys if not the state of Louisiana. "If he was a dog, he'd lean against a fence to bark," Miss Viola said many a time about Uncle Aubrey, whose idea of a good time was sitting outside and whittling all day long while he followed the shade around the house. As I juned around taking care of business in the mornings, I could hear Jamie thrashing around behind the walls of Jericho, yawning and moaning and gearing up for her first cup of coffee like she had a houseful of butlers and maids. However, after my first few days at the Hole in the Wall, I got used to her lazy ways and began to consider it a point of pride to have the place emptied by 8:00 A.M. or a quarter after at the latest and to accomplish it with a maximum of goodwill and a minimum of ass kicking. After all, I was staying there for free, and, furthermore, I sort of enjoyed the back-and-forth and carrying-on with the boys. Most of them were as frisky and prankish as puppies and these days I often think about some of the regulars like Hector and Juanito and Antonio and wonder whatever became of them.

Usually nine o'clock found me and Jamie having coffee—her first, my third or fourth—and looking over the paper.

One morning, she shuffled in scratching her head and yawning and said, "Oh, you got a call yesterday while you were out."

"Who from?"

"Buck. He wanted to say good-bye."

"I thought he already said that."

Jamie shrugged and poured coffee for herself. "He feels bad about everything. About fooling around with all those women. And especially Shirley Jack. I think he feels bad about everything in his life right now. He says he needs a change of scenery. Says he's definitely hitting the road for Alaska and he doesn't care if he never gets back."

When Jamie said that, I tried to visualize Buck driving off into the sunset alone and I couldn't. I tried to visualize him all alone, lost on a northbound blacktop, pulling over to the side of the highway to silently pore over a road map in hopes of finding a more direct route or one not quite so hectic as the interstate, but the picture didn't come to me. I tried to visualize him stopping at truck stops, the solitary wanderer punching out numbers on the jukebox, playing the Romeo with cute waitresses, and striking up conversations with strangers, and I just couldn't see it. The fact about Buck was that he was a man who required company at all times, somebody to take care of him and tie his neckties and share his troubles, and it struck me that, hmm, while I had had my reasons to stay with Buck all those years, he had had his reasons too: I was good company. Furthermore, because Buck was the way he was, it was a good bet, I figured, that he and Shirley Jack had not spent a day or night apart since I left Lake Gladys. Which would be enough Shirley Jack for any man. But if they were really finished with each other now, and it sounded as if they were, what plans did Buck have? It was something I could not help wondering about and that is what was on my mind when Aquanetta popped in. She sat down with one of Jamie's cats on her shoulder and there was a brightness in her eyes. She poured herself a cup of coffee and tried to keep her grin down to a manageable size.

"Guess what?" she said.

"What?"

"I'm going to be on TV."

I hit myself on the forehead and said, "I knew it! I *knew* it!"

She sat up ramrod straight and looked puzzled and astonished as only Aquanetta could look puzzled and astonished.

"No, Aquanetta, you're not going on television," I said while Jamie backed me up with a negative shake of the head.

"And why not?"

"Because you're nuts," said Jamie.

"That never stopped anybody else from going on TV," she said.

"You've been talking to Dr. Lazarus," I said. "Paco told Jamie all about it."

"So?"

Jamie said, "So we don't think he's on the level about wanting you on TV. He wants Shirley Jack back and maybe he just wants to use you to get her attention or maybe he's just pulling your leg. You don't know Leroy, Aquanetta."

"Aquanetta," I said, "listen, honey, he's not a man to be trusted. Dr. Lazarus would climb a tree to tell a lie before he would stand on the ground and tell the truth."

Aquanetta wasn't smiling but she wasn't licked yet. "Hey, look," she said, "I can handle Dr. Lazarus. This could be my big break. Can you imagine? The Esta Noche's own Aquanetta taking America by storm in the brand-new version of *Gospel Jubilee?* America's new sweetheart? I'd be a fool not to go for it."

Jamie and I slurped coffee and rolled our eyes.

"Well, wouldn't I?"

I said, "Look, Aquanetta, how do you know they're going to let Dr. Lazarus back on TV in the first place?"

"That's the whole idea," she said. "We get together a package—him preaching and saving souls and me singing my heart out in such a way that those sinners out there would forget they ever heard of Shirley Jack—hey, it would be a winning combination. And it's national TV."

"And you'd wind up getting hurt," I said. "Aquanetta, I've known Leroy Lazarus all my life. . . ."

Jamie said, "Aquanetta. Honey. As much as I like you and as much as I dislike Shirley Jack, I have to say there is one advantage—only one, mind you, that she has over you. And you know what it is, I guess."

She looked real surprised and said, "I do *not.*"

Jamie said, "Think about it, Aquanetta."

Aquanetta put on a big show of thinking. She crossed her legs and her arms and cupped her chin in her hand and stared at the ceiling with her eyebrows making a little steeple. Then she said, "Well, I'm sorry, girls, but knowing Shirley Jack only from the perspective of an avid television and gospel fan, I'm at a loss as to how she could out-class me in any way whatsoever."

I said, "Aquanetta. Dear. She's a real girl."

Aquanetta stared at me in amazement for a moment, then burst out laughing so loud and hearty that Jamie and I finally joined in although I, for one, wasn't quite sure I got the joke.

When she finally recovered from this display of hilarity, Aquanetta wiped her eyes and patted me on the hand. "You're cute, Raylene. I adore you. Are there any more like you in Lake Gladys?"

I gave her a look. I said, "Aquanetta. Honey. The word would get out. It always does. You're not exactly an unknown in this city. What about the tabloids? God, poor Dr. Lazarus would be ruined all over again."

Jamie sat up and leaned forward. She said, "Hey, that's right. Poor Dr. Lazarus. He should be warned about women like you."

Aquanetta said, "Hey, that's Dr. Lazarus's problem. I'd be bigger than ever."

"What a schemer!" said Jamie. "What a vixen! Clawing her way up the show business ladder . . ."

Aquanetta put on a real haughty look and corrected her. "The tel-evangelism ladder," she said, and sniffed for good measure.

"Same difference," Jamie said.

Aquanetta had a way of using body English to bring conversations to a close or at least change the subject. She stood up and put a lot of energy into straightening her skirt—a fluorescent red micro-mini-mini-mini from which the cheeks of her behind hung down like accessories to the outfit. Then, she hitched up her cheekless panties from

Frederick's of Hollywood with such a force that you could tell that Dr. Lazarus and all he represented was put aside, if not forgotten, for the moment.

Later, at the Patio Café, where Aquanetta treated us to a typical Castro Street brunch of chic little turkey crepes and mimosas, we sat in the sun and talked about our futures. As Dr. Lazarus's delightful sidekick, Aquanetta would be, she was certain, America's sweetheart in the very near future. And if an exposé scandal was part of the package (and she really didn't see how it could be avoided, considering her notoriety in San Francisco), well, hey, think of the publicity. She would be invited to appear on every talk show in the world, not to mention the fact that she would receive top dollar at every drag club. She couldn't miss, she declared as she slashed bloodred lipstick across her mouth and pretended to ignore the stares and murmurs of diners who recognized her from the Esta Noche, which I'm sure secretly thrilled her to the core.

"It's a cinch," she said. Then she leaned back and looked around at the other tables like she had just awakened in a strange and enchanted room and couldn't imagine how she got there. She waved at someone across the way and blew a kiss. She cut her eyes around to the next table, where a couple of blue-eyed sweater boys had greeted our arrival with, "Oh, look, there's Aquanetta!" She favored the guys with a faint smile to make up for snubbing them earlier, when she had been too absorbed in the business of making an entrance to give them the time of day.

She fluttered her fingers at them and said, "Hi, guys," and then, before her greeting had a chance to go to their heads, she got busy scoping out the rest of the room for interesting people. Since she found nobody else worthy of her attention, she focused on me and said, "Okay, your turn, Raylene. What's in the cards for you?"

I upended my mimosa and drained it while I chose my words, which as it turned out, would not have won any prizes in the originality department.

I said, "Aquanetta, whatever will be will be."

The words were no sooner out of my mouth than Aquanetta blew a raspberry that turned heads from clear out in the kitchen. Then she sang a chorus or two of "Que Será, Será," with Jamie chiming in while I sat there with a tight little smile and pretended to study a wine list that stood in the little wire rack that held the salt and pepper shakers. When Aquanetta quieted down and after the rest of the brunchers returned to their Bloody Marys, I said, "Don't laugh. There's a lot to be said for living life as it comes. I'm living proof of that, God knows!" All right, maybe I was climbing a little ways up on my self-righteous high horse.

Aquanetta said, "Oh, I see. So if circumstances cause you to miss connections with Armando in Seattle, well, whatever will be will be, huh? And you'll go on your merry way? Is that how it works?"

"That's different," I said.

Aquanetta settled into her seat. She licked her lips and clasped her hands before her on the table. It was lecture time.

"Different?" she said. "How so? Let me tell you something, Raylene," she said, and for a second I got an Alice from Dallas flashback from her tone of voice. "Correct me if I'm wrong," she said, "but what you're telling me if I'm reading you right is that you're willing to let circumstances rule your life."

I said, "Well . . ."

But Aquanetta held out her hand like a traffic policeman. She said, "No, listen, Raylene. When I talk about circumstances, I'm talking about a lot of different things. I'm talking about a person being in the wrong place at the wrong time, or being used as a pawn in somebody else's game, or just being caught in rotten weather. But you always have choices. You don't have to be a victim of circumstances. You can change, you can put your foot down and say, 'Not this girl,' or, hell, you can create your own circumstances. I mean, look at Jamie."

I looked at Jamie.

"No, don't look at me," she said. "I'm not a good example."

Aquanetta said, "Don't be silly. You're an excellent example."

Jamie said, "You think so? Well, thanks for the vote of confidence. Personally, I feel like I've been hibernating for a long time. But I think I'm waking up. I feel more alive than I have in a long time."

Aquanetta said she would drink to that and ordered another round of mimosas from the skinny blond waiter who came loping to our table at the sound of her whistle.

Jamie scanned the room, looking relaxed and happy, before she turned to me. "Really," she said, "your energy has been good for me, Raylene. I think I'm ready to start moving again."

I said, well, I was glad to hear that. Lord knows, Jamie did have a lot of room for improvement in the moving department.

She said, "Maybe I'll take a computer course at City College or join a gym or take cooking classes. . . . Maybe I'll get a job. I'd like to get away from the Hole in the Wall and get a real apartment with my very own bathroom. Oh, God, what a luxury that would be."

I said that sounded like a good idea to me.

Aquanetta said all Jamie needed was a new place and a new man.

Jamie said, "All in good time, my dear."

Aquanetta paid our bill and we walked out. Her behind hanging out of her short, short skirt drew stares at every turn and flounce, which was just the way she liked it, but otherwise, we strolled down the sunny sidewalks of Castro Street window-shopping and gossiping like three housewives out for an afternoon away from the kids. We dawdled for an hour, then picked up the free newspapers off the sidewalk racks and bought a few items at the drugstore and we were ready to head for home. The brakes on that Volkswagen of Aquanetta's were about shot and when she started slowing down a block away from the Purvis Hotel, they screeched so loud I gritted my teeth.

Jamie said, "And why are we stopping here?"

Aquanetta said she had something she wanted to give to Paco.

"What?" I said. I was a little impatient because I had half a dozen things I needed to do at home and we had already been gone for hours.

Aquanetta pulled over to the curb and said, oh, it was just some cologne that he said he liked and she wanted to give him a little something for introducing her to Dr. Lazarus. Jamie and I said we would wait in the car, but Aquanetta insisted that we come with her. "Don't you want to see what kind of room they gave him?" she asked.

"Not particularly," I said, but we followed her into the hotel rather than argue with her. Paco wasn't in the room that the desk clerk sent us to, but as we walked back down the stairs, we saw him coming in the front door. Oh, and who was the slightly older man by his side? That slightly rumpled, slightly faded gentleman whose looks fit in so well with the seedy decor of the Purvis Hotel? The good Dr. L. At the sight of us, he made a move as if to turn on his heel, but he recovered in about half a second and came striding toward us like there was nobody he was happier to see. He oozed all over Jamie and me, saying how great it was to see us again and so forth and so on and so on and so on. It wasn't for nothing he became a preacher. That man could talk. I gave him a constipated little smile but Jamie ignored him completely, which was fine since neither of us could have got a word in edgewise anyway. Meanwhile, Paco accepted his little bottle of cologne, an expensive one for a drugstore brand, with smiles and hugs for Aquanetta. He could be a charmer when he wanted. When Leroy invited us for coffee at a little dive of a café next door, Jamie and I said no right away, but nobody heard us because Aquanetta said okay much faster and much louder and practically dragged us along.

We got settled into a corner booth. I followed my instincts and sat as far from Leroy Lazarus as possible. Aquanetta wasted no time ordering coffee and tailoring the conversation to meet her needs.

"Well," she said to Leroy, "I've been thinking a lot about what we talked about the other night."

"Oh, yeah, what's that, baby?" said Leroy, who had not taken his eyes off her snowy white tits for more than a few seconds since he showed up. However, even a liberated woman such as myself has to admit that those things she had did present a focal point that was real hard to ignore. Even Jamie and Paco and I kept cutting our eyes around at Aquanetta's bosoms when she would jiggle them to emphasize something she was saying, such as, "Oh, look, there's a booth. We can (jiggle) fill it up."

Our future superstar looked only a little put off at Dr. Lazarus's poor memory, "Oh you know what we were talking about. About how you need a new chick singer to go on your new TV show with you to take Shirley Jack's place." The glance she gave me and Jamie was such a purely shy one and so completely unlike her that I felt like reaching under the table to squeeze her hand or something but the moment passed.

"Oh!" said Dr. Lazarus. "Oh, yeah, that." And then he laughed so long and loud and hard that I reconsidered and I did reach for Aquanetta's hand, but she drew away after a few seconds.

"What's so funny?" she said when Leroy's hee-haws subsided into tee-hees.

He said, gasping for breath between words, "Oh, I don't know, honey. I guess that would be something else, wouldn't it?"

"What? Me on TV?" With her mouth painted far beyond its perimeters and eyebrows tweezed to high heaven, Aquanetta's face did not exactly lend itself to blankness, but now it was about as perfectly blank as I ever hoped to see it.

Leroy said, "Well, who knows, maybe they could get used to a gal like you out there in the boonies (chuckle, chuckle, chuckle). But seriously, Aquanetta," he said. "Honey, I'm afraid you'd just overwhelm 'em out there in middle America. You're too good for 'em."

Everybody, even Paco, was silent. I was trying to look anyplace but at Aquanetta and thinking, oh, the humor of it all.

"Oh, I see, so you were just kidding, huh? Just having a go at me, as it were." Aquanetta's voice was as blank as her face.

Paco looked at a Budweiser clock on the wall and said, "Hey, Dr. Lazarus, we need to go. It's almost three. You know what I mean?"

Dr. Lazarus brushed him off and said there was nothing he'd like better (heh, heh) than having a go at Aquanetta, but what he needed to take Shirley Jack's place was somebody clean and wholesome, because they ate that up out there in Televisionland.

"Who can find a virtuous woman?" he hollered at the ceiling, demonstrating his style and sparking some flashes of recognition in a couple of elderly customers at the counter. "For her price is above rubies!" His bright eyes came to rest on Aquanetta, the blank Aquanetta who seemed like such a stranger.

"Yeah, virtuous is not my style," she said.

He said, "I tell you what. As soon as I get me some money lined up here, I'm gonna take you on a trip, Aquanetta. I'm gonna take you over the mountains and across the sea."

"Where's that?" she said.

"Away from here," he said. "Someplace where it's warm and we don't have to wear so darn many clothes."

She pulled at the neckline of her sweater and said, "Oh yeah, they are a nuisance, aren't they?"

"I want to go someplace safe. San Francisco makes me nervous."

"How come?" Aquanetta asked in a bored way.

Leroy's face swooped down in front of hers. "Why, *darlin'*, it's like Sodom and Gomorrah and half the people in town have got *AIDS.*"

Ms. Stoneface considered that a moment before she said, "Isn't it the truth?"

"Yeah, I'll tell you what, Aquanetta," he said. "We'll go down to Meh-hico and have us a time."

She said, "Oh, yeah? Starting when?"

Dr. Lazarus gave Paco a quick little wink. "Well, is tomorrow too soon?" he said.

"We'll see," she said.

He put on a big look of alarm. "Now you're not playing hard-to-get, are you, honey?"

"*Moi?*"

She seemed to be warming up to him for reasons that were beyond me. Jamie and I started making noises about how we really did need to be getting home. While we gathered up our purses and Paco agreed in a loud voice that, yeah, it was getting late, Dr. L. and Aquanetta exchanged a few more words, whispering into each other's ears this time. Jamie and Paco and I scooted out of the booth. At the door I looked back and Aquanetta was still in conference with Leroy.

I hollered, "Aquanetta, let's go. *Now!*"

She said, "Yeah, yeah, okay. I'm coming."

Well, she eventually did slither out of the booth, but not before giving Leroy's hand a squeeze.

One of the old codgers at the counter nearly choked on his coffee at the sight of the lower hemispheres of Aquanetta's rear end peeking out in such a saucy way from under her so-called skirt. She gave him a wink and we filed out the door. Tooling down the street in Aquanetta's VW, Jamie and I made efforts to smooth everything over. She was a lot better off not getting mixed with Dr. Lazarus, I told her, and Jamie was quick to agree, saying he was walking trouble. Aquanetta just watched the street over the steering wheel and smiled in a grim way as she raced the engine at every red light to keep it from dying.

"Don't worry about me, girls. I can hold my own with Dr. Lazarus."

I said, "What does that mean, Aquanetta? Does that mean you're not finished with him yet?"

She said, "Just don't worry, darling."

I said, "It sure looked like Ms. Aquanetta had some unfinished business. . . ."

Aquanetta kept her eyes on the street and kept silent for once. She dropped us off in Balmy Alley and I sighed with relief to finally be home where I could do the things I needed to take care of before the bachelors started showing up. Jamie, on the other hand, flopped on the bed and read a book.

I mixed up a special salt-and-pine-oil recipe that Miss Viola had taught me years before to clean the floor of any bathroom where any person of the male gender has set foot. "There's not a one of 'em born that'll hit the hole more than fifty percent of the time," she always said, but I daresay she would have turned over in her grave if she could have seen the truth of her remark on any given morning at the Hole in the Wall. When I finished the daily routine I had established of swabbing around the commode, there were plenty of other chores to take care of. I washed a bunch of dishes, changed the kitty litter, and picked two or three handfuls of cat hair off the couch. Then I loaded up a bunch of dirty laundry into a plastic basket and set off for the Laundromat a couple of blocks away on Twenty-fifth Street. I said hello to Mr. Rodriguez, the old blind man, who came shuffling down the alley, led by his giant poodle, Sheba. Then I stopped to admire the paint job a gawky-looking woman standing on a stepladder was giving her house. I remember the moon, full but wispy, that seemed to be forming before my eyes in the twilight sky over Bernal Heights as I trudged down the bumpy alley with my load. I can never take a casual look at a full moon. I always pay attention because I believe in them too much. I always find myself wondering what kind of stupendous changes or romance or fireworks it's going to bring into everybody's lives, especially mine. It never just sits there and does nothing. I know that from experience and I know it better than ever after this particular night.

I was at the Laundromat for quite a while, reading old tattered magazines, *People* and *Newsweek,* and socializing and thrashing out the pros and cons of a new antigraffiti plan with Mrs. Martinez, the neighborhood organizer. I was pretty well done in when I got home and was not overjoyed to see, standing there with his finger on the doorbell, Dr. Leroy Lazarus in trademark sharkskin and grinning like a tree full of possums as I came up the steps.

If he noticed how very unenthusiastic my greeting was, he sure didn't show it. Most people, I think, would take some kind of hint from the words, "Oh, it's you. What are you doing here?"

But Dr. Lazarus was a master of positive thinking and from the looks of things, you would have thought I had strewn rose petals in his path and greeted him with a bear hug.

"Raylene! The pride of Lake Gladys!" he yelled at me as I wearily poked my key in the door.

"Leroy, what do you want?" I said, and not in a lively, friendly way either, if in fact it is possible to say that in a lively, friendly way.

Jamie was still curled up with her book and the look she gave us was one of hard-core boredom as we muddled through the door. Of course, her look didn't bother Leroy. He went ahead on, as they say.

"Why, I just dropped by to say good-bye," he said, *"ladies."*

I was waddling toward the kitchen with the plastic tub that was about half my size, and not half paying attention to Leroy, but I did notice him shooting a meaningful glance at Jamie on this last word. She didn't miss the glance either.

She said, "What are you looking so happy about?" There was a challenge in the way she said it from her bed where she lounged like a harem girl at the mineral baths. Her book was closed but she kept one finger in it to mark her place while she studied Leroy through narrowed eyes.

His grin grew an inch or two wider. "Now why shouldn't I look happy, Miss Jamie?" he asked.

Without thinking very long, she managed to name off several reasons why he might have reason to be less than overjoyed, starting with the obvious ones—he had been kicked off the airwaves and lost his wife—and winding up with a couple that made me lift my eyebrows as I stood folding towels in the kitchen—his toupee was on crooked and he had chronic bad breath.

"Well," he said, "you're right. I've had a few setbacks in recent months and that's no secret, but I think my luck's about to change for the better. Change is definitely in the air."

At those words, I remember glancing up at the big yellow moon, framed in a wooden rectangle of window.

He said, "I've got a few things happening for me right now, got some irons in the fire, got some *ideas,* and that's what I came to see you about, Miss Jamie."

"Ideas?" I heard her say from my post in the kitchen. I was trying to look as busy as a person can look folding clothes and humming, just in case Dr. Lazarus glanced my way expecting hospitality. However, when he walked across the room and sat on the edge of Jamie's bed to talk about just why he had come to see her, I quit my humming and folded in silence. Then, Raylene Stout being Raylene Stout, I quit my folding and stood there with my ear cocked toward the living room, trying to pick up on what was being said. What I caught was a fast and low-pitched sales spiel of some kind on the part of Leroy and, as I peered through the door, a whole list of expressions on Jamie's face—surprise, hurt, anger, outrage—and then her whole face clouded over and all hell broke loose.

May 19

When Dr. Lazarus came calling, I was not as absorbed in a book of Italo Calvino short stories as I pretended to be. However, they were stories of considerably more charm than anything the good doctor could offer up, and I was not happy about the interruption. But he said he had come to say his farewells, and although I wondered why he had not taken that opportunity earlier in the day when we had met, I held my tongue. Instead of saying, "Okay. Good-bye Leroy and here's the door," words which anybody would be well advised to use immediately upon seeing his face, I played it passive, meanwhile making a mental note to perform, the minute he left, the old broomstick behind the door trick which had proved so effective with Shirly Jack. And so, Dr. Lazarus was allowed his parting remarks, or parting proposition, as it turned out.

"Miss Jamie, I want you to listen," he said as he sat down so heavily on my bed that I had to throw a hand on the mattress to maintain my balance, thereby losing my place in the book. "I've got some plans I want to lay out for your inspection and approval."

I didn't reply, which was fine with him, I assume, since he didn't leave a gap for me to talk anyway.

"Jamie, I've been busy since I got to San Francisco," he said. "Real busy. I bet you thought I had just been layin' around, just takin' it easy. Now tell the truth. Isn't that what you thought?"

I assured him that I really hadn't given the subject a moment's thought. And riffled through my book, looking for the page I had been reading.

"Jamie," he said, "I've been talking to your little buddy, Paco. He's a character, ain't he?"

It was not the kind of question that seemed to require a reply and, occupied as I was with the book, I didn't favor him with one. He paused a moment and when I glanced up he seemed to be studying my face and deciding the order, or perhaps weighing the wisdom, of his next words, which, when they came, came rushed and caution-to-the-winds.

"Jamie, Paco and me are putting together a little business deal with another gentleman you know, name of Chuy."

Well, this got my attention. Gentleman? Chuy? Since Leroy did appear to expect a reply this time, I said in a voice slightly above a murmur, "I know the gentleman. I know the deal."

He looked a little nonplussed. "Who you been talking to? Paco?"

"Leroy, get a grip," I said. "Paco was trying to cook up that same deal with me a week ago. It's not like this is any big secret."

"Huh?" he said, pushing Eustacia aside to get a better look at me. The cat yowled and Leroy pushed her onto the floor.

"The cocaine Chuy brought up from San Diego," I said. "I'm afraid it's old news, Leroy."

He made a gesture of dismissal. "Oh, that," he said, and produced a little snort that was better than a thousand words. "Seed money," he said, and winked.

"A hefty little dab of seed money," I said.

"Yeah," he said impatiently. "But, look, Miss Jamie, that's not the deal I'm talking about. What I'm telling you about is a little enterprise that I'm planning in Tijuana. A nice part of Tijuana, Chuy tells me."

Curiosity overcame my disdain of anything involving the dynamic duo of Leroy and Chuy and I had to ask him what kind of enterprise exactly he was talking about.

"Jamie," he said, and availed himself of a dramatic pause while he studied my face. "You know me. You've known me a long, long time and you know I'm not the kind of guy that'll call a spade a diamond."

"Only if there's money in it for you," I said.

He ignored me and went on. "The enterprise I'm talking about in Tijuana is, well, a whorehouse, Jamie. A very high-class whorehouse. Let's call it a bordello. That sounds better. I'm gonna buy this place, lock, stock, and hookers, and I'll be back in business again. No more begging from TV people for another chance, no more sucking up to Shirley Jack. Mexico can be a very pleasant place to live if you've got a little money, and I'll have more than a little real soon. By tomorrow, I would expect—"

Reacting mechanically, I cut him off without thinking. "Why are you telling *me* all this, Leroy?"

He leaned forward till we were practically butting noses. *"Because,* Jamie! Because how many whore . . . uh, bordellos, how many bordellos— and I'm talking top-ranking, high-class bordellos, mind you, no street-walkers—how many bordellos can offer a customer the novelty of a good-looking gal that used to be a fella?"

I was stunned, couldn't speak.

"Chuy says this place has a bathroom for every two bedrooms, and the best-looking women from all over, Jamie. He says they've got a gal from Denmark there that puts on shows with a German shepherd. They get a steady stream of customers from L.A. and San Diego. That's what Chuy says."

I still didn't speak, couldn't speak, but I must have turned a warning shade of red before I exploded because he quickly backed off and initiated a clumsy kind of damage control.

"Well, listen, Jamie, Paco said you were on the lookout for something new to occupy your time. He said you were ready to make some big changes in your life and, to tell you the truth, it was his idea that you might be interested in my enterprise and it seemed like . . ."

He might have gone on and on if I hadn't done something I have never done before in my entire existence, neither as male or female—I socked him. In the jaw. I didn't slap him. I *socked* him. I socked him so hard he fell back flat on the bed. I socked him so hard my knuckles stung with pain, and I automatically thrust my fist to my lips to soften the burn, while Raylene stood in the kitchen doorway, so wide-eyed and perplexed I almost wanted to laugh.

"Watch out, Jamie!" she hollered a second later, but it was too late. I felt the blow to my own jaw and, yes, it's true, I saw stars.

"You goddamn son of a bitch," the good doctor said in a tone decidedly unecclesiastical.

By the time I roused myself to a sitting position, Raylene had pounced on his back, thrown the toupee out the open window and was pulling the short fringe of hair around his ears. I leaped back into the fray, landing a kick right where it would do the most good, causing the doctor to double over with pain, but not before he waved a fist and roared, "You whore!" at me. Raylene scurried into the kitchen and emerged with the two cast-iron skillets that have been used as weapons on more than one night when the revelry at the Hole in the Wall has gotten a little out of hand. By the time Leroy straightened up again, still clutching his crotch with both hands, Raylene and I stood over him, each wielding a skillet over our heads in the attack position.

"You whore," he said again, this time in an ominous growl.

"Get out, Leroy," I said, managing a pretty good growl myself.

"Get out, Leroy," he mimicked me. "Get out, Leroy. I remember the last time you said that to me a long, long time ago. Remember all the trouble you caused that time, Jamie?"

I felt a burning in my stomach that seemed to radiate outward to the tips of my fingers and toes. I knew my face was on fire. I glanced at Raylene, whose look of bafflement in no way altered her threatening posture toward Leroy. I said, "I want you to get out of my house, Leroy."

Leroy looked to Raylene and to me and back again. "I bet Raylene doesn't even know what happened that night at the graduation party."

I could sense Raylene struggling not to ask what night. But I think we both knew questions were not necessary, that Leroy was hell-bent on full disclosure.

Suddenly he thrust a fist into the air and yelled, "Ye shall not lie with a man as with a woman! It is an abomination!"

"*Out!*" I hollered.

At that point I suggested again, applying my skillet rather forcefully to the general vicinity of Dr. Lazarus's ribs, that he vacate the premises. He did make it to the door this time, but not before landing a jab to my right jaw and a kick to the pit of my stomach that left me lying on the floor in the fetal position.

When I began to come around, Raylene was frantic. "Are you okay? Do you want a drink of water? What can I do?" she said.

"Hand me that telephone," I said.

I dialed the police.

twenty-two

Well, I found out things I didn't know, things I had often wondered about; no, let's get real here, these were things that had kept me awake nights my whole adult life—why Nick jumped off the bridge, my part in it, why Jamie left town. If Jamie had not socked Leroy, I guess I would still be wondering. And if Leroy had not threatened to tell his version of the truth about graduation night, a warped version I'm sure, Jamie might never have told it like it was.

I can't remember ever seeing Jamie so stomp-down mad as when Leroy left the house. I wasn't surprised when she went straight to the phone and called the police. She hung up the phone after barking out the particulars on Leroy: who he was, where he was staying, and what he was selling. She looked down at the phone a moment and sounded real tired—as who wouldn't be?—when she asked if I would make her a cup of tea. Sure, I said, but not before I set the broomstick behind the door, which didn't take me long at all. Just as I was plunging the fork into the broom, I heard Jamie.

"*Paco!*" she hollered. She bolted to her feet and ran to the phone. She ripped through that damn phone book till she found the number of the hotel. She punched out the numbers so fast her fingers were a blur.

"Is Paco there?" she yelled. I could picture the guy at the other end holding the phone out from his ear. She said, "Paco *who? Paco!* Paco who works there at night! The night clerk! You know Paco! Well, where did he go? Oh, God! Well, listen, this is very important. Please tell him to call Jamie the minute—the *second*—he gets back! *Jamie!* He knows the number. Please don't forget."

She hung up and collapsed on the bed before she turned to me with sort of an apologetic look. "I *forgot,*" she said. "I forgot all about Paco. They'll arrest him too."

I said, "Well, if he's not there . . ."

She said, "If he's not there, it will be even worse. Dr. Lazarus will put *all* the blame on him."

And I knew she was right about that. However, there was nothing to be done but wait for his call.

When the tea was ready, I found Jamie on her little back porch weaving a vine in and out of an old half-rotted lattice. When she finally spoke, she sounded exhausted but I could see she had a lot to tell me.

She said, "First of all, did you ever suspect about me and Nick?"

While these words were sinking in, she kept fiddling with the vine and lattice. I heard a car alarm go off somewhere in the neighborhood and then I heard a voice that sounded more or less like mine say, "Suspect? Suspect what?"

She peered inside her teacup and said, "Well, to tell you the truth, you kind of stole him away from me. We had sort of a thing going, Raylene. I was crazy about him."

I couldn't get the words out. "S-s-stole him away?" I almost turned my head to see where my voice was coming from.

"Yeah."

I said, "You mean you liked him, uh, that way?"

She gave me a shy look and said, "Well, he liked me too."

I said, "Well, I'm sure he did, Jamie."

"Yeah," she said, "but, Raylene, we were, well, *involved.*" For a moment, she focused on breaking off a decayed end of the lattice and seemed to forget I was there.

"Involved?" I said. "In a, uh, physical way?"

All right, I was thinking to myself, I'll just get the information now and I'll sit down and process it later.

She said, "Yes, Raylene. In a, uh, physical way. Before he started going with you, I mean." Then she smiled to show she wasn't making fun of me, or at least that the fun she was making was gentle.

"Where? When?" I said. I must have sounded pretty bleak.

"Oh, Raylene," she said, sounding real tired. "At my house, at his house, once even in the big house when Miss Viola was taking a nap."

That last part made my hand fly up over my mouth, but I recovered fast enough to pretend I was just scratching my lower lip. I was determined not to get hysterical about this.

"So how did Leroy know?"

She said, "He caught us. At the graduation party. Uh, kissing."

She told me the whole story in a low voice, watching her hands as they worked with the vine and the lattice. Every once in a while, she glanced up to see how I was taking it, but went on with her story till it was finished.

She and Nick, she said, were in the kitchen that night, hiding a carton of beer in the refrigerator. The only light was from the fridge and the screened porch outside the window. Nick was a little drunk, she said, and a little upset because Shirley Jack, who had hounded him into bringing her, was dogging his footsteps, and he had spent the evening trying to get away from her.

I said, "Was this before he talked to me that night?"

Jamie shook her head. "After. He told me he had tried to talk to you but Shirley Jack had interrupted."

Nick had not had a good day. His mother had gotten drunk in the middle of the afternoon and created an ugly scene with the neighbors for parking in her driveway. And then she had set fire accidentally to the living room drapes with a cigarette. However, there was some good news. He took out his wallet to show the surprise graduation present he had just received from an uncle in Texas—three hundred dollars.

She said, "I wasn't exactly cold sober myself that night, but I wasn't as far gone as Nick."

I said, "Jamie, you don't have to tell me all this if you don't want to."

"No," she said, looking me in the eye. "I want to. I want you to know exactly what happened."

And she went on. She said she was telling Nick something about the best place to hide the beer so Dot's mom wouldn't spot it, just rattling on, kind of nervous, but he wasn't listening.

She said, "Nick was just watching my face and suddenly, he told me he loved me. He just blurted it out. I was shocked that he had said it out loud like that. In a sort of public place. In Lake Gladys, Louisiana. Everything we had done together had been so secretive. I thought he would be shocked, too. I thought he would run away."

I said, "But he didn't, huh?"

"No," she said. "He didn't. And when he just stood there staring at me, I kissed him and he kissed back. And suddenly the lights went on and there stood Leroy looking very surprised and—well, it goes without saying—malicious, and going, 'What the *hell?*' "

Jamie's cats ran across the yard, one chasing the other. She watched them and waited till they disappeared around the corner of the house.

Jamie smiled. My first reaction was to holler, "Get out, Leroy!"

She said, "Nick and I were horrified, of course. It was impossible to deny what we were doing or pretend we were just kidding around, and we didn't try. We just stood there facing Leroy and waiting for whatever came next."

Jamie stopped and gave me a look that begged for understanding, and that's what I tried to give her with the look I gave back to her. I did understand. I had loved Nick myself. It wasn't hard to imagine Jamie, even the boy Jamie, feeling the same way. And I didn't feel all flustered or embarrassed at the idea the way I usually did when Jamie confided in me about this kind of stuff. I felt like I had made some kind of a breakthrough and I wanted Jamie to know, but, like a fool, all I could do was sort of grin and nod and hold on to my teacup.

Finally I said, "Well, what did come next?"

Jamie scooted her chair back from the table, crossed her legs, and stared at her hands clasped in her lap. She said, "Well, it was blackmail, pure and simple."

Leroy, she said, ranted and raved about queers till they begged him to lower his voice. He said, no, he wouldn't lower his voice. He was going straight to Coach Winfield, who was one of the party chaperones and whose views on queers were well known. Coach Winfield, he said, would throw them out on their asses. And then Leroy ever-so-casually mentioned Nick's mother, something about her being drunk on the job at the shrimp cannery where he worked part-time, something about her friends covering for her, something about the possibility of her losing her job if only Leroy spoke to the foreman, a great friend of his. And wouldn't she be surprised to find out her son was queer?

Jamie forced a laugh. She said, "I was thanking God for Dot's thundering stereo on the screen porch that drowned out any and all conversation. We offered to leave, but no, Leroy Lazarus, the class scuzzball, was in the driver's seat at last."

Leroy drew Nick into a corner and the two of them talked. About money Nick might have, about anything else of value that Nick might have. Jewelry or whatever. After several minutes, Jamie saw them reach some kind of agreement. Nick was reaching for his wallet when Jamie walked up and sloshed half a Dixie cup of beer in Leroy's face and walked out.

I was in the grip of the story. I said, "And Leroy never told anybody?"

Jamie shrugged. "Sure he did. I found out later that night that he made an anonymous call to my dad."

Jamie put her hands down at her sides and grasped the seat of the kitchen chair. "So now you know about me and Nick," she said.

"Yeah," I said, feeling as numb as a post, "now I know."

Jamie said, "So. Well. How do you feel about it?"

"I feel like . . . well, all's fair in love and . . . you know."

"Yeah," Jamie said, and kind of laughed. "Yeah, I guess so."

We both got real busy suddenly wiping counters and plumping up cushions till the bachelors started drifting in for the night. Hector brought his guitar and huddled in a corner and played a couple of quiet songs before he got involved in a card game in the kitchen. Big Victor dozed on the couch. A few of the boys sprawled on the floor in front of the television and drank beer and only swatted at each other during the commercials. Overall, a quiet night by Hole in the Wall standards.

Meanwhile Jamie and I sat on our beds with our chins on our knees and cleared up a few questions left over from the day's revelations:

Q: How did Uncle Aubrey react to Leroy's phone call?

A: With a fifth of Old Crow in one hand and an ax handle in the other. Jamie's battle scars included two black eyes and a chipped tooth.

Q: Where did Jamie run away to?

A: To a motel in Mobile with a traveling salesman who picked him up on the road. To Omaha with a truck driver who took him in when the salesman kicked him out. To New York with an AWOL sailor he fell in love with. To Rome and Paris with an archaeologist he met in a New York gay bar after the sailor was arrested and sent to the brig. To Barcelona with a flamenco dancer who promised him a job in an amusement park. And that was just the first year.

I was getting pretty wrapped up in Jamie's history, when the phone rang. Jamie grabbed it on the first ring.

Her end of the conversation was like: "Paco! Get out of the hotel. Now! This minute! What? What? What the hell are you doing *there?* Oh my *God!*"

This was shaping up as Jamie's most emotional day since I came to town. She looked at me like she had parted company with her wits.

She said, "He's with Shirley Jack at her motel! Had to take her some damn tequila!"

While Jamie sat there looking dazed, dabbing at a little scar Leroy had left on her jaw, I grabbed the phone and told Paco in no uncertain terms to get in his car and make tracks. I hung up the phone and said, "All right. Let's just calm down now. Let's cool out."

I went to the medicine chest to see what I could find for Jamie's face. Alcohol? Iodine? No, this was the Hole in the Wall, not the Mayo Clinic. I finally came up with a little hundred-year-old bottle of Absorbine, Jr., which I dabbed on her jaw with some toilet paper.

I said, "I hope Leroy didn't damage his manicure when he gave you this."

Jamie said, "It wasn't his nails, it was that damn pinkie ring. I saw it coming. Gleaming in the sun. Emeralds, I think."

I said, "Yeah, probably worth more than you and me make in a . . ."

Dab, dab, dab, dab, daab, daaaaab, daaaaaaaaab. I stopped dabbing and stood real still and said real quiet, "You're right. That pinkie ring of his is green. I bet it's emeralds."

"I think so. I don't know. I didn't really get a good look at it."

"Me, neither," I said.

I put the cap back on the Absorbine, Jr., and put it up.

"I'll be back in a little while," I said.

May 20

Last night was a night that will live in infamy. I was feeding the cats when I heard an uproar from the guys clustered in front of the television.

"It's Raylene!" yelled one of the boys.

"*Raylene!*" said half a dozen of them in chorus.

Big Victor sat up on the couch, looked at the TV, and said, "Raylene?"

I dashed over to the television and it was Raylene, all right. Gaping into the camera with her jaw dropped halfway to the floor. She seemed to have been surprised in the act of sliding a ring onto her finger. . . .

But behind her was the big show. As the cops elbowed Raylene aside, Aquanetta took over center stage and finally got her shot at the big time. National live television. I have to say one thing for A. loud and clear: This gal can wear anything and look quite stylish. In her own way of course. For instance, on this particular occasion, she sported an all-black leather outfit of a bra and a mini only slightly longer than the one she wore earlier that day. She appeared to be as composed as a housewife welcoming the local garden club instead of a SWAT team from the San Francisco Police Department. She did look a little put out at the intrusion, as who wouldn't be put out by half a dozen cops and a camera crew breaking down the door, but no more put out than she would be by the appearance of, well, the local garden club. I must say it didn't stop her from slowly waving a big leather whip in the air in a way that I can only call menacing. Or some might call it hammy. After all, this was television and this was Aquanetta. *"La publicité! La publicité!"* as she often referred to such situations, and not in a complaining way either. However, her few moments of stardom were brief, and I could see she wasn't happy about the way the camera crew shoved her aside in favor of the spectacle behind her. Dr. Leroy Lazarus. On the bed. Tied up hand and foot. Naked hand, naked foot, naked everything, it looked like, though the camera was quick to focus on his face. With a none too clean-looking tennis ball stuffed in his mouth. Looking distressed, you might say. He wriggled and bucked and snorted, but gagged and hog-tied as he was, he soon gave up and lifted his beseeching eyes to heaven in a way all too familiar to television audiences everywhere.

"That looks like Dr. Lazarus!" one of the bachelors yelled, breaking the spell that had plunged me into silence.

I said, "Yes, dear, I believe you're right," not tearing my eyes from the screen for an instant. "It must be his room at the hotel."

The boys whooped and yelled and giggled.

"Yes, dear, I believe you're right," I said again, as if I were talking in my sleep.

In one corner of the screen, Aquanetta now stood grimly holding her wicked-looking bullwhip upright in *American Gothic* style. In the other corner a couple of cops in SWAT windbreakers pulled out dresser drawers and looked under rugs, while, in the middle, Dr. Lazarus, his midsection covered with a sheet by this time, twisted from one side to the other as best he could with his arms bound with leather straps to the headboard of the bed. The look of pure terror he gave to first the cops, then Aquanetta, then back again, probably set more television viewers' feet on the straight and narrow than all the preaching he had ever done.

Finally, one of the cops pulled up a floorboard and hauled out a Pillsbury flour bag that appeared to be about half-full. Poor Leroy bounced several inches in the air when the same cop, as smug and blow-dried as any preacher, dropped to a sitting position on the side of the bed.

He said, "You gonna bake us a cake, Dr. Lazarus?"

Well, although I was frozen to the television, the bachelors, I can assure you, went wild, saying things in Spanish which translated roughly to "The jig is up" and clapping each other on the back. But up the jig was not. The show was just getting off the ground.

The tennis ball made a loud smacking sound when the cop pulled it from Leroy's mouth, and we all waited for the good doctor's explanation, which wasn't long in coming. He yelled about being framed and wanting a lawyer. The usual. But then he went too far. He gestured with his head and eyes toward Aquanetta. "It's her fault! It's her stuff!" he yelled. Not a wise ploy to try when Aquanetta is armed with a bullwhip.

Crrrrack! She landed a solid lash across his mid-section which could only have been very tender from his encounter with me that same afternoon. I almost felt sorry for Dr. Lazarus, but before I had a chance to sort out my feelings, he spouted more blasphemy.

"She tricked me! This harlot tricked me! Such is the way of an adulterous woman!"

Leroy was saved from another dose of the bullwhip only by the quick intervention of one of the cops, who grabbed it and twisted it out of Aquanetta's grasp. A look of surprise and fury crossed her face as she watched the cop pass her weapon to someone out of camera range. She fumed a second, then jumped directly in front of the camera so that the viewer was treated to a warts-and-all close-up of an enraged dominatrix.

"*I am not a harlot!*" she roared.

From behind Aquanetta came Leroy's answering roar. "*All wickedness is but little to the wickedness of a woman!*"

Aquanetta cast her eyes to the left and right and it was clear that a decision of some kind was in the making. And we didn't have to wait long to find out what kind. She jumped back from the camera and up on the bed straddling Leroy's legs, which resulted in an almost full-length view of our miniskirted star.

With a sly look at the camera, she grasped the hem of her skirt, pulled it upward, and yelled, *"And I am not a woman!"*

A very audible gasping sound filled the Hole in the Wall. It's something to hear a dozen young men gasp simultaneously along with a fairly worldly-wise transsexual. It sucked all the air out of the room. I'm sure there wasn't enough oxygen left to light a match. For just a second, before the screen went all snowy, Dr. Lazarus' face could be seen gaping in horror through the A-frame of Aquanetta's gorgeous gams. As television fans all all over America noted, Aquanetta was pretty well hung.

twenty-three

I knocked on Leroy's door so hard I thought it would break.

"Leroy, you better open this door, I know you're in there!"

I was in one of my feistier moods, but I swear and be damned, I like to have died when Aquanetta, all done up in her leather outfit, opened it and said, "May I help you, madam?"

I was just asking her what on earth she was doing there, when I looked into the room and saw Leroy all bound and gagged.

Aquanetta said, "Oh, the silly ass. You heard him say he was— yuk, yuk—mighty curious about this here S and M stuff, right? Well, I thought it was only fair that I should teach him what I know about the subject."

With that, she raised a big black bullwhip and brought it down across his thigh with a crack that sounded like a pistol shot. It was easy to do my business. While Aquanetta stood aside looking puzzled, I zipped into the room, lifted Leroy's hand, and checked out that pinkie ring. Uh-huh. Miss Viola's. Actually, I think Dr. Lazarus was not that sorry to see the cops arrive. He was in need of some relief by that time.

I guess there's hardly a soul in the USA, or probably the world, for that matter, who doesn't feel like he or she was a witness to the downfall of Dr. Lazarus. That's television for you. If you missed it live on *Police, Camera, Action!,* you caught it later, whether you wanted to or not, on every news program on every network and *60 Minutes* and every talk show you ever heard of. And you may have caught Raylene Stout, the mysterious woman in red, explaining just what part she was playing that evening when her face was flashed with no warning into ten million living rooms.

"Well, it's simple, Oprah. Dr. Lazarus had stolen a ring that belonged to me many years ago, blah, blah, blah . . ."

The more I told my story, it seemed, the more people's eyes wandered off toward the distant horizon and the more they seemed to be thinking, sure, lady. But who cares? It's like Aquanetta says, it doesn't matter what people say about you as long as it isn't true.

Oh, and by the way, speaking of Aquanetta, she became a household name within twenty-four hours, and she couldn't walk out the door for six months without being pursued by the paparazzi, which suited her just fine, of course. When she hosted *Saturday Night Live,* the ratings were second only to the Super Bowl, and when she posed for *Playboy,* the magazines were sold out the first day they hit the stands. A solid year after the incident, I would turn on the TV in some midwestern motel room and there she would be, explaining to David Letterman just exactly what all this S and M business is about, like she was the world's foremost authority, or modeling leather fashions for Sally Jessy or giving Geraldo the story of her life.

Of course, now everybody knows her as America's favorite HIV poster girl. Just as all the hullabaloo was dying down, she went public on the Donahue show about her HIV status and now she is in greater demand than ever at AIDS benefits all over the country. "The greatest role of my career," she crows on the talk shows, and swears she'll lick the deadly virus. It wouldn't surprise me. Nothing Aquanetta could do would surprise me, though she really didn't look her best last time we talked. She was getting dressed for a show and I was helping her squeeze into something that looked like an Imelda Marcos dress with the puffed sleeves, you know, and it also sported a little yellow tutu around the waist, Aquanetta's own design. Sequins all over, of course, including the shoes. Ever so chic.

I said, "You need to slow down, Aquanetta. You're looking a little thin."

"Honey, when they get one glimpse of me in this little yellow tutu, they're gonna decide they like 'em thin!" she shot back at me.

"Well, I was just worrying about your health," I said.

"Don't," said Aquanetta. "I'm in my glory, Raylene. Don't worry about me."

So I don't, though I stay in touch as much as I can.

Tuesday nights have become *the* night at Esta Noche and tourists are regularly lined up around the block for the weekly "Aquanetta's Follies." Sometimes she has to fly in from the East Coast—first class, of course—to make the show, but she has never missed a show and when Ooky looks up from counting his money, he seems mighty happy to see her. If my travels take me anywhere near San Francisco, I make a point of dropping in to see the old gal sashay across the stage.

Her first show after her encounter with Dr. Lazarus was one for the records. Scads of people were turned away at the door. Jamie, Big Victor, and I sat in a place of honor at a little hubcap-sized table next to the stage. We had closed the Hole in the Wall for the night and were laughing and carrying on and acting, in general, like people hell-bent on having a good time. Just about show-time, I almost choked on my bourbon and Coke when I looked up and saw Buck grinning and sweating and elbowing his way inch by

317

inch through the rowdy crowd. He suddenly grabbed an empty chair that a friend of Jamie's had just that minute vacated and before I could decide whether I liked the idea, the lights went down, the show started, and we were a foursome, Buck plunking himself down right between me and Jamie.

Well, hell, I thought, we're civilized people and at least he didn't drag Shirley Jack along. Buck ordered a round of drinks which I thought was awfully nice until it struck me that it was probably my money he was using.

So here comes Aquanetta up to the mike, telling a couple of jokes, dipping and swaying and mouthing a romantic ballad called "Put It Where It Was Last Night." I was pretty much wrapped up in the show when Buck leaned over to me and said, "Raylene?"

"Yeah?" I said, just cocking my ear toward him and keeping my eyes on the show.

"I'm through with Shirley Jack."

I said, "What?"

"*I'm through with Shirley Jack!*" he hollered so loud Aquanetta glanced down from the stage.

"Oh," I said. "Well, good."

He said, "I just wanted you to know."

"Okay," I said.

He scooted his chair an inch or two closer to mine and said, "It was just a temporary thing, you know. Just one of those things."

I said, "Buck, nothing in life is permanent. That's what I've learned."

I said that the way I say a lot of things—just to fill up dead space in a conversation. But as soon as I said it, the truth of it struck me and I thought about it a minute. Then, just acting on an impulse, I leaned toward Buck and said, "That's the truth. That's what I've learned, Buck. Don't become attached to things and they won't be able to hold you back or tie you down."

I might as well have been talking about the weather.

He said, "Uh-huh," and like to knocked over the table, stomping and whistling and clapping as Aquanetta wound up her show.

Big Victor pushed back his chair and said he had to go because he had an early wake-up the next day. Suddenly, I wanted to get away from Buck and I told Big Victor to wait for me.

May 22

Finally heard from Paco. He called from his godmother's home in Veracruz, where he says Shirley Jack is driving him crazy with her demands to be brought back to the States. He can't bring her because the police are looking for him and can't send her because there's no money. He is worried for Shirley Jack's safety as his godmother, fed up with her constant bitching, claims to have put an evil-eye curse on the former sweetheart of the airwaves, who is threatening to become an honest whore, instead of the hymn-singing kind, to make some quick cash.

He said she had been bored to death at the Econo Gardens and was as eager to get out of San Francisco as he was and practically raced him to his car. He balked till she produced a MasterCard and a Visa, both of which proved, once they were over the border, to be charged up to the max. He wanted to know what happened to Dr. Lazarus.

"In jail. Probably for a long time," I said, and promised to keep him posted.

Aquanetta, sitting at my elbow, grabbed the phone out of my hand.

"He's glad he's in jail. He's safe from Aquanetta." She allowed Paco time for a hearty long-distance laugh before she shyly simpered, "Did you fuck her yet?"

At his answer, Aquanetta's eyes opened in alarm. "What? *What?* Good-bye."

She hung up and turned to me. "He told Shirley Jack that he and I were engaged to be married soon as I get my sex change completed. She's settled for being just friends. Reluctantly. For the time being."

Aquanetta stayed till Raylene came home from her interview at the truck-driving school. Raylene was elated at the financial arrangements she had made to go now, pay later (although I'm sure these were not unusual arrangements for this school to make). I was glad to see her looking so rosy cheeked and sounding so chipper. She has been borderline glum lately, constantly seeking my reassurance about her affair with Armando. ("He's as mature as a thirty-year-old and I'm as immature as a thirty-year-old," she says.) Aquanetta sat her down and filled her in on all the news. One of her many admirers had posted her bail yesterday and was going to hire Melvin Belli, but it looked as if the case against Dr. Lazarus were so cut-and-dried that all charges would be dropped against Aquanetta, except, of course, the indecent exposure thing, which would probably result in a fine that could be entered into the "costs of achieving stardom" column and written off on her income tax. Meanwhile, the *National Enquirer* was ringing her half a dozen times a day.

While they talked and giggled, I slipped out to meet Buck at Café Boheme. He looks haggard. I think he's getting used to the idea that Raylene wants no part of him anymore. Yesterday, while Raylene was at the beach, he kept me on the phone for two hours while I commiserated with him about what a mess he had made of his life. And I do feel a lot of sympathy for him.

"It'll be different in Alaska," I tell him.

Then he gets that fatigued look. "It's such a long way to go, though," he says.

I tell him, "It sounds like a wonderful adventure to me."

He watches me closely when I say things like that. Appears not to recognize them as clichés. Appears to be committing my words of wisdom to memory. It's touching. I kind of like him.

twenty-four

With Dr. Lazarus in jail and most likely on his way to the state pen, things quieted down. And, of course, it was fine with me that Shirley Jack had gone south with Paco. With my plans all made to go to trucking school, I was feeling like a new person. I was always a good driver and all I would need was sixteen hours of classroom instruction and forty hours behind the wheel, which meant I could get my class A trucker's license in a couple of weeks. It was Aquanetta's idea—one of her better ones—that I should have some kind of skill to fall back on in case I didn't go back to the circus for whatever reason. I felt pretty satisfied with myself. Wouldn't Armando be impressed? And Carlotta too.

Speaking of Carlotta, a funny thing had happened. Twice. The first time it happened was a night when I had gone to bed feeling more at peace with the world than I had in a long time. I had happened to get a few days employment for myself and Big Victor and a couple of the other regulars; Mr. Willingham around the corner owned a big apartment house and needed it painted, so I wrapped up the deal and the fellows were real happy with me. We celebrated with tequila sunrises and a game of Texas, Hold 'Em (a combination which got me feeling all sentimental and nostalgic about Alice from Dallas, especially after about the third tequila sunrise). It was the night after that crazy night when Aquanetta showed her stuff to one and all, which seemed like such a dramatic event that everything that followed seemed relaxing and soothing by comparison. I was in bed sound asleep in the middle of the night and suddenly I wasn't asleep anymore. I had the feeling that something other than snoring bachelors had awakened me but I didn't know what. I was lying there with my eyes closed, and without making any effort whatsoever, I began to have a vision, all in Technicolor, mind you. Armando and Carlotta and Wally were all lying on a riverbank like in a French painting, sunny day, a lot of greenery, birds chirping in the trees, butterflies, red-checked tablecloth on the ground heaped with all kinds of food. They weren't talking but I could tell they were thinking about me. They were just pining for old Raylene Stout. It gave me such a peaceful feeling that I began to drift off to sleep just as natural as could be. However, I got to a point just a smidgin away from sleep but not quite there and for a few seconds, I seemed to be floating in a space between awake and asleep. It was the most soothing feeling, and I realized that I had felt it before on the night the twins came to see me. I could feel the most easy, carefree smile forming on my face. Suddenly I heard, just as clear and hollow as a raindrop, Carlotta's voice. Not like she was standing in the same room, but like she was broadcasting on that hard-to-get station that I loved to listen to.

"Raylene," she said. That's all she said, and she just said it once.

I waited for her to say something else but the only sound was . . . not an echo of her voice, but a silvery silence so complete that her one word hung in the air like the hum from a tuning fork. Oh, just listen to me. I sound like a crazy woman. But it's true. Don't ask me what happened to the snoring bachelors. I didn't even think of them till much later.

Now before I go on to tell about the second time this happened

323

I have to talk about what happened a couple of days later. I was out in Jamie's little playpen of a backyard getting a little sun and reading the paper and playing with the cats.

Jamie came to the door and said, "Oh, here you are. I've been looking all over for you."

First thing I knew, she sat down beside me and then I saw a shadow on the ground in front of me. I turned around and it was Buck. What they wanted to talk about was . . . right, going away together. To Alaska, for God's sake. I guess if I had been paying more attention to Jamie's attitude when Buck's name had come up over the last several days, I'm sure I would have been a lot more prepared for this news. But, as it was, I rose up out of that flimsy little chair like somebody who had been underwater a long time coming up for air. I looked from one of them to the other and I could see they were trying to put a name to the look on my face—anger, surprise, pleasure, confusion? Well, guess what? As I stood there on that sunny morning, I was doing the same thing, trying to identify and file in some kind of order everything I was feeling. Well. Hmm. I looked from one of them to the other, just trying to get my bearings, sort of, before my voice finally came in a squeak:

"Alaska?" I said.

Yes, I know Buck had never made any secret of his so-called intentions to go to Alaska. But here's the thing. Over the course of our marriage, Buck had, at various times, made plans for us to move to the following places: Las Vegas, because somebody told him a good twenty-one dealer could live like a king there; Little Rock, because Deke Jacks, his old rodeo buddy, had made good there in the real estate business and Buck wanted to try his hand; Fargo, North Dakota, because of the low crime rate (this being after Buck's car was stolen once, then found a couple of days later in New Orleans); San Antonio, because of the low cost of living. Now these were just a few of the places Buck had fantasized about for months on end. He called the chambers of commerce and got pamphlets and hotel advertisements sent to him. He went over road maps with a Magic Marker. He talked

324

it over with all his buddies. I just kept busy at the hardware store and waited it out. I knew Buck.

Jamie and Buck both nodded, solemn as a couple of owls. They were watching me, waiting to see if it was okay to smile or whether explanations were in order. I gave them permission to smile by smiling myself. Then I asked for explanations.

I said, "When did this happen?" and dropped back down with no more effort or thought than it had taken to stand up.

They both waited a couple of beats before starting to talk and then they talked at the same time. Buck made a little hand gesture that meant Jamie should do the honors, and so she did. She told me a story of long phone conversations and secret meetings and what she called "becoming friends." She wound up with a question. She asked me as plain and simple as could be, "Raylene, how do you feel about all this?"

When I didn't answer right away, she added, "I just want you to tell me the real truth. Please."

I looked at the sky. I looked at the ground. I looked at Buck's shadow stretching across the yard and up the slatted fence. When I answered, I was just as plain and simple as she was. "I don't know, Jamie."

I guess I was in shock. Jamie? Buck? Together? Well, the idea did require some thought. But after I thought about it a little, you know what? It suited me fine. Buck was definitely my soon-to-be ex-husband. It was just a matter of getting the papers. He and I had wound up our ball of yarn, and no hard feelings. That was one thing I liked about Buck; he did not hold a grudge. He didn't have a good enough memory. And, knowing him as well as I did, I couldn't hold a grudge against him either. Besides, there was some kind of poetic justice going on here, it seemed to me. Me stealing Nick. Her stealing Buck. Not that she wasn't welcome to him.

Without thinking, I reached out and took his hand. I said, "So you're worried about what I might think?"

He said, "Yeah, I sure am." Real quiet, real sober.

I said, "Well, I don't want you to be. I don't want you to be worried about me one little bit, Buck."

He looked like he wasn't quite sure if I was being sarcastic or not. I often confused Buck that way, come to think of it. I squeezed his hand and attempted one of these reassuring smiles which Shirley Jack with her experience in tampering with other people's emotions could probably have done a damn sight better. But he got the message and smiled back as shy as if we had never eaten with our feet under the same table.

I looked at Jamie and saw her as she really was. Not my cousin. Not a woman that used to be a man. Just a woman. Her face was all shut up like a morning glory, but the eyes were puffy, the fingers jittery.

I said, "Hey, Jamie, it's like I always say, all's fair in love and . . . hell, no, let's not mince words here, nothing's fair in love, is it?"

"No," she said, "but it's a nice thought. Keeps you sane. Sort of."

"That's right," I said. "It's just a matter of believing what you need to believe to get you through the night. Simple honky-tonk logic, which has served me as well as any in this life."

As I looked at her it struck me that I wanted nothing for this woman but the best things life could possibly bring her. And I wouldn't be at all surprised if my ex-husband felt the same way about her. Which was fine with me.

A cat poked his head through a crack in the fence and meowed. Wound up as we all were, we turned in that direction like some kind of precision drill team. Then I held out my free hand to Jamie and she took it in both of hers.

I looked her square in the eye and I said, "I hope you have the time of your life. I hope you and Buck go up there and find peace and get rich and have a house full of friends. I hope you wake up with a smile on your face every morning."

I stood up and she stood up with me.

I said, "Are y'all gonna drive safe?"

"Yeah," they said.

I said, "Are y'all gonna stay in touch with me?"

"Yeah," they said.

I said, "Can I come visit you sometime?"

"Yeah," they said.

And the three of us stood there in that little patch of backyard, holding hands and grinning and sniffling a little.

After we got all straightened out and went back inside, I noticed there was something new about Jamie. There was something about the way she sat and stood and walked that said, "Hey, lighten up, world." She seemed like such a different person I couldn't keep my eyes off of her. The other thing I couldn't help wondering was, well, just how "friendly" did these two get behind my back and for how long? If I had pulled Jamie aside and asked about it, I'm sure she would have told me but I minded my own business on that matter. And, to be honest, after thinking it over, I didn't really care. Their plans, if that's what you want to call a road map and a couple of grins, were not long in the making. Jamie sat at the kitchen table, brushing the hair out of her eyes while she measured the distance to Anchorage on the map with her thumb and index finger. After finger-walking up the Pacific Coast twice to be sure, she announced that it was a piece of cake. A week from now they would be all settled in and, with any luck (and she was feeling lucky, she said, and it showed), they would even be employed by that time.

"Employed as what?" I asked.

"Oh, whatever kind of jobs they've got up there. They probably can tuna or maybe blubber," she said in such an offhand and sassy way that I almost asked if I could go along too. We laughed a lot, the three of us, that day, as we talked about their upcoming trip and, as goofy as the pairing of these two had seemed at first, I began to think, well, hell, maybe they would make a good pair. Of some kind.

Out of the blue, sweet little Hector dropped off a bunch of shrimp and I got busy at the stove, whomping up a batch of farewell jambalaya to send Jamie and Buck on their way, because they were in no mood to wait around till tomorrow. They were itching to get on the road. In my Cajun mood, I started singing "La Jolie Blonde" sort of softly while I poured water and shrimp and oregano and whatnot into the pot. I got busy stirring my pot and wiping up spills and raiding the cabinets and refrigerator for everything that might make a jambalaya interesting. I could feel that a chapter of my life was coming to a sort of melancholy close, but I didn't want to think about it.

twenty-five

When they left a few hours later, I stood in a light rain and waved till Buck's car disappeared around the corner. I gazed down the empty street for a long time before I closed the door and started getting ready for the bachelors. The house was mine now, but that was no big earth-shaking change. The fellows came in and sprawled out in front of the TV or in the kitchen and only a couple of them even asked where Jamie was, since she never was exactly a live wire in the hostessing department. But I missed her. I sat on the couch with Big Victor while he delivered a twenty-minute speech about getting a bill for twenty-five dollars when he picked up the shoes he had got resoled on Twenty-sixth Street. He was fit to be hog-tied, all but tearing his hair out with frustration and anger.

He asked me, "You know how much new soles cost in Mexico?"

"How much?"

"Guess."

"Oh, I don't know, Victor. Five dollars?"

"Two! *Two dollars!*"

I pulled out all the stops to show my sympathy—clucking, shaking my head, going "Mmm, mmm, mmm,"—but my mind was on Jamie and Buck. How far would they have gone by now? Sacramento? Yreka? Maybe they had already had their first spat over the road map, because I knew Buck couldn't read a map worth a damn. But I hoped that wasn't the case. I wanted them to be happy.

After he got his consumer's complaint out of his system, Victor was in a talkative mood, full of news of a mostly upbeat nature. He had found a brand-new Giants cap in a dumpster. He had got a letter from his former sidekick Little Victor, who wanted to be friends again. He had heard somebody was going to hire a dozen guys for a big roofing job in Daly City. He wanted to go back to Mexico for his brother's wedding. I replied with smiles and these dreamy, dopey little nods, feeling sort of in an unusual mood myself which carried over into bedtime. I pulled the walls of Jericho around my bed and made myself comfortable and drifted off in the general direction of sleep. I wasn't the least bit surprised when Carlotta called my name again. In fact, if I recall right, I was sort of lying there, feeling just as blissed out as a well-fed cat, more or less *waiting.*

"Raylene," she said in a sort of everyday way, like she was standing at the door and was trying to see if anybody was home. Well, I was home all right. I didn't reply right away. I waited for the tuning fork effect of her voice to peter out.

Then I said, "Carlotta?" and I remember thinking, Gee, my voice sounds pretty tonight. The sound of my voice lingered for several seconds too, just like Carlotta's. I knew she had something else to say, and so again, I was just . . . waiting. Waiting there in the dark, feeling just as mellow and relaxed as could be and thinking, Thank you, God. I didn't have long to wait, but her voice, when it came again, snuck up on me. It didn't cut the air. It eased into the room, into my head. It seemed like her voice and the air were part of the same general program.

"Get up," her voice said. "Go out."

Now my first impulse was to say, "Huh?" But I didn't, because I knew what I had heard. However, I didn't get up either. Not right away. Then her voice came again.

"Ray*lene*," she said. "Get *up*. Go *out*."

She wasn't kidding this time. I got up and slipped into jeans and a sweater. Then I sat on the side of the bed a minute and wondered about the going out part. Go out *where?*

I closed my eyes for a minute and then I said, "Where?"

But my voice came out in its flat, everyday tone. I knew I wouldn't get an answer. I had lost the station. I thought of Alice from Dallas's method of finding a direction in the *Farmer's Almanac,* but I knew for sure there wasn't one of those around. The only book in sight was Jamie's diary, which I pulled out of the wastebasket where she had pitched it, along with a handful of bills. In fact, what she did take with her didn't amount to more than a couple of changes of clothes. She called it "getting a fresh start." I hadn't said anything, but I had my doubts about how fresh she would feel in a couple of days when she would need some clean clothes. However, since I inherited a sizable wardrobe I had no grounds for complaint. I picked the diary up from the bedside table, tiptoed to the window with it, closed my eyes, opened the book, slid my finger to the middle of a page. When I opened my eyes, my finger rested squarely beneath the words "Sincere Café" in a sentence about a conversation between her and Paco. Hmm. Okay. I can take a hint. I grabbed my coat. (Salvation Army thrift shop, two bucks. Cute, too. Wool. Kind of faded reddish.) Then I ran my fingers through my hair and pinched my cheeks and made my way over and around and past the sleeping boys and out the door.

That moon! It was like Balmy Alley was all lit up for a nighttime street fair and I walked along with a spring in my step. The night was peaceful, the way it can be in the Mission after a rain, cool and starry, no gunshots, no sirens, and the few people I passed smiled like they were glad to see me. Somebody was playing "Misty" on a saxophone, I remember, on the upper floor of an apartment house. I slowed down to listen to it and picked a fat, overblown pink rose off the humongous bush in front of Mrs. Martinez's house. I buried my face in the flower and smelled its sweet perfume while I thought about how the twins used to play that song over and over on a Johnny Mathis record. I walked on in my little tennies. Oh, I'll just stroll awhile, I thought. I don't want to waste this night. I wandered on down the rain-shiny street, checking out the specials in the windows of Woolworth and Walgreen's. A couple of teenage boys in baggy pants and 49er jackets passed me on the sidewalk and gave me the once-over. One of these little hot shots said, "Hey, mama!" which made me smirk in a way that was not really unfriendly, but also made me decide it was time to catch a bus, since the after-midnight streets were looking more and more deserted. I got on the night-owl bus at Twentieth Street and settled into the razor-slashed seat behind the driver. It didn't really occur to me that a woman getting up in the middle of the night to travel blocks away to the Sincere Café was anything out of the ordinary. I turned around to check out my fellow bus-riders—there was only a handful of them, faces with the life washed out of them by the fluorescent lights, which was just as well, because at this hour, these people looked too tired to put up a front anyway. Looking at them one after the other, I suddenly felt real close to those people going to and coming from God knew where. There was an old man in an overcoat at the very back of the bus who looked a lot like my granddad, the judge, and when I looked at him he seemed to nod at me in the most respectful way. Then I made eye contact with a Chinese woman in a quilted jacket right across the aisle from me and she gave me the very shyest of smiles, then looked away. I wondered where she could be going at this hour and I wouldn't be surprised if she wondered the same about me. I looked at the others, a sad young black woman chewing gum like she needed it to stay awake, a couple of young white kids wrapped in leather and laughing—we all seemed so much a *group* to me—all going in the same direction in that same old bus at the same ungodly hour—that I didn't want to leave them. But I did. I got off at Sixteenth Street and walked the half a block to the Sincere Café. The place had a pretty good after-midnight crowd, maybe a dozen people, most of them sitting alone at the counter. I spotted an empty stool near the door and headed for it, seating myself between an elderly Chinese man and . . . Armando. My first reaction was to scream so loud that the old Chinese man knocked over his cup of tea. Armando had been making these little cameo appearances in my mind all day long. I kept having these pathetic little doubts. Maybe he never wants to see me again. Then, the other side of my brain, the one that's got a little sense, would say, Oh, Raylene, try to see it my way. He cared for you as much as you cared for him. You're not so stupid that you couldn't see that. And it's right for the two of you to be together. It's only right.

And then there he was. Was I surprised? Well, obviously that first shock of recognition just about did me in. However, surprised? Well, not really. And was Armando surprised? Well, not as much as you might think, all things considered. Since I'm committed to telling the truth here, I'm not going to embroider the dialogue of the two long lost lovers who met again at the Sincere Café, although I will admit it was fairly silly.

"Armando!"

"Raylene!"

"Armando!"

"Raylene!"

"Armando!"

"Raylene!"

Hug, hug. Kiss, kiss. And then kiss, kiss, kiss, kiss, kiss. And then we were together again. And have been ever since.

I said, "How did you find me?" I was a little out of breath from kissing and crying and carrying on.

He told me he saw me on television, and, after conferring with Carlotta, jumped in his car and drove day and night from somewhere in Utah to find me. He said that since I had left, Carlotta had spent hours talking with him and she explained about the lie I told about my wealth, why I told it and so forth, and he still loved me.

I said, "After everything you still love me?" This was information I needed some strong confirmation on.

"Yeah," he said. "After everything."

I laid my cheek against Armando's chest and gazed out at the street, feeling more content than I ever thought I could. Then, he said that after Fabio told him about finding me and Tobias making love on the floor of Alice's trailer it took him a long time to forgive me, but forgive me, he did, because . . .

"Excuse me?" I said.

Well, I straightened that story out right away and even managed to wring a laugh out of the trouble that damn broken egg had created for me.

"How's Carlotta?" I asked him before the echo of our laughter had died away.

He said she was fine now, but had been crazy with regrets and worry the first couple of days after my unceremonious departure from the circus.

"Just the first few days?" I asked. I guess I felt a little put out. The ego of Raylene Stout, you know. He said she claimed to have got a thought message from me one night. A message that said I was okay, and after that she didn't worry about me. Hearing that Carlotta had actually received my message, I felt like I was glowing all over, but I didn't discuss it with Armando. It seemed like such a seriously personal thing between me and Carlotta. And besides, I had another question in mind for Armando.

"And what about you?" I asked, looking at him in a very level way. "Have you been worried about me?"

"You don't have to ask that, Raylene," he said. "You know the answer to that question."

And what was I doing at the Sincere Café at this time of night? I told him Carlotta sent me.

"She sent *me* here," he said, shaking his head.

Well, what about her hair, I wanted to know.

"What about it?" he said.

Well, I came within an inch of giving away Carlotta's big secret again. It's a curse, the love of talking. But I have to give myself credit for catching myself at the last moment and saying something like, "Well, that's where she had all her . . . uh, er, that's where she had all her *trouble,* you know. That's where everybody's trouble started. I mean, when Pooch cut Carlotta's hair, you know." The last thing I wanted to do was betray Carlotta again.

"Oh, yeah, Carlotta's hair," he said, "You know what? There was something interesting about that." And he laughed.

"Well, *what?*" I said.

He said, well, chuckle, chuckle, Carlotta had gone public with the problem about her hair. She even folded up her Madam Carlotta tent and took a job in a concession stand selling cotton candy and candied apples.

"Oh, no," I said, "I'm sure that didn't make her happy."

"Well, it didn't last long," he said.

After a week or so of her new job, Carlotta marched off to Woolly Wanda's trailer and started a series of hair treatments with Wanda's ginseng and Mentholatum formula and not only did her hair grow back in a matter of days, a foot longer than it was before, but her psychic powers were even stronger than before. But he wasn't finished with his story. He said Wanda was just as surprised as Carlotta at the astounding results of her hair formula, as she had only used it on her beard, where the results were nowhere near as spectacular. The happy ending to the story was that Wanda was forming a corporation with Carlotta to market the product. And Wally, all healed and back to work in the cannon, was helping them out, filling in for Wanda while she composed letters to her new pen pal in San Quentin, Dr. Lazarus. There's somebody for everybody, isn't there?

"What about us?" I asked Armando later over a huge pile of chow mein that we were splitting between us.

"What *about* us?" He said from under those long lashes that would belong to a woman if there was any justice in this world. "We're *together,* Raylene. That's the end of our story."

We talked and talked about the things that had happened to us and the things we were going to make happen, such as my plans for truck-driving school. He told me that the foot Pooch shot him in was still not in tip-top condition. Not good enough for risking his neck on the trapeze every night, but plenty good enough for driving a truck, he said, while my heart fluttered at the vision of Armando and me rolling off to the edge of the continent in a big old semi, then bouncing back to the other coast. Just me and him, through rain, sleet, snow, and sunshine. I thought about some yellow rain slickers with these cute little hats that I saw at Arik Surplus on Mission Street. We'd be a pair in those.

I said, "Oh, Armando, do you think we could do that?"

He said, "Sure, as long as we're together," and never looked up from his pancakes. You know how men take these things in their stride.

I got a marriage proposal that night at the Sincere Café. After we filled up on pancakes and coffee and hugs and kisses and sweet nothings, it seemed like the most natural thing in the world for Armando to say, "Let's get married."

And you know what? It also seemed pretty natural to me to say, "Not now, Armando."

The words just came tripping off my tongue and sounded right when they landed on the table. Although I will say that it didn't seem to be the answer that Armando was expecting, judging from the way his thick, black, sexy eyebrows shot up toward his thick, black, sexy hairline.

"Not *now?*" he said.

I said, "That's right. Not now, and don't start in about those pygmies."

I explained to him that number one, I was still married on paper, although eventually Buck and I would get a divorce. And number two, I *liked* being the free and independent Raylene Stout. I told him that was the person he fell in love with and that was the person I wanted to stay. At least for now. Poor Armando! To be at the mercy of the dazzling Raylene Stout. I felt for the boy.

He said, "So what does this mean? We can't be together?"

I grabbed him by the scruff of the neck and dragged him out of the restaurant.

I said, "Hell, no. It means we're going to a motel and do all the things we used to do plus a few little extras that I've been dreaming up in my spare time."

Which is exactly what we did. We went to a place a few blocks away called the Mission Hotel and I wouldn't be surprised if they had customers asking for their money back that night, because if what went on in room 201 didn't disturb the peace, I don't know what would. The luxury of a queen-size bed! I can't tell you! Of course, what we were doing didn't really require all that much room. Well, unless you count one little maneuver that Armando had dreamed up in *his* spare time, something called the One-Legged Dutch Girl, which had me cartwheeling all over the bed and afforded me several opportunities to view the young man upside down. And in regard to what Alice from Dallas said about 'em all looking the same from that angle, I say we gals should be so lucky. (And I'm going to shut up right now about all this business, else Dot's mama would scalp her and me both.)

Around sunup, I called Big Victor and told him I would be a little late getting home.

He said, "Is everything okay?

"Yeah," I said, "everything is really okay now, Victor."

He said, "Why do you sound so happy?"

I said, "Just practicing, honey. I've got to get used to it."

epilogue

Going to truck-driving school was a good idea and it was fun with
Armando by my side. Big Victor was happy to take over the Hole in
the Wall and when we left San Francisco, he was fixing up the upstairs of the house to make it livable or at least sleepable. He said that
with both floors he could easily sleep forty guys in the place. Occasionally, he picks up a little extra money serving as Aquanetta's body-
guard when she's off to a premiere or supermarket opening or what
have you. He's doing okay. And so is Jamie. She and Buck are still up
in Nome, where they run a bait shop. Happily.

It's been a year now. So has Raylene Stout been happy with her
young husband? Yes. For the most part. Which is fine, because like
an old Navajo Indian woman told me once in the Arizona desert,
there's no such thing as happiness; there are only moments of happiness. And Armando and I have certainly had our moments and enjoyed
them. Once, we drove down to Mazatlán for a week and every evening
we stood in the water with our arms around each other without say-

ing a word and watched the sun sink inch by inch till it disappeared way out there in the Pacific. And once I won a two-thousand-dollar jackpot in the quarter slot machine in Reno and we lived it up for three days in the best hotel in town. Another time, we camped out in Yellowstone National Park and told ghost stories while sharing a sleeping bag beside a campfire.

There have been other moments too. For instance, one night we stopped over at a motel in Oelwein, Iowa, and Armando stayed out all night at a poker game with an old circus buddy who lived nearby. He said. It was our first night apart since our reunion at the Sincere Café, and I couldn't help thinking he sure splashed on a lot of Aqua Velva just to visit an "old buddy." Around midnight I started getting really mad, sitting on the motel bed, playing solitaire, but after I fumed and cussed a bit, I got to thinking about what Alice from Dallas said about possessing being the same as destroying. That kind of settled me down a little, right? I mean, that's how it works, isn't it? In the middle of your life, things are not working out, so you run away from home and you meet new and different people who drop little gems of wisdom on you that make you think about your existence in a different way and suddenly everything clicks into place and finally your life makes sense, right?

I wish.

I did chew on Alice's words the night of this poker game and, washed down with a couple of bourbon and Cokes, they did sort of enlighten the situation and help me make it through the night, as they say. In fact, by sunup, when Armando got back, I was almost asleep. I didn't kick up a fuss, because we had to get to Des Moines to pick up a load of washing machines bound for Minneapolis, and I don't let anything get in the way of me getting my business done. A woman in the trucking business, or in most other businesses for that matter, has to be twice as good as a man, and I'm sure you women out there won't argue with that. So I let Armando's first night out pass, in the interest of both interstate commerce and being a more enlightened person.

The fact is, if you've got a brain in your head, you do pick up a few basic truths as you stagger down the highway of life. Advice—that's one thing people are always willing to part with, isn't it? And you do think about these little gems of knowledge as you go along and they do make you feel better for a little while and then you drop those little jewels into a mental jewel box or slap 'em on the bumper of your car and one little jewel begins to look a whole lot like all the rest.

But if you feel like you have earned some words of wisdom after bearing with me this long, I say use those gems when you need them, but meanwhile, get your damn washing machines to Minneapolis and try to get 'em there on time. And while you're at it, relax and expect the best, but don't be surprised if the truck throws a rod. There's always going to be some "urgent situation" ready to foul up the works, but I must say, the more mileage I get on me, the more the definition of an "urgent situation" changes. These days, I try not to worry about any situation short of one that requires a tow truck. Maybe letting go of worry is the beginning of something like wisdom, though let's face it, all wisdom really is, is keeping other people from finding out what a damn fool you are. All I can tell you is I'm alone in this motel room tonight and I'm not sure where Armando is, but I'm not ripping my hair out with worry. I know where he said he would be—at an all-night Unocal station, getting the brakes relined on the semi—but I don't know for sure that's where he is. I do know for sure that there's a dishwater blond waitress at Soapy's Truck Stop, six miles down the road, who nearly passes out with pleasure every time we walk through the door, and this is the third time we've passed this way in the last two months. She is one of these brisk, chirpy little gals just out of high school, who's always saying "Right on!" and "Go for it!" (the truck stops of America are full of 'em). But Tara—that's her name—seems real sweet, though she's way too young to be calling everybody "Hon" and wearing those big squarish Sophia Loren glasses that always look like you've got 'em on upside down. However, she's a good waitress. I have to say she's the quickest draw in the Midwest with that coffeepot. I have to hold my hand over the cup between sips to keep from setting her off. Actually, Tara seems like a nice girl and she looks real cute in her little pink uniform and her French twist. I don't know why I'm having these suspicious thoughts about her tonight. Well, I do, too. It's just that, number one, she can't seem to keep her eyes off of Armando, and number two, he's been gone for hours. But, is my blood boiling? No. Am I wrecking the furniture? No. So I guess I've learned a little about letting things be, about letting life happen. I'm not really worried. Much. All right, I'm worried a little, because I love him and love is something you have to hold on to if you can, though, I must say, it hardly ever seems like you've got just exactly the right amount of it from exactly the right person, does it? And, yes, Armando and I do have our little power struggles from time to time. Which is fine. Show me a couple who don't go toe-to-toe every now and then and I'll show you a couple that just aren't communicating.

Armando's foot is all healed now and he talks about rejoining his brothers in the circus. I guess he will pretty soon because he's an artist and he has to do what he has to do. If he goes, I'll go with him, and who knows? Maybe I'll be shooting through the air with the greatest of ease again. I like to keep all the options open. But for now, I'm happy driving a truck and seeing the country and meeting new people every day and being with Armando.

So that brings us up-to-date and not a minute too soon because I have to take a break to answer the phone.

I picked up the phone and said, "Hi, Armando."

"Raylene?"

"Hi. So you're not coming back tonight?"

He didn't answer my question right away, but after thinking it over, he said, "Oh, yeah, baby, they're about to finish the job. Those brakes were really shot. I'll be back pretty soon," he said, and he paused again before he said, "Probably."

Well. My whole life rolled before my eyes while I twiddled with the cord of the venetian blinds and looked at the lights of a place called the Lie and Brag Saloon across the highway.

Finally, I said, "Okay, Armando. I'll be here. *Probably.*"

I said "Good-bye" as friendly as could be and laid the receiver down just as gentle as a mother putting her baby down for a nap. I looked at myself close-up in the dresser mirror and put on lipstick the way Jamie taught me, using the tube and a pencil both. (You don't just smear it on there, girls.) I stood there smacking my lips and rolling my eyes and experimenting with a few frowns and a few smiles and a few come-hither looks. I ran my fingers through my hair and kind of fluffed it up. Miss Viola's dog ring caught the light for a second and reminded me that she was right there with me. Always had been, always would be. I wrote Armando a note and told him to meet me at the Lie and Brag.

Well, I think I've said about as much as I need to here. As the buckaroo used to say, it's time to piss on the fire and call the dogs. I've been running my mouth all night and having a beer sounds like a damn good idea right now. And I'd like to see some people. And laugh. And act a fool. And run my mouth some more. It's just too dreamy a night to stay in. Seems like a special night. I'm looking out the window at that sky so full of stars and there's a dry Oklahoma breeze rustling the leaves on the chinaberry tree outside my window. I wouldn't be surprised at anything that happened tonight. I wouldn't be surprised if Armando rushed into that bar and swept me up and told me he loved me more than ever. And, of course, I hope he does.

But if he doesn't, I'll get over it.